A CAGE OF CRYSTAL

PROPHECY OF THE FORGOTTEN FAE
BOOK TWO

TESSONJA ODETTE

A Cage of Crystal

Cover design by Covers by Combs

Map and header images by Tessonja Odette

RISA
NORUN
THE WALL
TOMAS
VINIAS
KHERO
SELAY
MENAH
SYRUS
ZARAS
SOUTHERN
ISLANDS
Balma
Sea
CARTHA

LELA
DELANY
CAMBRON PASS
RIDINE CASTLE
Khero
ISHVONN WOODS
CENTERPOINTE ROCK
Selay
DERMAINE PALACE
VERLOT PALACE
Menah
BRUSHWOLD
N
W
E
S

1

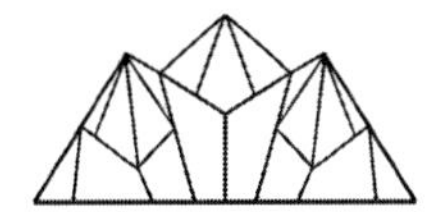

Aveline Corasande Caelan had been a prisoner before, but never in so lovely a cage. By appearances, she was in a luxurious bedchamber. It was twice as large as her childhood bedroom with white marble floors bedecked with opulent carpets and walls papered in a white and gold rose motif. Despite the room's comforting display, Cora knew the truth. She was stuck here. The room was certainly an improvement upon the wagon she'd been kept in after she was captured at Centerpointe Rock, but it didn't change the fact that she was on trial. It was a quiet trial, one of secret conversations and endless questions held behind the closed doors of this gilded prison, but it was a trial nonetheless.

And Cora was getting godsdamned tired of it.

She strolled from the mahogany bureau to the plush bed, ignoring the quiet company of the ever-present guard who stood before her closed door. With an aggravated sigh, she sat at the edge of the mattress. The comfort of her seat helped take the edge off her restlessness, not to mention the slight throb she felt in her still-recovering ankle. Thankfully, getting trapped under a dead horse had resulted in only a few sprains and not fractures.

Almost a month had passed since the battle at Centerpointe Rock. After her injuries had been tended to, nearly every waking moment had been spent trying to prove her identity and the—at least partial—innocence of her brother, King Dimetreus. They'd both been hauled off the battlefield and taken into custody. King Verdian of Selay had become their captor. Nameless men and women had become her inquisitors, asking her to recount everything about Duke Morkai, his magic, her childhood, and her brother while they listened with intimidating silence. She was certain the only reason she and Dimetreus hadn't been sent to the dungeon upon arriving at Verlot Palace was because Teryn Alante, Prince of Menah, had intervened on her behalf.

Thoughts of Teryn did strange things to her heart. She wasn't sure if he made it sink or flutter. Both perhaps. She was sure of one thing though; she needed to stop thinking of him as a prince. With his father dead, he was king now. Or would be soon. She hadn't a clue how he'd fared since the battle. When last she'd seen him, he'd been wounded. It hadn't been the deadliest of wounds, but it didn't stop her from worrying about him. No matter how many times she'd hounded her captors with inquiries, no one would say a damn word about Teryn's well-being.

Today no one had said a word to her at all. This was the first day she hadn't been visited by inquisitors at the crack of dawn. She couldn't help but assume the worst. That King Verdian had made his decision regarding Cora and her brother's fate.

Panic rippled through her, mingling with a flash of anger. Curling her fingers into fists, she pushed off the bed and marched to the nearest window. At least, she intended to march. As her first hard step on her right leg sent a sharp pain through her ankle, she forced herself to slow. Keep her steps even. Careful. She'd only been given the go-ahead to walk on it this week. She supposed she should feel grateful that her wounds had been tended to at all.

She reached the velvet-draped window and tugged the curtain aside. Morning sunlight winked back at her, rising over the sprawling mountains in the distance. Her nerves stilled at the sight of those mountains, at the thought of those forests. What she wouldn't give to be transported straight there, to escape these stifling walls and fill her lungs with early summer air.

Can't I? a small voice inside her asked. *Can't I just...leave?*

She remembered what she'd done at the battle, how she'd somehow managed to cross time and space, bringing her from beneath the dead horse that had pinned her legs, to the rock where the duke had stood. It had happened in the blink of an eye.

And yet, the more time that passed between then and now, the more she began to doubt it had truly happened that way. Surely there was another explanation for it. She'd heard of witches who could astral project and astral travel, but those powers were rare. What were the chances Cora had accomplished such a feat?

Besides, even if she could disappear, she knew she couldn't. She'd made her choice. Now she had to see it through. At least there was one way she could experience what stood outside her prison. Sort of.

Pressing her forehead to the cool glass, she closed her eyes and extended her senses outward. It didn't take long to connect to a sense of warmth. Hoofbeats echoed the pound of her heart. She could almost feel the soil beneath her feet, smell the dew-speckled leaves glistening beneath the morning sun. Then a voice came to her, formed from feeling, shaped into words.

I'm still close by.

Her lips curled into a sad smile. Even though she was a prisoner, it gave her comfort to know that Valorre, her unicorn companion, was free.

The door opened behind her, and her connection to the unicorn vanished. Forest trees and dewy leaves dissipated as her senses returned fully to the room. She turned away from the window just as a young woman entered.

"Is this her?" the girl asked the guard. She appeared to be perhaps fourteen or fifteen years of age with dark blonde hair and blue eyes. She was dressed in maroon velvet; a simple gown but far too fine to mark her as a lower servant.

The guard nodded. Without a word, he exited the room and left the two women alone.

Well, that was a first. Save for her use of the toilet, there was always a guard around, even while she slept. Or tried to. For someone who once had to rely on a sleeping tonic to achieve some semblance of peaceful slumber, trying to rest while being watched was no easy feat.

The girl dipped into a deep curtsy. Her face was alight with a bright smile as she rose. "It's wonderful to meet you, Princess Aveline."

"Cora." The word slipped from her mouth before she could take it back. She'd gone by *Cora* for the last six years. *Princess Aveline* still felt foreign to her. Forgotten. Forbidden. She hadn't even liked the name before she'd fled her childhood home and had preferred the nickname her mother had given her. After she'd started her new life with the Forest People—a commune of witches and Faeryn descendants who scorned royals—she'd discarded her former title. Buried it deep alongside her past.

But she wasn't with the Forest People anymore. She'd relinquished her chance to return with them after the battle when she'd chosen to defend her brother instead. In doing so, she'd turned her back on magic. On her true self. On *Cora*. But Cora had never belonged with the Forest People. Not truly. Had they known she was a princess when they'd found her wandering the woods alone as a child, they never would have accepted her into their midst. The question now was: did she belong with the royals either?

"Cora," the girl echoed. "Ah, that's what the prince calls you, isn't it?"

Cora's pulse kicked up at her mention of the prince. Of Teryn. Her mouth fell open, her tongue prickling with the questions she was desperate to ask. How was he? Had he recovered from his wounds? But the girl was already speaking again.

"I'm honored you would allow me to call you Cora in private," she said, smile widening. "I assume it's a name reserved for your dearest friends, and I do hope you will consider me a friend, for we will be spending much time together. As for me, my name is Lurel."

Cora frowned. "Why will we be spending so much time together?"

A blush rose to her cheeks. "Silly me. I should have explained myself better. I'm your new lady's maid."

Cora's pulse hammered. If she'd been given a lady's maid, did that mean...

She swallowed her hope before it could fully rise. Until she met with King Verdian himself and heard from his lips that she and her brother were pardoned, she would assume nothing.

A knock sounded at the door, and Lurel bounded over to open it. Three older women entered the room, bearing several boxes each. They paused to curtsy, then proceeded straight for Cora. She stiffened as they set their boxes down at her feet and began to assess her with furrowed brows. Emotions flooded her at once, an odd mixture of aversion, curiosity, and dread. She realized then that her mental shields were down; she'd lowered them to connect with Valorre. The emotions she was experiencing now were coming from the three women who were circling her with furrowed brows, *hmm*-ing, huffing, and whispering amongst themselves.

With a deep breath, Cora focused on the marble floor, firm beneath her feet. She imagined the air around her thickening, growing denser and stronger until it felt like a protective shroud. With her mental shields back in place, the unwanted emotions faded away.

Being a clairsentient witch had its benefits, but there were times when it was highly inconvenient. Her empathic ability to feel the emotions of others had served her numerous times, but in everyday situations, it was a hassle that required constant vigilance to block out unwanted outside stimuli.

And now that she was trying to reclaim her place as a princess amongst royals who feared magic, it was a secret she kept to herself.

The women continued to circle and assess her like a horse up for auction, making her discomfort grow. Were they determining her coffin size? Deciding on which length of rope to use at her hanging? Perhaps she was jumping to ridiculous conclusions, but if someone didn't explain why she was the sudden object of these women's scrutiny, she would lose every last shred of good sense.

"Pardon, but what is your purpose in being here?" Her

voice came out sharper than she intended, but the three women didn't balk.

"I'm so sorry," Lurel said, wringing her hands as she approached. "I'm off to a terrible start at being your lady's maid, aren't I? I'm so used to serving Princess Mareleau, and she—well, I forgot that you haven't lived as a princess for quite some time."

Cora clenched her jaw to keep from snapping at the girl, who still hadn't answered her question. One of the women lifted Cora's arm and ran a measuring tape from her armpit to her wrist. That was when Cora understood. She hadn't been fitted for clothing since she was a young girl. "You're seamstresses."

Lurel nodded. "You're being fitted for a new wardrobe by Princess Mareleau's personal dressmakers. Ordered by King Verdian himself."

She raised a brow. "Why would he do that?"

"Rumor has it that Selay and Khero are allies now. He's helping you reclaim your title as princess. Of course he would want to help you look the part. You can't return home looking like that."

Home. She was...going home?

"I'm surprised you weren't offered finer clothing sooner. Or a bath." Lurel's tone was devoid of disgust or condemnation, but it made Cora bristle just the same.

She glanced down at the plain gray dress she wore, one she'd received upon arriving at the palace, along with a nightgown and undergarments. She'd been given a daily ewer for washing, but her hearth was never lit unless she requested it. Since she was too proud to beg anyone here for help, she'd donned her cloak on cold mornings instead, and today was no exception. It was the same cloak she'd worn during the battle, and the wool was stained with soil and blood. She splayed her hand, noting dirt caked under her nails as well as the loose strands of frizzy hair that floated about her face.

Now she understood the emotions she'd sensed from the seamstresses. If they were used to fitting the Princess of Selay, they had their work cut out for them with Cora. They didn't bother having her undress and they seemed loath to touch her or her filthy clothes more than necessary.

After a few more basic measurements were taken, the women stepped back and began holding bolts of fabric and even some finished dresses next to her as if testing the colors against her skin tone.

"These are Princess Mareleau's old dresses, Highness," one of the seamstresses said, addressing Cora for the first time. She held up a gown of gold taffeta and squinted at it before giving the dress a nod and taking it to the bed.

"More like rejected designs," the eldest woman muttered, a wry smirk on her face. That earned a titter from the other two.

"I can't imagine why Mareleau would reject any of these," Lurel said, tone wistful as she watched the women lift dress after dress and hold it next to Cora. The seamstresses were careful not to let any of the gowns come within an inch of her current ensemble.

Once they seemed satisfied, they packed all their things back in their boxes. "We'll have these gowns hemmed and adjusted by evening, Highness," one said. "They won't be perfect but they'll do until you get home to your own dressmaker."

There was that word again: *home*. She tried to associate it with Ridine Castle but forest trees and archery seemed more suited to it.

She shook her head. Maybe someday she could return

to just being Cora, forest witch, friend to unicorns, and poisoner of enemies. Not yet. She'd chosen her brother. The safety of Khero. Until she knew both could flourish without her, she had to stay. Had to be Princess Aveline.

"You must be exhausted after everything you've been through," Lurel said, rousing Cora from her thoughts. Only now did she notice that the seamstresses had left and had been replaced with servants hauling in a large washbasin and pitchers of steaming water. "Now, come. Let's get you washed and styled. We'll have you feeling like a princess again in no time."

2

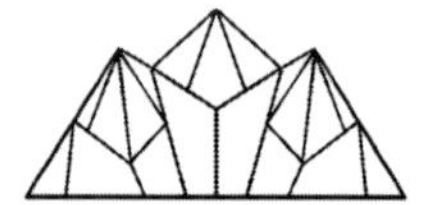

The bath was heavenly. Aromas of jasmine filled her senses while the enormous tub accommodated enough water to let her submerge up to her neck. The only part of her bath that was less than ideal was Lurel's presence. She hadn't bathed in front of an attendant since she was a child, but the girl had only scoffed when Cora suggested she wait outside her room.

"Nonsense," she'd said. "You won't get those tangles out of your hair without aid."

Lurel had been right, and Cora was now suffering from it as the knots were combed from her dark strands. Cora could feel the other girl's frustration, even with her mental shields in place.

"I've never met a more stubborn knot," Lurel said through her teeth.

"You can cut more of my hair," Cora offered, ready for her torture to end.

"I already cut six inches, Highness. I'll take no more."

Cora made no further argument. By the time her hair was combed, her scalp felt like it had been grated off. But when she ran her hands through her silken tresses, she thought perhaps the torment had been worth it.

"We must hurry," Lurel said as she ushered Cora out of the tub and behind a dressing screen. "Your bath took far longer than I expected and you have a meeting to attend."

Lurel left Cora to dry herself with a plush towel, then returned with her arms full of cream-colored silk and linen, which turned out to be a shift, corset, petticoats, and stockings. Cora's cheeks heated as the girl took Cora's towel and began dressing her in undergarments as if it were the most normal thing in the world. She supposed it was for a lady's maid.

"A meeting with whom?" Cora asked as Lurel flounced off again, this time returning with the gold taffeta gown the seamstresses had left behind.

"With King Verdian, of course," Lurel said.

"I'm meeting with King Verdian?" Her voice was muffled as Lurel pulled the dress over Cora's head.

"Of course. Hasn't anyone told you?"

When Cora's head popped above the bodice, she gave the girl a pointed look. "You're the first person I've had any lengthy conversation with who isn't an inquisitor."

Lurel paused, her face going a shade paler. "Oh. I hadn't realized—well, there I go being a rotten lady's maid again. No wonder Mareleau offered me up to you. I may be her cousin, but she doesn't like me much."

I wonder why, she thought with sarcasm, but chastised herself. Lurel may be a bit vague but she was kind. That's more than she could say for the inquisitors. They had been some of the most abrupt, skeptical people she'd ever had to converse with.

Once Lurel secured the laces at the back of the dress, she rounded the front and assessed Cora through slitted lids. "It will have to do. The dress is a bit too modest for your age, but it was the only one that would fit without being hemmed first. It belonged to Mareleau when she was eleven."

Cora glanced down at the gold and cream taffeta, the ivory lace at the hem and sleeves. The bodice was high enough to leave no sign of cleavage, but it wasn't terribly modest. Then again, her ideas of fashion were likely out of date.

Lurel's words suddenly dawned. "You're saying I have the body of an eleven-year-old?"

"An eleven-year-old *Mareleau*," Lurel corrected. "She's much taller and curvier than you are. You really ought to wear a crinoline or a bustle—but we don't have time for that. Your hair! Oh, it looks terrible."

She wasn't sure if she should feel offended by Lurel's comments, but she pursed her lips and let the girl finish her flustered ministrations.

Cora felt more like a peacock than a princess as she left the room. Her hair had been woven into four braids that had been pinned around the crown of her head and dressed in feathered ornaments to hide that her tresses were still damp from her bath. Rouge colored her lips and cheeks, but she'd managed to convince Lurel to forgo the face powder and kohl. She hadn't been this overdressed since she was a child and never had she been expected to wear cosmetics.

A pair of guards flanked her as they escorted her down the elegant halls of Verlot Palace. She tried her best not to gawk at the splendor around her, but this was the first time she'd been allowed out of her room all week. Equally as distracting were the many curious eyes that looked her way, the courtiers who stared shamelessly as she passed.

The guards stopped outside a pair of double doors. Her heart raced as they opened them, and she fisted her hands in the folds of her skirt. She found the room beyond to be a study, with the familiar face of King Verdian standing behind a large desk. He looked different from how he had on the battlefield. Instead of short gray hair, he now wore a powdered wig, and instead of armor, he bore a regal gold and white coat emblazoned with Selay's rose sigil over his breast. An imposing-looking woman sat to his left, her golden hair arranged in a tight coronet, lips tightly pursed, eyes hard and assessing.

The guards closed the doors behind Cora, and she dipped into a curtsy several seconds too late.

"Princess Aveline," King Verdian said, tone flat, "this is Dowager Queen Bethaeny."

Cora blinked a few times. She'd assumed the woman was Verdian's wife, Queen Helena. Instead, it was...Teryn's mother. Now that she reassessed the woman, she saw some similarities between her and the boy she knew. While Teryn favored his late father's looks with his green eyes and dark hair, his tresses glinted gold in the sun, a similar shade to the queen's.

More surprising than the unexpected presence of Queen Bethaeny, though, was the figure that rose from his seat. She hadn't noticed him behind the high leather back of his chair, but as her brother faced her with a worn, tired smile, she couldn't look anywhere else. Her heart skipped and lurched, just how it had when she'd first seen him at Ridine Castle over a month ago. It seemed her emotions still didn't know what to make of Dimetreus. For too many years, she'd hated him for believing she'd killed his wife. She'd despised him for ordering her to a dungeon cell without remorse. Only after she'd been captured by Duke Morkai had she realized her brother was being controlled by the mage.

At the end of the battle, her brother had been surrounded by soldiers, called a traitor for having attempted to conquer Selay and Menah. Dimetreus, however, hadn't had a clue as to what the accusations were about. Morkai's death had severed his magic and the multiple glamours he'd woven. Once the glamours had been lifted, Dimetreus—and all the others who'd been freed from the mage's hold—had been confused. Lost. His memories a tangle of truth and lies.

Cora still blamed her brother for many things, primarily for letting Morkai into their lives in the first place and not being strong enough to withstand the mage's glamour. But she knew he wouldn't have waged war on Selay and Menah if he hadn't been under Morkai's spell.

At least, she hoped that was the case. It was the gamble she'd taken, the sole reason she was here and not far, far away, basking in the solitude of the woods. If Dimetreus was innocent, he deserved to keep his crown, and she owed it to their kingdom to ensure that happened.

She assessed him, noting the dark circles that still hung beneath his eyes, the wrinkles he was too young to have, and the thin gray hair that should have been lustrous and black. These telltale signs of Morkai's abuse fueled her conviction. There was no way he'd have endured Morkai's sorcery willingly. He *was* innocent.

"Aveline," he said as he walked toward her, voice strangled. His dark eyes glistened with tears, reminding her too much of how they'd looked when under the sheen of the glamour. He extended his arms, inviting her into an embrace, but she couldn't bring herself to move.

A flash of memory shot through her, of him storming

into Queen Linette's room, of the rage on his face when he'd turned to Cora and blamed her for his wife's death...

Slowly, he lowered his arms and gave her a knowing nod. "I'm so sorry, my dear sister."

Cora shook her head to clear it and tried to summon a smile. All she conjured was a subtle flicker of her lips. "It's all right," she whispered. Then, with a deep inhale, she took her brother's arm and allowed him to escort her to the desk. Her breath caught when she felt how slim his arm was. Her momentary resistance drained, leaving only sympathy in its wake. She looked up at him, this time managing an almost-full smile. "I'm glad you're well. You seem to have recovered from the wounds you sustained at Centerpointe Rock."

"I have. As have you, I presume?"

"Yes," she said, and they separated to take their seats.

Verdian's expression remained hard, unmoved by their reunion.

Queen Bethaeny spoke first. "My son has done much on your behalf, Princess Aveline. He's been tireless in proving your identity and corroborating your story. I was curious to meet the woman who had my son so transfixed that he'd delay both his coronation and the burial of his father."

Heat flooded Cora's cheeks, her heart flipping in her chest. It took no small effort to keep her voice level. "I am grateful for everything Prince Teryn has done, and for Your Majesties' willingness to listen."

She meant every word. Trusting Teryn had been another gamble. He knew her secrets, knew she was a witch. Knew that she'd poisoned an entire camp of hunters and that she had a dark history with Morkai. The things he knew could have condemned her. She'd put blind faith in him the last few weeks, trusting he'd say only what the royals needed to hear and nothing more. She knew from firsthand experience how convincing he could be, even to someone who could sense emotions. She'd been on the receiving end of his lies when he betrayed her to Morkai. If anyone could keep a secret, it was him.

"Have you been treated well?" Bethaeny asked. "I was told my son demanded that you were."

Cora paused, debating her answer. "My accommodations have been fine, but I much prefer the freedom to leave my room."

The queen gave a smile that didn't reach her eyes. "You must forgive us for the lengthy questioning period you endured. Even with my son so invested in your plight, precautions were necessary."

"After what we've been through, we weren't willing to take any chances," Verdian said, his tone far brusquer than Bethaeny's. "Lives have been lost. We couldn't risk the possibility that either of you posed the same threat the duke had."

"I assure you," Dimetreus said, speaking slowly, carefully, "I hold none of the ambitions the former Duke Morkai held, nor do I believe any of the lies he once fed me. I only wish to return to Khero and set everything to rights. As I've promised, I will do whatever it takes to secure the trust of Selay and Menah."

"Yes, we've heard your promise," Verdian said, "but now we need the princess' word as well."

"I feel the same as my brother," Cora said. "I will support him in any way I can."

Verdian leaned back in his chair, pinning Cora with an icy look. "First, I must remind you what is at stake. Even though we're willing to believe Dimetreus was not acting of his own free will, those who fought at Centerpointe Rock saw him as a traitor. Rumors have spread, and even citizens of his own kingdom have reasons to doubt him. It would be no difficult task for me to seize control over Khero during this time of unrest for the kingdom's own good. If you and your brother fail to agree to our terms, I will enact this plan, and you will remain hostages here. Any resistance from you as hostages, and you will be executed."

Cora clenched her jaw. This was the first time she'd been referred to as a hostage. She'd known that was what she'd been all along, but it was one thing to know it and another to hear it stated outright. Not to mention his threat to seize her kingdom as his own. A fiery rage sparked in her chest but she breathed it away. "What are your terms?"

"Your brother will be allowed to resume his place as King of Khero, but his council, staff, and military will be selected by me. All positions will be filled by men from Selay. Dimetreus has already agreed to this."

Cora met her brother's eyes. He gave her a resigned nod, and her muscles began to uncoil. Those terms weren't terrible.

Verdian continued. "But we need something from you too. Based on the widespread belief of your death, as well as your questionable...*history*...we've struggled with how best to secure trust with you."

He glanced briefly at Cora's forearms where a hint of black ink trailed over the tan skin above her silk gloves. Lurel had wrinkled her nose when she'd first caught sight of the tattoos during Cora's bath, her feelings made clear despite how she'd insisted she thought they were *pretty*. Cora hadn't argued when Lurel dressed her in gloves before leaving her room. She tugged the silk a little higher now, pursing her lips against the indignation that colored her cheeks.

Verdian didn't know that the tattoos were *insigmora*, a

Faeryn tradition meant to convey what level of the magical Arts one was practiced in. Hiding her tattoos—and her magic—felt like a betrayal, but these were secrets she needed to keep. She'd already drawn enough suspicion when she'd admitted to having lived with the Forest People. Even though they'd fought against Morkai at Centerpointe Rock, there was no denying their use of magic. Everyone on the battlefield had witnessed them wielding roots and vines like weapons. During Cora's questioning, she'd sensed the inquisitors' fear and disgust for all things magic. That was when she'd decided to bury that side of her. Hide it. Ignore it. Pretend she was just a princess. Just a girl eager to restore her title and save her brother's crown. It was the only way to convince them she was who she claimed to be.

Verdian spoke again. "While our current terms have established trust between Selay and Khero, you and Dimetreus owe Menah a debt as well. It is imperative that we forge an alliance between all three of our kingdoms, so that true peace can be secured between us."

"My son has come up with a proposal," Bethaeny said. "A solution that will bind you to Menah and forge that trust we seek."

Sweat slicked Cora's palms. "What proposal would that be?"

"Marriage," Verdian said.

Cora froze. She repeated their words in her mind to make sure she understood them correctly. *Teryn has proposed...*

"Marriage?" she echoed.

Verdian and Bethaeny nodded in unison.

"To me."

Another nod.

Emotions clashed in her heart, anger warring with

something softer. How dare Teryn propose marriage without asking her directly! She...she...she would stab him for this. Surely she deserved a far better proposal than one of contractual obligation. But of course he didn't *want* to marry her. This was a matter of politics and alliances, as all royal marriages were. It was all for the better this way. She wasn't certain she wanted to keep her title longer than it took to reestablish her brother's rule. A marriage of the heart would only complicate things.

Still...he'd come up with this plan for *her*. That had to amount to something. Perhaps he did want the union, for reasons other than necessity.

Warmth crept into her chest, barreling through her anger, her shock. Memories of the kiss they'd shared in Ridine's dungeon came to mind, of that moment of pleasure and desire that had ended in trickery. He'd kissed her to trick her. He'd tricked her to force her to leave him behind. She'd resented him for using her own hidden desire against her, but...

Could he have wanted the kiss as much as she secretly had?

Verdian's voice was an unwelcome distraction from her thoughts, especially with the taunting lilt to his voice. "Your betrothal contract will be drafted at once. You will marry the Prince of Menah in one year."

Cora frowned, puzzling over the mocking way he'd said *Prince of Menah* and that he'd referred to Teryn as *prince*. Bethaeny had said Teryn postponed his coronation, but Verdian had begun calling Teryn *king* as soon as the battle was over. A cloud of dread began to sink her stomach.

"Once you agree, we will speak with Prince Larylis," Verdian said. Then, with a smirk, he added, "I doubt he'll have any qualms over it. He's lucky to be a prince, much less marry a princess."

Cora felt as if the floor had opened a gaping hole beneath her. Her disappointment was so heavy, it made her head spin. "Just so we're clear," Cora said, her voice trembling, "I am to marry Teryn's brother...Larylis."

"*Prince* Larylis," Bethaeny said, tone brimming with disdain. "Thanks to my late husband's last wish."

Cora curled her fingers around her chair's armrests.

Teryn hadn't made a proposal of marriage between himself and her. He'd made it between her and his *brother*.

Every soft feeling that had awakened inside her dissipated beneath the new wave of fury that roared through her. She wasn't mad at Teryn. No, what he'd done made sense. He was already engaged to Princess Mareleau. He had no romantic inclinations toward Cora. Her anger was with herself. For that pathetic spark of hope she'd allowed herself to entertain.

"Oh, Highness," Bethaeny said, voice soft, "you didn't think..."

Cora met her eyes and found the queen's expression held equal parts sympathy and amusement. It was the latter emotion that had Cora's chest heaving. She tore her gaze from Bethaeny's and turned her attention to Verdian. "Is that all?"

"There are finer points to this arrangement," he said, sharing neither Bethaeny's sympathy nor her amusement. "Should Dimetreus fail to secure a proper bride and provide a suitable heir, rule will pass to you upon his death or abdication. If Dimetreus' council deems him incapable of the crown at any point, he will be forced to abdicate at once. If this occurs before you and Larylis have officially wed, you'll need to formalize your marriage immediately. Your council will not recognize you as Dimetreus' heir until this marriage alliance is secure."

Cora glanced at her brother again only to find resignation in his eyes. This was another term he'd already agreed to. What else was there for her to do but resign herself to it as well? She was too angry to think things through, too irritated by her own fickle heart to do anything but say, "I accept. All of it. Whatever it takes. When can we return home?"

Verdian tilted his head back as if he hadn't expected her to agree so readily. "We've arranged transportation and lodgings. My brother, Lord Kevan, will host you at his estate for a few days while we finish preparations. He will serve as Dimetreus' Head of Council and will escort you and some of your new household staff to Ridine—"

"Great," Cora said. She was disturbed by how much had already been arranged before she'd agreed. More than that, she was desperate to end the meeting. "We will leave for Lord Kevan's estate at once."

"Very well," Verdian said. "The sooner we can bring stability to Khero, the better."

With her cooperation secured, she took the opportunity to excuse herself. She felt a flash of guilt for abandoning her brother, but she needed to get out of there. To breathe. To be alone—

"I hope you didn't think it was going to be that easy."

Cora had just left the closed doors of the king's study behind her when a tall female figure blocked her path. She expected it to be one of the guards who had brought her here, but she spotted both of them waiting farther down the hall. Instead, she was confronted by a woman dressed in a turquoise silk gown with a plunging neckline that revealed an ample bosom. Her skirts flared out at her waist in every direction. Her silver-blonde hair fell in perfect curls over one shoulder. Cora blinked at her a few times. "Excuse me?"

"Don't get comfortable," the girl said, blue eyes flashing with menace. "You aren't marrying Larylis."

She wanted to say that she didn't give two licks about Larylis, or her, or anyone here. Instead, she lifted her chin to meet the other woman's eyes. Batting her lashes, she said, "Should I know you?"

The blonde's cheeks heated with indignation. The truth was, Cora knew exactly who she was. It didn't take a genius to guess this was Princess Mareleau Harvallis, the woman who'd spurned her engagement to Teryn and sent him on a hunt for unicorns. Until this moment, Cora hadn't realized just how much she already despised her.

Mareleau took a step closer, hands on her hips. With a cruel grin, she looked Cora up and down. "Nice dress. Do you always wear children's clothes?"

Cora gave her an innocent smile. "When my only options are the leftovers from some spoiled harpy with poor taste in fashion, yes." With that, she skirted around Mareleau and stormed down the hall, her fury burning hotter with every step she took.

3

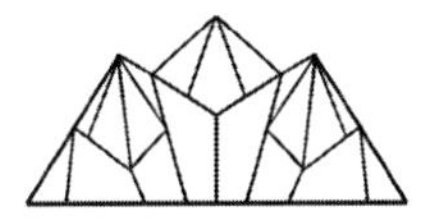

There were few things in life Teryn Alante truly despised. Sitting still for any extended period was one of them. His disdain for inertia had sprouted when he'd been kept prisoner by Duke Morkai before the battle at Centerpointe Rock. He'd been helpless. Powerless. Unable to prevent what came next. Those feelings had only worsened after the battle. After his father's gruesome demise.

Now if he stayed still too long, his mind would fill with blood.

With screams, cries, and the clash of steel.

With his father's lifeless eyes.

He'd found a way to channel his angst, and it was in fighting for Cora's freedom. After his injuries had been tended at Centerpointe Rock, he'd requisitioned a coach and followed King Verdian's retinue to Verlot Palace.

For that was where Cora had been taken.

His half brother Larylis had remained by his side. When Teryn's fractured rib kept him from writing, Larylis wrote for him. Together, they'd recorded everything Teryn knew about Cora, Morkai, and Dimetreus—anything that could prove Cora's identity and innocence.

Once he'd arrived at Verlot Palace, he'd redoubled his efforts, dogged in his determination and refusing to return home to Dermaine Palace until the matter was settled. Not even his own coronation nor his father's burial could tempt him away.

Not yet.

Not until she was safe.

Not until he'd fixed everything he'd nearly destroyed.

Teryn stood in the Great Hall of Verlot Palace, anxiety tickling the back of his mind. The emotion was a constant passenger and would be until Cora's fate was sorted. He tried his best to ignore it, however, as a friendly face came bounding toward him.

"Prince Lex." Teryn greeted his friend with a grin.

"Come to see me off?" Lex asked as they grasped each other's forearms in a gesture of camaraderie. After the battle, Lex had come back to Verlot Palace. He'd done more than his share to confirm everything Teryn had said about Cora. And to keep quiet about all the things Teryn had left unsaid.

Teryn nodded. "Thank you for everything you've done."

Lex gave a halfhearted shrug. "I had to make up for tricking you into thinking I'd abandoned you at Ridine Castle."

"I would think fighting with our armies was already more than enough." He glanced around the Great Hall. The gilded walls and marble floors echoed with sound, as the palace was already bustling with activity this morning. He caught several courtiers looking at him and Lex as they passed. Lowering his voice, he added, "But I do appreciate everything you've done for Cora."

"Yes, well, I figured going the extra distance might remind you of a certain discussion we once had. One regarding Aromir wool."

Teryn's expression fell. He'd almost forgotten their bargain. It had begun as an offer from Lex to help Teryn win the Heart's Hunt in exchange for inclusion into Menah's most exclusive trade contract. After they'd met Cora, Teryn had renewed the promise to Lex, as long as he'd agree to come with them and rescue unicorns. Now that Menah was no longer in debt to Cartha, Teryn could afford to reward Lex's loyalty. Still, he wasn't officially king yet. He wasn't sure what promises he could make.

Lex chuckled and slapped Teryn on the shoulder. "I'm kidding. I didn't come to Verlot because of our alliance but because you're my friend."

Hearing Lex call him a friend warmed his heart. It was almost enough to quiet the incessant buzz of anxiety that fluttered in the back of his mind. "What about your father? Won't he be cross that you've returned home empty-handed?"

Lex's mirth faded. "Hopefully he'll be proud enough that I helped save the damn world. Though, I bet he'd sooner chastise me for not hiding from the conflict. Either way, I hope you think of Tomas as an ally."

"I do. Menah is yours as well."

"What about Selay?" Lex asked with a grimace. "How much does King Verdian hate me?"

Teryn released a sigh. "No more than he dislikes me." Proving Cora's royal identity had required them to confess that Lex had withheld information from Verdian when he'd brought news of Morkai's plans. It meant Selay could no longer carry the full blame for Teryn's imprisonment at Ridine Castle. Teryn had learned that his father had decided to let Verdian think the Heart's Hunt had been the sole reason Teryn had crossed paths with Morkai. It would be an understatement to say Verdian had been furious to learn the fault lay more with Teryn's attempt to collect Cora's bounty.

Lex squinted at Teryn. "Have you told her yet?"

"Told who what?"

"Cora," Lex said, in a too-loud whisper. "Or Aveline, or whatever I am to call her now. Have you told her how you feel?"

Teryn didn't know what to say. He hadn't realized Lex still believed Teryn had feelings for Cora. He'd allowed his friend to believe as much when they'd first met her. It had been a ruse to convince Lex to join her unicorn rescue mission without Teryn having to admit the real reason he wanted to travel with her—to turn her over to the crown as an outlaw. He wasn't sure why he kept quiet now. Perhaps because the lie no longer felt so false.

"You should tell her," Lex said.

"I will." It came out too fast, his cheeks suddenly too warm.

With that, they said their final farewells. Teryn watched his friend leave the Great Hall. As soon as he was out of sight, his fluttering sense of urgency crept back up. Dread filled his bones as it did during every quiet moment, every time he stood still without any direct destination toward which to move his feet. He bit the inside of his cheek just to feel something else. Something—

"Your Highness."

Teryn found Captain Braze of his personal guard beside him. He'd sent the man to check on Cora. His heart climbed into his throat. "Do you have news of her?"

The man nodded. "She's been released. She's meeting with King Verdian now."

TERYN MOVED SO FAST, HIS SIDE ACHED WHERE HIS STITCHES strained against the full breaths he took. He turned down the hall that led to Verdian's study—and halted. His entire body froze save for the mad thumping of his heart.

It was the first time he'd seen Cora in nearly a month, and he was overjoyed to find her hale and whole, uncowed by her imprisonment. He'd been worried she might have been mistreated despite his orders, but the way she walked with her head held high, carving a line through gaping courtiers like a wildfire surging through a forest, he knew she held the same spark she had before. Perhaps more of it. Her dark eyes were fierce, her rouged lips and cheeks doing nothing to soften the intensity of her gaze. She walked on swift feet, leaving no sign of the injuries he knew she'd sustained, and with the confidence of someone who'd never stopped being a princess. Two guards trailed in her wake, but she paid them no heed.

Her eyes landed on him, noticing him for the first time, and she pulled to an abrupt halt.

His lips spread into a grin while her face flashed with surprise. He nearly bounded over to her but stopped himself as her expression turned hard. Cold. Not a look he was unaccustomed to, but one he hadn't expected to find upon their reunion. She closed the lingering distance between them, stopping a few feet away. Everything inside him begged to reach for her, to turn her head this way and that to assure she remained unharmed. If he discovered anyone had laid a finger on her…his blood boiled at the thought. He fisted his hands at his sides to keep them still.

She tilted her head back to lock her eyes with his. "Am I just a pawn to you?"

Teryn inhaled sharply, her tone so barbed she might as well have slapped him. "What?" It was the only word he could utter.

"You proposed marriage," she said, voice quavering, "which you had no right to do."

Heat crawled up his neck. "What—how do you know—"

He couldn't find the words to finish. He'd brought up the idea of a marriage alliance between Khero and Menah to his mother just two days ago, but he hadn't spoken to Verdian yet. There were still details to work out. Bonds to break. New ones to forge. Most of all, he'd wanted to talk to Cora first.

"Your mother told me," she said. "I had to hear it from her. Meanwhile, you didn't even ask me if that was something I wanted." The tears glazing her eyes struck him like a blow to the chest. He was torn between the pain that came from knowing he'd once again hurt her and the weight of her rejection. He hadn't had the chance to ask her himself. Perhaps it was best that he hadn't.

"I wanted to talk to you about it," he said, unable to meet her eyes. "I didn't think…" Confusion tangled his thoughts, stalling his tongue. Why the hell had his mother intervened? What he'd conveyed to her had only been the barest idea. A hint to test her response. A seed that would first require Cora's acceptance before it could grow.

Cora shook her head. "You didn't think what? That this would hurt me?"

Teryn opened and closed his hands, his fingers desperate to reach for hers, to comfort her, to seek forgiveness. When he'd come up with his idea, he'd known there was a chance it could strain things between them, especially if she said no. However, he'd hoped they could at least remain friends if that ended up being the case.

Then again...were they *ever* friends before?

They'd exchanged as many smiles as they had blows, verbal and physical alike. They'd been enemies. They'd been allies. He'd betrayed her. He'd kissed her.

Where did that leave them now?

Not for the first time, the memory of their only kiss played through his mind. In the moment, he'd been driven by desperation. On one hand, he'd wanted her to leave him behind at Ridine Castle and flee while she had the chance. He'd known shocking her with a sudden kiss would work in his favor. On the other hand—and more importantly—he'd wanted to feel her lips against his. Wanted to give in to the spark of desire he'd felt. It was the desperate last wish of a man who thought he'd never see her again.

Whispers drew his attention back to the present. To Cora's tear-filled eyes. To the courtiers who surrounded them, muttering behind their hands. He took a step closer and lowered his voice. "Can we speak in private?"

She shook her head. Her voice calmed as if she too had noticed their audience. "What more is there to say? The only way for me to get my kingdom back is to resign myself to a loveless marriage."

The last part stung worse than he could have imagined. He swallowed hard. "You really think it would be loveless?"

She let out a humorless laugh. "I'm such a fool. I'm always such a fool when it comes to you." With that, she brushed past him.

His throat constricted. He knew he should let her go. End this scene before they stirred more gossip than they already had. Against his better judgment, he turned and took a step after her. His fingers closed softly around her wrist.

She stopped at once, frozen midstep. Then, after a glance at his hand, she slowly lifted her eyes to his. A sad smile curled her lips. Her voice was small, fragile. "For one moment, I thought she meant you."

His breath caught in his throat. He was so stunned that when she tugged her wrist from his grip and stormed off, he could do nothing but stare after her. Dread crept into his heart. What had she been implying by her last statement?

I thought she meant you.

Teryn fought the urge to chase after Cora and turned his attention to the other end of the hall. Toward King Verdian's study.

4

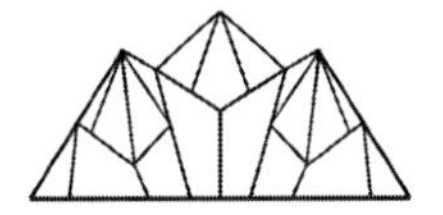

Mareleau Harvallis stood before the closed doors to her father's study several moments before gathering the courage to enter. King Dimetreus had already taken his leave, which meant now was her chance. Yet she lingered, still stewing after her interaction with Princess Aveline. She required a clear head to do what she had to do next, so she needed to rein in her emotions. She'd been planning this for weeks. She wouldn't let her plan fail now.

It was time to utilize her *magic trick*. She planted a false smile on her lips and envisioned the persona she wanted to project. Confidence. Dignity. Authority. Not that manipulating her outer composure ever really worked with her father. King Verdian and Queen Helena were amongst the few who often seemed immune to her charms. Still, it was worth a shot. She needed all the pretend magic she could muster for the reckless actions she was about to take. With a deep breath, she pushed open one of the doors.

"Princess Mareleau." Dowager Queen Bethaeny greeted her with a warm smile. It took no small effort not to sneer at the woman as Mareleau lowered into a polite curtsy. Mareleau had never had a reason to dislike Bethaeny before, but after the meeting she'd overheard, she found it hard not to despise her. She knew the queen wasn't to blame for the proposed marriage between Larylis and the lost princess. According to Bethaeny, it had been Teryn's idea. His mother had only played messenger. Either way, it gave Mareleau yet another reason to hate Teryn Alante—her fiancé—from the depths of her soul.

Once she rose from her curtsy, she faced her father's desk.

King Verdian gave her an impatient look. "I did not summon you, daughter."

"Yet I came anyway."

"I am expecting someone else."

She cocked her head innocently to the side. "Who might that be?"

He released a sigh and pinned her with a pointed glare. "Prince Larylis."

"Oh, how convenient. He's exactly who I came to speak to you about." She opened her mouth to say more when the study doors opened again. Her pulse kicked up as she expected Larylis to enter the room. Instead, she gritted her teeth at the sight of Teryn. Her sneer was lost on him, for he didn't so much as look at her. His eyes were locked on his mother.

His rigid posture—broad shoulders tense, chest heaving—stripped Mareleau's mind of all previous thought. She'd never seen him looking anything other than the arrogant, composed prince he was. What in the name of the seven gods did he have to be so enraged about? More than that, did he not realize he was interrupting a very important meeting? One she'd plotted with stringent care?

Teryn's voice came out strained as he spoke to Bethaeny. "Mother, did you offer a marriage alliance to Princess Aveline?"

She gave a gracious nod. "I did."

"Between Aveline and whom?"

"Between Aveline and Larylis, of course."

Mareleau internally roared with anger, but before she could let it out, her father cut in.

"Was it not your idea?" he barked.

Teryn's jaw tightened as he looked from Verdian to Bethaeny. "It was my idea to form a marriage alliance between Menah and Khero. I had suggested nothing beyond that."

Bethaeny skirted around to the front of Verdian's desk and laid a placating hand on Teryn's arm. "Darling, I simply executed your idea in the best possible way."

"I didn't ask you to do that, nor did I express the intricacies of my plan."

The queen gave Teryn a knowing look, one Mareleau couldn't quite decipher. "I had some inkling as to your *intricacies*," Bethaeny said, tone terse.

Teryn returned the look, green eyes flashing with anger. His words were clipped as he spoke through his teeth. "Clearly you didn't."

"I have something very important to discuss with my father," Mareleau said, giving Teryn and Bethaeny an exaggerated smile that probably looked more like a snarl. "You'll excuse us, won't you?"

They both ignored her.

"Princess Aveline is not marrying Larylis," Teryn said.

Mareleau blinked at him in surprise. When she managed to find her voice, she rushed to say, "I agree. She most certainly is not."

Teryn frowned at her as if he hadn't realized she was there until now.

"The princess has already agreed," Verdian said.

"She agreed under false pretenses," Teryn argued. "It was never my intention for her to marry Larylis."

Verdian released a grumbling breath. "Then who did you intend for her to marry?" When Teryn didn't answer, the king continued. "If Queen Bethaeny hadn't brought your idea to my attention, I would have come up with a similar solution myself. We need more than spies and allies at Ridine Castle. To ensure Khero is never again a threat—"

"Cora isn't—" Teryn shook his head and started again. "Princess Aveline isn't a threat."

"To ensure that is the case," Verdian said, enunciating each word, "we need a stronger alliance. Your marriage to my daughter will seal peace between Selay and Menah. Aveline's marriage to Larylis will do the same between Menah and Khero."

"Aveline cannot marry Larylis," Teryn said. "And I...I cannot marry Mareleau."

Mareleau's eyes shot to him. Never had she heard sweeter words. She shuttered her eyes, certain she was hallucinating. "You...can't?"

He met her gaze with a sympathy that almost made her bark a laugh. "I'm sorry."

She huffed. "Don't waste an apology on me. If you weren't going to end it, I was."

Verdian rose from his seat. "Have the two of you lost your minds? What is this?"

Bethaeny's cheeks flushed pink as she took her son's hand in hers. "What are you thinking, my dear? This marriage alliance has been secured for three years."

He quirked a brow. "I think we can all agree that this

marriage alliance has been anything but secure. I will sign a treaty for peace. I will promise my kingdom's loyalty. But I will not go forward with this marriage."

Mareleau lifted her chin, mildly disturbed that she was agreeing with the man she'd been fighting against for three years. "Nor will I."

Verdian scoffed and planted his hands on his desk. "You have no say in this."

"I do," she bit out, despite her father's warning glare. She knew she should stay silent. With Teryn's refusal to go through with their betrothal, her most pressing battle was won. But there was something left to fight for. Something she'd given up on once before, only because she'd been tricked. This was her chance to try. "*I'm* marrying Larylis."

A vein pulsed at her father's temple. "You've gone mad."

"You knew I wanted to wed him three years ago. Did you think my heart would change because you and Mother stole my letters and forged a mockery of my words?"

His face paled. It was the only confirmation she needed; both he and her mother had been involved with intercepting her letters. He revealed no shame as he spoke. "We've been over this. You are not marrying a bastard."

Her blood boiled at the word. That despicable, hateful word. It had driven her and Larylis apart three years ago when Uncle Ulrich caught them kissing in the stables. Moments before, they'd confessed their love for each other, their wishes to marry. Then, just like that, their dreams had been murdered, buried beneath the headstone of *Bastard*.

Larylis' parentage hadn't mattered to her then, and she wanted to argue that it didn't matter now. But she knew it wouldn't move Verdian. Her father didn't care what she wanted or how she felt. He only cared about his throne and his legacy. Well, if it was a legacy he cared so much about, she'd play that card.

"Larylis Alante is not a bastard, Father. He's been legitimized. He's a true prince now."

Verdian shook his head. "It may have been Arlous' last wish to give Larylis the Alante name, but it doesn't change the boy's origins. You are my heir, Mareleau. As a woman, your claim to the throne is tenuous."

"*As a woman*," she echoed, every word laced with venom. She curled her hands into fists to keep herself from shaking. "You do realize that if you were dead, Mother could run this kingdom just fine. Perhaps even better."

He snorted a humorless laugh. "That might be true, daughter, but Helena will not rule after I'm gone. My heir will. However, both of your uncles would rather see themselves on my throne than you. Should you marry someone of questionable blood, you won't stand a chance. The crown will never make its way into your hands. Not unless you make a proper match. Teryn is that match. He is a king. You will be his queen."

She threw her hands in the air. "How can I be queen of one kingdom and heir to another? Are you simply trying to get me out of the way so you can give your crown to one of my uncles? Are you so desperate to be rid of me as your heir?"

"You are my heir and I plan on keeping it that way," he said, with so much conviction she was partial to believe him. "Whether you keep my crown after I die is dependent upon your standing in the eyes of your competition. Should you marry a crown prince, or even a second or third son of distinguished royal lineage, that would be enough. Anything less..."

"Anything less...what?"

He ran a hand over his face. "Do you know what happens to monarchs with a weak claim?" He walked around to the side of his desk, stopping when he was a few feet away. "Queen Marion, 29 Year of the Fox, ruled for fifteen days before she was beheaded by her younger brother. Queen Jesebel, crowned 76 Year of the Sheep, overthrown in her second year of rule and imprisoned until her death. Princess Vilas, 102 Year of the Tiger, disappeared three days before her coronation as queen and was never seen again. Her cousin took the throne. Do you understand?"

Mareleau suppressed a shudder at what her father was insinuating. She'd never been overly fond of her uncles, and they bore very little love for her. But...did he really think they'd do something so sinister? The names he'd listed filled her mind, followed by other famed monarchs in history who'd been overthrown by powerful relatives. She kept her voice level as she said, "You underestimate my own cunning."

"You may be cunning, daughter," her father said, tone softening, "but I cannot risk your safety. You think I've been hard on you, but I will not set you up to fail. It is better that you are strong and safe. As Teryn's queen, you will be. Upon my death, you and Teryn will merge two kingdoms into one. Forge a power so great your uncles won't stand a chance. Even if they did manage to wrest Selay from your control, you would still have Menah. My legacy would die in this kingdom, but it would live on through you elsewhere. That would be enough for me."

Her heart shattered at the care she saw in his eyes. It was the first time she considered that his unwavering austerity toward her could have been fueled by something other than cruelty. And yet, she couldn't give him what he wanted. "I can't marry Teryn."

Verdian's composure hardened once again. "You will marry King Teryn. The two of you will rid your minds of this nonsense."

"I don't love him, Father. You know this. I love Larylis."

"We're not talking about love. We're talking about politics. About your own safety."

Her stomach churned. It was time to play the card she'd been keeping close to her heart. One she knew would damn her soul as soon as she uttered it aloud. Folding her hands at her waist, she met her father's eyes with contrived calm. "I will marry Larylis, Father, for it is the only reasonable course of action now that I'm with child. *His* child."

Silence echoed in the wake of her words, the tension so thick she thought it might smother her. Then a sound cut through. The only sound that could shatter her composure, her resolve, and her heart all at once.

Larylis' voice trembled from behind her. "What did you say?"

Slowly, she turned to face him. He stood in the doorway, his expression brimming with a flurry of feeling. Confusion. Anger. Guilt. Hurt.

His emerald gaze turned to steel, hardening on one final emotion.

Betrayal.

5

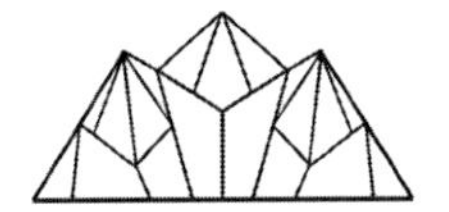

Teryn didn't know what to feel. His first reaction upon hearing Mareleau agree not to marry him had been relief. It hadn't been the biggest surprise, considering her previous attempts to court other suitors. But when she'd spoken of her love for Larylis, he'd been...shocked. Ashamed. Embarrassed.

He realized now that she hadn't spurned their engagement all this time because his kingdom was poor, nor because of his father's scandal. She'd done it because she was in love with someone else, and Teryn had stood directly between them. For the first time, he saw himself the way she must have seen him all along. An unwelcome interloper.

Did his brother see him the same way? The thought made his chest feel tight.

"You aren't serious, Mareleau." Queen Helena's voice teetered between disbelief and hysteria. Teryn hadn't noticed her enter behind his brother, but now she swiftly closed the study doors, eyes darting quickly around the room as if to assess who'd heard Mareleau's scathing admission.

"She isn't." Verdian's voice was almost a growl. His face was so flushed it was almost purple. "This is just another one of her games. Another childish attempt to flee an engagement."

"I think we've heard enough," Bethaeny said, taking Teryn's arm to pull him away. His feet were rooted to the spot.

"It's not a game," Mareleau said. Her words were for her father, but her eyes remained pinned on Larylis. She'd gone pale since his arrival, and her composure seemed shaken. "I'm pregnant with Larylis' child. It's a truth we no longer have to hide."

"No." Larylis' voice broke on the word. "We never..." He turned toward Teryn. "We didn't..."

Teryn studied him, searching for layers of truth behind his pleading eyes, between the words he wouldn't say.

Larylis had once admitted to having kissed Mareleau, but according to him, it hadn't meant anything. The disdain Larylis had demonstrated for the princess over the last three years had only served as evidence to support the claim.

But Teryn could still recall the pained look on Larylis' face during the poetry competition. During every conversation where Mareleau had come up. It was the same expression Larylis wore now.

The look of a man whose love was equal only to his agony. Both of which he tried to hide.

How had Teryn not recognized this before?

Was it because he'd never been in love?

If so...why did he recognize it now?

His mind went to Cora, but he couldn't think of her without recalling how he'd failed her. Betrayed her. He'd chosen duty over friendship. Lies over truth. He'd tried to fix his mistake but only when it was too late.

He would never be too late again.

Not for anyone.

Larylis took a deep breath and gathered his composure. "It isn't what you think, Teryn. I promise you, we never—"

"You don't get to speak, bastard," Verdian roared.

Mareleau rounded on her father. "Don't you dare talk to him like that!"

"You shouldn't talk at all."

"No, she *should* talk," Helena said, forcing calm into her voice. "Let her take it back. She knows better than this. Such a false statement would ruin her."

Mareleau lifted her chin with defiance. "I won't take it back."

Verdian opened his mouth, but Helena rushed to him and put a hand on his arm. "Let us not say a word more. Our daughter needs some time to contemplate—"

"There's nothing to contemplate. I am with child. Larylis is the father."

"Nonsense," Helena barked, her composure shattering into fury. "Your moon cycle—"

"My moon cycle is late. Ask my maids about my laundry. They will confirm it. Larylis and I conceived the night of the Heart's Hunt."

Larylis stepped forward. "Mareleau, stop. Please."

Helena shook her head, setting loose a graying brown curl from her towering updo. "That's not possible. I made sure to keep the two of you separate."

Mareleau shrugged. "You think I don't know how to navigate the servants' passages?"

Verdian's lips peeled back from his teeth. "You've ruined yourself!"

Mareleau didn't respond to her father's statement. "If you'd like proof of further indiscretions, just ask Lurel. She left me and Larylis alone in the drawing room adjacent to the library after the war meeting. I threatened her to keep it a secret."

"Seven gods, Mareleau," Larylis said as he ran a hand over his face. His shoulders drooped with fatigue. Or was it remorse?

Teryn realized he still hadn't moved. Still hadn't spoken. His blood stirred with a sensation he'd grown accustomed to over the past weeks. A desperation to not be idle. To fill every possible silence with a flutter of activity. To work, to strive, to fix.

This...he could fix this too. Before it was too late.

Teryn cleared his throat. It took a few attempts to find his voice. "Do you love her, Larylis?"

His brother opened and closed his mouth, eyes darting between Mareleau and Teryn. "We didn't..."

He repeated his question, tone firm. "Do you love her? The truth."

Larylis' throat bobbed. "Yes."

Teryn nodded. "Then you should marry her."

"You don't get to make that choice," Verdian said. "She's my daughter and she will not marry that—"

Teryn cut him off before he could say the word *bastard* again. "Why? My brother has been named an Alante. He's a prince. You were willing to see him wed the Princess of Khero. Why should he not marry the Princess of Selay?"

"The Princess of Khero isn't my daughter. Aveline's kingdom has no other contenders for the throne. Prince Larylis will suit fine for our purposes there. Here..." Verdian shook his head. "He does not have the respect required to allow my daughter to keep my throne after my death. Unlike you, he can offer her nothing else. He cannot merge our two kingdoms, nor can he make her a queen."

Teryn's stomach sank. As much as he hated to admit it, Verdian was right. Mareleau was Verdian's heir. His only child. He wanted his daughter made queen at any cost. Kept safe at any cost. And Larylis...well, he may have been given the Alante name, but he was still only a prince.

"It humbles me greatly to say this," Verdian uttered through his teeth, "but you're her only hope now. Should you find it in your heart to take my daughter as your bride and bury this scandal—"

"How dare you suggest such a thing." Mareleau's voice quaked as tears gathered in her eyes. "I love Larylis. I'm pregnant with *his* child."

Verdian's voice took on an empty quality. "If Teryn agrees to marry you, no one need know of your shame. Otherwise, you are ruined. You will neither be queen nor my heir."

"If I'm so ruined, why not just let me marry the man I love? Disinherit me. Make one of my uncles your heir. Do whatever you must, just—"

"I will not reward you for what you've done!" Verdian's voice boomed from wall to wall.

Another silence fell, and in its wake Teryn felt that familiar itch return. To move. To act. To fix. He opened and closed his fists as he worked up the courage to do what must be done.

Finally, with a trembling sigh, he said, "I abdicate my claim to the throne."

~

LARYLIS ALANTE NEVER IMAGINED HOW AWFUL IT WOULD FEEL to have his deepest desires come true. When he'd dreamed of earning the Alante name, he'd always imagined it would come about through perseverance, through gaining the respect of Queen Bethaeny, through his own merit. Not seconds before his father's death—a fate that was delivered by his own words.

When he'd dreamed of being with Mareleau, he'd never imagined it would come through deception and lies. Never imagined the woman he loved would twist their forbidden ardor into a tale of some treacherous liaison. Never imagined he'd be offered a crown in exchange for their perceived indiscretions.

He'd never—*ever*—dreamed of being king.

The thought of being given a throne he didn't deserve made his shoulders feel as if they bore leaden weights. There was only one reply he could give to Teryn's outrageous statement.

"No."

The word was shared with everyone else in the room, save Teryn and Mareleau. Verdian, Helena, and Bethaeny all looked at Teryn as if he'd gone mad. Teryn, meanwhile, stood taller, prouder, as if he'd already shrugged off the burden of their father's crown. Was that why Larylis suddenly felt so heavy?

"I won't take it," Larylis said, as if his refusal could shift the weight back where it belonged. He caught Mareleau's injured expression from the corner of his eye, but he couldn't bear to look at her. Not because he was angry. He certainly *was* angry, but he was more concerned that—should he meet her eyes, should he remember the desire in them when they'd shared their last kiss, should he recall the sweetness of her lips—he might be tempted to play along with her lie.

"It seems the boy has some modicum of sense after all," Verdian muttered.

"What I said stands." Teryn's voice was stern. "I abdicate, and that is final. I will gather Menah's council to make it official, but I have made my choice." In that moment, he reminded Larylis so much of their father, he thought his heart might shatter in two. Teryn held Verdian's stare with the same conviction Arlous had demonstrated when he'd first referred to Larylis as an Alante.

It was too much.

His throat closed up, seared by blood, by battle, by the words that had condemned their father to die.

We refuse to surrender.

"This will not stand," Verdian said. "You are King of Menah—"

"I've yet to be crowned," Teryn said. "Larylis will be in my stead."

"No." Larylis ground the word through his teeth.

Mareleau took a step toward him, her expression begging him to be silent.

"No," he said to her as well.

Teryn rounded on him. "I'm trying to fix this."

"There's nothing to fix." His lungs felt too tight. He could almost smell the blood on the battlefield, could almost hear the clang of steel. Red filled his vision. His next words came out in a rush. "I will not be rewarded for killing him."

He felt empty in the wake of his confession. It was the first time he'd spoken the truth out loud. That he'd killed King Arlous.

Teryn's expression flashed with pain, but it quickly hardened. When he spoke, his voice was cold. "You don't get to carry that burden on your own, brother. Father traded his life for mine."

"But I'm the one who refused to surrender." He hated

the way his voice trembled. Hated how small he felt in that room, despite being one of the tallest there.

Teryn's tone softened the merest fraction. "You did what I wouldn't have had the strength to do. You made the choice only a king would make. That's why Father put you in charge of that decision. That is why you will take my place."

Larylis shook his head. "You don't understand what you're giving up. What you think Mareleau and I have done—"

"It doesn't matter. Take the crown. I will not be swayed otherwise. If you won't take it as your right, then take it as your punishment."

His punishment.

There was something about that concept that silenced any further argument. There was a rightness about it. A cruel justice.

Perhaps it was what he deserved. To bear the crown of the man he killed. To win the hand of his beloved not through love but lies.

It would hurt so much more to accept than to refuse. It would hurt more to be king than to watch Teryn make all the impossible decisions from now on. It would hurt more to start a marriage based on deception than simply loving Mareleau from afar.

It was that pain, that aching punishment that drove him to finally say, "I accept."

6

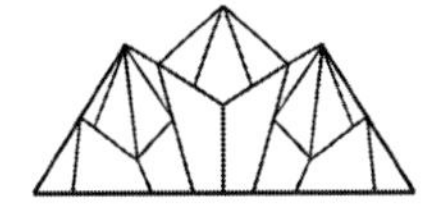

Teryn felt every muscle in his body uncoil. He hadn't realized how badly he hadn't wanted his father's throne until he felt the responsibility slip from his hands. His lungs felt stronger. His heart lighter.

As he assessed his brother, he knew why. Larylis now bore all that Teryn had shrugged off. Guilt sank Teryn's gut. He knew his brother didn't want it. Knew Larylis held much of the same anguish over their father's death. Perhaps it was cruel of Teryn to do what he'd done—to give him a crown he didn't want—but it was the only way he could think to fix the mess they found themselves in. This way, Larylis could marry the woman he loved. And Teryn...

He shuddered at the void that stood in the space his father's crown once filled. Without the mantle he'd been raised to bear...who was he?

The itch returned. He fluttered his fingers and shifted his stance just to feel his body move. He faced Verdian. "We've made our choices, Your Majesty. What's yours?"

"Choice," Verdian said with a scoff. "You've hardly given

much thought to your so-called *choice*. How will your brother keep his rule strong?"

He felt Mareleau's eyes burning into him, a silent plea for him to answer well. She'd gone silent since Teryn's announcement, as if she feared any word from her would shatter what Teryn was attempting to fix.

Teryn glanced at Larylis. He stood as still as a statue, jaw set. His eyes were unfocused as if he were only half there.

Turning his gaze back to the king, he said, "Larylis' rule will be strong, for he will have all our support. Selay's. Khero's. We're already in the process of forging a peace pact between our three kingdoms. Let us write these new terms into it. If you're determined that Selay and Menah will merge as one kingdom upon your death, then we'll write it into the pact. That way anyone who defies Mareleau or Larylis will draw the wrath of all three kingdoms. As for other allies, I'm sure even the Kingdom of Tomas will support him, thanks to Prince Lexington. I too will support Larylis as my king with all my heart, and..." He swallowed hard as he glanced at his mother. "He'll have Dowager Queen Bethaeny's support as well."

She paled, stunned silent. Then color pinked her cheeks. "You reckless, insensitive boy," she said, voice trembling with restraint. "You ask too much of me. Too much of my heart."

A lump rose in Teryn's throat as he watched her turn on her heel and flee the study. He wanted to run after her, to explain, to apologize, but he needed to see this through.

He returned his attention to Verdian and continued. "King Larylis will be crowned on the fifth of July. If you would like your daughter to be made queen the same day, I suggest you accept these new terms."

Queen Helena brightened at that. Gone was her

previous disdain as she smiled up at Verdian. "The fifth! That's only a few days from now. Our Mareleau could be queen so soon."

Verdian ignored his wife and huffed a laugh, his eyes still trained on Teryn. "Is that when you were supposed to be crowned? You're cutting it a little close to still be here."

He was right, but he'd had his reasons. "I didn't want to return home until I was assured of Princess Aveline's safety."

With a grumble, Verdian returned to the other side of his desk and sank into his chair. "And what shall we do with Princess Aveline?"

Teryn bit the inside of his cheek before answering. "I will marry her, pending her acceptance. The marriage alliance will be just as we'd planned before. Only a change of groom will be required. But I implore you, do not speak of this to her until I have spoken to her first." His heart ached to recall her anger at him when they'd met in the hall. He couldn't bear it if she learned of yet another development made without her prior knowledge.

Verdian rubbed his brow, sending his powdered wig slightly askew. Teryn held his breath as he awaited the king's answer. Finally, he spoke, his voice brimming with grudging resignation. "Very well. But I have conditions."

Mareleau stepped forward and took one of the chairs on the opposite side of his desk. She perched at the edge of her seat, fingers clawing into the armrests. "What might they be?" she said, her voice barely above a whisper.

Verdian spoke only to Teryn. "Following Mareleau's coronation, my daughter will leave for Ridine Castle. She will travel with Lord Ulrich. He's already planning to lead the rest of King Dimetreus' new staff and council to Ridine anyway."

Mareleau lifted her hands from the armrests to

anxiously weave her fingers through a lock of her silver-blonde hair. "Why would I go to Ridine?"

Verdian met his daughter's eyes. "I want someone there who can get close to Aveline. Someone she will feel comfortable enough to confide in. I'd previously had it in mind that Larylis would stay at Ridine during their period of courtship and act as a spy."

Teryn took a step forward. "Then I will take Larylis' place."

"No," Verdian said, his lips lifting into a smug grin. "You must stay with your brother. Now that you've decided to turn over your crown to someone who is wholly unprepared, you'll need to guide him."

"But I'm pregnant," Mareleau said, lifting her chin. "I can't travel."

Helena stood by her daughter and rested a hand on her shoulder. "She's right. She's in no condition to travel all the way to Ridine. It's bad enough that she'll have to journey to Dermaine Palace."

"Have some sense, Helena," Verdian barked. "She isn't far along. Besides, no one knows she's with child yet. She'll need to keep up the ruse that she conceived on her wedding night. Until it is proper for her to announce her condition, she will act as normal."

Mareleau rose from her chair. "That's unfair."

Verdian pinned her with a hard look. "Those are my terms."

Mareleau's eyes darted from Verdian to Helena, then to Teryn, as if hoping one of the latter two might intervene. Teryn knew better than to argue now. Finally, her gaze locked on Larylis. He still stood frozen, hands behind his back like an obedient soldier. Her expression flickered with hurt.

Verdian followed her gaze. "What do you think about my terms, King Larylis?"

Teryn bristled at his mocking tone, but Larylis was unflustered. "I will agree to whatever terms you deem necessary."

Mareleau pursed her lips as she burned Larylis with a glare he refused to meet. Turning back to her father, she said, "How long do you intend for me to stay there?"

Verdian rubbed his jaw, eyes unfocused, before he answered. "Until the end of July. On the final day of the month, we will convene at Ridine Castle to sign the official peace pact, solidifying these terms we've discussed. That will give us a chance to ensure once and for all that Aveline and Dimetreus can be trusted. Until then, keep close to Aveline. Report on her actions. Once the peace pact is signed, you may return home with your husband. Do you agree?"

She resumed weaving her lock of hair until her mother laid a hand on her fingers to still them. Mareleau dropped the tangled braid and folded her palms at her waist. "Yes."

"Then I suppose it's time to draw up a marriage contract."

Teryn released a sigh. He'd done it. He'd managed to fix something before it was too late.

But there was still more to do. More amends to make. And a very important question to ask.

THE DOORS TO CORA'S ROOM SPRANG OPEN. CORA HALTED her pacing before her window and turned toward the door, grateful to have some distraction from her thoughts. She was desperate to rid herself of the memory of Teryn's stricken face when they had spoken in the hall, of the courtiers who'd watched them with amused grins, of the betrothal she'd agreed to.

Lurel skipped into her room, a large box in her hands. The girl's smile grew with every step she took toward Cora. "I have so much news to share with you, Your Highness!"

"What news is that?"

"First of all," she said as she set the box on Cora's bed, "everything is settled for your journey to my father's estate."

Cora furrowed her brow. "Your...father?"

"Lord Kevan," she said.

Cora recalled the girl mentioning she was Mareleau's cousin, but Cora hadn't realized Lurel was the daughter of the man who'd be accompanying her to Ridine.

Lurel spoke again. "My next piece of news is even better! I'm coming to Ridine with you. I get to remain as your lady's maid even after you leave here! I wasn't sure Father would let me come, but since he'll be going to Ridine too, he gave me permission. Isn't that great?" The girl bounced on the balls of her feet. Her excitement was somewhere between endearing and annoying.

Cora gave her a weak smile. "How wonderful."

Lurel beamed and lifted the cover off the box she'd brought. "This is my next piece of news." From inside the box, she extracted a cloak of teal wool with brown leather running along the front seams and bottom hem. "It's your new riding cloak, made from the finest Aromir wool. Do you love it?"

Cora stepped closer to examine it. She ran her fingers over the wool, finding it impossibly soft yet dense. Aromir wool wasn't something she'd had access to when she'd lived with the Forest People, for it was more of a luxury than a necessity. When it came to practical use, regular wool sufficed.

But when it came to a garment fit for a royal...

"It's perfect."

"Try it on," Lurel said, already draping it around Cora's shoulders. "The seamstresses will have a riding habit hemmed for you within the hour. If you're still set on leaving tonight, we can depart by early evening. My father's estate is only an hour away, so we'll make it there by nightfall."

"My brother is prepared to leave tonight as well?" A pinch of guilt squeezed her chest. After her confrontation with Teryn, she hadn't had the courage to leave her room, which meant she hadn't seen her brother since she'd abandoned him at the meeting.

"He has left it up to you, Your Highness." Lurel straightened the length of the cloak while Cora secured the clasp. She noted its shape—a purple oval with a black mountain. Khero's sigil. She hadn't worn something bearing her kingdom's sigil since she was a child. It made her throat feel tight. Lurel's voice called out from behind the dressing screen. Cora hadn't noticed when she'd flitted over there. "Can we throw this one out then?"

Cora frowned at the stained garment Lurel held by the tips of her fingers. She took the battered cloak from Lurel, her eyes falling on the torn hem where she'd cut a bandage for Teryn's wound after the battle at Centerpointe Rock. She remembered how he'd looked at her then, how he'd placed his hand on hers after she'd finished wrapping the wool around him. The thought was quickly replaced with the pain she'd felt at discovering he'd bargained off her hand to his brother.

"Might as well burn it." Gritting her teeth, she folded up

the cloak with far more force than necessary and strolled over to the hearth and the warm blaze within. Now that she'd officially reclaimed her title as princess, she didn't have to beg for her hearth to be lit; it was simply done. She folded the cloak tighter and prepared to toss the bundle on the flames when she felt something hard beneath her palm. Frowning, she paused and searched for the source. From within one of the inner pockets, she extracted a large amber crystal.

Her heart leaped into her throat. Murky energy thrummed against her palm—

"What is that?" Lurel appeared at Cora's side, eyes wide.

"It's nothing." She threw the cloak into the fire. As Lurel's eyes followed the garment, Cora stashed the crystal into the pocket of her new cloak. Her mind reeled. How had she forgotten that she'd taken Morkai's crystal from the battlefield?

Lurel looked back at Cora, eyes searching her now empty hands. She opened her mouth, but a sudden chime of bells drowned out whatever she was about to say.

"What is that?" Cora asked. The bells resounded far too many times to mark the hour.

Lurel clasped her hands to her chest. "That must have to do with my next piece of news! I heard the gossip on my way here. Princess Mareleau is getting married. Well, those chimes must be announcing that it has already happened. It seems there will be no fuss or ceremony. It's rather last minute, don't you think? But her engagement has already lasted three years. It makes sense they would wed so fast, I suppose. There is to be a feast tonight. We cannot go, for we will be on the road by then. Unless you want me to ask my father to postpone?"

Cora tuned out the girl's voice as she spun on her heel.

Her steps were slow and heavy as she made her way to one of the windows. She watched as courtiers chatted animatedly in the garden below, probably gossiping about the princess' surprise nuptials. Something dark heaved in her chest, but she refused to let it out. She was too afraid it might be a sob.

No, she wouldn't cry.

She wouldn't.

Why should she, anyway? Had she not admitted that a loveless political marriage would be better for her? If Teryn had wanted her hand, it would only complicate things. Her feelings for him represented something she wasn't ready to accept—surrender. Should she marry for love, she'd have to give a piece of herself away. Her magical self. She knew she'd never be accepted as both a royal and a witch. Should she forge any heartfelt ties beyond what was necessary for the safety of her kingdom, she'd never have the option to return to the woods. She'd be nothing but Princess Aveline forevermore.

No, that was not something she could give in to just yet. While she knew she no longer belonged with the Forest People, she didn't fit with the royals either. Her place was yet to be discovered. In the meantime, she'd play the royals' games. Agree to their terms. Serve her kingdom. So long as she kept one foot out the door, she'd have means for escape. For freedom. For a future where she could be herself again.

Lurel came up beside her and handed her a folded piece of parchment, sealed with a simple, unmarked blot of wax. "Here is my final piece of news, though I can hardly call it that. I don't know what it is. A servant brought it to me and asked that I deliver it to you."

Cora took the note from the girl and flicked the seal with

her thumbnail. She unfolded the paper to find a short letter that read:

Cora,
Meet me in the garden after dinner.
Please.
–Teryn.

"What does it say?" Lurel asked.

Cora crumpled it into a ball and brought it to the hearth. "Nothing important. Come. Let us prepare to leave. We'll make no fuss about it either. Tell your father to keep our departure quiet. We wouldn't want to take away from the princess' happy day." She said the last part with no small amount of malice and tossed the letter into the flames.

7

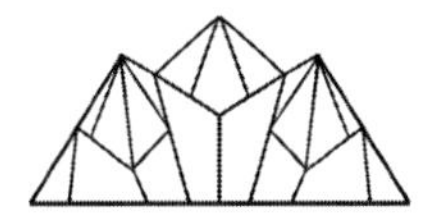

Mareleau Harvallis had never felt so anxious as she did now. Her stomach was a swarm of butterflies. Her heart the rapid pulse of hummingbird wings. She walked down the dimly lit halls of Verlot Palace next to the man she loved. The man she was now married to. The man who hadn't so much as looked at her since they'd marked their names side by side on a binding contract.

That was all her wedding had been.

No ceremony. No Godspriest. No elaborate gown. Not even a kiss to seal their nuptials.

Just a quill, a contract, and a flurry of bells.

Her mother had convinced Verdian to agree to host a dinner at least, but Mareleau could have done without that. The last-minute formality meant Mareleau had been pulled away from Larylis immediately following the signing of their marriage contract to be fussed over by her lady's maids. They'd cooed congratulations while whispering behind their hands when they didn't think she was listening. They'd worn smiles while they'd styled her hair, dressed her in the prettiest gown she owned, then smirked and gossiped over the suddenness of her wedding and her unsettling choice of groom.

Dinner had been more of the same. She'd endured cold congratulations, perplexed stares, and too-loud whispers as her dinner guests speculated upon why she'd married the bastard and whether it was true he was now King of Menah in lieu of Teryn. She'd suffered it all with a tight-lipped grin, her composure curated to hide the mess of emotions tangled within. All the while, Larylis—her husband, her beloved—had sat mute by her side. Not once had they gotten the chance to speak. Not once had he turned to her with a smile or a kiss. Her dread had only grown from there.

Now that dinner was over, she and Larylis were forced to engage in one of the most barbaric and outdated traditions Mareleau's kingdom observed during royal marriages. The procession to the wedding chamber.

The corridor echoed with strains of violin, shuffling feet, and muffled whispers. Thankfully, their retinue wasn't overlarge, but even the dozen or so spectators were more than enough to tie Mareleau's stomach in knots. She and Larylis were near enough to touch as they walked with slow steps. That they didn't so much as brush fingertips showed her what efforts Larylis was taking to prevent it. She no longer tried to catch his eye, for she was too preoccupied with her own dread and humiliation. Surely, if she'd been denied a formal wedding ceremony, she could have been denied this ridiculous tradition as well. But no matter how hard she'd argued against it, her mother had refused to hear a word of it. *This is more important than the wedding*, Helena had said. *Especially where you're concerned.*

Mareleau had guessed what her mother had been referring to. The procession to the wedding chamber was meant to prove a royal marriage was consummated. She could only thank the seven gods that her kingdom had long ago done away with the requirement that the consummation be witnessed by a Godspriest. To think that was ever considered civilized!

They reached the end of a short hall where a pair of red and gold doors stood. Mareleau had never entered them before. She'd never had need to, for the room was reserved specifically for newlyweds. Mareleau had to resist the urge to fiddle with her hair as they paused before the doors. She hazarded a glance at Larylis just as he did the same to her. Her heart climbed into her throat, sending it thudding even faster. Too soon, he looked away and faced the crowd behind them.

Mareleau did the same. She kept her eyes fixed firmly above everyone's heads, grateful for how dark the hall was. Breah, one of her lady's maids, stepped forward with a curtsy, then loosened the laces of Mareleau's gown and removed pins, jewels, and sashes from her ensemble. Breah helped her out of her dress next, leaving her in her petticoats, corset, and shift. As she let down Mareleau's hair, a young man went to assist Larylis out of his jacket and waistcoat.

Mareleau swallowed hard and briefly scanned the crowd. She found her other two lady's maids—Ann and Sera—as well as her mother. It was no surprise her father was missing, for he'd hardly deigned to join her wedding feast. His actions spoke clearly of his disdain for her marriage, regardless of his grudging acceptance.

Once Larylis was left in only his shirt and trousers, the audience rumbled with polite applause. Everything inside her wanted to curl forward, to fold her arms over her chest, but she forced herself to stand tall, to lift her chin, to exude the confidence she didn't feel.

Queen Helena clasped her hands to her heart and faced the crowd. "It is now time for the bride and groom to become true husband and wife. Wish them many blessings, so they may bring forth an heir." Another wave of applause. A few disbelieving snickers.

Breah curtsied once again, bowing her blonde head. "Is there anything you desire to be brought to you before we bid you goodnight, Your Highness?"

"Wine." The word came out in a rush.

Helena cut a glare at her daughter, then glanced suggestively at Mareleau's abdomen.

It took no small amount of restraint to keep from rolling her eyes. "For my husband," she amended, lifting a hand toward him. She nearly alighted it upon his arm when she remembered they hadn't touched since their stolen kiss over a month ago. She folded her hands at her waist and gave her mother a demure smile. "My husband would like wine. I do not."

Breah nodded and scurried into the crowd, returning with a bottle and glass. Breah handed both to Larylis.

Helena gave a satisfied nod, and two servants opened the pair of doors. As Mareleau and Larylis turned toward them, her pulse kicked up. She was relieved to escape the eyes of the spectators, but she dreaded what would come next. Not the consummation they were expected to perform but something far more mundane.

A conversation.

She'd been desperate to speak to him all night, to explain, to apologize, but as she entered the wedding chamber and heard the doors close behind them, she wished she were anywhere else. The longer Larylis had avoided speaking to her, the more certain she'd become of his displeasure. He had every right to be upset, of course. Hopefully his love for her was stronger than his anger.

Silence hung heavy as they stood just beyond the closed doors. They studied the walls, the bed, looking everywhere but at each other. The candlelit room was relatively small while the bed was enormous, piled high with plush pillows, silk sheets, and velvet blankets in the deepest shades of red and gold. Old-fashioned tapestries adorned the marble walls, displaying romantic scenes of courtship and lovemaking.

Mareleau couldn't help but wrinkle her nose. "This is the most hideous room I've ever seen."

Larylis snorted a laugh. The sound was so familiar, so cherished, it had Mareleau's chest warming. She glanced his way to see if he held a smile on his lips, but he was already turning away from her. He strolled over to the bedside table and set down his armload. With slow moves, he poured the deep ruby wine into the glass. She expected him to drink from it, but he didn't. Instead, he set it back down and moved to the sole window in the room. He drew back the crimson curtain and stood silent, hardly moving but for the rise and fall of his chest. The blush of the setting sun streamed through the window, amplifying the red and gold glow of the room, glinting off the copper tones in his dark hair.

Mareleau watched him for a few moments, studying the broad expanse of his shoulders, the slim taper of his waist visible beneath his untucked shirt, the way his overlong hair curled at the nape of his neck. She was desperate to break the silence, but no words would come. So she swept over to the glass of wine, drained it in two gulps, then filled another. The burn of the fiery liquid warmed her stomach and muted her swarm of thoughts. She closed her eyes as she took another sip, relishing the way her muscles unwound.

"What about the baby?" Larylis' voice had her eyes flying open, his tone equal parts taunting and condemning. He watched her from the window, lips pressed into a tight line.

Her heart hammered so hard, she was surprised her entire ribcage didn't shatter in her chest. With trembling hands, she set down the cup and took a few steps toward him. She immediately set to braiding three strands of hair, hating how her stomach turned beneath his unyielding scrutiny. She paused and considered wielding her *magic trick* to summon one of her false personas. It would make it easier to have the conversation they needed to have, but...it wasn't right. Larylis deserved her true self now.

"I'm so sorry I lied, Larylis," she said.

"Why did you do it?"

She frowned. "Why do you think I did it? I had to get out of marrying Teryn."

He shook his head. "You could have gotten out of your engagement a hundred different ways. Why did you bring me into it? With a lie, no less. One that made me look like a traitor to my brother."

She bristled at his rising tone. Her own voice grew sharper. "It was the only way I could think that would finally allow us to be together."

"You should have asked me first."

"You would have said no."

He took a step closer. "And you'd have had my answer. What are you going to do in a few months when it's clear you aren't with child?"

"I have plans for that," she said slowly. "In a few weeks, I will announce that my condition came to...to an end. My parents won't expect me to mourn, for I am supposed to be hiding my supposed pregnancy."

She expected some relief to show on his face after hearing she had it all under control. If anything, he looked angrier. "You shouldn't have done this."

She narrowed her eyes. "You'd have let me go so easily? Even after everything we confessed in the drawing room, after learning what had happened to our letters...you'd have let me go? Answer me honestly."

He opened his mouth only to snap it shut. With a slow sigh, he dragged a hand over his face, and his expression finally eased. His tone turned soft. Resigned. "Only on the outside. Inside...inside, I would have held you tight and never let you go."

"Well, I'm not quite so noble as you. I wasn't willing to let you go inside or out. I had to fight for you, whether it damned my reputation, ruined my chances at inheriting my father's crown, or had me cast out as a traitor. I had to try. I had to risk everything."

Again, he opened his mouth only to say nothing for several breaths. Finally, he whispered, "It was wrong. We shouldn't...we shouldn't have been rewarded for your lie. I shouldn't have been rewarded for what I did to my father."

Her heart clenched at that. She remembered what he'd said in her father's study, how he'd taken the blame for his father's death. She'd heard the details of what had happened during the battle. Had she been less wrapped up in her own schemes, she might have reassessed the timing of her plan. She bit her lip and took a few steps closer. Her hands begged to reach for him, but she was too afraid he'd evade her touch. "It wasn't your fault."

He averted his gaze. "You weren't there."

"I didn't have to be." She stepped closer again, and this

time she did reach for him. Her hands shook as she pressed them to his chest. His heart thumped against her palms. Despite their years of animosity that had resulted from her parents' trickery, touching him now felt like coming home. Like she hadn't spent three years thinking he'd abandoned her. "I know you, Larylis. You are the most intelligent man I've met. You do nothing without analyzing the alternatives first. You make no choice without weighing it against histories, facts, and probabilities. You are selfless and are constantly trying to make those around you happy and comfortable. You think too little of yourself, but I see you. I know about the difficult choice you made, and I know you made the only one you could."

He looked down at her, a flash of surprise in his eyes. Then his expression fell, and he looked away from her again. "I can't help but wonder if it was the wrong decision."

"You can't go back." She lifted a hand from his chest and placed it on his cheek. "*We* can't go back. I'm sorry for what I did and for all the pain I've caused. I'm sorry for the rift I may have driven between you and your brother, but..."

She gently turned his cheek until his eyes met hers. Lifting her chin, she spoke with fierce truth. "I don't regret it. I'd do it again a hundred times if it meant no one would keep us apart again."

His eyes widened. Mareleau wasn't sure if they held awe or terror. She didn't care. This was the real her. If he was to be her husband, he should know she wasn't a pretty flower. She was a dragon. She would consume the world and burn it to ash to get what she wanted.

Right now, what she wanted was him.

She stepped closer until her chest brushed his. He stiffened but kept his eyes trained on hers. "Tell me this is wrong," she dared him, angling her head back. "Tell me you don't want this. Say the word and I'll step away from you. We can be husband and wife in name only. You can punish me for my lies and punish yourself for your own perceived crimes."

He said nothing.

She ran her thumb along his jaw, feeling the slightest hint of stubble beneath the pad of her finger. "Tell me, Larylis."

His breaths turned sharp and shallow, his wide chest pulsing against her breasts. She refused to widen the space between them, refused to give an inch unless he told her to. His moss-green eyes swam with a hunger that sang through her blood, echoing the desire thrumming in her core.

Finally, he slid an arm around her, his palm skating over the laces of her corset. His other hand covered hers—the one still pressed against his cheek. It sparked a memory from the last time they'd stood this close, the last time he'd placed his hand over hers. They'd been in the drawing room, and she'd been working to frantically undress him when he'd stilled her hands and pulled away.

Her heart lurched as she expected him to do the same now. She held her breath, bracing herself for his rejection—

His lips came down to hers, soft and slow and hungry. She gasped with surprise, with relief, and wound her arms around his neck. They were a tangle of limbs as they moved away from the window. She opened her mouth to deepen the kiss, felt his tongue caress hers. Her legs trembled from the desire that coursed through her, gathering in a burning warmth low in her belly. She gave more and more of her weight over to him, let him lift her beneath her thighs and carry her the rest of the way to the bed. Her back met the plush mattress, the velvet blankets soft against her bare shoulders.

She tugged Larylis closer, searching for buttons to pry loose. He pulled away from her long enough to shrug free from his shirt. She lifted herself on her forearms, desperate not to let the distance between them grow too vast. When he returned to her, his hands moved to her back. With one hand, he untied the laces of her corset. With the other, he unhooked the front closures. Once she was free, he threw the garment on the floor. Her petticoats went next, leaving only her cotton shift to cover her naked flesh.

He paused and pulled back, eyes roving the length of her. The desire filling his gaze was so heady, it emboldened her. With slow motions, she reached for the top of her shift and slowly slid it down her shoulders. Inch by slow inch, she let the cotton skate down her skin, baring her breasts, her torso, her stomach. Finally, she slid it over her hips until she was fully naked before him.

He assessed her again, then leaned in to claim her lips. She pulled back and shook her head. "It's your turn."

His lips quirked into a crooked grin—the first smile she'd seen from him all day—and it was the most beautiful sight she'd ever witnessed. Her hands moved to the buttons of his trousers. He trailed kisses down her neck, over her collarbone, over the crest of each breast, as she freed him from his pants. Then, slowly, he lay beside her on the bed, his hands roving her side, her hip, her upper thighs. His gaze turned suddenly timid, but his touch was fire, igniting everywhere their skin met. She bit her lip as his hand curved around her bottom.

"Larylis." His name came out with a tremor. "I need you. So badly, I need you closer." She meant it in more ways than one. She wanted his body in this moment more than she'd ever wanted anything. But she wanted his heart too. His mind. His love. The coldness that had stood between them today was too sharp to endure again. They'd already been pulled apart for three years. Now they would be separated again in a matter of days. She'd be stuck at Ridine Castle for at least two weeks, and that didn't include the travel time to get there. She needed to know a chasm wouldn't grow between them in her absence. "I need you to love me."

He drew his hand back up the length of her body, over her thighs, her stomach, her breast, her neck, until he cradled her cheek. Locking his eyes with hers, he said, "With everything that I am, I love you."

She pulled him down to her and lost herself in his lips, his limbs, his touch. Their hearts met. Their bodies tangled. Amidst the web of lies she'd spun, through the cracks rent by the ferocity of her affection, love dug roots and bloomed.

8

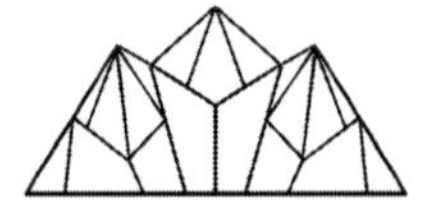

Dinner had been over for two hours, and still Teryn waited. He stood in the courtyard just beyond the doors that led from the palace to the garden, ensuring he wouldn't miss anyone who entered. No matter how many times footsteps resounded on the stone steps, not a single pair belonged to *her*.

His heart had sunk with the sun, and now that night had fully fallen, he wasn't sure he dared hope any longer. He glanced away from the palace doors to the windows of the upper levels. Music streamed from the open balcony of the ballroom, where a celebratory dance was being held. The newlyweds had already been escorted to their wedding chamber, but it seemed the festivities being held in their honor were ongoing. Teryn scanned other balconies, most of them dark, seeking Cora's room. He knew he could go to her, but there was a reason he'd asked her to see him in the garden tonight. Yet the longer he stayed out here, the more pathetic he found his reason to be.

He released a heavy breath. "Was it really so foolish of an idea to think I could romance her?"

The only answer he received was a sharp peck on his cheek. With a grin, he glanced at Berol, his peregrine falcon. She was perched upon the leather pad he wore over one shoulder, strapped across his dinner jacket. He dared not go outside without it, for Berol refused to let him out of her sight when he was outdoors lately. The falcon had found him the day he'd arrived at Verlot Palace after leaving Centerpointe Rock. Teryn's relief at seeing her both alive and having forgiven him for yelling at her to go away during the battle had nearly been enough to bring tears to his eyes. He'd been willing to upset her at Centerpointe Rock if it meant keeping her safe, but her short absence had been almost as painful to endure as his physical wounds.

He gave her neck some scritches, which she returned in the form of more nibbles to his cheek.

The sound of a door opening caught his attention, followed by the swoosh of skirts and the patter of feet. Hope bloomed in Teryn's chest as he angled himself toward whoever had come—

His shoulders slumped as he found his mother strolling into the garden. He should have recognized the cadence of her steps. Dread replaced his hope, for it was clear she'd come to talk. He owed her an explanation for what had happened today, for how he'd claimed she'd support Larylis' rule. However, he'd hoped he'd have more time to prepare for it.

Her lips were pursed as she walked up to him. Berol launched off his shoulder as if she dreaded the scolding as much as Teryn did. What Teryn wouldn't give to sprout wings and fly away too.

"Mother," he said with a nod.

Her eyes blazed with fury as she spoke. "Everything I've

done, I've done for you. In a single sentence, you've done away with all of it."

"I'm sorry," he said, filling his voice with the full weight of his apology. He didn't regret abdicating, but he was agonized over how much it must have hurt his mother.

"What is your apology worth now? They've won. They got what they wanted all along."

Teryn frowned. "Who won?"

"Lady Annabel and your father," she said through her teeth. "Why do you think I sent Larylis away all those years ago? My ladies heard Annabel bragging that her son would one day be king. Her ambition had become dangerous, so I fought hard against it. I fought with everything I had to protect you. To protect your crown."

"I never asked you to protect my crown," he said as gently as he could.

"I'm your mother. My protection comes with or without your request or permission. Now that you've turned your crown over to Larylis, everything I fought for has been for naught." She let out a humorless chuckle. "With Arlous' death, *we'd* won. You and me. Even with Larylis named prince, we'd still won."

Teryn shook his head. "I'm tired of war, Mother. The battle of crowns was never one I wanted to fight. I never wanted to be pitted against my brother. I never wanted to be torn between you and Father."

She huffed. "Are you saying I was wrong to fight for my crown? I was defending my right and yours."

"I could never deny you that right, nor could I have condoned what Father did when he tried to replace you. You're my mother. I love you. But...I loved Father too. And Larylis."

"Your love won't make him a good king."

"I believe in him."

"What about me? Have you no sympathy for what this means for me? With Larylis as king, Lady Annabel will have the run of Dermaine Palace. She'll be Queen Mother Annabel. I'll be relegated once more to my little palace, never again welcome in the place that once was my home." Her voice broke on the last part.

Teryn's heart sank. He gathered his mother's hand in his. "You will be welcome."

She turned up her nose. "Larylis could ensure I'm not."

"He's better than that. He's better than Annabel, and you know it."

She turned her head but made no argument.

"He and I will both take care of you." He hesitated before saying the next part. "There was once a time when you took care of him. Until you banished him from Dermaine, you were far more of a mother to him than Annabel was. He hasn't forgotten the kindness you once showed him."

Her shoulders drooped. She met Teryn's eyes briefly before shaking her head. "I couldn't let myself love him. It was too dangerous. He won't forgive me for banishing him."

"He will. It's himself he'll struggle to forgive. Besides, Larylis and I have seen true danger. We met it on a battlefield. We fought wraiths, a monster, and a blood mage. This...this is just politics."

"You're really willing to let go of your birthright so easily?"

"I won't say it's easy, but I believe it's the right thing to do. If you trusted me to be king, then I ask you to trust me with this too."

Silence fell between them. Finally, she squeezed his hand. "I can't say my heart isn't broken, but I...I'll support your brother's claim to the throne in name only. Do not ask me to do anything more on his behalf."

"That's fair," he said, trying not to sound too shocked that he'd won her agreement.

She released his hand and made to leave. Just as she turned away, she whirled right back around. "Who are you waiting for?"

"How do you know I'm waiting for anyone?"

"You've been out here for two hours, my son. It's the longest I've seen you stay in one place in weeks. So tell me. Who is it?"

He couldn't help the flush that heated his cheeks as he spoke her name. "Princess Aveline."

His mother's eyes flickered with a sympathy that seemed suspiciously feigned. "Did no one tell you? She already left."

Teryn's muscles went rigid. "When? Why didn't I hear about it?"

She gave a flippant shrug. "One of my ladies told me the princess left while everyone was at dinner. Rumor has it, she didn't want to take away from such a special occasion with her hasty exit."

He rubbed his temples as if it could grind away his disappointment too.

"My suspicions were correct," Bethaeny said, an edge to her tone. "You have feelings for the princess. You intended to wed her when you proposed the marriage alliance."

He gave her a pointed look. "Yes, and you shouldn't have intervened."

"Like I said, Teryn. I am your mother. My protection does not need permission. I was worried you were about to make a hasty decision and destroy your engagement to Mareleau. That was before I knew the girl was a scheming harlot, of course."

"I fear your protection has made things far more difficult," he said, trying his best to keep his voice level.

"Tell me this, son. Is *Cora*, as I've heard you call her, worth giving up your crown for?"

"I didn't do it for her." His words were true. He'd done it for Larylis too. He nearly left it at that but there was a deeper truth yet to be said. "But yes. She's worth it."

"Do you love her?"

His heart hammered at the question. Heat crawled up his neck, his cheeks. He was grateful that night had fallen to hide the blush that had certainly taken over every inch of his skin. "One step at a time," he said, trying to sound nonchalant. "First, I need to make sure she doesn't try to shoot me in the heart with an arrow when she sees me next. Which...I don't know when that will be."

"Promise me you will not go after her," she said with a stern raise of her brow. "Promise me you will be there for your brother. You owe it to him and your kingdom."

He hated that she was right; Larylis needed him. His brother had a heavy responsibility he'd never expected to take on. And yet, Teryn couldn't find it in his heart to make the promise his mother asked for. He'd long since learned not to utter promises he knew he wouldn't keep. "I'll do what is needed of me."

She narrowed her eyes but made no argument. Seeming satisfied with his answer, she left him alone. Berol flew back to his shoulder. He fed her a strip of duck he'd taken from dinner, but in his mother's absence, the uncomfortable itch to move returned. He'd managed to keep it at bay while he'd been waiting for Cora, but now that he knew he wouldn't get to see her tonight, he was back to feeling unsettled. Stuck.

With a heavy sigh, he turned from the palace doors and headed deeper into the garden, past the candlelit alcove where a single table stood, upon which sat a bottle of wine and a pair of glasses. He couldn't bring himself to look at it. Cora probably would have hated it anyway. He walked past the harpist and shook his head. With a nod, the musician rose from her seat at the edge of the fountain and departed. Cora would have hated that too. They'd danced to a harpist once, but...what had he been thinking? She'd hated him then. She probably hated him still.

And yet...

For one moment, I thought she meant you.

Damn it all, it *was* him. It had always been him. He couldn't tell her now, and maybe he couldn't tell her any time soon. But he would. Eventually...he would.

Deeper and deeper, he walked into the garden, Berol his lone companion, determined to walk until he was tired enough to sleep and forget the hollow ache in his heart.

9

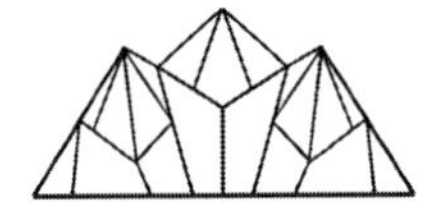

The smell of the forest was so soothing, Cora almost wept. Aromas of earth and pine surrounded her, carried by the mild breeze. Closing her eyes, she tilted her face to the sky, basking in the morning sun that warmed her skin. If it wasn't for the dozens of hoofbeats that echoed on the road around her, she could almost pretend she was deep in the woods, riding one of the Forest People's horses alongside Maiya. Instead, she rode a borrowed palfrey alongside her brother on their way home.

She still didn't know how to feel about the word *home*, nor the pain that lanced her heart at the thought of Maiya. She hadn't communicated with any of the Forest People since the battle, and she was desperate to know how they fared. They'd come to her aid, fought Morkai's wraiths, defended royal soldiers. All in the name of protecting fae magic. They'd come out victorious, but she knew not all the Forest People had survived. She'd seen Druchan's dead body. Witnessed Roije get his arm severed by Morkai. Had he survived such a grave wound? And if not...would Maiya ever forgive her?

She shook the question from her mind, for it would only plague her to no end. Perhaps someday soon she could seek out the commune, at least for a visit, but this was not the time. Right now she needed to be Princess Aveline.

She turned her face away from the sun and opened her eyes. Her gaze landed on a less pleasant view—Lord Kevan's backside. He rode ahead of her while Dimetreus kept to her side. Guards took the lead and rear, while dozens of other horses, wagons, and coaches filled the middle of their entourage. Lurel rode in one of the coaches, alongside other handpicked servants and staff, all selected by Lord Kevan.

Cora and Dimetreus had stayed at Kevan's estate for three days while their preparations had been finalized. That had given Cora more than enough time to set her opinion of her kingdom's new Head of Council. He was gruff, short tempered, and the complete opposite of his bright and bubbly daughter. The more she got to know him the harder it was to believe they were related. Even their looks were at odds. Where Lurel was willowy and fair, Kevan was a brutish bear. He was barrel-chested with piercing blue eyes, gray-brown hair that framed his face like a wild mane, and a thick beard. He was never short on cutting remarks and made no effort to venerate Cora and Dimetreus more than necessity required.

Cora had been eager to get out of his home and on the road to more neutral territory. Yesterday, she'd gotten her wish, and today had brought them to the forest road. To pine and birdsong and a mountainous view beyond a sea of endless green. It was the closest she could get to the forests she craved.

Closing her eyes again, she focused on her breath, on the air caressing her nostrils, brushing her cheeks, dancing over her gloved hands as she held her reins. She let the horse beneath her root her to the earth, every hoofbeat serving as an anchor. The warmth of the sun connected her to the element of fire while her emotions, her blood, and the aroma of dew-speckled leaves connected her to water. The elements thickened around her, feeding her mental shields.

Her shields had been especially necessary lately. Without them, she'd likely have a migraine by now from all the emotions she'd have picked up from the strangers around her. But that didn't mean she couldn't let them down for at least a moment...

With a slow exhale, she pried the smallest hole through her mental shroud and extended her senses outward, beyond the road and her retinue, reaching deeper into the woods that flanked their path. Finally, she located what she'd been searching for.

Warmth greeted her like a friendly wave.

I am nearby, Valorre said. She smiled at the feeling-thought that was his voice, although she could sense a tinge of impatience with it. The unicorn was not overly fond of how slowly her entourage traveled. He'd already galloped ahead and doubled back several times. *You will be pleased to know I have found no hunters.*

That's good, she thought back to him. However, she wouldn't be fully comforted until they left northern Selay and confirmed the forests in Khero were empty of Morkai's hunters as well. She figured word of their master's death had likely driven them to abandon their efforts, but she couldn't be certain. Unicorn horns were still a rare commodity. And unlike many of the soldiers who'd awoken confused on the battlefield after the duke's glamour had been severed, the unicorn hunters Cora had once pitted herself against weren't being controlled by dark magic. Instead, they were mercenaries and convicted criminals. Cora wasn't sure what Verdian and her other new allies were doing to sway public opinion about her brother and present him as an innocent victim, but if Morkai's men thought Dimetreus was still in league with the duke's former plans, they might continue their work.

That was yet another thing Cora was determined to see finished before she considered leaving Ridine Castle to find the Forest People—unicorn hunting had to be abolished. Not just in Khero, but across the continent.

"You used to love to ride." Her brother's voice roused her from her thoughts. Closing her mental shields, she turned and met his grin. It was the same tired smile he'd greeted her with in Verdian's study, but the fresh outdoor air seemed to be doing him some good. His complexion had regained some of its golden-tan hue, the blotches that had once marred it now fading. Her heart tumbled with the same confused reaction it always gave when she looked at him—love and hate. Fear and sympathy. She stiffened as he reached across the space between their horses to squeeze her hand. "Do you still love to ride?"

His tone was so much like how it had been when she was younger—soft and slow, like he was speaking to a child. She didn't have it in her to be offended. His last clear memories of her were as a young girl. It was the only way he knew how to talk to her. They'd have to get to know each other all over again.

She gave him a nod. "I do."

"I remember that," he said, a note of pride in his voice. He returned his hand to his reins. "More of my memories are coming back. I recall almost everything clearly from... from *before*."

He didn't have to elaborate. She knew he meant before Morkai had come into their lives. The duke—though not a duke yet at that time—had arrived at court two years after she and Dimetreus had lost their parents to a plague. She wondered how soon Morkai had begun using his magic to influence her brother...

A chill ran over her, so she tucked her hand into one of her pockets. A deep pulsating beat thrummed against her gloved palm—the energy of an object she'd forgotten was inside. She extracted the hand faster than if she'd been burned. Repulsion swept through her, as well as annoyance that she kept forgetting the crystal's presence. Even more frightening was the thought that it might be enchanted. Though it would explain why she found herself surprised by its existence, it was too unsettling to think Morkai's magic might linger beyond his death. Still, it wasn't an impossibility. His glamours had been severed, but those had been woven using his Roizan, which had died along with its master. That didn't mean all Morkai's spells had dissolved. It stood to reason that any magic he'd made without the Roizan could remain.

She hated keeping the crystal on her person. She'd chuck it into the woods if she didn't suspect it was too dangerous to discard so carelessly. It undoubtedly held vast darkness, but when she'd first touched it on the battlefield, she'd felt something else. Some unfamiliar energy. Whatever it was, the crystal needed to be cleared by magical means. The Forest People had taught her several ways to clear objects of unwanted energy, but she didn't dare do it until she had ample privacy.

"What else do you like, Aveline?" her brother asked. "Do

you like when I call you Aveline? I've been told Prince Teryn calls you Cora, like...like our mother used to." His eyes turned down at the corners.

She could be honest and tell him she strongly preferred being called Cora, but she was supposed to embrace being Princess Aveline from now on. "You can call me whatever you prefer."

He opened his mouth but his words were halted when a rider came up alongside them, edging in beside Lord Kevan. The messenger was not from their entourage, for he bore the white and gold rose sigil of Selay. Cora's retinue rode beneath Khero's standard—the black mountain on a purple background. "Message from King Verdian," the rider said.

Cora watched as Lord Kevan took a letter from the messenger. He scoffed as he read it, then looked over his shoulder at Cora and Dimetreus. He offered a grin that looked more like a sneer. "It appears a guest will be joining us after we arrive at Ridine."

"Who?" Cora asked.

"Queen Mareleau," he said with a mocking laugh. "She is to serve as your companion while you get settled back into your role as princess."

The news couldn't have been more unfavorable. Her sole encounter with Mareleau had been enough to turn her heart against the girl until the end of time. Now that the brazen harpy was married to Teryn, Cora despised her even more. Before she could dwell on her sudden spike of jealousy, she bit out, "Why?"

Kevan nodded at the messenger, dismissing him, before returning his attention to Cora. His lips curled into a cruel smirk. "Probably to punish her for marrying a bastard." He chuckled and faced forward again. "Pardon, I meant *King Larylis*."

Cora nearly dropped her reins in her shock. She blinked a few times, her mind reeling over what he'd said. "Lord Kevan, are you saying Mareleau has wed...Larylis Alante? Not Teryn?"

"So it would seem."

Her mind flashed to the letter Lurel had delivered. The one she'd ignored, crumpled, and tossed into the hearth. She'd thought he'd wanted to meet with her as a married man, a friend seeking a fond farewell. She'd been too angry to respond, too hurt by the unwanted engagement he'd orchestrated, too desperate to leave Verlot to consider...

Regret pierced her heart, but she hardened it against the sting. It didn't matter now. Whatever marriage politics had befallen Teryn, Larylis, and Mareleau, it was none of her concern. At least it meant she no longer had to marry Larylis.

And yet, a marriage alliance might still be required between Menah and Khero. It was one of Verdian's terms.

Teryn might...*no*.

She shoved him from her mind. Never again would she give in to hope without due cause. Never again would she let her heart distract her from the reality at hand. She'd already established that love was the last thing she needed. Love equated to permanent attachments. To vulnerability. To giving up on who she really was.

She tried to focus on her current reality. That gave her far more pressing matters to concern herself with—getting home, ensuring her brother could make peace with his lost memories, helping him reestablish his role as king, and...

She gulped.

Tolerating the company of Mareleau.

Despite her best efforts to distract herself, her mind and heart conspired against her, forming a solitary wish: that she could go back in time and stay long enough at Verlot to hear what Teryn had wanted to say.

10

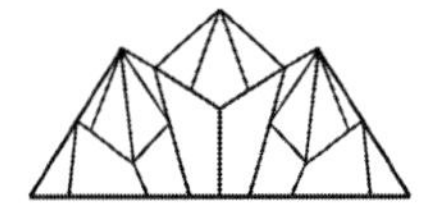

Mareleau had enjoyed one night of bliss, one night of passion, one night to experience the pleasure of being fully and completely loved. It had been beyond anything she'd imagined, anything she'd ever had a right to hope for. Now she stood to lose everything.

Well, perhaps not everything. Larylis was her husband and nothing could change that. But if he didn't show up for his own coronation, she wouldn't be crowned either.

She paced the length of the hall outside the Godskeep at Dermaine Palace, grateful that the only witnesses to her panic were a handful of guards and her three lady's maids. Breah trailed after her, keeping the long train of Mareleau's white silk dress from touching the ground. Whenever Mareleau would pause, Ann and Sera would rush to her, dabbing her face with powder, patting her hair, or straightening her red velvet cape.

Seven devils, where was he?

Sounds of chatter slipped beneath the Godskeep door. The room was full and the audience had already been waiting for fifteen minutes. If Larylis didn't show up soon, the courtiers, nobles, and guests would have more to gossip about than Teryn's unexpected abdication and Larylis' equally unexpected marriage to his brother's former fiancée.

She reached for her hair, seeking a lock to braid, but found her tresses out of reach. Her maids had done her hair in an elaborate updo specifically suited for the crown she'd be given. *If* Larylis showed up.

She'd seen less of him than she'd wished over the last few days. The morning after their union, they'd hastened to leave for Dermaine. Everything that followed had been rushed activity and travel. They'd slept separately at night, traveled separately by day. They'd exchanged only a few stolen glances and too-short embraces. Even the one night they'd spent together after arriving at the palace had been brief, with Larylis being called into a meeting with his council until well after Mareleau had fallen asleep. Still, their sparse interactions had been enough to show her the melancholy he'd returned to.

What if he'd changed his mind about becoming king? She imagined what that would mean for them. If they weren't king and queen, if her marriage to Larylis lost what little credibility her father was willing to see in it, if she was disinherited...

For one moment, she felt the strangest twinge of relief. If they were no longer beholden to their parents' thrones, they'd be...free. They could run away together, live a simple life—

She shook the thought from her head. Wherever Larylis was, he hadn't chosen to bring her along. Besides, she may have enjoyed the occasional fantasy about living the simple life, but she knew as well as anyone that she was not a simple woman. She enjoyed her luxuries. Already, the walls of Dermaine Palace felt too close compared to the wide halls of Verlot. The lights too sparse, too dim. The floors too plain. Her footsteps too loud. Her pulse too fast.

She paused her pacing and steadied her breaths. Sera came to powder her forehead, but Mareleau slapped her hand away. “I’m fine.” The girl took a step back and exchanged a glance with Ann.

“He’ll be here,” Breah said, tone calm. Mareleau wanted to believe her, but Breah didn’t know a damn thing.

The Godskeep door opened, sending Mareleau’s heart leaping into her throat. Hope bloomed in her chest but she crushed it even before the figure emerged from the other side. It couldn’t be Larylis, for he was supposed to be entering the Godskeep, not emerging from within it. If he were already inside, she wouldn’t be an anxious mess.

Teryn stepped into the hall and closed the door quickly behind him. “He still hasn’t shown?”

“No.” Mareleau put her hands on her hips. “Do you know where he might be?”

Teryn’s eyes unfocused. “I think I have an idea.”

LARYLIS NEVER IMAGINED HE’D FIND SOLACE AMONGST THE dead, but the crypts beneath the Godskeep were oddly soothing. It was the quiet that comforted him, something he used to only find in libraries. But with Dermaine Palace so busy in the wake of his and Teryn’s return, his favored haunts were devoid of their usual silence.

He placed his hands on the cool stone of his father’s sarcophagus. The sides bore an intricately carved relief of seven faces to represent the seven gods. The top was carved with Menah’s eagle sigil. Arlous’ effigy was still being carved, but soon it would grace the sarcophagus as well. Footsteps echoed from the entrance to the crypts, telling Larylis his respite was at an end. Teryn came up beside him.

"I figured you were down here," his brother said without a hint of reproach. Instead, Teryn's voice sounded as tired as Larylis felt. It was an exhaustion that no amount of sleep seemed to dissolve.

They stood in silence for several moments before Larylis found his voice. "We laid his body to rest this morning, and by afternoon I'm expected to take his crown."

"I know."

Larylis realized this was the first time they'd been alone since the meeting in Verdian's study. Before Teryn gave up everything and laid it at Larylis' feet. Slowly, he turned to face his brother. "I'm sorry, Teryn."

Teryn released an exasperated sigh. "What are you apologizing for?"

"You know what I'm apologizing for. I've taken everything from you."

"You've taken nothing that I did not freely give. And it's nothing you don't deserve." His voice held an edge that wasn't lost on Larylis.

He certainly *did* deserve it. Deserved whatever scorn his brother held.

Teryn's expression softened. "I'm not mad at you."

"I can't imagine how you could feel anything but hate for me."

"I could never hate you. You're my brother." He turned to face their father's sarcophagus. "It's myself I'm angry with. I should have known how you felt about Mareleau. I should have seen it, even when you told me you didn't love her."

Larylis' stomach turned. "No, I should have been honest. It's just...it was complicated. I didn't think I loved her anymore, nor she me. I didn't think we could ever be together, didn't think I'd ever be worthy of her. And it was your duty—"

"My duty can go to the seven devils," Teryn said with a dark chuckle. "I've made more mistakes in the name of duty than I care to admit." He turned to face Larylis with a pointed look. "It's your duty now. One you're rather tardy for."

Larylis' fingers curled into fists. "How can I wear his crown after what I've done?"

"I meant what I said before. You made an impossible choice."

"What if I'd surrendered? He could still be alive—"

"We don't know that," Teryn said, tone sharp. "We will never know what might have been. If you're worried about being worthy of Father's crown, then *be* worthy. Stop asking if you are. Just be the king he'd want you to be."

Guilt and shame twisted in his heart. Teryn was right. "I've done a terrible job of accepting my punishment, haven't I?"

Teryn's eyes turned down at the corners. "I didn't mean it when I said you should take the crown as your punishment. I only said that because I needed you to accept. Because I knew your capacity for self-hatred was greater than your willingness to be happy. But that's not what Father would have wanted."

Larylis opened his mouth to argue but couldn't find the words.

"I've seen what you're doing, Larylis. You've been distant with your wife. You're refusing to let yourself enjoy one of the best things life has to offer. Carry Father's crown like a burden if that is your wish, but...don't shun love."

"Weren't you the one who always said love is for the weak? That duty is greater when you're a royal?"

"I told you how I feel about duty. Besides, you're lucky. Your wife is both your love and your duty. Don't push her away. And don't you dare say you don't deserve her. She deserves *you.* A woman who's willing to fight for your sorry ass deserves better than a cold bedfellow."

Larylis' cheeks flushed. His and Mareleau's one night together in bed had been anything but cold. Yet Teryn was right. He'd gone to great lengths to distance himself from his wife ever since. The warmth of his love, the depth of his joy at being near her...it terrified him. He was so afraid to give in, to revel in the love he'd been given, to take pleasure in anything that had come from either his treachery or hers. What exactly he was afraid of, he wasn't sure.

He met Teryn's eyes. "You've changed...since before..."

"Since before I betrayed someone I cared for and got myself captured by a blood mage? I know."

"The person you care for...that's Cora, isn't it?"

Teryn's throat bobbed. He gave a curt nod.

"She's the reason you've been acting like a maniac, isn't she?"

"What do you mean?"

"Don't think you're the only one who's noticed odd behaviors, brother. I've seen what you're doing too. You're constantly in motion, constantly fixing things you don't need to fix."

"I just want to be useful."

Larylis leveled a look at his brother. "You helped fix a wagon wheel on the road. We pay people to do that, yet you aided repairs with your own hands. When we arrived home, you organized the study. You cleaned Father's desk. You alphabetized correspondences by sender, then rearranged them by date received instead."

Teryn shifted from foot to foot. "I'm supposed to be helping you."

"But you'd rather be somewhere else."

A flush crept up Teryn's cheeks. His voice was low when he spoke. "I need to talk with Cora about our...potential engagement. I don't want her to find out in a letter, nor do I want it arranged before she's had a chance to say yes. And if she says no, then we need to find another way to formalize an alliance with Khero." He said the last part in a rush.

Larylis recognized something in his brother. Something he'd never seen in Teryn, only in himself. He wasn't sure if Teryn knew just yet, but his concern over Cora was more than politics. More than alliance. More than friendship. A flash of treacherous joy crept into his heart, but for once he didn't try to tamp it down. Surely he could stand to be happy for someone else, couldn't he?

"You should go to her," Larylis said.

"I will. Perhaps in a few months after you're settled—"

"No, you should go to her now. Leave in the morning with Lord Ulrich."

Teryn blinked a few times, shifting from foot to foot again. "I can't go now. You need me. There's so much I haven't told you about running our kingdom, so much I've yet to pass on. Moreover, Lord Ulrich would never allow me to come. Verdian is determined to punish us, and I doubt Ulrich would act against his brother's wishes."

Larylis' heart sank. Teryn was right. Verdian wanted his daughter punished by sending her to Ridine. He wanted Larylis punished by keeping him from his wife. And Teryn... did Verdian realize keeping him from Cora was punishment too? Larylis wasn't even sure Teryn realized as much. Whatever the case, he didn't think he was ready to face Verdian's wrath. Larylis may soon be king, but Verdian was his father-in-law. He'd witnessed both the power and rage such a familial tie could bring when Queen Bethaeny's father threatened war when Arlous tried to divorce her. But still... Larylis' crown had to be good for something.

"Then wait a few days and leave on your own. You are the least beholden to Verdian. And is it not essential we secure an alliance with Khero? If you're determined to do it in person, then I say it's a pressing matter."

Teryn's expression brightened, his lips quirking into the ghost of a grin. "You really think so?"

Larylis straightened, shoulders squared. "As your king, I command it." It felt like a mockery to refer to himself as king, but he supposed he should start getting used to it.

"Very well," Teryn said, "but if I am to listen to a damn word you say, you better get to the Godskeep before Mareleau wears a hole straight through the floor with her pacing."

Larylis forced a smile. "Deal."

Together, they left the crypts and ascended the stairs to the hall outside the Godskeep. There he found his wife, a vision in white silk, her shoulders adorned in a velvet cape. A queen's cape. Just as Teryn had said, she was pacing frantically across the floor. She paused when she caught sight of him. His heart lurched in his chest as their eyes met. Her gaze held a question steeped in worry, laced with trepidation.

He knew then how much his distance these last few days had hurt her. Knew how selfish he'd been in clinging to his pain. He wasn't ready to let go of it completely, but he could push it aside, just enough so she could fit beside it.

His valet approached him with the royal cape—red with

sable trim to match Mareleau's—while a servant darted forth with a brush for his coat, frowning at the thin layer of dust Larylis had accumulated from the crypts. Larylis stepped past both of them, heading straight for Mareleau instead. He didn't stop until she was against him, until both his hands had framed her face, and her soft lips were pressed to his. She met his kiss first with tense surprise, then with yielding. He felt her smile against his mouth, felt her grip tighten around his waist. With every tender brush of his lips, he conveyed his apology, his love, his promise.

I'll never push you away, he thought. *I'll make today count. And when it's time to go to Ridine for the signing of the peace pact, I'll be ready to bring you home.*

His valet cleared his throat while Mareleau's ladies giggled. He reluctantly pulled away from the woman he loved. She smiled at him and he let himself grin right back.

This. He'd let himself enjoy this. He may not deserve it, but damn it, Teryn was right. *She* did. His fierce, beautiful, devious wife deserved his love.

They faced the closed doors and let their servants clean them up once more. Then they entered the Godskeep hand in hand and claimed their burdensome crowns together.

11

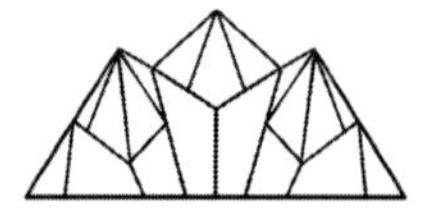

Cora's arrival at Ridine Castle felt less like coming home and more like stumbling upon a traveling circus. The location was familiar but had been transformed by the uncanny. As she entered the great hall with her brother, she found it looked nothing like the understaffed castle Morkai had brought her to, nor the dark, chilling place of her once-constant nightmares. It bustled with activity, much like it had during her childhood, but with unfamiliar faces.

Servants and staff bowed low as Lord Kevan barked orders and made introductions. Chests and furnishings were brought in from the wagons that were being unloaded in the courtyard. The chaos was so unsettling, Cora found her shields weakening. She took a deep breath to steady her nerves and forced herself to focus on the latest introduction.

An older man with a slim build and kind face greeted her and her brother with a bow. "Your Majesty. Your Highness. I am Master Arther, your new steward."

Cora nodded in greeting, then faced Lord Kevan. "Has Lord Ulrich already come?"

"No," Kevan said, "we are not expecting him for another three days at least."

Cora furrowed her brow. If Ulrich hadn't arrived with the rest of their newly appointed staff and councilmen, then who were all these people? Neither Master Arther nor half of those scuttling about the halls had come with her retinue. None showed any familiarity with Dimetreus but seemed well enough acquainted with Kevan. That meant they hadn't served under her brother when Morkai had had the run of the castle. Considering how empty Ridine had been the last time she'd been here, it was no surprise it required an overhaul of staff. Still, she hadn't expected it to have been done in her and Dimetreus' absence.

When Kevan didn't elaborate, she turned a questioning look to her brother.

Dimetreus released a grumbling sigh. "King Verdian seized control of Ridine immediately after the battle," he said, speaking low. "He'd already had it restaffed before we'd come to our agreement."

A spike of indignation surged through her blood. While she understood Verdian's suspicion over her brother's involvement with Morkai, it felt wrong that he'd taken over Ridine Castle so prematurely. It served to remind her that until the peace pact was officially signed, she and Dimetreus were essentially on probation. Should they give Verdian—or his brothers—any reason to doubt their innocence, he could pull Khero right out from under their grasp.

Kevan narrowed his eyes at Dimetreus. "Yes, and you should be quite thankful for my brother's generosity. Had he not acted when he did, you'd be coming home to cobwebs."

"I am ever so grateful," Dimetreus said through his teeth. This was the first sign Cora had seen to suggest he might share in Cora's annoyance. For the most part, he'd demonstrated nothing but eager submission and a willingness to comply with whatever was demanded of him. She studied him closer and saw a tic forming at the corner of his jaw.

Lurel bounded up to Cora, her face alight with a wide smile. "You're home, Your Highness! How does it feel? I bet you missed it greatly. You haven't been back to Ridine in so long, have you?"

Cora nearly admitted that it hadn't been long at all but decided against it. She hadn't shared many personal details with her lady's maid, so all the girl knew about Cora's past was whatever was being said through gossip. Kevan had urged Cora and Dimetreus to speak little of recent events until they could hold a council meeting and agree upon the official story that would be publicly shared. That meeting, however, couldn't commence until the rest of the council arrived with Lord Ulrich.

Lurel glanced around the great hall, her smile shifting into something like a grimace. "It's rather...different from Verlot, isn't it?"

"Different is a word for it," Cora said. She'd been too consumed with her and Dimetreus' fates to appreciate the luxury of Verlot Palace, but as she stared at the plain stone walls, bare wooden beams, and flagstone floor, she couldn't help but admit Ridine left much to be desired.

Lurel bounced on the balls of her feet. "We can spruce things up, Highness. You're the lady of the castle. It will be up to you to bring a..." She trailed off, frowning at a faded tapestry bearing a gruesome hunting scene that hung on the wall beside them. Her expression brightened as she met Cora's eyes with a hopeful smile. "A feminine touch. That is what you'll bring."

"Your composure, Lurel," Kevan said, tone gruff.

Lurel pursed her lips, steeling her features. In a softer voice, she said to Cora, "Might I take your cloak and riding gloves, Highness?"

"Oh...yes." Even after spending over two weeks with a lady's maid, she was still unused to being waited upon. Lurel unclasped Cora's cloak and slid it from her shoulders while Cora peeled off her riding gloves. As she handed them to Lurel, she caught sight of Kevan staring at her bare hands, her tattooed palms now visible.

His lip curled behind his bushy beard as he addressed his daughter. "From now on, Lurel, be sure to keep an extra pair of gloves on hand so the princess always has something to change into."

Cora bristled at the disdain in his voice. Was the sight of her tattoos so repulsive to him? Her palms tingled as if the magic thrumming through her veins wanted to show him exactly what he should fear. But the fiery urge quickly cooled to a simmer. She'd already chosen to bury her magic when she'd asserted her innocence before the inquisitors, convincing them her *insigmora* were simply traditional markings borne by the peaceful commune that had provided her sanctuary for six years. When she'd been pressed for more information regarding their magic, she'd feigned ignorance, claiming she knew nothing of magic herself. She'd sensed her questioners' approval then, which had made Cora wonder if they cared less about the truth and more about her delivery of acceptable answers.

A rebellious fire burned in her belly. Holding his gaze, she rolled up the sleeves of her riding habit, showing off more of the black ink.

With a derisive snort, Kevan gave a shallow bow and departed.

"Your Majesty, Your Highness, shall I show you to your

rooms?" Master Arther said. "I imagine you must be tired from your journey."

"I may have what many consider a befuddled mind, but I know how to find my own living quarters," Dimetreus said, tone sharp enough to stiffen Cora's spine.

Arther paled. "Yes, Majesty, I understand. It's just...very few of the rooms had been kept with much care. We've focused our efforts on preparing living spaces for our most prominent residents, but not all rooms are ready for occupation. We are awaiting delivery of fresh linens before we can finish the rest of the rooms. In the meantime, we have assigned sleeping quarters that may not be what you were used to."

Dimetreus rubbed his brow and forced a smile. "Of course. Lead the way."

Cora eyed her brother as Arther led her, Dimetreus, and Lurel upstairs. Dimetreus seemed to have grown fatigued since stepping foot inside the castle. The tic still pulsed at the corner of his jaw, and his shoulders were nearly to his ears. "Are you all right?" she whispered.

He grunted his assurance, but Cora wasn't so convinced.

She continued to watch him carefully as they proceeded past a dimly lit portion of the keep which was clearly uninhabited. The only light came from the pink blush of the setting sun that peeked through the occasional window.

Lurel wrinkled her nose and muttered something about a draft. She edged closer to Cora, hugging Cora's cloak close to her chest. "I certainly hope the whole castle isn't always this cold. It is summer, after all."

They approached a well-lit hall that Cora was quite familiar with. One end led to her childhood bedroom, the largest guest bedrooms, and the king's suite. As for the other end...

Cora's pulse quickened as Arther turned to the left and entered another corridor.

Her feet rooted in place. Shadows gathered at the corners of her vision, her heart thumping with a dread she hadn't felt since her last nightmare. Her sleep had been mostly dreamless since Morkai's death, but now her mind rang with echoes of the past.

She knew where this hall led. Knew it ended in a single door. A bed.

And blood. So much blood—

Dimetreus stumbled, his hand clutching his chest. In an instant, Cora's mind returned to the present. As her vision regained its focus, she found her brother's face, twisted with anguish.

Arther doubled back, seeing that they were no longer following him. "Is everything all right, Your Majesty?"

Dimetreus' voice came out strained. "Why isn't there a wall here?" He blinked hard several times. "I...I thought there was a wall. This hall isn't supposed to exist."

Arther frowned. "There was no wall, Majesty. This hall was crowded with dusty furniture, but—"

Before Cora could think to stop him, Dimetreus charged past Arther into the corridor. Belatedly, she started after him, ignoring how the walls felt as if they were closing in on her. On trembling legs, she reached the dreaded door.

And found her brother slumped in the doorway.

Cora's first reaction was relief. The room inside looked nothing like the one from her nightmare. The bed had been moved from its previous location, the linens elegant and new. Violet brocade curtains were drawn open to welcome the last glow of sunlight as it dipped behind the Cambron Mountains.

Cora's muscles uncoiled as every remnant of fear faded

away. In its place, calm settled over her, and her attention narrowed on her brother. She approached him with slow steps.

He held his face in his hands while his shoulders heaved with sobs. "Linette!" he wailed.

Cora reached out a timid hand and let it hover just above his shoulder. She wasn't used to comforting others. Over the last six years, she hadn't allowed herself to become close to anyone but Maiya and Salinda. Sympathy had become something she'd refused to accept. In turn, she wasn't sure if she knew how to give it.

Then she recalled the way she'd opened up to Valorre as her friend. The softness that had melted her heart when she and Teryn rescued the baby unicorn. The fierce protectiveness she'd felt when Teryn was wounded at the battle.

She had been capable of sympathy, kindness, and care, even when she hadn't meant to be.

Right now, her brother needed that from her.

She let her hand fall the rest of the way onto his shoulder. "Dimi."

He cried harder as he angled his head toward her. "I remember. I remember it, Aveline." He pointed to the room. "You were there. And I thought...oh, seven gods, I let him convince me..."

"It's all right," she whispered over the lump in her throat.

"You tried to tell me. You tried, and I...I ordered you to the dungeon. I condemned you to die."

"It's over now."

He leaned against the doorframe, shoulders slumped. "But then...then I saw your body. You'd died too." His eyes met hers, and there was a wild quality in them. "You'd died, Aveline. I saw that too. I saw—" He blinked hard several times, his body trembling with convulsions.

Lurel came up beside them while Arther wrung his hands farther down the hall. Lurel's face was pale as she watched the king. She pointed a thumb over her shoulder. "I should go. I must tell my father the king is unwell."

An urgent feeling, a clairsentient warning, had Cora rounding on the girl. She wasn't sure why she was suddenly so panicked, until something dawned on her.

Verdian's threat echoed in her mind.

If Dimetreus' council deems him incapable of the crown at any point, he will be forced to abdicate at once.

"You will not," Cora said, pinning the girl with a hard look. "This is a private matter. The king is grieving."

"But...but my father asked me to report to him if—"

"I don't care what he asked of you. You will not embarrass the king in his time of need. You will stay here until he has recovered and speak not a word of this incident."

Lurel worried her lip. Even through her shields, Cora could feel the girl's conflict. Lurel desperately wanted Cora to like her but knew better than to disobey her father.

Cora softened her tone. "I'm sure your father only had the king's best interests in mind when he asked you to report on his actions, but this isn't the kind of situation he meant. This is simply grief. You don't understand my brother's complex past nor the dark history this castle bears, and to spread word of this would be a great dishonor to the king you now serve."

Lurel sank to her knees, head bowed. "Forgive me, Highness. I didn't mean to offend you or the king. I'm sure you're right."

Cora stalked past Lurel toward the steward. "Master Arther, how about we show *you* where our rooms are, and if they are not ready for us, then do whatever it takes to have them prepared by the end of the day." She was surprised at the demand in her voice. It was a tone she hadn't spoken with since she was a child. Or perhaps the few times she'd argued with Teryn.

Master Arther straightened and gave her a nod. "It will be done, Your Highness."

Satisfied that she had the situation under control, she returned to her brother. Doing nothing more than resting her hand on his shoulder, she let him cry. Let him grieve the memories that pained him and rail against the ones he'd lost. She kept her eyes dry, her composure strong.

Later, she told herself. Later she'd let herself cry too.

Now there was work to be done.

12

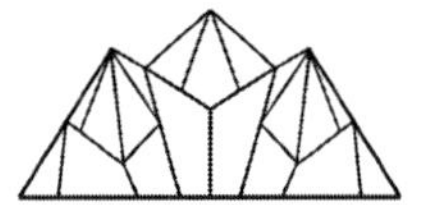

Mareleau never imagined she could be so physically close to a person yet feel so lonely. But as she rolled from side to side on the old mattress, sandwiched between her lady's maids, lonely was all she felt. She wanted her husband. The bed they'd shared at Dermaine Palace. Not these three snoring harpies and a stale bedroom.

She rolled onto her opposite side, wincing as the wooden bedframe creaked in response to her movement. Ann mumbled in her sleep, Sera erupted with a gasping snore, and Breah's arm flew across Mareleau's face. Mareleau sat up with a scoff and cut a glare at the three sleeping girls. How could they sleep in accommodations as shoddy as this? Their rooms back at Verlot were almost as nice as her own. Yet there they were dozing like three baby pigs in a stall.

A stall. Yes, that was all she could say of this room. It certainly wasn't appropriate for a supposedly pregnant woman, much less a queen. This wasn't the first time she'd been relegated to such accommodations during her recent travels either. Instead of staying at grand estates and being hosted by lords, viscounts, and barons, she's been shuttled from one inn to the next. They were fine inns, she supposed, but they were nothing like what she was used to. She wasn't sure whether she had her father's malice or her new kingdom's lesser financial wealth to blame for her environment, but she suspected it was the former.

She gritted her teeth as her eyes shot to the closed door of the tiny bedroom. She was tempted to stomp across the hall to Lord Ulrich's room, pound on his door, and demand he find private lodgings for her at once. But she knew it would do no good. Her uncle never had much patience for her before, and his opinion of her seemed little improved now that she was queen. If anything, it had the opposite effect. At least they were finally nearing the end of their journey.

An unsettling question came to mind. Would Ridine be any better? It was a castle, not a palace, after all. A structure built for defense. With a sigh, she laid back down only to find Breah had taken up more space in Mareleau's absence. Cursing under her breath, she stood and grabbed her cloak, wrapping it tightly around her as she crept from the room.

The hall outside was chilly, lit with a single lamp. She made her way down the stairs and into the empty dining room. The clang of pots and pans and the giggling voices of maids echoed from the kitchen. Dinner had been hours ago, and since Ulrich had had the decency to buy out the inn for the night, there were no other guests lingering about. She went to the hearth and pulled up a chair next to the dying embers. A shiver ran through her, and she pulled her cloak even tighter around her nightdress.

Now that she was fully alone, her annoyance began to

fade, replaced with the full weight of what lurked just beneath it: loneliness.

Mareleau had never considered herself a friendly person. The last friend she'd had—a former lady's maid named Katra—had dallied with one of her suitors. She wouldn't have cared much, had the man not been the only person she'd been even remotely attracted to after Larylis. The memory filled her with guilt now that she and Larylis were together at last, but at the time, that mild attraction had felt like hope. What Katra had done had broken something inside her. She hadn't realized it before. She'd been too preoccupied with the Heart's Hunt. Then the threat of war. Then her plot to marry Larylis.

In the wake of everything she'd won and everything she'd risked, now that she was away from the man she loved and the two parents who despised her, she felt that gaping void like never before. It was a hollow ache, one that made her shrink into herself as if that could close it.

She hugged her arms around her torso, then startled as the kitchen doors swung open. In an instant, she sat up straight, evoking her *magic trick* to help her appear calm. Collected. Regal. A maid left the kitchen, arms full of clean plates, and tossed a snide remark over her shoulder. It was met with much laughter from the other maids. As the girl fully entered the dining room, she caught sight of Mareleau. The smile disappeared from her face. In a rush, she set the plates on the counter and hurried to Mareleau. With a low curtsy, she said, "Forgive me, Your Majesty. We weren't expecting anyone to be awake. What can I get for you?"

"It's all right," Mareleau said curtly. "I need nothing but what you cannot provide."

The girl took that as her dismissal and scurried back into the kitchen. Mareleau heard no more giggles or gossip from behind the door after that. She settled back into her chair, sulking into the backrest, and reached into her cloak. From within, she withdrew a folded piece of parchment. The sight of her name written in a familiar script was enough to fill her heart with warmth and longing in equal measure. Larylis had pressed the letter into her hand before she'd left Dermaine for her journey north. She'd waited until she'd been alone the first night before reading it. Gods, was she glad that she did. For no sooner than she'd read the first sentence had her chest heaved with a sob.

With a deep breath, she opened it now. Tears welled in her eyes as she read the words her heart had already committed to memory.

Mareleau,

For all the letters we didn't write over the last three years, I will write you a thousand more. For every kiss we didn't share while we were apart, I will give you a million kisses more. And every moment you doubt my love, remember my heart is yours. These seconds may be torture while you're away, but my love will only grow.

It will grow, Mareleau.

I will be waiting.

Writing.

Loving you.

Forever and always yours,

Larylis

She reread the words over and over until her eyes were raw and her lungs were sore from silent sobbing. When she could no longer handle being so ridiculously pathetic, she refolded the paper with care and tucked it back into her pocket. Wiping at the moisture on her cheeks, she stood to return to her room—only to sink back into her seat as the dining room door opened.

The old innkeeper entered, followed by a hooded traveler. Mareleau kept still in her chair, hoping they wouldn't notice her in the dark room. After crying like a wailing babe, she had no desire to speak to anyone, nor did she have the energy to control her composure. "We weren't expecting you, Your Highness," the innkeeper said, his tone laced with anxiety. "You didn't arrive with the others."

"Others?"

Mareleau's spine went rigid. The voice was gratingly familiar. She turned in her seat, getting a clearer look at the newcomer as the innkeeper led him through the dining room. Sure enough, just as they turned toward the stairs, she caught sight of his profile.

She rose to her feet and planted her hands on her hips. "What the hell are you doing here?"

Teryn startled. With a frown, he faced her.

The innkeeper shrank down, eyes darting between the two of them. "Is the prince not of your party, Your Majesty?"

"That depends," she said through her teeth. "Did he come alone?" Hope threatened to swell in her chest as she awaited his answer. *Please say Larylis is here. Please.*

"Yes, I came alone."

Her heart plummeted to her feet, and rage funneled in its place. "No, he does not belong to my party, and my uncle gave you orders not to allow anyone else to stay here tonight."

The innkeeper opened his mouth but Teryn spoke first. "Might I have a word with the queen?"

She lifted her chin, tempted to deny him. She wasn't even sure what drove her sudden rage. Teryn was only guilty of the same crime she'd always accused him of. Not being Larylis. But he wasn't a threat to her happiness anymore, was he?

"Very well," she said.

The innkeeper bowed low and rushed from the room as if he were eager to be anywhere else.

Mareleau repeated her question. "What are you doing here?"

Teryn gave her a bewildered look. "What are *you* doing here? Ulrich has you staying at an inn? I thought you'd be hosted by nobles."

She crossed her arms. "You don't need to rub it in. Besides, I asked you first. I am your queen, remember?"

He glanced around the empty room, then released a heavy breath. "I'm heading for Ridine to speak with Princess Aveline. I'd meant to follow behind your retinue and arrive afterward, but it appears I've caught up too quickly. Promise me you won't tell your uncle I'm here."

"Why shouldn't I? I was ordered to go on this journey against my will, and you were told to remain at Dermaine. Why should I, the queen, follow orders while you get to break them? Why should I be separated from my husband —" She cut off as her voice broke on the last word.

His face softened. "Larylis wishes he were with you, trust me. I haven't seen him so morose, since…ever. He doesn't want to risk going against your father. I, on the other hand, have less to lose. For now."

She averted her gaze. "It isn't fair, you know."

"I know it isn't." He took a few steps closer. "I also understand why you resent me. If I'd known about you and Larylis..." His lips quirked into a wry grin, one that reminded her too much of his brother. "Please don't take this the wrong way, but I never wanted to marry you either. I found the prospect just as awful as you did."

She was overcome with a sudden urge to bark a laugh. Her animosity softened at the edges, making her wonder if Teryn hadn't been her enemy all along.

"Can we be allies? We are brother and sister now. Plus, you owe me." His smile turned devious.

She could tell he was teasing, but she didn't feel generous enough to play along. Instead, she pursed her lips and burned him with a scowl.

He wasn't the least bit cowed. "Don't you agree? I helped you marry the love of your life."

That managed to weaken her resolve.

"Can I count on you to keep my presence here a secret from your uncle? I promise not to show up at your next stop. I'll simply stick to far finer establishments."

She snorted a begrudging laugh at that. "That will certainly keep you from wherever Ulrich has me sleeping."

He raised a brow, reminding her she had yet to answer his question.

She rolled her eyes. "Fine, I won't tell Ulrich." It was almost painful to say. Everything inside her wanted to see him punished as badly as her. But she reminded herself of what he'd given up. He'd abdicated, set aside his crown, his birthright, for Larylis. To clear the final obstacle that had kept them from being together. Uncrossing her arms, she let her shoulders relax and tried to smile. All she managed was a grimace. "So...I have a brother now?"

"Unfortunately for us both, you do."

"Ugh. I never wanted one." She brushed past him and

ascended the stairs. Despite her abrupt last words to him, she was surprised to find the aching void in her heart had lessened. Whether it was due to reading Larylis' letter or entertaining the prospect of having a new—albeit unwanted—brother, she knew not. All she knew was that, as she climbed back into bed between her annoyingly peaceful lady's maids, she felt a little less alone.

13

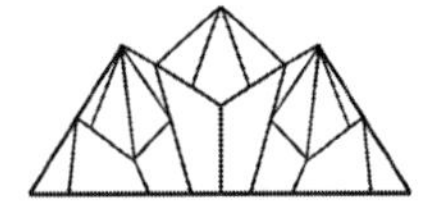

Cora wasn't sure why she chose to return to her childhood bedroom. She could have had her pick of rooms, ones that didn't bear memories of the last time she was here, dressing in a gown in preparation to meet her brother for the first time in six years, only to find him controlled by dark magic. Nor the time before that, when she'd pouted on her bed after pretending to curse the queen. The queen who'd later died...

She shook the morbid memories from her mind and returned her attention to the present. She sat at her vanity while Lurel brushed her hair. Even after two days back at the castle, she still wasn't used to being waited on like this. Dressed. Brushed. Bathed. Forced to sit idly while others served her. It aggravated her, reminded her that this princess persona was all an act, made her want to flee the confines of the castle walls and leave this curated world of cruel politics and false politeness behind.

This is all for Dimetreus, she told herself. *It's for the sake of Khero.*

Lurel continued to comb Cora's hair, a task that seemed

endless despite the girl tending to it twice a day. Cora's eyes darted toward the window and the glow of the setting sun. It was a most welcome sight, for as soon as night fell, Cora had plans to escape the castle and throw off the guise of princess. Temporarily, of course, but the thought had her antsy with anticipation.

She was desperate to be surrounded by trees, close to the elements the Forest People had taught her to revere. To feel her magic buzz around her so she could embody the witch she was. It was a part of herself she couldn't fully let go of, only hide, betray, and publicly refute. All for the sake of being a princess and proving to those who distrusted her that she was nothing like Morkai. If only she could trust *them* to understand that there was a stark difference between witch magic—*quiet magic*—and the sinister sorceries the duke had dabbled in.

But no, they did not understand. Which meant if she wanted to utilize the Arts in any obvious way, she needed to do it where no one would see her. That was exactly what she intended to do tonight. Once she was in the woods, she could perform a clearing ritual on Morkai's crystal.

There was an additional reason she was eager to sneak out tonight: to see her unicorn friend again.

Her knee began to jiggle, and she sat on her hands to keep from fidgeting. What she really wanted to do was shake off Lurel. The sooner the girl bid her goodnight, the sooner Cora could proceed with her plan. Still, she knew her maid was ordered by her father to keep a close eye on her. The last thing she needed was to cast herself under a suspicious light.

Lurel, though, seemed perfectly oblivious to Cora's anxious state. "How can your hair get so tangled after just a day?" she said with a grunt as she worked at a large knot at the end of Cora's dark tresses.

"Is that abnormal?" Cora asked.

"Perhaps I'm only used to Mareleau's hair. Her hair is always tangled in random braids by the end of the night, but her hair is smoother than yours and easier to brush."

Cora tried not to take offense at that, but any mention of Princess Mareleau—no, Queen Mareleau now—set her teeth on edge. She still couldn't shake their first meeting and the woman's icy demeanor. Worse was the fact that she was expected to arrive at the castle in the next few days.

"Why was the king so distraught yesterday, Your Highness?"

Cora tensed at the unexpected question.

When Lurel received no answer, she elaborated. "When we went to...to that room. You said he was grieving and that I didn't understand his complex past or the castle's dark history. What did you mean by that?"

Cora considered not answering. It wasn't Lurel's business, after all. But if it helped the girl understand the king, then perhaps she'd take her duties to spy on Cora and Dimetreus less seriously. "His wife died in that room."

"Oh my. Queen Linette, right? That was a tragedy. But you were said to have died that night too. If you're still alive...what really happened?"

Cora narrowed her eyes at the girl's reflection in the mirror, wondering if she was testing Cora's response at the command of her father. Lord Kevan had insisted she not speak about her false death, disappearance, or resurrection until after their council meeting could commence. Cora opened her senses to her maid but found only naive curiosity in her emotions. Regardless, she'd follow Lord

Kevan's rules. Until the peace pact was signed, she had to toe a fine line. "I'm not at liberty to say."

Her lips curled into a frown. "Father won't tell me either. All I hear is rumors from the staff. Is there anything you *can* tell me? Is it true what they're saying about your brother?"

Again, Cora's muscles tensed. "Who's *they* and what are they saying about him?"

"Well, I've heard some of the servants whispering that a sorcerer had chained the king in the dungeon for several years and was acting as the king in his stead, and that the mage is the one who instigated the battle at Centerpointe Rock, not the king. Others say the king was working alongside the sorcerer and truly wanted to conquer Menah and Selay. The oddest rumor is that the king was being puppeteered by dark magic and hasn't had control of his mind or body for countless years. Almost all accounts claim Duke Morkai was the evil mage. That paired with the tales I've managed to overhear about the battle makes me wonder if it's true. Were there truly...ghosts on the battlefield?"

Lurel paused her brushing and met Cora's eyes in the mirror. Her face was pale but there was a note of excitement playing around her mouth.

"Again, I am not at liberty to speak on such matters until I've had further counsel with your father."

Lurel resumed brushing, shoulders slumped. "I thought you might say that. Well, what about the rumors regarding the North Tower Library?"

Cora's blood went cold. "What about it?"

"Is it truly haunted? I heard we aren't allowed to go in there. Naturally, some of the servants are speculating that there's a ghost in the tower, and that if we open the door, it will come out and terrorize the castle. Sometimes I think I'd give anything to see a ghost. It would be a fright, but...oh, there's just something so romantic about a haunted castle, isn't there?"

Cora couldn't agree. She'd seen wraiths, souls of the dead reanimated to fight living men. There was nothing romantic about watching men get cut down by spectral blades.

"You must have been to the tower yourself. This was your childhood home! Tell me, is there really a ghost? Perhaps the spirit of the dead queen—"

"Lurel." Cora whirled in her chair to face the girl, pinning her with a stern look.

Lurel took a step back, cradling the brush against her chest. "I'm being insensitive, aren't I? I'm so sorry, Your Highness. Mareleau was always saying as much, so I suspect it must be true. I was always either annoying, insensitive, or too weak-minded, according to her. I beg your forgiveness, Highness. I seem to forget myself around you."

Cora clenched her jaw at being compared to Mareleau. She gentled her tone. "You're just getting a little carried away. The North Tower Library is not haunted."

"Then why are we forbidden from entering it?"

Cora imagined it was because Morkai's belongings were still there. She remembered what the room had looked like when the duke had brought her there for a tense chat. He'd turned the library into his personal study and filled it with an array of ominous-looking books and vials of strange liquids. With Master Arther so focused on preparing the living quarters in the castle, it stood to reason that other parts of the castle had yet to be touched. She couldn't blame anyone for wanting to avoid the library for as long as possible.

"The library is dirty, that's all," Cora said. "Until the room has been cleaned, it poses a hazard."

Lurel's expression fell as if the answer disappointed her. Cora turned back around to face the mirror and let Lurel resume brushing. The girl's moves were slower this time, distracted.

Finally, Lurel spoke, her voice small. "Can I stay in your room again tonight? I know I only stayed last night because I didn't have a room of my own yet, but all this talk about ghosts has me frightened."

Cora assessed the girl in the mirror with a quirked brow. "Your room has been furnished now. Besides, I thought haunted castles were romantic."

"Yes, but in a morbid sort of way, and...well, if I'm being honest, Father told me to stay with you again."

"To spy on me."

"Highness, please don't hate me for what he's asked of me. I have no intention of betraying you, but—just like my cousin has always said—I am weak of mind, and I find it rather difficult to say no."

Cora's lips flattened into a line. She just had to bring up Mareleau again. Every mention of the woman had Cora itching to prove she was the opposite. She sat up straighter. "You aren't weak-minded, Lurel. Your father is a powerful man and he has his reasons for distrusting me and my brother."

"But I don't distrust you in the least. Either way, you're a princess. Should you demand it, I'll go to my own room. Although...I really have put myself ill at ease about the ghosts, especially now that I know about...about the queen's room." Lurel's voice climbed higher until it ended in a squeak. "My quarters are in that hall."

Cora nibbled her bottom lip and cast a glance at the setting sun once more. Lurel's presence would put a hitch in her plans. It was why she hadn't snuck out to clear the crystal the night before. But at least she'd determined that Lurel was a deep sleeper. The girl had spent most of the night snoring from the other side of the large bed. Cora had tested her ease of waking when she'd left the room to visit the toilet, but Lurel had remained in the depths of slumber.

Cora released a resigned sigh. "You can stay."

IT WAS NEARING MIDNIGHT WHEN CORA FINALLY LEFT HER room. Dressed in her shift and teal riding cloak, the amber crystal weighing down one of her pockets, she entered the hall outside her room, finding it empty. Her shields were down, allowing her to sense nearby emotion, but every strain of feeling that reached her was calm. Muted by sleep. On silent feet, she crept down the stairs. Unlike when Morkai had the run of the castle, there weren't guards pacing every corridor, so she didn't have to worry about evading them. In contrast, the castle was far more heavily staffed than it had been under the duke, which made the servants' passage a risk. So instead, she kept close to the walls, kept her shields down, and made her way straight from the keep to the kitchen.

Her heart climbed into her throat as she tiptoed out the same door she'd fled through when she'd escaped the dungeon, following the same path that led to the ivy-covered gap in the castle wall. She wrapped the elements around her, concealing her, masking the sounds of her steps. It might have been an unnecessary precaution, considering she'd yet to come across anyone, but the memory of what she was doing now echoed the escape she'd made almost two months ago, reminding her of when sentries stalked the wall, when a beastly creature shadowed her steps, pursuing her into the crevice—

She took a deep breath, forcing herself to pause and look around. This was not the Ridine Castle she'd escaped from. Morkai's men weren't patrolling the wall this time, only a few bored sentries near the gate. And the Roizan wasn't nipping at her heels. It was gone. Dead. Like Morkai.

With her nerves settled, she proceeded the rest of the way to the wall and located the opening. The narrow crevice wasn't the most welcoming of places, but it was her ticket to momentary freedom. Shoving the ivy aside, she plunged into the dark fissure.

14

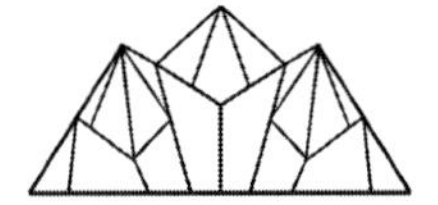

Anxiety tickled Cora's chest the deeper she went into the pitch-black crevasse, but soon a calming presence cut through every dark emotion.

I'm here, Valorre said from the other side of the wall.

Emboldened, Cora rushed the rest of the way out of the opening and found her friend standing on the other side. The moonlight glinted upon the slender horn at the center of his head and sent his white coat gleaming. Her heart swelled in her chest as a sudden wave of emotion constricted her throat. This was the first time she'd laid eyes on Valorre since the battle.

She was so relieved, so overjoyed at seeing him that she ran to him at once. He startled only a little as she threw her arms around his thick neck and buried her face into his hide. It wasn't something she'd done before. Valorre wasn't a pet, after all, but a fae creature. A person. And his temperament wasn't always cuddly. But Cora couldn't find it in her to care. Not with his soft coat pressed against her cheek, the aromas of dirt, leaves, and soil surrounding her, wrapping her in a blanket that felt so much more like home than a dusty castle did.

Yes, I am quite soft, aren't I? Valorre said, bumping her shoulder with his muzzle. *You will find the base of my ears are soft too. Perhaps you can scratch them?*

With a chuckle, she stepped back and gave in to his request. "I missed you, Valorre. I...I think you're my best friend."

Ah. That's nice. Teryn is my best friend.

She halted her scratching, mouth falling open as her euphoric joy turned to indignation. "Teryn? Why the Mother Goddess is he your best friend? You hardly know him."

He rippled with something like laughter. *I think it's called humor.*

She blinked at him a few times, at the twinkle in his russet eyes, and arched a brow. "You were teasing me."

It was fun.

"Then I am your best friend, right?"

Yes, I suppose you are.

She rolled her eyes at his begrudging tone. "So, you've been so bored without me that you learned humor in my absence. How does that work? Aren't fae creatures unable to lie?"

That sounds false to me.

"Well, it was a very rude joke. Teryn, of all people." Her heart stuttered. Even saying the prince's name brought to mind their last encounter. The anger she'd expressed to him. Her humiliation over having been promised to his brother at his behest. The note he'd sent that she'd thrown in the fire. The meeting he'd requested that she never attended. What was it he'd wanted to tell her?

You miss him too. Like you missed me.

She forced her thoughts away and scoffed. "Why would I miss him?"

Well, your heart gets quite loud and thuddy whenever you or I mention him. And I know you often think about that time when he put his mouth on your mouth—

"How do you know about that?"

Ah, yes, and then you get angry and admiring the same way you did whenever you saw him without a shirt—

"Let's stop talking about Teryn."

Valorre obeyed her request for all of five seconds. *But you do miss him, don't you?*

"No. I...why does it matter?"

You're my friend. He's my friend.

Cora waited for him to continue, but it seemed his explanation ended at that.

I'll make a bargain. Admit you miss him, and I'll let you ride on my back. He lifted his head, radiating pride if not a little arrogance.

Cora hadn't intended for a midnight ride when she'd planned on sneaking out of the castle. All she'd wanted was to greet her friend, surround herself with trees, and drink in moonlight. That and find a quiet place to perform an energy clearing ritual on the crystal, of course. She'd made a habit of shoving her hand in her pocket to remind herself of its existence. It continued to unsettle her how easy it was to forget.

Still, it wasn't absolutely dire that she perform the ritual right away. She could ride first. In fact, it might help her find the perfect place to proceed with her chore. The thought of speeding through the trees on Valorre's back, neither racing for their lives nor traveling with any destination in mind, was too good to resist.

However, something told Cora the unicorn wasn't going to compromise on his terms.

"Fine, Valorre," she muttered through her teeth, "I miss Teryn." She'd meant for her words to be meaningless, a way to get Valorre off the subject, but as soon as she said it, a thrum of truth warmed her chest, steadying her. Memories melted over her, of her and Teryn rescuing the baby unicorn. Of the two of them standing close while she used her magic to hide them under the tree. Of his lips on hers before she escaped the dungeon. Of the split second when she thought Queen Bethaeny was proposing a marriage alliance between Cora and Teryn.

I thought she meant you...

"I miss him, all right?" she said, voice firm and devoid of the emotions still playing inside her. "Are you satisfied now?"

Quite. Now climb up and I will remind you why I am so much stronger and better than the brainless creature you traveled here upon.

A wry grin curled a corner of her mouth. He really was a prideful creature. But if it garnered her a stolen moment of unbridled freedom, she'd play into that arrogance.

Valorre ducked his head, allowing her to gather his mane in her hands. No sooner than she was properly seated did he take off into the night. Shadows streamed past as the thud of the unicorn's hooves filled her ears, resounding against the beat of her heart, the exhilarating rush of her blood. Moonlight speckled the forest floor, and Cora let herself pretend—for a short time at least—that this was all that mattered.

~

CORA WAS FULLY READY FOR SLEEP BY THE TIME VALORRE returned her to the castle wall. The ride had been exactly what she'd needed, and now she felt rejuvenated in a way that left her equally exhausted. Only when she was halfway back to the castle, hand tucked in her pocket, did she realize she'd never performed the clearing ritual. She'd forgotten about the crystal again.

She halted, glancing back at the wall. Her bones begged for sleep, and she had to admit her weary state would likely hinder any ritual she'd perform. Starting back toward the castle, she told herself she'd have to try again the next day. A day that was soon approaching dawn, now that she considered how long she'd been out. If she didn't get some sleep soon, she'd be miserable come morning.

And yet...

A strange feeling settled over her. Not for the first time she wondered whether the crystal was enchanted, making it slip from her mind far too easily. Just the thought of being touched by leftover strains of Morkai's magic made a shudder run through her. Her eyes flicked up to the North Tower Library, barely visible behind the other turrets and crenellations—

She froze, her heart leaping into her throat. Subtle illumination flickered beyond the library window, soft like candlelight. It was so faint, she tried to convince herself she was imagining it. But the longer she looked, the more certain she was. Someone was inside Morkai's tower.

IT'S PROBABLY NOTHING, CORA TRIED TO TELL HERSELF AS SHE made her way through the lower levels of the castle, past the kitchen and the staircase that led to the keep. But the hair bristling at the back of her neck, the hollow pit in her stomach, told her it wasn't nothing. This feeling wasn't just a tinge of unfounded fear. It was a clairsentient warning.

She hoped she was wrong. She hoped there was a reasonable explanation for why someone would be in the library—the very room Lurel had claimed was forbidden to castle staff—well after midnight. And someone *had* to be in there. Why else would there be a candle burning in a forbidden room at this hour?

Nausea turned her stomach as she reached the dark stairwell that led to the tower. She placed one foot on the bottom step but found her body unwilling to move. Breathing deep, she called upon the elements to steady her—air to fill her lungs, earth to anchor her feet, water to calm her emotions, and fire to fuel her resolve. It smoothed the edges of her growing fear, but pain pulsed at her temples, pounding with the effort it took to ward off darker memories...

Of her and Morkai, sitting in the room at the top of these very stairs...

The hulking shape of the Roizan curled on the floor...

The duke confessing secrets she still didn't understand...

His claim as an Elvyn prince.

The reasons behind his war.

A prophecy.

The unicorns. The mother. The child. Who do you think you are in that prophecy?

His offer to give her half his heart.

His threat to bind her fate to his in a blood weaving—

Cora closed her eyes and flung out a hand, pressing it to the cool stone of the stairwell. Her palm thrummed with the steadying energy of the stone. She felt it move through her hand, her arm, warming the inked designs of her tattoos until she managed to catch her breath.

He's gone, she told herself. *It's over. There's nothing to fear from him any longer.*

Swallowing hard, she forced herself to take the next step. Then the next. Soon the library door came into view. It was left partially open, and the same flickering light she'd glimpsed outside shone from beyond the door. Daring to open a hole in her mental shields, she extended her senses, seeking whoever might be inside. She connected with a familiar energy, someone she knew—

The door flung all the way open, and Lurel's silhouette shone against the candlelight behind her.

Cora sagged with relief. She wasn't sure what—or whom —she'd expected to find, but now that she saw her lady's maid, all her fears seemed embarrassingly irrational. *I'm a witch, damn it. I'm supposed to be stronger than fear.* Perhaps suppressing her magic, betraying her true nature, had made her soft.

Her internal chiding turned to concern as Lurel came rushing down the stairs, her shoulders trembling with silent sobs. Her moves were so erratic, so panicked, Cora feared the girl would tumble down the stairs.

"Lurel," Cora said softly, so as not to frighten her.

The girl let out a startled squeak, but as soon as she saw Cora—or whatever she could see of her in the dark stairwell —she heaved an audible whimper and rushed the rest of the way to her.

Lurel threw her arms around Cora in a relieved embrace.

Cora was stunned at the sudden hug, and for a few moments, she didn't know what to do. Then her softer instincts took over, ones she admittedly wasn't too well-practiced at, and she returned the embrace with a few consoling pats on the other girl's back. She kept her tone gentle as she asked, "Lurel, what are you doing here?"

"You were gone when I awoke," she said, heaving a sob. "You didn't come back and I...I couldn't sleep. I was worried about you so I went looking to see where you might have gone. Then...then I kept thinking about the tower. I was scared."

Cora placed her hands on Lurel's shoulders and gently put space between them. Lurel reluctantly released Cora. The faint candlelight still streaming from inside the room at the top of the stairs cast half of her maid's face in shadow, but it was enough to show the streams of tears running down her cheeks. "So you came to the very place you thought was haunted?"

"You said it wasn't, so I wanted to prove to myself it was nothing! Besides, what if it *was* haunted? What if you'd been taken in your sleep by the ghost? But then...I saw...I saw all those things..." She gestured toward the open door, eyes wide, and shuddered.

Cora nearly did the same at the haunted look in Lurel's eyes, but she forced herself to keep her composure.

Lurel wrenched her gaze from the room and returned her attention to Cora. Her face twisted as her sobs renewed. "I'm so sorry. I shouldn't have gone in there. Please forgive me."

A pinch of sorrow struck Cora's chest. She wasn't sure if it was her own emotion or Lurel's, but it softened her feelings for the girl. Lurel may be irritating at times, but she was sweet. Kind. Determined to be liked. And the poor thing was trembling with fear. Cora forced her lips into a reassuring smile. "It's all right, Lurel, you're not in trouble."

Lurel shook her head. "Something happened. I pricked

my finger on a book when I tried to open it...and..." The girl wobbled on her feet, and one slipped off the edge of the stair. Cora caught her, but Lurel grew heavy in her arms, sinking down until she planted her bottom on the step.

Even sitting seemed too hard for Lurel. Her head hung low and she slumped against Cora. "I don't feel well, Highness," she said, voice weaker now.

Dread filled every inch of Cora's body. She shifted to the side and propped Lurel's shoulder against the wall of the stairwell. "Stay here. I'll get help—"

Lurel's eyes shot to Cora's. "Don't leave me."

Terror froze Cora in place. The candlelight from above still cast most of Lurel's face in shadow, but the portion it illuminated revealed her tears had grown tenfold.

No. Not tears.

Blood.

Rivulets of dark crimson turned black by the shadows of the stairwell trickled from the girl's eyes, her nose, the corners of her lips.

Lurel whimpered, then hung her head once more.

Cora couldn't cry, couldn't scream, couldn't move, could do nothing as she felt the emotion, the energy, and the life leave Lurel's body.

15

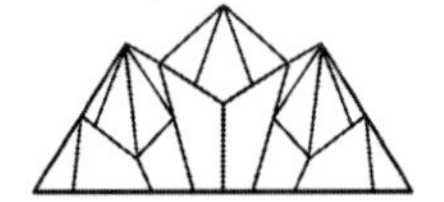

Cora was no stranger to death. It had first entered her life when her parents died. Next, it had arrived courtesy of Morkai when he'd murdered Queen Linette. More recently, she'd delivered several souls to death's door; first with Erwin, the hunter who'd tormented Valorre with an iron-barbed whip, then a camp of hunters, their rum poisoned by belladonna placed by Cora's own hand.

But this...

Lurel was different. Her death was senseless. Unfair. Untimely. Just like Cora's parents' deaths had been. Linette's too. And yet, Lurel's carried the same weight Erwin's and the hunters' did.

Because this too was Cora's fault.

Words of blame echoed around her, shouted by Lord Kevan. They resounded up the stairwell—now lit by several lanterns and the first blush of dawn peeking through the windows. All she could do was accept his condemnation. She couldn't refute what Lord Kevan was saying.

"She was supposed to stay with you. She was not to leave your side. Why was she in the tower? Why? *Why*?"

Because I told her it wasn't haunted, she said to no one as she let Kevan continue to shout at her. *Because I left the castle. Because Lurel woke up alone and came to find me.*

Her eyes stared sightlessly at the space where Lurel had lost her life. A stair now empty after the girl's body had been hauled away. By the time Cora had shouted for help, it had already been too late. Lurel had taken her last breath in Cora's arms.

"Look at me and give me a reason why my daughter is dead."

Cora managed to tear her gaze away from the empty stair to take in Kevan's stricken face. He stood several steps down from her, still dressed in his nightgown and robe. A robe that bore a crimson stain from where he'd cradled his daughter's face to his chest with a wail Cora could still hear piercing the air. His face was pale, his eyes rimmed with red. Sorrow poured out of him, slamming into Cora's threadbare mental shields and pummeling her with emotions that were not her own. Or perhaps they were. She was in a state of shock. Of numbness. Of feeling everything and nothing at once.

"Tell me why you're dressed in a riding cloak in the middle of the night."

The lie would be a simple one. *Lurel left my room in the middle of the night. I donned my cloak to go look for her*. But she couldn't utter the words.

Lord Kevan took a forbidding step up the stairs, his face contorted with rage. "Tell me why my daughter had blood streaming from her eyes! Give me an explanation, or for the love of the seven gods—"

"Lord Kevan."

Cora stiffened at her brother's voice. He hadn't been awoken when the chaos erupted, which meant he might not yet know what had happened. Kevan whirled to the side, revealing Dimetreus at the base of the stairs, shadowed by two guards.

"Watch your tone with my sister," Dimetreus said.

Kevan's chest heaved as he stared down at Dimetreus, but he managed to cut off his tirade.

"I've been informed a great tragedy has befallen us," Dimetreus said with gentle calm as he ascended the staircase, stopping when he was next to Cora. Placing himself at her side was a silent statement, demonstrating his support of Cora while reminding Lord Kevan of his place. Or what should be his place. Dimetreus' demeanor reminded her so much of the confident monarch he used to be that it cleared some of the grief clouding her mind. "You have my condolences, but please do not take your sorrows out on my sister. We are lucky she found Lady Lurel."

Kevan huffed. "Lucky. Perhaps you, Majesty, can shed some light on why my daughter was in the tower in the middle of the night."

"It is a fool's errand to seek such explanations, trust me." A note of sympathy deepened his voice. "My only guess is that she couldn't sleep. The library is stocked with ample reading material—"

"Reading material," Kevan echoed. "What in the name of the seven devils would she possibly have wanted to read in there? She was forbidden from stepping foot inside the cursed room. And...trust you? *Trust* you? You were in league with a sorcerer. Perhaps you still are. Perhaps you're the reason my daughter wept blood when she died."

"Wept blood," Dimetreus whispered, his face going a shade paler. "Cursed room."

Cora's stomach bottomed out. Whatever Dimetreus had been told about Lurel's death, he hadn't been given the whole story. A dark dread crept over her, clearing the remainder of her somber fog. This was not the time to get lost in her grief. In her guilt. She took a step closer to her brother and laid a gentle hand on his forearm. "Dimi."

He flinched at her touch and whirled to the side, casting a glance at the closed door at the top of the stairwell. His eyes grew wide. Haunted. "What significance does this room hold? Why was Lady Lurel forbidden from entering the North Tower Library?"

Kevan gave a disbelieving shake of his head. "You're going to claim ignorance about that too, then? That you had no idea your own library had been turned into a sorcerer's lair?"

Dimetreus flinched at his words, and he began to shrink in on himself. His regal demeanor drained to match the sudden pallor of his skin. "Sorcerer's lair?"

Cora put a hand on his shoulder and tried to turn him away from the door. "Dimi, let's leave the man to grieve alone," she whispered.

He ignored her, rounding on Kevan. "You said your daughter died with...with tears of blood. And that...that..." He gestured at the closed door, his throat bobbing. "Beyond that door is...*his* lair."

Kevan said nothing, only narrowed his eyes.

A tangled web of emotions—terror, confusion, panic—flooded Cora with a force that nearly made her knees buckle. She was still too raw, too drained, to strengthen her shields, but she breathed as much of the unwanted energy away and gripped her brother's arm tighter. "Dimetreus, we should go—"

He wrenched himself from her grip and cast another glance at the closed door. He trembled so hard he slipped down a step but caught himself against the wall before he could stumble down another. "He's here," the king muttered. "He's still here. We'll never be rid of him."

A low chuckle slipped from Kevan's lips, expression smug. "Ah, and now the king unravels. I've been waiting for this moment."

A spark of rage lit Cora's blood, burning away all her sympathy for the man. Her voice came out with a sharpened edge. "You are dismissed, Lord Kevan."

"I think not, Highness. It is my duty to make a sound judgment on the king's stability. You agreed to the terms. You know what will happen if your brother proves ill-suited to the crown."

She did know; Dimetreus could be forced to abdicate at any time.

Oblivious to her and Kevan's conversation, Dimetreus leaned against the wall and lowered himself onto one of the stairs. Cora tried not to think about how Lurel had done exactly that before she'd—

Cora shook her head, patting her brother's shoulder as he began to weep, his sobs punctured by a single name. "Linette. Linette. Oh, gods, I remember the blood."

Kevan lifted his chin and opened his mouth, but before he could utter a word, Cora said, "If anyone is incapable of sound judgment right now, it's you. You're grieving, Lord Kevan. Go tend to your daughter's death rites and keep your nose out of business you don't understand."

"Oh, I understand—"

"You understand nothing." Her voice rose nearly to a

shout. Movement shifted at the bottom of the staircase, reminding her of the presence of the two guards who'd followed her brother. She clenched her jaw, hating that there were witnesses to the king's current state. The guards may have been assigned to Dimetreus, but they were appointed by Verdian and Kevan, and likely held a stronger allegiance to them than to the king they now served.

She descended a few steps closer to Kevan until they were nearly at eye level. "Had you a sympathetic bone in your body, you'd recognize the king's sorrow and understand where it was coming from. But seeing as you choose to berate a grieving man rather than confront your own pain tells me you are in no position to judge us. Go, Lord Kevan. I've no need for your council at this time."

His face burned crimson, and a vein pulsed at his temple, but he made no argument. Whirling on his heel, he stomped down the stairs. "To the seven devils with you."

Cora's muscles uncoiled with every step the man took. Once he was out of sight, she released a heavy sigh and turned toward her brother, taking a seat next to him. For a while, that was all she did, sitting in silence while she let him cry, not forcing him to move or talk or leave. She caught the two guards exchanging a wary glance or two, but at least they left them alone.

"Aveline," Dimetreus said, acknowledging her presence for the first time since his breakdown had begun. He lifted his head and turned his tear-stained face to her.

Her breath caught in her throat as she recalled Lurel's face, eyes leaking crimson tears. She almost expected her brother's to look the same.

But the moisture on the king's cheeks was the benign sort, sending her panicked memories to the back of her mind. Shifting her focus to the cold stone beneath her, she anchored her energy and rose to her feet. "Come," she whispered softly to her brother, extending a hand. "Let's get you back to your room."

And away from the godsforsaken tower.

THE SUN HAD FULLY RISEN BY THE TIME CORA RETURNED TO the stairwell. As much as she never wanted to step foot there again, she knew she needed to. She couldn't rest until she saw what Lurel had seen. Until she had some inkling as to what had led to her death.

Rumors had already circulated the castle regarding Lurel's demise. The official story was that she'd taken a tumble down the stairs, but whispered gossip told of the cursed tower, tears of blood, and a vengeful ghost. Cora wanted to flay whoever was spreading the latter rumors, no matter how close to the truth they were. Only the guards who'd been summoned to help would have seen Lurel's body. Known where she'd lost her life. Which wouldn't make it difficult to pinpoint exactly who had broken Lord Kevan's order to keep quiet.

But that wasn't the task that took precedence in Cora's mind. She crept up the North Tower stairwell, thankful it was devoid of guards. Her throat tightened as she reached the closed door at the top of the staircase. At least the daylight made it harder to conjure images of what had happened earlier that morning. Made it less daunting to turn the handle and step inside the room...

Cora shuddered as she took in the circular library. It was dimmer than the stairwell, each window covered by a tapestry—the same as it had been when Morkai had brought her there to talk. In fact, everything was exactly as she remembered it. There was a tea table and a pair of wing-back chairs by the empty fireplace, a cluttered desk shoved haphazardly against one of the many bookcases that lined the walls, books upon books upon books bearing spines with titles she hadn't been able to forget: *The Art of Blood, Grimoire Sanguina, Mastering the Ethera*. Then there was the table that stood at the center of the room.

Her gaze lingered there, and she crept toward it. Upon the table she spotted the one item that had not been in the room before—Lurel's candlestick holder, the candle's wick extinguished after having burned down to the base. Beside it sat an open book.

Lurel's words echoed through Cora's mind: *I pricked my finger on a book when I tried to open it...*

Cora's heart hammered as she stepped closer to the table, to the book. She dropped her mental shields, assessing the energy in the room, and immediately felt the air darken, its weight prickling the hair on her arms. It was condensed around the book, saturating the metal clasp that hung from the cover, crawling over the page it had been opened to.

Cora breathed away the darkness and maintained focus on the stone floor beneath her slippered feet, rooting herself to the earth, to safety, to protection. Careful not to touch anything, she lifted a hand above the book. Her inked palms tingled against the darkness, buzzing against her flesh in an almost painful way. Her stomach churned the closer she let her hand drift to the book. The energy thrummed near the clasp, and as Cora leaned closer to investigate, she caught a glint of sharp metal protruding from the top edge. That must have been where Lurel had pricked her finger. The clasp must have been fitted with a mechanism that pricked anyone who tried to open it. Anyone aside from Morkai, perhaps, for how else would he have accessed the book? And it was certainly his; it writhed with the sorcerer's essence, as potent as his living presence had been. But how did Lurel die?

A hollow feeling drew her attention to the open page of the book. It was one of the first pages. On the left was blank paper, but on the right...

Cora launched a step back as bile rose in her throat.

Rust-colored ink crisscrossed the sheet, almost too faint to see beneath the dim lighting. It was a pattern of intersecting lines like a tapestry.

A blood weaving.

She understood then that the book had been enchanted to kill anyone who dared open it. The clasp had pricked Lurel's finger, drawn her blood, and woven it with whoever's this page contained. Perhaps even Queen Linette's, considering the similarity of their deaths—blood that seeped not from any ordinary wound but the eyes, nose, and mouth.

Cora's breaths grew sharper as panic threatened to seize her. But she couldn't give in. Neither to panic nor to sorrow. She needed to be strong. For her brother. For Khero. For the safety of Ridine Castle.

She swallowed her fear and let anger take its place, let it crawl down her arms, spiraling through the inked sigils she bore, driving the dark energy away from her, shoving it back, back, until it retreated into the pages of the book. Then she slammed the cover down, containing the energy. She sneered down at the closed book, the dark leather cover hiding the blood weaving that marred the inner page. She turned her scowl to the vials littering the table, then to the volumes of books cluttered upon the bookshelves around her. The objects leered, taunting her, but unlike their master, they were easily destroyed. One simply had to know how. And Cora did. She was the only person in the castle who could make this room safe again.

She'd been wrong when she'd told Lurel the tower wasn't haunted. It was. Now she was determined to rid every last scrap of Morkai's memory, his essence, his energy, if it was the last thing she did.

16

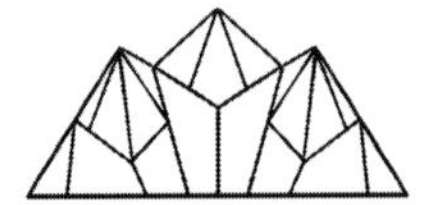

Mareleau blinked several times as if that could help her make sense of the words that just left Uncle Ulrich's mouth.

"My cousin," Mareleau said.

Ulrich nodded, not bothering to look at her from his seat opposite her in the coach they rode in.

"Lurel."

Another nod.

"She's...dead."

"A tumble down the stairs, the letter says. Just a few days ago," he said, tone distracted. His attention was consumed by the letter in question, although not by the subject matter Mareleau expected. While she continued to reel over the upsetting news, her uncle was already mumbling his approval that the council meeting would commence upon their arrival at the castle that afternoon as planned.

Mareleau blinked at him again, willing his countenance to reflect her internal unrest. But no, he remained unflustered, his grin stretching above his clean-shaven double chin, his gray eyes free of sorrow. Surely he should do more than say *a tumble down the stairs* before moving on. The girl was his niece, after all.

"My condolences," Breah said. She was the only other person in the coach with them, as Mareleau's other two lady's maids were riding separately. Mareleau turned a furrowed brow to the girl beside her, trying to determine if she too was reeling despite her simple words. Breah had served alongside Lurel. Even though she'd shown a stronger preference for Ann and Sera, she must feel the way Mareleau did. She must feel...

Well, how did Mareleau feel? Shocked, she supposed. Lurel was younger than she was. She'd been perfectly fine and healthy when last they'd spoken. Which was, of course, when Mareleau had informed her that she'd selected the girl to serve Princess Aveline. Mareleau's decision had been an easy one. Of all her maids, it pained her the least to part with Lurel.

But now it struck her that she'd had an indirect hand in Lurel's fate. Much as had been the case with Prince Helios' death. She hadn't felt as sorry as she should have that her Heart's Hunt had gotten one of her champions killed. There was little that could fluster her. Little that could shake her composure. She'd experienced her share of grief, of life's unfairness. But this was the closest Mareleau had ever come to feeling death's touch.

Lurel, her irritating, naive, endlessly prattling cousin... was dead. And Mareleau, the ever-unshakable, ever-scheming, ever-resilient newly crowned queen, felt smaller and weaker than she ever had before. What was this horrible feeling? Guilt? Grief? It felt almost as bad as when she'd broken Larylis' heart with her lie.

Her hand went to the nape of her neck, seeking loose strands of hair. She was desperate to move her fingers, to wind them through a braid like she often found herself mindlessly doing, but her silver tresses were pinned in a coronet.

"Stop touching your hair," Ulrich snapped, glancing up from the letter and tucking it into his waistcoat pocket.

She dropped her hands to her lap. Heat rose to her cheeks at having been chastised by her uncle. *At least I have hair to touch*, she wanted to say. His dark tresses, cropped just below his ears, looked more like an upside-down bowl that did his dour face no favors.

"Lurel was Princess Aveline's lady's maid," he said. "Now that she is once again without a proper attendant, you might loan her another one of yours."

Panic constricted Mareleau's chest. She had to choose another girl to serve Aveline? Make another choice that would lead to consequence, for better or worse?

"Certainly not me," Breah said in a rush, sitting up straighter. Ulrich arched a brow at her, so she swiveled toward Mareleau. In a much more composed tone, she said, "Sera would do a wonderful job, Majesty. She's much more skilled at serving a princess than a queen. Wouldn't you say? I can't imagine you'd be able to part with *me*."

Mareleau had to admit Breah was right. If she had to keep only one of her maids, it would be Breah. She was the only sensible one of the bunch. That didn't mean she considered the girl a friend. Katra was the last lady's maid she'd called *friend*. And that girl had betrayed her by trysting with her suitor.

The memory made her stiffen and reminded her why she kept her maids at a distance. Why she refused to coddle them. Katra's betrayal had broken Mareleau. It had taught her the futility of friendship and the necessity of being sharp. Suspicious. Relentless. In a way, she was grateful. The experience had made her cold enough to fight for what she deserved. To care less about those who only pretended to care about her. To extend her heart only so far as she was willing to let it be broken.

She'd done enough of that lately with Larylis. Now it was time to be a queen. A leader. Someone who could sit tall in the face of tragedy instead of wanting to curl up and plait her hair like a child. She couldn't fall apart just because a family member took a tumble down the stairs.

Her heart pulsed in rebellion at such an unfeeling statement, but Mareleau swallowed the treacherous feeling down. Donning the graceful mask that was Queen Mareleau, she said, "I suppose I can live without Sera. Temporarily, of course. I assume Princess Aveline will soon have her own ladies appointed to her?"

"By the time you're done serving as her companion," Ulrich said, "she'll have new ladies. For now, it is in our best interest to keep her circle of influence small and controlled."

Mareleau bristled at how her uncle referred to her task as *serving* the princess. She was queen now. She should have to serve no one. Up until this morning, she'd hoped her father would see that and take back his insistence that she complete this ridiculous errand. But today was the last day of their journey, crushing all hope that Verdian would have a change of heart. Her entourage would arrive at the castle in the next couple of hours. Once she was there, her sentence would begin.

It's really going to happen, she thought, watching the dense forest flanking the road fly by in a blur of brown and green. *I'm going to be stuck at Ridine Castle for at least two weeks.* The trees seemed to extend claws toward the coach in answer. They were so tall, so dark for such an early hour, that she couldn't help but see them as sinister. Not to mention the Cambron Mountains leering behind them like a sleeping giant. Such a dreary backdrop lacked both the elegance of the snow-dappled mountains in Selay and the charming green hills she'd glimpsed in Menah. What she'd seen of Khero so far was rugged, rough, and far from enchanting.

"Aveline needs your help, Majesty," Ulrich said, drawing her attention back to him. "She hasn't lived as a princess for six years. She's likely forgotten the rules of royal propriety and tradition. You must teach her your wisdom."

She couldn't tell if he was being earnest or not, especially with that flippant tone of his. Ulrich had never treated her like she held even an ounce of wisdom. There were times when he was downright disrespectful. After everything her father had said regarding her lack of safety as his heir, she had even less reasons to trust her uncle's sincerity.

"Princess Aveline is so lucky to have you, Your Majesty," Breah said.

Mareleau wasn't certain the princess would feel the same. Their first and only encounter had been rife with tension. Now that everything with Larylis was settled, she could admit she'd been perhaps a little brusque with Aveline. She'd all but accused her of trying to steal the man she loved. When she looked at the situation objectively, it was clear Aveline had no ulterior motive and was simply agreeing to terms that had been delivered to her. It had been desperation, not desire, that had driven the princess to agree to a marriage with Larylis.

Mareleau was a jealous creature, but she could try to forgive the princess for having posed a short-lived threat to her happiness. Couldn't she? She'd at least have to pretend.

Breah's words took on a conspiratorial tone. "I heard

she's been living in the forest this entire time. Raised by wolves if you can believe it."

Ulrich released a disapproving grunt and opened his broadsheets. The messenger had delivered the paper alongside the letter bearing word of Lurel's demise. His voice came from behind the front page. "She was raised by a group of covert operatives tasked with keeping the princess safely hidden from the traitorous duke."

Mareleau couldn't help but note his rehearsed-sounding tone. She wasn't privy to all the details of the battle with Duke Morkai, the truth of King Dimetreus' captivity, or the secrets of Princess Aveline's faked death, but every rumor she'd heard involved dark magic shrouded in secrecy, all of which her uncle constantly refuted. It would have been a comfort to hear such claims dismissed had Mareleau not known Ulrich's very duty was to create official statements for public consumption. In other words, everything he'd just said to her could have been a lie.

"Act kindly to Her Highness," Ulrich said, "but do not let your guard down. Remember that your job is not to be her friend but her confidante."

She sniffed, not bothering to respond. If anyone understood her duty, it was she. Mareleau knew she was a spy and nothing more, entrusted with a task that would earn her father's trust. Or whatever was left of it.

Under no circumstances did she intend to make friends.

17

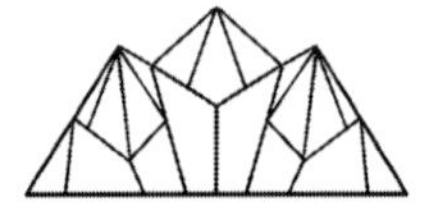

For the third time that day, Cora strolled past the stairwell to the North Tower Library. Just like the first two times—and every time she'd come here the last two days—a sentry patrolled the entrance. The guard noticed her approach and offered a stiff bow. She nodded in reply before gritting her jaw and scurrying past. Once she was around the next corner, she paused and slumped against the wall. Damn. She'd hoped she could sneak back into the tower library, but she'd had no such luck.

She supposed she should feel grateful for the guards, if only for the fact that it meant Lord Kevan understood the threat the tower posed. But stationing sentries in the stairwell day and night was not a sustainable solution. Sooner or later, one of the guards would get lax. Leave their post. Someone would get too curious. Too brave. Or perhaps too skeptical. Whatever the case, so long as the tower remained as it was, someone could get hurt. Or worse.

Cora hadn't let herself look around much when she'd come the morning after Lurel's death. It wouldn't have been safe. Not until she had the items she needed for a clearing ritual. Earth for grounding. Water for cleansing. Fire for transmutation. Air for dissipation. By the time she'd pilfered a few items from the kitchen, the guards had taken their posts. Cora had lost her chance to do her work unseen.

She glanced around the corner toward the stairwell and spotted the sentry's armored shoulder peeking from the archway. Opening her senses, she caught strains of boredom mingling with discomfort. She wondered if there was anything she could do to inflate the latter emotion and trick him into leaving his post. But what good would that do? Cora needed ample time to do what she needed in the tower. It would take days. Weeks. Months perhaps.

It left her only one option; she'd have to propose her plan to Lord Kevan.

She grimaced at the thought. After their argument in the stairwell two mornings ago, she'd done her best to avoid him. Maybe he was avoiding her too. Still, until she and Dimetreus established firm trust with their new allies, the castle was essentially under Lord Kevan's command. The guards listened to his orders. Followed his rules.

"Mother Goddess," she cursed under her breath, leaning her head against the wall behind her. If only she could repeat the strange feat she'd accomplished at Centerpointe Rock. Then she could cross the distance from here to the tower room with no one else being the wiser. That is, if she'd truly done what it had felt like she'd done. Despite her growing doubt over the singular incident, she'd attempted to replicate her feat of spontaneous transportation a few times. She'd tried to will herself to the other side of her bedroom. To the forest. To...anywhere. But it hadn't worked. She couldn't determine what was missing.

In the past, her magic had grown each time she'd overcome a personal challenge regarding the Arts. It was a concept the Forest People were well acquainted with. When a witch would overcome a point of resistance along their path with the Arts, their magic and abilities would grow. Cora had experienced this a few times now, and it had always come from doing what had felt the most difficult in any given moment. So far, her challenge had always been to tune in to her Art. To get out of her head and trust her magic. To release her skepticism and believe she was capable of doing more than she dared dream of. Lately, though, the most difficult thing she'd had to do was publicly reject her relationship with magic. It would have been so much easier to run away. To flee to the woods and let her brother sort out his own problems. Didn't that mean she was doing the right thing?

If so, her magic should be growing now. Instead, she felt like it was being smothered by a heavy weight in her chest. Sure, the base functioning of her clairsentient magic remained. She could open her senses, feel others' emotions, and raise or drop her mental shields, but those were all things that had become inherent to her. She tried to remember what it was like to be the witch who had rendered her and Teryn invisible. Who had manipulated matter and opened a locked door. The witch who had crossed a distance in the blink of an eye and killed a sorcerer. She simply...couldn't.

It reminded her of when her magic had become muted after getting captured by Morkai. Her anger over Teryn's betrayal had smothered her connection to her Art. If that was happening again, why? Was it guilt over leaving the Forest People? Anger over having to pretend to be someone she wasn't?

All she knew was that she'd felt somewhat like herself

again when she'd faced Morkai's deadly book and vowed to destroy all that was left of him. If she could perform a clearing ritual in the tower, she could connect to her magical side. To the witch she couldn't be until her duty as a princess had been served.

"Your Highness, there you are."

Cora startled at Master Arther's voice. The steward came marching toward her, shoulders tense. She pushed away from the wall and took on a more regal bearing. "Greetings, Master Arther. I was just—"

"They're here, Highness," he said, wringing his gloved hands. "The queen's entourage. You must greet her and Lord Ulrich at once. His Majesty and Lord Kevan are already in the courtyard."

Cora paled, her throat going dry. She'd been so focused on trying to get back into the tower that she'd forgotten the upcoming arrival of Queen Mareleau. The last thing she wanted to do was greet the prickly woman. "You'll have to send her my sincere apologies. I'm not feeling well—"

"The council meeting will commence as soon as Lord Ulrich exits his coach. You cannot leave the queen to such a cold welcome."

Cora bit off all further argument. Queen Mareleau could have the iciest welcome for all she cared, but her brother's first council meeting wasn't something she intended to miss.

"Very well," she said, "I shall greet Her Majesty."

Relief smoothed the furrows in Master Arther's brow, but it was short-lived. His eyes swept over her ensemble. "Are you going to greet her in that, Highness?"

Cora glanced down at the green wool riding habit she wore. It was one of her simplest outfits, and the easiest to don without assistance. Master Arther seemed to realize exactly that and took a sharp inhale. "Highness! Oh, dear. You must forgive me for neglecting my duties. I…I never…"

She knew what he was struggling to say. In the aftermath of Lurel's demise, she hadn't been appointed a new maid. Servants had come to call on her, but she preferred tending to herself. She wasn't about to bring any attention to the quiet solitude she'd been granted the last couple of days.

"It's all right, Master Arther," she said, lifting her chin. "I'm perfectly content to greet the queen in my riding habit."

"I suppose there's nothing to be done about it now," he muttered and led the way toward the front of the castle, past the dining hall, and out to the courtyard. As soon as they exited the front doors, a flurry of activity erupted around them. Several coaches pulled before the stone steps of the entryway, followed by dozens of wagons and countless figures on horseback. Cora's mental shields faltered beneath the weight of so many new faces, new energies, new emotions. She breathed deeply, strengthening the elements around her, and shifted her stance to root her energy into the stone under her feet.

Only then did she make her way to the bottom of the stairs to take her place next to her brother. He greeted her with a smile while Lord Kevan, who stood on the king's opposite side, didn't bother glancing her way at all. She wondered how he'd look at her once she brought up her plan…

"It will be nice for you to have a companion, don't you think?" Dimetreus asked in that doting tone that echoed how he'd spoken to her as a child. "Queen Mareleau is your same age, I believe."

Cora internally groaned. She'd almost forgotten the purpose for Mareleau's visit. While most of the people were here to serve as the remainder of the king's staff and council, the queen was to act as her companion and help Cora get acquainted with her role as princess. When Lord Kevan had relayed this information to her, she hadn't dared argue, but that had mostly been due to shock over having learned that Teryn hadn't married Mareleau. She could try to convince herself the queen might not be as bad as their first impression had suggested, but after everything Lurel had said about her...

Sympathy tugged Cora's chest at the thought of her lady's maid. While Cora had only known the girl for a short time, she was Mareleau's cousin. Despite whatever tense relationship Lurel had suggested they'd had, they'd been family. Mareleau might be grieving.

"Ah, here comes Lord Ulrich," Dimetreus whispered.

Cora's eyes fell on the nearest coach from which a stout, middle-aged man exited. He bore some resemblance to Verdian and Kevan but was the shortest of the three and had the most unfortunate bowl cut. With a bored expression, he extended a hand to help the next passenger exit the coach. White silk gloves grasped his leather ones, which reminded Cora that she wasn't wearing any. She hid her hands in the folds of her skirt, certain Mareleau would likely faint if she saw Cora's tattooed palms.

The queen in question exited the rest of the way from the coach in a waterfall of pale blue silk patterned with chrysanthemums, followed by a blonde who appeared to be one of her maids. Mareleau's wide skirts made Cora wonder how she'd even managed to fit inside the coach without smothering her traveling companions. It also negated the chance that the queen was deeply mourning her cousin's death, for blue certainly wasn't an appropriate color. Even Cora knew that, and she'd spent the last six years with the Forest People, who did not observe such traditions.

Then again...had the queen heard the news yet?

Ulrich escorted Mareleau up the stone steps to greet them. "King Dimetreus, Princess Aveline, may I present to you Queen Mareleau Alante." His words lacked sincerity, much like Lord Kevan's did whenever he spoke of Mareleau. Cora, her brother, and Kevan sank into obeisance.

"Gather the councilmen that have just arrived," Kevan said to Master Arther before Cora had even risen from her curtsy, "and direct them to the council room. The rest of us will wait there for them."

Arther rushed down the stairs while Kevan, Ulrich, and Dimetreus turned and marched inside. Cora felt a flicker of betrayal strike her heart at the sight of her brother's retreating back. Hadn't he thought of including her in the meeting?

Well, it didn't matter. She was going to go regardless—

An unwelcome figure blocked her view, mostly due to her ridiculously wide skirts and much taller height. Mareleau looked down at Cora with what was clearly a false smile. "Charming castle."

"Thank you, Majesty. Now if you'll excuse me—"

"We met under less-than-ideal circumstances at Verlot Palace," she said, tone placating, "but we can put that behind us, can't we? I am determined for us to be cordial. Besides, you heard what my uncle said. I'm Mareleau Alante now, Queen of Menah, and Larylis is my husband."

Cora bristled. She could hear the smug taunting in Mareleau's voice, as if...as if Cora should envy her. Over Larylis! Her preoccupation with following her brother fled as her mind became consumed with how best to convey just how little she cared about the queen's husband. Before she could sort out the most cutting retort, Mareleau spoke again.

"Congratulations are in order."

Cora blinked back at her.

"To me," Mareleau clarified. "You should have congratulated me on my coronation and my marriage. It would have been the appropriate response. We only have two weeks to school you in the proper behavior of a princess, so we'd best start now. Your curtsy must be improved upon. What you greeted me with was more like a half curtsy, not at all appropriate for meeting a queen. You should have dipped another six inches lower."

Cora bit back a humorless laugh. This was what Mareleau had meant when she'd said she was *determined for them to be cordial*? Fire heated her blood, and she let it rise, let it lift her chin and pull her to her full height despite being several inches shorter than the other woman. "That would be true, Majesty, if you were *my* queen. In that case, I'd have been required to lower in the appropriate twelve-inch curtsy, but since you are merely a visiting monarch from a neighboring kingdom, I need only demonstrate respect."

Heat flushed Mareleau's cheeks, and she pressed her lips into a tight line. She reached for the nape of her neck and twirled a wisp of hair around her finger before she abruptly folded her hands at her waist.

Cora extended her senses far enough to feel the queen's flustered state.

"You are correct, Princess," Mareleau said through her teeth. "I was merely doing my duty in helping you—"

"I honestly don't have time," Cora said, finally managing to skirt around her. "There's a council meeting about to begin."

She marched inside but found Mareleau keeping pace with her. "You aren't serious. They aren't going to let us sit on the council."

Cora halted and whirled toward the queen. "No, of

course they aren't going to let *us* sit on the council, for you do not belong to this kingdom. But *I* do, and I have every right to attend."

Mareleau gave her a pandering grin. "If it were that simple, I'd have attended every meeting at Verlot Palace. You do realize those are *my* uncles leading your brother's council, don't you? Do you know how many times they've refused me?"

"Many times, I'm sure, but this isn't Selay, nor is this Verlot Palace, and this isn't your father's council. I'm going to that meeting."

She turned away from the queen, nearly colliding with Master Arther. He was leading half a dozen men down the hall, but upon seeing Cora and Mareleau, he paused and directed the men to continue toward the council room.

Cora made to follow in their wake, but Master Arther shadowed her steps. "Your Highness, perhaps now we can settle on new linens for the remainder of the bedchambers."

She suppressed the urge to roll her eyes. Approving linens. Of course that was all a princess was good for. With an exaggerated smile, she gestured toward Mareleau. "You know who would do a wonderful job at selecting linens? Her Majesty."

Determined to let nothing more distract her, she marched away.

Master Arther called after her while Mareleau let out an affronted gasp. The last thing she heard before she reached the council room door was Mareleau's purposefully too-loud voice. "Linens. What nerve. Very well. Show me the most hideous linens I can choose from."

18

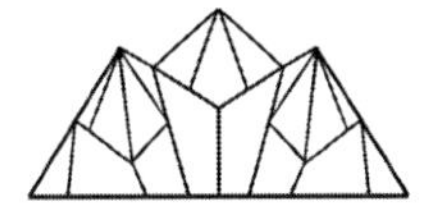

By the time Cora entered the council room, all the other members had taken their seats. She was momentarily stunned by the look of the room, for it appeared almost exactly as it had the last time she'd been inside. Not that she'd had much reason to enter it as a child. Still, she'd always been impressed with its imposing grandeur. She felt the same now as she studied the walls of dark wood, carved with reliefs of battle scenes. These were interspersed with portraits of previous kings from the Caelan bloodline, including her father, whose portrait stood at the far end of the room. Beside it hung a purple standard bearing Khero's black mountain sigil. The head of a large rectangular table was placed directly beneath it, where her brother sat now. Several smaller tables covered in maps and books lined the room.

Cora strolled straight for the table. A trio of servants fluttered about it, filling glasses with wine and water while the councilmen got situated. Conversation filled the room, masking the sound of Cora's steps. After the servants finished filling the last glass, they hastily made their exits, closing the door behind them. No one noticed Cora's approach until she placed her hand on the back of the empty chair at the far end of the table and slid it out.

Dimetreus was the first to rise to his feet. Others belatedly followed, some offering hasty bows, while Lord Kevan stood less out of respect and more out of annoyed surprise.

The king rushed over to her. "Oh, darling Aveline," he said, voice low. "You don't need to worry yourself with this meeting. I daresay it will be tedious and rather bleak of topic."

She tried not to feel offended by his tone or his words. When would he stop treating her like the twelve-year-old girl he last knew? Had she not been the one to comfort him all week? To play parent to him and soothe his emotions, all while controlling the narrative surrounding his sudden breakdowns?

Cora did her best to keep her voice level, but she didn't bother meeting his low volume. "Yes, dear brother, but you should recall that many of these bleak topics have to do with me. Lord Kevan has reminded us of this meeting's importance time and again, and that we are to say little about anything regarding our pasts and recent events until our stories have been agreed upon by your new council. That is precisely why I'm here."

Kevan's voice shot across the table with unmasked ire. "You're supposed to be showing hospitality to the queen, Highness."

"I showed her what hospitality was due. Right now my place is at this table."

Kevan's cheeks reddened, his mouth falling open.

Before he could speak, Dimetreus addressed the council. "Consider the oversight mine. I should have invited Princess

Aveline to attend our meeting from the start. She is right. Today's agenda involves her."

That silenced further argument from Kevan, but Lord Ulrich's snicker still carried across the table. Whether he was amused at his brother's irritation or laughing to undermine Dimetreus' authority, Cora knew not. Her nerves were wound too tightly to allow her to extend her senses.

Dimetreus faced Cora with an apologetic smile. "Forgive me," he whispered, giving her shoulder a gentle squeeze.

Her heart softened. "Of course."

The king returned to the head of the table and Cora finally lowered herself into her chair. She glanced around the table, meeting a few stares from the men around her—some curious, others icy—and held their eyes without falter. All looked quickly away, turning their gazes to the king. The council was comprised of twelve men total, aside from the king, half of whom had arrived today with Ulrich. Kevan and his men sat on one side of the table while Ulrich and his sat on the other.

"Shall we get started, Your Majesty?" Lord Kevan said, tone curt. "Perhaps we shall begin with the topic of Princess Aveline. Then she need not stay for the duration—"

"We shall," Dimetreus said, cutting Kevan off. "Lord Ulrich, I've been told you bear the responsibility of forging the official statements we'll be making to the public. What shall we say to prove my sister's assumed death was false?"

Cora was impressed with how effortlessly her brother spoke on a topic she knew distressed him. It bolstered her conviction that she'd done the right thing in aiding his return to the throne. Regardless of the trauma that continued to afflict him, he *was* king. Without Morkai's influence, he could be a great king.

Lord Ulrich shuffled the stack of papers before him.

Selecting one, he leaned back in his chair. His casual posture contrasted Kevan's tense demeanor. "The official statement," Ulrich drawled, "is that six years ago, King Dimetreus learned of a threat to the crown. While it had been too late to save the queen, he was able to spirit the princess away and fake her death to protect her."

Cora's gaze locked on her brother, seeking any sign that mention of his wife's demise was causing him anguish. The last thing she needed was for him to fall apart before the council. Thankfully, all she noted was a slight twitch beneath his eye.

Ulrich continued. "She was raised in a secret location in the Cambron Mountains by a group of operatives tasked with keeping her safe until the threat could be dealt with. That is why claims of her death are now being refuted."

"What is being said to clear our king's name?" asked a man with thinning auburn hair and a heavy mustache that hid his upper lip. Cora recognized him as Lord Danforth, one of the councilmen who'd journeyed with her retinue from Lord Kevan's estate.

Ulrich rifled through his papers again and selected a new one before returning to his slumped pose. "Although His Majesty first learned of the threat six years ago, it took almost as long to uncover its source. He nearly lost his life when he and his spies uncovered Duke Morkai's sinister motives, but he was able to flee to Selay. There the king and his allies from Selay and Menah rallied a force to confront the duke, which resulted in the battle at Centerpointe Rock."

Dimetreus furrowed his brow. "The people are accepting this story?"

"Yes, Your Majesty," Ulrich said. "It seems the duke kept very few witnesses at the castle, save for those who served him. We've questioned the survivors from the battle. Most had minds too addled to understand anything that had occurred, much like you'd claimed. Only a small handful knew of the lie Morkai had fed you about Selay's and Menah's involvement in your wife's death. The general public has no clue that Khero was ever pitted against Selay and Menah, and any rumors will quickly be smoothed over by our official statement. The worst crime your citizens see you as guilty of were your aggressive recruitment attempts, but those too will be forgiven when word spreads that you'd been countering a coup all along."

"What of the prisoners taken at the end of the battle?" one of the men from Ulrich's party asked. "Have all the soldiers who served under Morkai been put to death?"

Cora's blood went cold. While she knew Morkai had earned the loyalties of some of his soldiers, there had to have been countless more who'd simply fallen under his glamour.

"Many have," Kevan said, running a hand through his thick beard. "Any who revealed hostility or unwavering loyalty to the departed duke were executed at once. Their families have been informed that they died in battle serving the king. As for the rest, we're taking it one day at a time. We can't release a host of soldiers claiming to have lost their memories. And those who have retained their memories know of certain facts we can't let them share. Should too many similar tales begin to proliferate—"

"You can't kill them all." The words burst from Cora's lips. "Most have been afflicted in the same way my brother has. Duke Morkai's dark magic is to blame, not his victims."

Kevan pinned her with a glare. "If you'd waited until I'd finished, you'd have heard me state just that. Considering this is your first time sitting with a royal council, your childish behavior is excusable, Highness, but going forward do respect the speaker and wait your turn."

Heat rose to Cora's cheeks. She hated being scolded by him but arguing would only further his point. Pursing her lips, she funneled her rage by gripping the armrests of her chair.

"And going forward," Dimetreus said, steely gaze on Kevan, "you will speak to the princess as befits any other man on the council. Understood?"

Kevan's beard twitched as he shifted his jaw side to side. It seemed to pain him greatly to offer the king a tight-lipped, "Understood."

Ulrich sat a little straighter, amusement dancing in his eyes. "What my brother was going to say is that we are aware that we cannot execute all the soldiers who fought at Centerpointe Rock. Many have only good things to say about their king. We are going to use their confusion in our favor. We've begun feeding them a tale that the duke had utilized a chemical poison during the battle which resulted in hallucinations and memory loss. Those who accept this story are being sent home, honorably discharged from service, after a thorough interview."

Cora relaxed at that, and she regretted her earlier outburst.

"That will help explain away all mention of ghosts and monsters," one of the men said with an approving nod. "Even if rumors do spread, the official statement will counter it."

"A similar story has been fed to the soldiers who fought for Menah and Selay," Ulrich said. "Since they lack the memory loss of those who'd been controlled by the duke, their conviction over what they witnessed is stronger. But it's less important that they believe the story and more that they understand to keep quiet. No civilians were present at Centerpointe Rock, only military personnel. Anyone caught spreading rumors about dark magic and sorcery will be dishonorably discharged."

This time when Cora spoke, she kept her tone neutral. "So all word of magic is being stripped from the official story?"

"Yes," Kevan said. "There is no point in frightening the public. Now that the duke is dead, magic can return to being a thing of myth."

"But magic is real." Cora's heart hammered at the confession.

Some of the men paled while others shifted uncomfortably in their seats.

"No, it is not," Lord Danforth said with a sniff. "Whatever happened at Centerpointe Rock was a singular occurrence. Our story about chemical poisons and hallucinations very well might be true. It makes a hell of a lot more sense than sorcery."

Cora lowered her shields to sense the emotions coming from the men around her. She was struck with fear, discomfort, and dissociation. Conflict writhed through them, a war between the terrifying truth and the far more comforting lie.

Only now did it strike her that no one had referred to Morkai as a sorcerer or mage, only a duke. They were not only lying to the public...but to themselves.

With her shields back in place, she sank against the back of her chair, regarding the men before her. They knew the truth. They knew dark magic existed, yet they were content to pretend it had never happened.

She supposed she shouldn't have expected anything more. The average citizen didn't believe in magic, and anything deemed *too different* was often met with suspicion.

Which included witches—people born with one of the six sensory magics. If their Art caused them to reveal strange tendencies, keen senses, or miraculous abilities, they were often cast out of society. That was the very reason the Forest People, who'd once only been comprised of Faeryn descendants, began to welcome witches into the commune. Just like they'd welcomed Cora. Nurtured her Art.

A heavy sorrow filled her chest as she realized she was right back where she'd been as a child—hiding her magic lest she be judged for it.

It doesn't have to be forever, she reminded herself. *In the meantime, there are still things I can do. Issues only a princess can solve.*

She sat up straighter. "What of the unicorns?"

"What about them?" Kevan asked. "They are no more evidence of magic than a horse is. They are simply an ancient species that has recovered from extinction."

He was wrong about that. Unicorns were fae creatures, and where they'd suddenly returned from remained a mystery. However, that was not the topic she wanted to discuss. "What is being done about those who hunted them? I'm sure you've been told in the final report compiled by King Verdian's inquisitors that I came across multiple parties of unicorn hunters who served Morkai."

It had been a necessary truth to confess since it explained how she and Teryn had crossed paths. Of course, she'd neglected to admit anything about having poisoned a group of them. Teryn, it seemed, had stayed quiet on the subject as well.

Ulrich answered. "A proclamation has been publicly made against any hunters continuing work in the duke's name, and bounties have been offered in exchange for the recapture of the criminals the duke had freed."

Cora narrowed her eyes. "Has unicorn hunting been abolished? It is a cruel practice and should not be allowed, especially when a species is endangered, as Lord Kevan has pointed out."

"You can rest assured," Lord Danforth said, "that unicorn hunting has been strictly regulated."

A sinking sensation struck her gut—a clairsentient nudge. She pried a hole in her shields, just enough to sense Danforth's emotions, and found him lacking sincerity. He was...hiding something. She glanced from Danforth to Ulrich, then to Kevan. They wore smug expressions and writhed with greedy energy.

She could feel the truth then. *They* were continuing the hunt. They'd probably only issued warrants to lessen competition. Her mouth fell open, her tongue tingling with accusations...

But what could she possibly say? What could she accuse them of without confessing to her Art?

She'd have to wait and bring the subject to her brother alone. Not that he'd ever listened to her clairsentient warnings before. He may not have condemned her strange abilities the way Linette had, but he hadn't understood them either.

Damn it. I'll have to warn Valorre.

"Now, Highness," Kevan said, tone mocking, "do you have any other pressing matters to bring to the table? Perhaps the welfare of dragons and pixies?"

A rumble of laughter echoed over the table. He could laugh at her expense all he wanted. She was about to see that jovial expression stripped clean off his face.

Sitting straighter, she locked her eyes with his. "I do, actually. I'd like to discuss the North Tower Library."

19

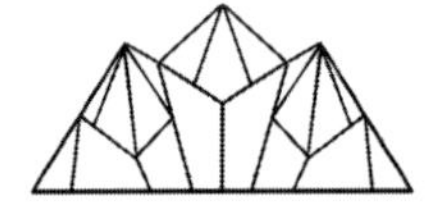

Silence fell over the council table. Not all eyes turned to Cora, for only the men who'd already been at Ridine knew the significance of the North Tower Library. But the faces that had locked on hers were ashen.

Lord Kevan, on the other hand, grew flushed. He spoke through his teeth, each word clipped. "What about the library?"

She kept her tone neutral, her composure steady. "I'd like to oversee its..." She paused to consider the best word to complete her sentence, knowing she needed to tread carefully with this topic. "Renovations."

Kevan scoffed. "There will be no renovations of the North Tower Library. The door has been locked and the stairwell leading to it will be guarded night and day."

"How long?" Cora countered.

"I just stated night and day—"

"Yes, but for how long? Forever? Shall guarding the stairwell become some grand tradition passed down through every ruler to come?"

With the hole still open in Cora's shields, she could feel

his growing discomfort. Not because the topic was related to his daughter's death, but because he had no answer to give.

She arched a brow. "You haven't thought it through, have you?"

Ulrich lifted a hand from his slouched position. "Is this stairwell the same that Lady Lurel took a tumble down?"

Cora flinched at his careless tone. Even she would have had more tact out of respect for Kevan's emotions. She wondered how much love the brothers shared. Perhaps very little.

Kevan glanced across the table at Ulrich. "Yes, and I am determined to see that her fate goes unrepeated. Meanwhile, Her Highness wants to gallivant around hanging tapestries."

"You mistake me, Lord Kevan," Cora said. "When I said renovate, I did not mean redecorate. I meant that I want to dispose of every item in that room."

Kevan had nothing to say to that. She slid her gaze to Dimetreus. He'd been quiet since she'd brought up unicorns and now the library. But when she met his eyes, he gave her a solemn nod.

Emboldened by his approval, she addressed the council. "What most of you don't know is that the North Tower Library was once the duke's private study. It is full of deadly items."

"What kinds of items?" one of Ulrich's men asked, tone skeptical. "Knives? Swords? A guillotine?" He grinned at the councilmen across the table but none shared his amusement.

"Grimoires," Cora said. "Poisons. Traps. You may have decided to dissociate the duke from magic, but that won't change the things he left in that room. We must get rid of them."

Ulrich waved a flippant hand. “So we’ll haul everything out and burn it.”

“Not everything can be burned. Besides, some things are too dangerous to be touched by those unaware of the threats the objects pose.” She was tempted to tell the truth about Lurel’s death, but it wasn’t her place. Kevan was the girl’s father, and regardless of how much Cora despised him, he was grieving. She couldn’t bring herself to illustrate the gory truth if Kevan didn’t want it known. She’d let him stick to his tale about a tumble down the stairs if that’s what he needed. So long as it didn’t prevent her from doing what needed to be done, that is.

Kevan spoke, and this time his tone was tired. Empty. “Which is why I’ve decided to keep the room locked instead.”

“Which is admirable,” Cora confessed, “but not sustainable. The only way to make that room safe is to destroy everything inside it.”

“But you just stated that the room is too dangerous,” Ulrich said.

Cora nodded. “For those unaware, yes.”

He quirked a brow. “But you are…aware?”

“Yes.”

“How?”

Cora’s pulse quickened, her heart rocketing in her chest. It was time to take the conversation into more dangerous territory. Should she make one wrong move, she could undo all the work she’d done to get Dimetreus back on the throne. She could contradict all the necessary lies she’d told the inquisitors to convince them she wasn’t a witch. Maybe she should wait to ruffle feathers until after the peace pact was signed, when Verdian’s threats to seize her kingdom could no longer bear fruit.

But this couldn't wait.

A little bit of truth. A little bit of lie. That will keep me safe.

Her words came out slow. Careful. "I've been trained to detect and dispose of the threats that are in that library."

Silence fell over the table once more. She couldn't bear to look at anyone but her brother, and when she met his eyes, she found a flash of confusion in them.

One of Ulrich's men broke the silence. "Clarify for me, Highness, but are you talking about magic?"

Her throat felt dry as she worked out her answer, but before she could speak, Kevan's icy tone struck her. "You told the inquisitors you harbored no magic. That you were not like those...those *people* we saw during battle."

She stiffened, knowing he was referring to the Forest People. She'd wanted so badly to keep them out of the inquisitors' report, but the soldiers from Menah and Selay had seen them. They'd witnessed them wielding roots and vines—a stunning feat only the descendants of the Faeryn could do with their Magic of Soil, and something Cora hadn't even known was possible until she'd seen it with her own eyes.

Every other Art Cora had witnessed before that had been quiet magic: a clairvoyant witch's vision of a future event that came to pass, a Faeryn's miraculous ability to track prey long since gone, a claircognizant witch's keen knowing that something was true, a Faeryn's gift to nourish poisoned soil and bring dead plants back to life. All things that could be easily explained away. Cora often felt that way about her own magic.

But what the Faeryn had done at Centerpointe Rock... that kind of Art was the opposite of quiet. It had been loud. Obvious. Irrefutable. And the only way to protect the Forest People had been to admit that they'd been on their side.

That they'd seen Morkai as an enemy and used their magic to aid Menah and Selay.

Lord Danforth shifted uncomfortably in his seat. "Are we referring to the...the vine witches?"

Sweat prickled the back of Cora's neck. She knew it was a losing battle to try and explain what a witch truly was, that they didn't deserve the fear and scorn they received. Instead, she confessed what might be a little easier to swallow. "The people who aided us at Centerpointe Rock—the people who kept me safe from Morkai for six years—are descendants of the Faeryn people."

"Faeryn people," Ulrich echoed with a laugh. "We're talking about faeries now?"

"The Faeryn are the same as the unicorns are," Cora said. "An ancient race that has survived extinction."

"And can wield deadly magic," Kevan said. He threw his hands in the air. "Why the seven devils are we talking about the library when we should be discussing how to round up these dangerous earth mages?"

Cora shot forward in her seat. "They aren't dangerous."

"Those who were at Centerpointe Rock will disagree."

"They fought on *our* side."

"This time," one of Ulrich's men muttered. "Who's to say they won't fight against us next time?"

"They are living on the king's land," another man said, "paying no taxes, no dues. They must be hunted down."

"No!" Cora shouted, but her voice was drowned out by sounds of agreement.

"Especially if they taught the princess magic," Danforth said.

One of Kevan's men looked at Cora sidelong. "They may have planted her here to claim the dead princess' identity."

She rose to her feet, her palms slamming against the

edge of the table. "My identity has already been determined."

Kevan narrowed his eyes. "Perhaps my brother made a mistake. A mistake he still has time to remedy."

Rage coursed through her, burning through her mental shields. Strains of emotion slammed against her—suspicion, repulsion, amusement, fear. The energies threatened to overwhelm her, to pull her down and override her self-control, but her anger somehow steadied her. That and the feel of the table's hard edge beneath her curling palms.

She honed her attention on Kevan, the instigator of this sudden chaos, and felt a violent pull toward him. Every inch of her body felt the ease with which she could take a single step—not the twenty or so paces she'd have to travel by foot, but a singular move through time and space—to reach the man and strangle the stubbornness from his bearded neck. Her palms tingled, as if she could already feel his flesh—

"Enough!"

Dimetreus' voice bellowed through the room, leaving tense silence in its wake. He stood at the opposite end of the table, hands planted on the table much like her own. His chest heaved as he glared from one man to the next. When he spoke, his voice came out with a deadly chill. "What kind of circus has King Verdian appointed to my council table?"

The men had the good sense to keep quiet.

"My sister's identity is not up for debate. Fail to respect that and I'll dismiss you from this council at once. Should King Verdian have a godsdamned thing to say about that, he can take it up with me, as *I* am his equal. I am King of Khero. This is my kingdom, my home, and my council. Don't you dare forget it."

Cora's rage began to melt away, leaving her trembling as she attempted to steady her breathing. Slowly, she lowered herself back into her chair. Thoughts of Kevan's neck beneath her hands filled her memory. For a moment there… she'd felt like she was about to use her mysterious ability again. Or had that simply been a violent fantasy? Whatever the case, it left her head spinning. Closing her eyes, she touched upon the elements and let her shields wrap around her.

When she opened her eyes, her brother spoke again. "We can try to pretend magic doesn't exist, and I agree that for the public, it is safer if we do. But not here. Not behind these closed doors where such matters are tantamount to this kingdom's safety. Six years ago, I ignored the possibility of magic, and I ended up ensnared in its web. Duke Morkai was a sorcerer, and my ignorance allowed me to be controlled by him, my mind invaded, my memories altered. I will not let that happen again. Not to me. Not to anyone else."

Dimetreus returned to his seat. "Now, we are not here to talk about the people who gave sanctuary to my sister. Yes, they used magic. Yes, they fought on our side. We will do our due diligence to ensure they pose no threat to this kingdom, but we want them as allies, not enemies. So we will not be hunting them down or rounding them up. Once this council has proven itself capable of good sense, then perhaps we'll send an envoy to open peaceful talks between us and them."

Cora's chest warmed. Despite his shortcomings, both recently and in the past, she was growing more and more impressed by him.

Kevan opened his mouth, but Dimetreus continued before he could utter a word. "We will return to the topic Her Highness has brought forth. While she has been considerate of your sensitivities to the subject of magic, I will not be. The North Tower Library is filled with dark magic, poison, and enchanted objects. If Princess Aveline has a way to neutralize the threat, we must hear her out. Sister, please continue."

Twelve sets of eyes turned toward Cora. She didn't need to lower her shields to feel the tension in the room or know that the councilmen gave her their attention begrudgingly. It didn't matter, so long as it allowed her to do what needed to be done.

"My brother is correct," she said, doing her best to keep her voice calm. Even. "The library is filled with dark magic. It doesn't matter if you believe that to be true or not. Should you care only for science, then let me tell you that there are violent compounds in that room, ones too dangerous to discard in a lake or pour onto the earth. Additionally, there are secret traps laced with poisons. Ones too small to see with the naked eye but deadly enough to kill. For example, following Lady Lurel's unfortunate accident, I investigated the room and found a book affixed with a needle hidden in its clasp. The needle had been laced with poison, pricking anyone who opened it and resulting in a quick death."

She met Kevan's gaze to see if he understood that she was describing how Lurel had died. The only sign he gave was a slight widening of his eyes. Of course, she still hadn't told the full truth. She'd left out the part about the blood weaving and replaced it with poison, as that was something Kevan and the other councilmen could accept.

Lord Danforth's throat bobbed. "How are you able to detect traps and poisons?"

She took a deep breath. *A little bit of truth. A little bit of lie. Focus on the things they can easily understand.*

"The Faeryn descendants I lived with for the last six years taught me many things. Healing practices. Herbal remedies. Living so deep in the woods required many precautions. I was taught to smell for poisonous herbs and flowers. How to detect hidden traps laid by hunters. I know the signs. I know the scents. Most importantly, I know how to safely discard these things. I know how to navigate a trap without setting it off. I know which compounds can be burned, which can be diluted in water, and which must never be opened under any circumstances. The duke's poisons bear labels only I can decipher with my knowledge of plant species."

"It's too dangerous," Kevan said, speaking slowly as if any inflection might spark Dimetreus' wrath again. "You're the king's heir. Or you will be once we've formalized the peace treaty." He rushed to say the last part.

Cora blanched. His words reminded her of the marriage alliance she'd agreed to, one that would secure her position as Dimetreus' heir in the eyes of his council. Now that Larylis had married Mareleau, would she be paired with... no, she couldn't let herself think of that. Matrimony was the least of her worries.

"I appreciate your concern over my safety," she said, trying not to sound too mocking, "but this is something I *must* do. Even if we keep the stairwell guarded, the day will come when one of the sentries makes a mistake. Someone will grow too daring. Or a guard will leave his post and let a curious servant slip past. Keeping the room locked and shrouded in mystery will only draw more attention to it. We cannot risk another *accident* happening again. The sooner you agree to support my work, the sooner we'll truly be free of the last vestiges of Morkai's influence."

The councilmen exchanged glances while Cora looked to her brother again. His face had grown wan, which told her his composure was beginning to dissolve.

"If we support this plan," Ulrich said, "I must insist that the room remains guarded at all times for your safety."

She pursed her lips to keep from smirking; she knew he cared less about her safety and more about having her under surveillance. It didn't matter. They could watch all they liked. She'd be using quiet magic. No one would be able to claim she was up to anything sinister.

"As long as no guard steps foot beyond the threshold of the room," she said, "I am grateful for the protection you offer."

"I approve of your proposal, Aveline," Dimetreus said. His lips flickered with a sad smile. "Please be careful."

She dipped her chin in a gracious nod.

Kevan released an irritated grunt. "Shall we conclude and reconvene tomorrow? I think we'd all benefit from a fresh start in the morning."

Without you, his glare told Cora.

It didn't matter. She'd leave the councilmen to their own devices on the morrow. While she was far from finished regarding the hunting of unicorns, she'd at least succeeded in regard to Morkai's tower.

The meeting ended, and she scurried out of the council room, unable to stop the victorious smile that curled her lips.

Maybe a witch can *be a princess.*

20

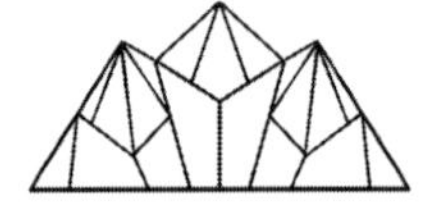

Mareleau had known from the start that her time at Ridine Castle would be time poorly spent, but she'd underestimated just how pointless it would be. She sat on an old-fashioned divan—furbished in a mauve brocade that had already been out of date last year—in her appointed room, doing the needlework she was supposed to be teaching Princess Aveline. Mareleau had been at the castle since yesterday, yet not once had the princess paid a visit. And Mareleau certainly wasn't going to call upon *her*. Aveline had proven herself quite capable of reciting proper protocol for royal behavior, which meant she damn well knew she owed Mareleau the first visit. Perhaps an apology too. Come to think of it, she never did receive the congratulations she'd been due, and she'd fully spelled it out for Aveline.

Gritting her teeth, she pushed her embroidery needle through the linen with more force than necessary, pricking her finger on the other side. Dropping her embroidery hoop to her lap, she brought the stinging finger to her mouth. She glanced at her two ladies, Breah and Ann, to see if they noted her distress, but they were too embroiled in gossip at the other side of the tea table, their own embroidery hoops barely touched in their laps. Not that she wanted their attention. She hated when they doted on her too much. Thankfully, Breah was too practical to get flustered by small things and Ann was too vapid to care more than she should. If anyone would fret over the queen's pricked finger it would be the simpering Sera, and she was officially serving the princess now. She supposed Lurel would have made quite the fuss too, but she...

Mareleau's heart sank. She still couldn't reconcile that her cousin was no longer living. Time and again, she found herself forgetting, found herself expecting her cousin to pop around the corner and chide Mareleau over some perceived wrongdoing. As annoyed as Mareleau had been with the girl most of the time, she now realized that much of that annoyance had been tangled with a thread of affection. It struck Mareleau as cruel that she'd never get to say goodbye. And since she hadn't had the foresight to have her ladies pack mourning attire, the closest she could get to showing outward respect for her loss was the navy gown she wore today.

She removed the injured finger from between her lips and found that it had already stopped bleeding. Setting aside her hoop, she left the divan and wandered to the window, winding three strands of hair between her fingers as she went. The view outside revealed the dense forest beyond the castle wall, crowned in a misty morning fog. It wasn't the most spectacular view, but it was tolerable enough to make her wish she could curl up on the ledge and press her forehead to the window glass, much like she often did in her favorite alcove at Verlot. Even if the sill was large enough to sit on—which it wasn't—she couldn't show such unqueenly behavior in front of her ladies.

She glanced back at them, still chattering away. Breah's blonde head bobbed as she laughed at something the crimson-haired Ann had said. Mareleau envied Ann's red hair and Breah's slender, willowy form. More than that, she envied the ease with which they laughed. Mareleau hadn't laughed with such unbridled restraint since she was much younger. Perhaps not since before she and Larylis had first been forced apart three years ago.

Her heart pulsed with longing for her husband, sending a wave of sorrow so strong, it nearly tore a sob from her throat. She gripped the edge of the windowsill hard enough to distract her, to steady her while she breathed away the urge to cry.

She would not let a tear fall.

Not a single one.

When her sudden grief had passed, she found anger in its wake. Whirling from the window, she faced her ladies. "This is incredibly unfair."

Breah and Ann halted their chatter and turned wide eyes toward the queen. Ann shifted anxiously in her seat, then began winding her embroidery floss around her finger. Meanwhile, Breah set aside her needlework and rose from her chair. "What can we do for you, Majesty?" she asked.

"You can tell me why the seven devils we're here," Mareleau said, marching past Breah to Ann and lifting the girl's embroidery hoop from her lap, "doing *hideous* needlework while the princess does gods know what."

Ann frowned at Mareleau's insult. "It's a bird."

Mareleau frowned just as deeply at what she'd been certain was a misshapen mountain. She dropped the hoop back onto her lady's lap and sank down onto the edge of the bed. It was bedecked in the same outdated mauve brocade as the divan. "Why am I in a room rumored to have belonged to a dead queen? One who died in this *very* room, no less?"

Breah nodded. "It's in rather poor taste, Majesty. But it might just be a rumor."

Ann swiveled in her seat to face them. "I heard it repeated by at least four—"

Breah silenced the girl with a glare.

"You're right," Ann rushed to say, "it's probably just a rumor."

"I had a plan," Mareleau mumbled. "I was supposed to at least *pretend* to be useful here."

Despite Mareleau's dread over having to spend two weeks at Ridine, she'd managed to give herself some sense of purpose. During her travels, she'd organized lists of all the wisdom she'd share with Aveline, all the etiquette, manners, and feminine arts she could pass on. She wasn't normally a fan of anything considered *feminine arts*, nor was she one to go to such great lengths to help others, but her mission at Ridine was a scheme of sorts, and scheming was something Mareleau excelled at. If she was forced to be a spy, she'd be a damned good one.

"It's only been a day, Majesty," Breah said. "Aveline will come to call soon enough, and you'll be able to chastise her for her poor behavior."

Ann rushed to stand beside Breah. "Have you asked your uncles where she is?"

Mareleau scoffed. She *had* asked her uncles, and when she'd inquired how the seven devils she was supposed to get close to the princess when the girl wouldn't even observe respectful protocol, they'd told her there had been a development. According to Kevan and Ulrich, the princess was in charge of refurbishing some library that Mareleau was forbidden to step foot in. When she'd asked for more of an explanation, they'd refused.

Never before had it been clearer; her purpose at Ridine was less about being her father's spy and more about being punished.

A knock sounded at the door, and Mareleau's heart leaped, half with hope, half with dread. While she was eager to busy herself with something—even if that *something* was a princess whom she didn't exactly get along swimmingly with—the thought of conversing with Aveline set her teeth on edge. She'd humiliated her yesterday, going on about how Mareleau wasn't *her* queen, and she didn't belong to *this* kingdom. Mareleau was almost of a mind to take everything back and feel gratitude for her state of boredom, but when Breah opened the door to reveal an unfamiliar face that did not belong to Aveline, Mareleau felt her anger return.

How dare the princess still not visit! *She* was a queen.

Breah closed the door without inviting the caller in and brought an envelope to her. "You have a letter, Majesty."

Mareleau tore it from the girl's grasp and rushed to the window. All prior thoughts fled her mind as she flicked open the seal without even looking at it, hoping to see a familiar script—

She pursed her lips. Why she wasn't used to disappointment by now was a mystery. She should have known better than to expect a letter from Larylis. Not because he hadn't been writing, but because she'd already received one from him that morning. She rarely went a day without one, and they'd become the singular bright spot in her current state of existence. If she could reread them all day, she'd never suffer from boredom. However, along with joy, her husband's letters brought sorrow too, simply because they were apart. Her emotions had already grown volatile as of late; everything seemed to bring her to the edge of either tears or rage. Should she spend all day reading her beloved's words, she might forget how to keep her composure at all.

She scanned the brief letter with a scowl, then tossed it on the windowsill. "Teryn," she said between her teeth. "Have I not done enough for you as it is?"

The answer rang through her, a clear *no.*

While she'd kept her word and made no mention of Teryn's secret travels nor his appearance at the inn to Uncle Ulrich, she knew in her heart that she'd always be in his debt. Nothing could repay him for what he'd done. She didn't know whether he'd acted out of love for his brother or dislike for Mareleau, but it didn't matter. He'd been on her side when no one else had been. He'd abdicated his right to the crown so Larylis could be king, erasing every last obstacle that stood between her and the man she loved.

Her heart softened, smoothing the edges of her ire. She glanced back at the discarded letter. Its contents relayed a request for another favor. Since it was a scheme of sorts, Mareleau supposed she could oblige. He was her brother now, and if she couldn't do her duty as a spy, she could assist her unwanted sibling's request to get him into the castle without being intercepted by her uncles.

With a soft smile curling her lips, she turned away from the window. She was about to exit the room for the sake of reconnaissance, but the look on her ladies' faces pulled her up short. Breah's eyes turned down at the corners while Ann wrung folds of her silk skirt in her hands.

"What?" Mareleau bit out.

Breah and Ann exchanged a look but said nothing.

"Out with it."

Breah worried her lip before taking a step closer to the queen. "It's just…I was wondering…is it strange?"

Mareleau's irritation returned in a flash. "Is *what* strange?"

"Being married to…to King Larylis instead of Teryn?"

"Why the seven devils would that be strange? Strange would be being wed to Teryn."

"Because Teryn isn't king?" Ann said.

"Because Teryn isn't my husband."

"But you wanted him to be, didn't you?" Breah asked. "The two of you were engaged for three years."

Mareleau barked a laugh. "What gave you the impression I'd *wanted* to be engaged to him? Banish it from your minds."

Ann shifted from foot to foot and let out an awkward laugh. "I did find it strange that you were always courting another suitor."

"Courting other suitors went against my will, just as much as being engaged to Teryn did. The only man I've ever loved was Larylis."

Breah's eyes bulged from their sockets. "Truly?"

Mareleau was perplexed by her ladies' shock. Hadn't they known about her friendship with Larylis when he'd lived as a ward to Uncle Ulrich? The budding feelings she'd begun to develop? Then she recalled that she'd only confided in Katra, the lady's maid she'd trusted most. The one person aside from Larylis that she'd considered a friend. Before Katra had betrayed her, of course.

No wonder her maids knew nothing of her true feelings. She'd kept them well hidden. Now she felt a little self-conscious that she was sharing so much. Being at Ridine truly was messing with her emotions. Either that or—

That's right!

Her moon cycle was due any day now. Her pregnancy ruse was coming to an end. That explained her irritation, her fraying nerves.

She studied her ladies through slitted lids. She supposed it wouldn't hurt to tell them the truth about her feelings. The last thing she wanted were rumors spreading that the queen had only married Larylis because he'd been named king. She needed the world to know of her love. Of her victory.

"Yes," Mareleau said, lifting her chin, "I've only ever loved Larylis. I've never had an ounce of feelings for anyone but him. I would have given up my royal right for him, would have burned down the world for him. And now he's mine and I'm happier than I've ever been. Or I will be, once I leave here and go back home to Dermaine Palace."

Ann brought a hand to her lips while Breah blinked a sheen of tears from her eyes.

Mareleau threw her hands in the air. "Now what?"

Ann lowered her hand to reveal that she was grinning like an idiot while Breah bounced on the balls of her feet. "It's just," Breah said, "we've never heard you speak like that before. You've never talked about love or romance, or feelings at all. It's so good to know you're happy."

"I am," Mareleau said, but the words formed a sudden lump in her throat. Tears welled in her eyes, and a sob was building in her chest, too heavy to suppress.

Breah's lips curled into a sappy smile, and she took a step forward to reach for her hand.

Mareleau whirled back toward the window before the girl's fingers could make contact with hers. Blinking furiously to clear her eyes, she managed to say, "Find me chocolate. Both of you."

"I already have, Majesty," came Ann's voice. "The cook said she didn't have any."

"Ask again," Mareleau ground out between her teeth. "And if she still doesn't have any, tell her to order some. While you're at it, bring me a slice of cake."

"Yes, Your Majesty," both girls said in unison. A swish of skirts followed, then the close of her chamber door. Only then did Mareleau release a heavy sigh. Only then did she let a tear slip over her cheek.

21

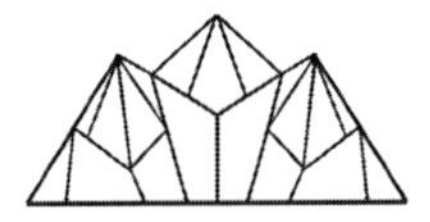

Cora could only guess how long it had been since the North Tower Library last felt the touch of sunlight. Now that the windows had been freed from the heavy tapestries that had covered them, the room looked half as sinister as before. She wiped her hands on the apron covering her simple wool day dress and gave the room an approving nod. She could work with half as sinister.

Warm afternoon air wafted through each open window, bringing with it the smell of the not-too-distant mountains mingling with the hawthorn, laurel, and rosemary burning in the hearth. The herb smoke and sunlight, along with the droplets of spring water and rows of salt lining each sill, would ensure any dark energies that managed to escape the room through the open windows would be purified.

Earth, fire, water, air.

That was all a witch needed to cleanse an item of energetic impurities. Her efforts were working. Already she could feel the room growing lighter, brighter, clearer. A safer space to navigate. But that was just the room itself. As for objects in the library...well, that would take far longer. The predicted weeks of emotionally draining work lay ahead of her. Luckily, it was work she was well suited to.

She'd spent the last day and a half gathering supplies—herbs, plants, spring water, and stones—to accompany the items she'd already taken from the kitchen. This morning, she'd spent a few hours taking energetic inventory of the room, wandering from wall to wall with her palms extended, sensing beats of pressure, darkness, enchantments. The strongest pulse had come from the book that had killed Lurel. It remained closed as Cora had left it, but one of the first things she'd done this morning was carefully slice the leather strap that attached the metal clasp to the cover and toss it in the fire. The hidden needle was the only trap she could sense on the book, and she wasn't willing to risk anyone else being pricked. She couldn't guarantee that the blood weaving Morkai had armed the book with could only be forged once.

She glanced at the book now, sensed it thrumming with the murky darkness contained between its covers. With her shields only partially up—for protection only—she could sense fluctuations in the energies around her. She had every intention of purifying and destroying the book, but she knew it would be a challenge. Something with that much dark energy would fight her. While the Forest People had taught her and all the other witches and Faeryn descendants how to clear energies, she'd only had experience with small items. A patch of earth here and there. Her tools and weapons. Never had she been responsible for an undertaking like this, and it would doubtless be a draining endeavor. Until she'd warmed up to the process and assessed her energetic stamina, the book would remain as it was.

Her gaze slid to the amber crystal resting beside the book. She couldn't count the number of times she'd forgotten it by now, but today, when she'd found it in her apron pocket, she'd refused to remove her hand from it until she'd entered the room. Then she'd set it on the table, out in the open where she wouldn't be able to forget its existence, regardless of the enchantment Morkai had placed on it. She squinted at it, then at the two copper basins on the floor before the fireplace. One held salt while the other would soon be filled with water. She could try the crystal first...

A rushing sound reached her ears, of wings beating wind. She caught sight of a dark silhouette from the corner of her eye and nearly jumped out of her skin as a large bird landed in one of the open windows, opposite the row of salt lining the ledge. There it stood, head cocked to the side. Backlit as it was by the bright sun, she couldn't clearly make out its distinguishing features. She blinked a few times and took a few steps closer, trying to get a better glimpse.

Its size, its form, the emotional energy she was just beginning to connect with, slowly took shape as something familiar...

Could it be?

"Berol—"

"I've brought another jug of spring water, Highness." The disgruntled voice of Cora's new lady's maid sent the bird flying from the sill and out of sight.

Cora whirled toward the doorway just as Sera began to duck beneath the dangling bundles of rosemary hanging from the doorframe. All thoughts of the bird fled her mind. "Do not take a step inside this room," Cora barked, her voice harsher than she'd intended.

Sera pulled up short, muttering under her breath. "Like I even want to be here at all."

Ignoring the girl's retort, Cora met her at the doorway. With a poorly hidden scowl, Sera handed her the jug of spring water beneath the hanging rosemary.

"What is this anyway?" Sera asked, casting a wary glance first at the rosemary, then at the row of salt sprinkled in a distinct line over the threshold. The girl seemed more annoyed than curious, wrinkling her nose in distaste. Then again, Cora had never seen Sera looking anything other than displeased. She was starting to wonder if that was simply due to her face. She had a small mouth, an upturned button nose, and a pointed chin a little too sharp for her rounded cheeks. There'd be something cherubic about her looks, were she not always looking at Cora like she'd rather be anywhere else.

Cora noticed movement farther down the stairwell where one of her guards—or Kevan's spies, more like—awaited. He was around her brother's age, perhaps nine-and-twenty, but his shrewd expression made him seem much older. Another sentry stood at the base of the stair-well, but the man upstairs was tasked with keeping an eye on her at all times. His gaze narrowed on the bundled herbs as if he too sought an answer to Sera's question.

Cora relayed her lie with practiced ease. "Since I've been ordered to keep the door to this room open while I work, I've had to take precautions to ensure no one but me enters. It is for everyone's safety that I be the only one allowed in here. Should I see smeared granules of salt across the floor or hair tangled in the rosemary, I'll know someone has been inside."

Sera nodded absently, accepting Cora's fabricated tale while she twirled a strand of straight brown hair around her finger. The guard seemed to accept her story too and averted his gaze from the doorway.

Cora turned away, smiling to herself with satisfaction that quiet magic could so easily be masked with logic. The true purpose of the salt and rosemary was to keep the energies contained to the room, utilizing the magical properties of the herbs. They acted as a ward of sorts, preventing the dark energies from fleeing down the stairwell and into the rest of the castle. If the energies wanted free, they'd have to depart through the windows where they could be purified upon crossing the sill.

She crouched on the floor before the water basin and reverently poured the spring water from the jug. A tingle of euphoria moved through her. Mother Goddess, this felt good. Not so much being surrounded by Morkai's dark items, but embodying her magical side, even if only in secret. To think she used to scoff at quiet magic, used to undermine its soft and unassuming effects in favor of weapons. Now she was grateful to be surrounded by the invisible Arts. It made her feel powerful. Useful. A witch hiding in plain sight. A princess with a purpose.

"You don't need me anymore, do you?" Sera asked from the other side of the threshold. Then, as an afterthought, tacked on, "Your Highness."

Cora rolled her eyes. Ever since Lord Kevan had hauled Sera into her room and deemed her Cora's new lady's maid, the girl had made no secret that she'd rather be with her beloved queen. It served Cora well, though, for it made Sera easy to get rid of. And she'd certainly need her gone before she could get started. It was already bad enough having a guard hovering at the top of the stairs.

"You may go," she said over her shoulder. As soon as the words left her mouth, she felt Sera's emotions lift into bubbly excitement.

"Do you need me to return at all today? Perhaps not

until this evening when I ready you for bed? In the meantime, I really should check on Her Majesty. It must be dreadful managing with only two of her ladies. She really needs me, you know. Especially because of the baby." The last part came out as a loud whisper.

Cora shifted slightly toward the door. "The queen is with child?" This was certainly the first time Cora had heard of the news.

Sera continued to wind a strand of hair around her finger. Taking on the telltale tone of someone relaying a juicy bit of gossip, she said, "According to Queen Helena, yes. The morning we left Verlot, she told us she was absolutely certain her daughter had conceived on her wedding night and ordered us to forbid the queen even a single glass of wine while she was away. I daresay she must be right, for of course Her Majesty would conceive easily. She is queen, after all, and knows her duty is to bring Menah's next heir into the world. Her son will be heir to two kingdoms because when her father dies, she'll inherit Selay too. Can you imagine how great a kingdom she'll have when Selay and Menah merge as one?" She lowered her voice to a whisper again. "Much larger than your own kingdom, Highness."

Cora stared blankly at the girl. That was the most Sera had ever spoken to her. Apparently, if the topic was Mareleau, she'd be impossible to stop. Well, that was a subject Cora could do without.

Before Cora could dismiss her once more, Sera spoke again, eyes going suddenly wide.

"Is it really possible to know if one's pregnant immediately after one's wedding night?" Trepidation and a hint of panic wafted from the girl. "Or one's...*you know*...night?"

The guard let out a cough to mask what had started as a bark of laughter.

Sera stiffened, cheeks turning pink as if she'd forgotten the man's presence.

Cora debated the best answer she could give—one that wouldn't undermine whatever Queen Helena had said while also convincing Sera to leave her alone already—when a clairsentient feeling struck her, telling her she was on the verge of a truth she wasn't supposed to know. She shouldn't care; this situation had nothing to do with her. But the niggling feeling had her stringing facts together in her mind: Queen Helena's certainty that her daughter had conceived, Mareleau's sudden marriage and surprising change of groom, her aggressive protectiveness over Larylis...

Mother Goddess, Mareleau and Larylis had had an *affair*.

It was the only explanation that made sense. Why else would Teryn not have married her? Why else would Larylis be King of Menah in Teryn's stead? There was no way Teryn would have *chosen* such a thing were it not a last resort.

The thought tied her heart and stomach in knots.

"Never mind," Sera said with a huff, clearly frustrated by Cora's lack of answer. "I was only asking for a friend. *I* trust Queen Helena's judgment." Then, without offering any kind of formal farewell, she turned on her heel and rushed down the stairs.

Cora roused herself from thoughts of Mareleau, Larylis, and Teryn.

And Teryn.

Teryn.

She shook her head, forcing him from her mind at last. She had a vital task to perform, one that required a clear head and emotional fortitude. Rising from the floor, she strode to the table, retrieved the amber crystal, and brought it back to the water basin. With a deep breath, she dropped it beneath the surface and gave herself over to the miracles of quiet magic.

Until quiet magic turned to blood.

22

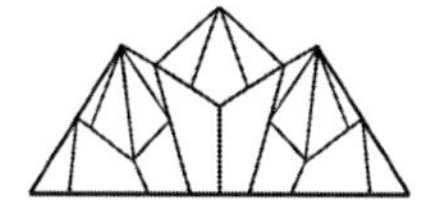

Cora watched with terror as the water in the basin turned crimson. She wanted to believe it was a trick of the light, the orange glow of the crystal reflecting off the copper bowl, deepening into scarlet. But she knew the truth. It filled her with a sickening certainty.

The crystal was leaking blood.

It shouldn't have surprised her. She knew this was Morkai's crystal, remembered how it had dripped blood when she'd found it on the battlefield, broken off from his cane dagger. She'd suspected that he'd somehow used the crystal to store the blood he'd stolen for his weavings.

And now it was filling the basin, flooding it with the essence of countless victims, most of whom were probably dead.

Her own ball of blood was likely in the pool, swirling, mingling...

Bile rose into her throat, but she couldn't look away. Couldn't move. Her shoulders began to tremble, her mind reeling between shock and panic. The water was so dark, the crystal was almost invisible now.

Cora.

Valorre's familiar energy reached through her frazzled emotions, cleaving through her panic, and separating her from her fear. She hadn't been out to see her unicorn friend since the night of Lurel's death, but he'd come close enough to the castle walls to check in with her now and then.

Are you all right?

She forced herself to her feet, averting her gaze from the basin. Then, focusing on the elements—on the heat from the hearth, the smell of herbs wafting from the fire, the feel of solid stone beneath her leather slippers, the glittering dewdrops lining the windowsill—she drew her shields tight around her. She'd need to lower them again before she got back to work, lest she fail to sense hidden dangers, but for now they served as a sense of safety.

I'm all right, she conveyed to Valorre.

I worry, he said from somewhere in the forest.

So do I. But I'm fine now.

With a slow exhale, she glanced back at the blood-filled basin. The sight still repulsed her, but she could think objectively now. Of course the crystal leaked blood. And it was a good thing. It meant the cleansing was working. All that was left for her to do was empty the dirty basin, bring it back inside, refill it, and start again. She'd do it over and over until the water ran clear.

She'd made a mistake in starting with the crystal, assuming it would act like an ordinary stone. Had she wanted to start off easy, she'd have chosen something far less personal to Morkai. But she'd already begun and now she would see it through.

Setting her jaw, she bent down and hefted the basin in her hands. Thankfully, it wasn't overfull, even with the blood. She'd purposefully poured only one jug of spring water inside it, knowing she'd have to change the water frequently over the course of her work. Even so, she kept her steps even, determined not to let even a drop of the basin's repulsive contents get within inches of the bowl's rim. Then, keeping her composure nonchalant, she ducked beneath the hanging rosemary and strolled past the guard. He stiffened at the sight of what she carried, but she commented, "Rust," and left it at that.

Every step felt tenuous as she descended the stairs. Her heart slammed against her ribs, making her arms shake. She dreaded even the slightest stumble. If she got even a drop of that vile blood on her, she'd retch. She managed to reach the bottom of the stairwell without any incident and proceeded through the castle. The guard's footsteps sounded behind her, echoing the pound of her racing heart, but she paid him no heed. She had no choice but to let him follow her.

She moved more on instinct than design, making her way outside past a familiar courtyard, then through a door in a low wall, stopping only when she reached the charred field that once was Ridine's garden. Her composure began to crack at the sight of it; it was somehow even more sorrowful under daylight. Morkai had sacrificed the life that had once grown there to animate his wraiths. It remained as she'd seen it last, an expanse of black earth dotted with gnarled stumps.

A shudder ran through her as she recalled the duke's demonstration. How he'd killed two prisoners, one slaughtered by his wraiths, the other murdered by a blood weaving. She understood now why her instincts—no, her Art—had drawn her here. While she couldn't change what had happened, couldn't bring Morkai's victims back from the dead, she could return the blood he'd stolen. Give it back to the earth where the dead belonged. Feed the land where Morkai had taken. Killed. Destroyed.

Crouching at the edge of the field, she emptied the basin until every last drop of blood seeped into the charred soil.

IT TOOK TWO MORE JUGS OF SPRING WATER BEFORE THE crystal stopped bleeding. Her chest unraveled with relief. Even more so when she dried off the stone and buried it in the bowl of salt. She half expected the salt to turn red, but it remained untainted. Blowing out a breath, she shifted her weight and sat back on her heels.

You can stop being such a mother hen now, Valorre, she relayed to her friend. With her shields lowered again, she could practically feel the frantic pacing of his hooves along the outer length of the castle wall.

Hen? I am no hen, came his affronted response. *Nor am I a mother.*

Her lips quirked into a weak smile. *No, you are a valiant unicorn. But I'm all right. Truly.* Her heart sank with regret. As much as she liked knowing he was always nearby, she felt guilty too. The only reason he kept close was because of the choice she'd made. He could go wherever he wanted. Roam the woods. Find more of his kind. Instead, he chose to stay near Ridine, for a person who hadn't had the decency to visit him more than once—

Valorre's voice cut in on her thoughts. *I am not to be coddled. I stay because we are friends. You think I need to see your face to be your friend?* He scoffed into her mind. *You confuse me with a pet.*

She blinked a few times, surprised at his sudden ire. His presence waned, and she sensed him trotting off. A flash of concern pinched her heart, but it quickly abated. Her too-proud companion would be back. In the meantime, he was giving her the space she'd inadvertently requested.

And she needed that space. That silence. That focus.

Returning to her kneeling position before the salt basin, she smoothed her hands over her apron, then reached inside the bowl and retrieved the crystal. She rinsed it briefly once more and brought it before the hearth. A fresh bundle of herbs burned alongside the cedar logs, filling the space with the heady aroma of woodsmoke, hawthorn, laurel, and rosemary. She ran the crystal through the smoke, turning it in her hand so every facet could feel the heat of the flames and the gentle touch of the smoke. Now that every element had done its work—earth for grounding, water for cleansing, fire for transmutation, and air for dissipation—she took it to the empty tea table and placed it at the center. There she'd formed a protective sigil using twigs and stones, shaped in overlapping triangles and circles, much like her *insigmora*.

The tea table was far enough from the doorway that the guard, or anyone watching from the other side of the threshold, wouldn't see the strange symbols. With her back facing the door, she could hide what she did next. Not that she was about to do anything impressive. It was only that some aspects of quiet magic looked odd to those ignorant or fearful of magic.

Her inked palms tingled as she closed her eyes and lowered her hands around the crystal, not touching it but sensing. *Feeling* with her Art alone. She extended her senses, connecting with the energy of the crystal. An energy she hoped to find vibrating with pure light—

Disappointment sank her stomach.

She opened her eyes and frowned down at the crystal. While the stone's energy certainly felt lighter, there was still a weight to it. A murky energy mingling with something she couldn't identify. Something that felt alive. Trapped. And not necessarily dark.

Cora released a frustrated sigh, sending loose tendrils of tangled dark hair off her forehead. What could she do next? A normal stone would be cleared by now, but this wasn't a normal stone. Perhaps heat from the fire hadn't been enough to fully transmute the energy. She could throw it in the flames. But would it melt? If so, would that be a good thing? She supposed that all depended upon what exactly that trapped energy was. Not to mention the murky energy beside it that felt far more malevolent.

Curiosity had her furrowing her brow. She reached into her apron pocket and retrieved the paring knife she'd taken from the kitchen. Bending over the table, she held the crystal in place with one hand and carefully pressed the blade's edge into the stone with the other. No matter how much pressure she applied, the crystal didn't so much as splinter. That meant it was only amber in color, not composition. That didn't mean it couldn't be broken. Still, breaking it should be a last resort. It would be best if she could purify more of the murky energy before doing anything that could either destroy the neutral energy or release the darker.

But what else was there to try? She was running out of tools in her arsenal. The Forest People hadn't taught her much beyond this, for whenever they'd come across something that required extra care in regard to clearing, it had been handled by an elder. If only she'd taken magic more seriously when she'd been with them. If only she'd accepted Salinda's invitation—

No. She could not allow her thoughts to get tangled up in *if only*. The truth was, had she taken her magic more seriously and accepted Salinda's offer to take the path of elders, she wouldn't be where she was now. She'd have gone to the Beltane ceremony instead of the hot springs the night she met Valorre. It was impossible to say if fate would still have led her to leaving the commune, meeting Valorre, or crossing paths with Teryn. All she could do was accept that *this* was the path she'd taken. She'd have to solve the puzzle of the crystal with the skills she had at her disposal.

With a groan, she swiped the crystal off the table and stormed back toward the basins. As she passed one of the open windows, a beam of sunlight caught the object in her palm, sending glittering light across her vision. She halted in place and faced the window.

"Sunlight," she said under her breath, realization dawning. While heat from the fire might have been too mild and flames too strong, sunlight could be just what she needed. Taking a step closer to the open window, she lifted her hand and let the warm glow of the afternoon sun fully encompass the crystal. It glittered with light, casting the walls and floor in shards of rainbow luminescence.

Why did Morkai have to use something so beautiful for such sinister purposes?

She rotated the crystal, allowing another portion to face the sun, but when she held it still, she caught movement swirling at the stone's center. With a frown, she watched closer as the crystal's amber depths undulated, its movements like slow honey.

"What are you?" she whispered, tilting the crystal higher, creating more contrast between the sunlight and the stone's core.

Her palms thrummed in warning.

Her heart echoed with a heavy beat.

She lowered the crystal, forcing her eyes away. But when she blinked into the light of the room, her vision was blanketed in white.

23

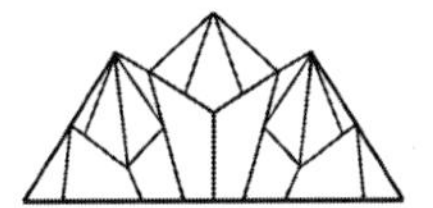

The white that surrounded her was blinding, like the forest after a heavy snow, masking every tree, every blade of glass, turning the world shapeless. Formless. Panic crawled up her throat, seared every nerve. She tried to focus on the ground beneath her, to root her energy through the soles of her feet, but...there was no ground. No sense of purchase beneath her. It felt more like she was floating.

In nothingness.

Trapped.

Without shape.

She glanced down at her body, her hands, her feet and saw...

Nothing.

Nothing.

Nothing.

"It's all right, it's all right," came a soft feminine voice. The white light dimmed, muted hues bleeding into it like watercolors on a canvas, painting the scene in earth tones. Of stone and wood and sunlight. The tower library took shape around her, but there was something hazy about it. Tenuous.

"This is where you are, isn't it?" the voice asked. Cora looked around for the source, feeling another spike of anxiety when she saw no one.

"I'm here."

Cora faced forward again, and this time she saw a figure standing before her. She was unfamiliar to her, a woman perhaps a year or two her senior. Her skin was deep brown, her hair falling in black curls that just reached her shoulders. Shoulders Cora now realized were bare, as the woman wore a silky gown that hung from her neck and fell in sweeping folds to her ankles. The dress was unlike anything she'd seen before and certainly wasn't suited to this climate.

This climate, her mind echoed.

But what was *this climate*? Her eyes slid from the woman to the room, and a feeling of wrongness struck her. The warmth of summer no longer touched her skin. *Nothing* touched her skin. Panic threatened to seize hold of her again, but the girl's calming voice stole her attention.

"Don't focus on anything but where you are."

"But why am I in this room at all?" Cora startled at the sound of her own voice. It was hollow. Flat. "I…I can't remember why I'm in the tower library." She took a step toward the woman, but the stranger leaped back at the same time, palms facing Cora in warning.

"Be very careful not to touch me," she said.

Cora froze. Despite her sudden inertia, a tingling sensation hummed all around her. Through her. Like she was no longer a solid being.

"Remember what you were doing just a moment ago. Start with what you were wearing."

She glanced down at her body and saw that she wore a

gray wool dress covered in a linen apron. In one hand, she held a paring knife. Her mind flickered between sharp memories and hazy confusion. She chased the former, trying to recall why she was in the tower library. What had she been doing with the knife? She glanced at her other hand but found it empty. Hadn't she been holding something?

"The knife," the woman said. "Focus on the knife."

She did as told, but as she studied it, the color of the hilt flickered from black to brown and back again.

"Don't focus on what it looks like. Focus on how it feels in your hand. Close your eyes and *feel*."

Cora didn't want to close her eyes. She wanted to understand what the hell was happening. "Who are you? Where did you come from?" Again, the hollow sound of her voice struck her as wrong. Why didn't it echo even the slightest?

"You cannot focus on me," she said, a note of panic in her tone. "Focus on you. Focus on your body, your surroundings, your breath. Focus on—"

The woman's eyes darted to the side, and a flash of fear crossed her face. Cora shifted to follow the stranger's line of sight, but she barked, "Don't look."

Cora halted, but this time she couldn't stop the panic from tightening her chest, her lungs. Her eyes remained on the woman, but she could sense something behind her. Something dark, murky...

"Focus on yourself, Highness," the woman said, but the terror in her voice was palpable. "Please. You must remember where you are. Focus on the knife. Focus on your breath."

Cora tried to do as the woman suggested, but the dark energy building behind her grew too strong to ignore. Against her better judgment, she cast a glance over her shoulder. At the center of the room, the air vibrated, shuddered, like an enormous fist was slamming against an invisible door.

The woman rounded Cora until she stood between her and the strange phenomenon warping the center of the room. She angled her head until Cora was forced to look at her. "I can't keep us locked here for much longer. You must focus on yourself. Close your eyes."

Just then, a sound like breaking glass pierced the hollow silence around them. Where the air had shuddered, there now was a crack. A crack in what, Cora didn't know. It splintered the center of the tower room as if her surroundings weren't real but something reflected behind a mirror.

Another thud. Another crack. Then wisps of black smoke oozed through the cracks.

On instinct, Cora lifted her blade...

But her hand was empty.

"No," the woman said, reaching for Cora without touching her. "The knife. Remember the knife! Feel it!"

Cora opened her palm. Closed it. Felt nothing. Nothing.

The tower room began to drip and bleed, returning to the blinding white. The woman was nowhere to be seen, only the darkness that continued to spill through cracks that were now invisible. It took shape before her, swirling from the ground up to form legs, hips, a torso, a pair of shoulders—

Cora opened her mouth to scream.

WITH AN INTAKE OF BREATH, SOUND AND COLOR RUPTURED around her, bringing with it the heavy awareness of her body, her limbs, her hands, things she'd been disconnected from a moment ago. Another body pressed close to hers, touching her, shaking her. She curled her palm around her paring knife, and this time she felt its hilt, a comforting weight in her hand. In a flash of movement, she flicked the blade up and pressed it to her assailant's throat.

She blinked several times, clearing them of the haze lingering in the wake of the change of light, until a familiar face took shape before her.

Dark hair flecked with gold. Chiseled cheekbones. Green eyes the color of moss.

She had the strangest sensation that this wasn't whom she'd been expecting.

But whom had she been expecting?

What had she been doing?

Why was she holding a paring knife...to Teryn's throat?

His hands went still on her shoulders, throat bobbing as his lips curled into a hesitant smirk.

"This brings back memories," he muttered.

Cora's chest heaved with sharp breaths, her knife hand trembling. Her emotions shifted between terror and relief. Confusion and shock. Part of her wanted to scream while the other wanted to collapse into Teryn's arms and sob with relief. Then she recalled he had no reason to be there. He *couldn't* be there. He was supposed to be at Dermaine Palace. No matter how hard she tried, she couldn't reconcile this moment with the one that came before it. Both were equally impossible, but one was slipping from her mind with every beat of her heart until...it was gone. *Now* was all she had left.

Teryn looked down at her with the most tender concern. "Are you all right?"

Cora gave a shaky nod.

"Then will you lower the knife?"

She'd forgotten about the blade. Forgotten why she'd been driven to defend herself with it. Why was she so shaken up? Had Teryn simply startled her while she'd been concentrating on her work? But what had she been working on? Hadn't she been holding something other than the knife...

"Highness," came a voice from behind them. It belonged to Cora's guard, and his tone was laced with the frantic impatience of someone who'd been repeating himself to no avail. "Is everything all right?"

"Yes," Teryn called over his shoulder.

Cora drew back her knife and took a step away from Teryn, just in time to see the guard's head ducked beneath the rosemary, his foot planted over her line of salt.

Solid sense eradicated the remainder of her disorientation. "You can't be in here," she shouted at the guard. Then her eyes slid to Teryn, going wide when the implications of where she was—where *he* was—began to dawn. "Damn it, Teryn, you can't be in here either."

Her pulse kicked up, propelling her to return her knife to her apron pocket and press both hands against Teryn's chest. She blushed at the feel of his solid torso beneath her palms, but she blamed it on her fury. Forcing him around, she pushed him toward the doorway.

"Have you any idea how dangerous it is in here?" she said to his back as she shoved him by the shoulder blades. "How did the guard let you in?"

"I didn't exactly give him a choice," he said, voice low. "And...you weren't moving. You were just standing frozen. Unresponsive. I was worried about you."

She paused. *I was frozen?* For the life of her, she couldn't recall what might have had her so transfixed. Never mind that. The thought of Teryn meeting Lurel's same fate just to save her had her redoubling her efforts. Hands on his lower back, she pushed him the rest of the way out the door. Had he wanted to, he could have set his feet and laughed while she tried to move him without gain. They may have been well matched with weapons, but when it came to size and strength, Teryn was the indisputable winner. So it wasn't lost on her that he let her push him, let her guide him out the door and into the stairwell.

Cheeks flushed, she stepped over the threshold and faced Teryn with her hands on her hips. With him standing on the top stair and she on the landing before the doorway, their bodies were noticeably close. She lifted her chin to meet his eyes and found that she didn't have to lift them far. With him a step down from her, they were nearly eye to eye. Lips level. Chests close enough to collide—

"What are you doing here?" she bit out, her voice laced with fury. Whether her ire was driven by lingering worry over him having crossed such a dangerous threshold or resentment over their last meeting, she knew not.

Teryn opened his mouth then snapped it shut, steely gaze moving to the guard that hovered on the stair beside him. He arched a brow. "Do you mind?"

The guard glanced from Teryn to Cora, then moved down a few steps.

Teryn returned his gaze to hers. His emotions slammed into her, buzzing with trepidation, timidity, and...something warmer. Softer.

Cora took a deep breath and fully raised her shields.

"I...I came to speak with you," he finally said.

"About what?"

A flush crept into his cheeks.

Even with her shields now fully in place, she knew the answer. She'd been half expecting this, though she hadn't let herself dwell on it. A marriage alliance still needed to be made to secure trust between her and her new allies. Teryn was here to forge that alliance. Between himself and her.

She startled at the happy trill that sang through her chest, but she smothered it down. *I'm his only option*, she told it. He was not here for a love match, just politics.

A heavy disappointment clawed at her heart.

Another thing she smothered down.

He lowered his voice. "Can we go somewhere private?"

Her stomach tightened. He wanted to go somewhere private to...to ask her to marry him. It was a fact. Logical. She *felt* in her deepest core that this was happening. Knew it *needed* to happen.

This is just a cold, calculated alliance.

Then why the Mother Goddess did it send her heart hammering?

Her throat constricted, forcing her voice higher than she intended. "Right now?"

"Yes, right now."

She angled a thumb over her shoulder. "I...I have work to do—"

"Then we'll speak here if we must. I'm not willing to let this matter stretch on a second longer. I've gone to great lengths to ensure no one and nothing will come between us —between this matter at hand—until I've said what I've come to say. I'd prefer we speak before Verdian's brothers return."

Cora focused on the last part of his statement, not the parts that made her heart feel like it might take flight from her ribcage. "Where are Lord Kevan and Lord Ulrich?"

"Hunting with your brother and his council."

She pulled her head back. "Hunting?"

"Yes, in the royal forest."

That cured some of the fluttery madness writhing through her. Dimetreus had gone out hunting with the council...and he didn't even tell her! What was he thinking? Should he even be going on such an excursion? What if something happened? What if he had another breakdown in front of those men—

She closed her eyes and forced the thoughts from her mind. Her brother may not be in the most stable of states, but he was king. He'd proven that he could hold his own at the council meeting. Royal hunts were expected of a monarch. What was the worst that could happen?

Her stomach sank. Perhaps she shouldn't let her mind go there. Plenty of things could go wrong, but—

The blood drained from her face.

Valorre!

She cursed under her breath. Valorre was out there somewhere, well beyond the castle wall. She extended her senses to try and connect with him, but it seemed he'd yet to return to close range. If Kevan or Ulrich caught sight of him...

She remembered the clairsentient warning she'd felt at the council meeting; she knew some of the councilmen were eager to continue hunting unicorns.

"Are you all right?" Teryn whispered.

Her eyes snapped to his, and she was forced to recall just how close he stood to her.

"Yes," she said in a rush, caught between worry for Valorre and anxiety over what Teryn had come to talk to her about. Perhaps she could handle both issues at once. She swallowed hard and gestured down the stairwell. "Very well, Teryn. Let's go speak in private."

24

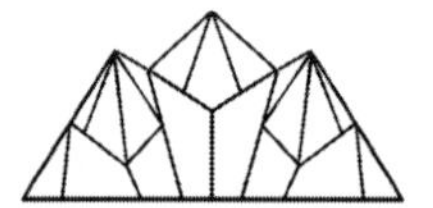

The air between Cora and Teryn crackled with tension, thick enough for Cora to feel even through her shields. They walked side by side down a narrow path through the woods just outside the castle walls. The three feet of space between them meant their shoulders were in no danger of touching, yet she felt Teryn's presence with every fiber of her being as if he were pressed to her side.

She'd brought Teryn outside so she could check on Valorre and ensure he hadn't crossed paths with her brother's hunting party. But with Teryn so close it was hard to focus on anything else. Not even the presence of the two guards who tailed them lessened her awareness of him.

Shaking thoughts of her distracting companion from her mind, she extended her senses and sought Valorre's familiar energy. She'd tried it several times since exiting the castle to no avail, but this time she felt their connection snap into place. He was just barely within their communication range.

Valorre! Where the hell are you?

She felt a tinge of annoyance coming from him, but it melted away. Softened. His voice reached her without an edge. *I'm not too far.*

My brother is in the royal forest with a hunting party. I don't trust his councilmen when it comes to your kind. You haven't crossed their path, have you?

He scoffed, and she could almost see him puffing his large white chest with pride. *They are a pathetic hunting party. They could never find me or my kind. I could trot beside them and they'd pay me no notice. They rely on hounds to alert them of prey, not their brains.*

They have hounds? How is that supposed to comfort me?

Hounds like me.

She waited for him to elaborate, but that was the only explanation he gave. *Fine. Just be careful.*

Who's being the female chicken now? he said with a smug chuckle.

The phrase is mother hen—never mind. I guess we're even.

Her lips curled into a small smile.

Cora startled as something brushed her hand. A glance to the side revealed Teryn had stepped in close, and his knuckles lightly skated over hers.

He threw a look over his shoulder at the guards, then lowered his voice. "Is Valorre nearby?"

She suppressed a shudder at the way his deep, whispered tone rumbled through her. "He is."

"I thought so." He took a small step away, but not far enough to regain all the distance he'd closed. "You had that look on your face just now. The one you often got during our travels. I always felt like you and Valorre were sharing some secret language."

She pursed her lips. She never did confess just how well they could communicate. "What about Berol?"

He tipped his chin toward the sky.

Cora glanced up and saw a dark silhouette circling high above them. Realization dawned as she recalled the bird that had landed in the tower window. *That had been Berol after all!*

"So..." Teryn sidled slightly closer. "Should we talk about—"

"Not yet," she said, heart leaping into her throat. "Not until we get to where we're going."

"Ah, so you do have a destination in mind. We aren't simply wandering the woods until you find an ample cliff to shove me from?"

"Oh, we are heading for a cliff. I'm undecided whether I'll be shoving you off it." She met his gaze with an easy smile and found him grinning right back. The sight made her pulse quicken. When had she last seen him smile like that? For a moment, it felt as if they'd slipped back in time to just under two months ago, when their banter and arguments had begun shifting into friendship. The echo of the past unsettled her. It felt...wrong. But why? Because they were less than friends now?

Or because they were more?

She couldn't help but think of their kiss. Or before that, of the moment they'd shared beneath the tree when she'd rendered them invisible. Or at Centerpointe Rock when her hand had stilled on his torso after she'd bandaged his wound. Her mind lingered over that moment now, remembering how his eyes had flickered as he'd looked down at her, stirring the energies between them into something new. Even more so when he'd placed his hand over hers and caressed the back of her hand with his thumb.

That moment had felt so heavy. So meaningful.

But then everything changed. Cora had gotten herself captured by Verdian.

And Teryn...

Teryn had proposed an engagement between her and his brother. Regardless of the reason that had brought him here now, she couldn't let herself forget that she hadn't been his first choice. He was here because he had to be.

The forest path split into a fork, and Cora paused to recall which way led to her destination. After a moment of hesitation, an internal tug pulled her to the left. "This way," she said, starting off down the left-hand path and taking the opportunity to place another foot of space between them.

Keeping her voice nonchalant, she changed the subject to neutral territory. "How did you know my brother and his council had gone hunting?"

Teryn's smile no longer brightened his face. "Mareleau told me."

"Mareleau?" A spike of annoyance shot through her. So his former fiancée was simply...Mareleau. Not Her Majesty. Not Queen Mareleau. Cora wasn't sure how to feel about that, but the jealousy that clouded her chest was most certainly uncalled for. But that didn't stop it from growing.

Teryn nodded. "She'd discovered my plan to come here and speak with you. I begged for her silence and requested her help in getting me inside the palace while her uncles were away."

Cora arched a brow and cast him a disbelieving look. "She helped you? As in...she did something for another person?"

"More like she sent me a curt letter informing me of her uncles' hunting excursion, and I took advantage of their fortuitous absence."

"Why did you ask for her help and not mine?" Cora

wished she could swallow her accusing tone, but it was too late. *I shouldn't care. It shouldn't matter.* She cleared her throat. "If your business at Ridine involves me, you could have sent me a letter informing me of your visit. Why the secrecy?"

Teryn cast her a sideways grin. "I wasn't sure you'd reply. Worse, I thought perhaps you'd tell me not to come at all."

He had a point.

But still…

"So instead, you schemed to infiltrate my home and sneak up on me unannounced?"

"Technically, I didn't infiltrate the castle. Master Arther greeted me and—" His voice cut off and his expression turned serious. "I was willing to do whatever it took. I told you, Cora. I wasn't going to let anything come between us again."

Us.

The word sent her pulse thundering.

She shifted her gaze ahead and saw the trees thinning, opening to a familiar sight. One she hadn't seen since she was a child. She picked up her pace, pouring all her focus into her destination to distract herself from Teryn.

From the way he'd said *us*.

Teryn kept pace at her side while the sound of the guards' footsteps lagged farther behind. Finally, they reached a small clearing at the edge of a low, grassy cliff. Beneath it spread a wide meadow dotted with wildflowers in every shade imaginable. A smile stretched Cora's lips. It was even more beautiful than she'd remembered.

She halted a few feet before the cliff's edge and breathed in the fresh summer air. A shadow crossed the sun as Berol descended and landed in a nearby tree.

Teryn came up beside Cora. His knuckles caressed hers

again, making her breath catch. He made no move to pull his hand away, only let their fingers brush once more before he said, "It's beautiful."

She angled her body to the side, sliding her hand out of reach. "I used to come here with my brother when I was a child. It was our secret place."

He met her eyes, sunlight catching his emerald irises. His mouth lifted at both corners. "Thank you for bringing me here."

Her shoulders tensed as a sudden wave of self-consciousness swept over her. She hadn't considered the implications of bringing him to a special place to have their private chat. To be honest, she hadn't thought of where to take them until they were several minutes into their forest stroll. It was the only place she could think of that was close enough for the guards not to make a fuss but far enough away to give her the time she needed to mentally prepare for the matter at hand.

Teryn faced her fully. His throat bobbed once. Twice.

She held her breath, knowing what he was preparing to say...

"Why didn't you meet me in the garden at Verlot Palace that night?"

She blinked a few times. Those weren't quite the words she'd expected, but they filled her with no small amount of anxiety. She opened her mouth to answer, but her eyes darted to the side, taking in the bored postures of the two guards who stood several feet away.

Teryn released an aggravated grumble and addressed them. "Can you *please* give us some damn privacy?"

The guards exchanged a glance but begrudgingly obeyed, taking a dozen or so paces out of the clearing to flank the forest path instead.

Teryn returned to face Cora, brow raised in question.

It seemed he wasn't going to let her off that easy.

She resisted the urge to fidget and hid her hands in the folds of her skirt. Only then did she realize she still wore her apron and her dress was embarrassingly plain. She'd had to borrow it from a servant just to have something comfortable enough to work in. She was likely covered in salt, herbs, and soot as well. Not to mention what her hair must look like. Meanwhile, he was dressed like a true prince. A man who'd almost been king. His dark trousers were clearly made for riding, but the way they hugged his thighs told her they were custom tailored to the finest precision. His waistcoat was leather, but not in the style worn by a hunter. His was of a supple blue suede, embossed with Menah's eagle sigil. Not even the rolled-up sleeves of his shirt or the cravat hanging loose around his neck belied his title.

He was a distinguished royal. *She* was a witch playing pretend until she'd served her purpose as a princess.

Besides, it didn't matter what either of them looked like. He was only here for politics. It was better that way. She'd already determined that a political alliance was all she could commit to. A love match represented danger. The potential for heartache. She wasn't yet ready to let go of the life she'd had with the Forest People. Of freedom. The Arts. If she married for love, she'd have to give that all up. Be Princess Aveline forevermore.

But isn't Teryn the one person I can be both a witch and a princess with?

She banished the thought and reminded herself he was still waiting for an answer. She supposed he deserved one.

Forcing herself to meet his eyes with a neutral expression, she said, "I didn't think it was proper to meet with what I assumed was a married man alone in a garden at night."

"You thought I'd married Mareleau."

Cora shrugged. "She was your fiancée."

"No, Cora, everything changed—"

"I know what changed. I know about Larylis and Mareleau. Or...her pregnancy at least."

Teryn frowned. "You do?"

She let out a halfhearted chuckle. "One of the queen's maids—well, I suppose she's my maid now—isn't the keenest when it comes to discretion. Or even logic."

Teryn looked relieved that she'd freed him from the burden of having to explain. Perhaps she should free him from the rest of his burdens too. They might as well get this over with.

Turning back toward the edge of the cliff and the bright meadow beyond, she said, "I know why you're here, and I know what you came to say. What you came to ask me. I agreed to an alliance with Menah, one that will be solidified in a peace pact at the end of the month. Its terms include a betrothal to Menah's prince and will result in an official marriage one year from now. But there's been a change of groom. Now I must be engaged to you to secure trust with my allies. Marrying you is the only way my brother's council will recognize me as his heir. Until Dimetreus remarries and has children of his own, I'm the only heir he has. Which makes our engagement necessary on all fronts."

Teryn was silent for a moment. Then he came up beside her. She could feel his gaze burning into her profile, but she refused to meet his eyes.

"You don't have to marry me, Cora," he said, voice low, somber. "You have a choice. Should you wish to refuse me,

I'll convince Verdian of some other way to secure trust. I promise."

She let out a humorless laugh. "Have you learned nothing about the folly of making empty promises? King Verdian is your queen's father. He's threatened to take my brother's birthright away if I so much as step out of line. You can't go up against him."

"Try me."

Cora couldn't help but look at him then. His expression held no jest. She didn't dare open her senses to him, to feel the intensity hidden behind his words.

"It doesn't matter," she said, forcing her composure to remain cool. Calm. Disconnected from emotion. "My answer is yes."

"It is?" When she gave him nothing but a curt nod in reply, he lowered his head and pinched the bridge of his nose between his fingers. "This isn't going how I'd imagined."

"Were you expecting me to say no?" She clenched her jaw, a flash of fury sparking in her veins. "Do you...want me to say no?"

"It's not that. I just thought...I thought this would be a bigger deal to you."

"Well, it's not. You're giving too much weight to a small matter. You didn't need to come here, Teryn. You could have written this all in a letter—"

"I didn't want to write it in a letter," he said, voice rising. "I came so there'd be no mistaking my intentions...and yet of course you're mistaking them anyway because I'm a blundering fool..."

His words dissolved into a string of muttered curses. With a sigh, he ran a hand over his face and looked out at the meadow. Cora's brow furrowed as she took in his tense shoulders, the fist planted on one hip, the sharp rise and fall of his chest. She wasn't sure she'd ever seen him so flustered.

"You may be content to agree to a cold, loveless betrothal," he said, opening and closing one hand as if he didn't know what to do with it. "If that's what you prefer, I'll respect that, but I don't want you agreeing to a thing until you understand my side of things."

"What's your side?" she asked, almost terrified of the answer.

Slowly, his eyes returned to hers and he held her gaze without falter. His voice came out slow, broken only by the slightest tremor. "When last we spoke, you said you'd thought my mother had meant for you to marry me when she conveyed my proposal."

Cora shrank back, wishing she could disappear entirely. Her cheeks flooded with heat. "I...that's not—"

"It *was* supposed to be me. It had always been me."

Cora's breaths grew sharp, her pulse rioting. "I don't understand."

He took a step closer. "I told my mother of my idea to forge a marriage alliance between Khero and Menah, but that was all I'd said. She had no right to take my proposal and offer it to you before she fully understood—no, that's giving her too much credit. She did understand my heart and interfered on purpose. She never should have done that. It was supposed to be you and me from the start."

Teryn's words did strange things to her chest, her stomach, threatening to upend the balance of the entire world. She felt a flicker of hope—one that had proven traitorous before.

Shoving aside all warm feelings, she latched onto steely logic instead. "That's impossible," she said, voice calm. "You couldn't have meant to marry me from the start. Not until you found out about whatever scandal befell Mareleau and your brother. You were engaged to her. Had you rejected her without due cause—"

He stepped even closer. "I wasn't thinking about her. Not for a moment. I was only thinking about you. About us."

Us. There was that word again.

A corner of his mouth quirked up. "Thankfully, my unwanted fiancée had secrets that aided my own."

Her gaze lingered on his lips, on that crooked smile. On the mouth that just confessed he'd wanted her from the start. That he'd intended to choose her over the woman he'd been promised to.

Again, that flicker of hope tried to spark into a blaze, but she breathed it away. She crossed her arms over her chest and lifted her chin in defiance. "You've tricked me before. Used my own emotions against me."

His smirk stretched wider, revealing the depths of his amusement. "Are you talking about our kiss?"

She pursed her lips. "I don't see anything funny about it."

"The only thing funny about it is that you think I did it to be cruel." He stepped in closer, forcing her to take two steps back. He shadowed her retreat, but she refused to let him close—

Her breath caught as she felt her back come up against the trunk of a tree.

He stared down at her with unbridled intensity. "Do you honestly believe my only motive for kissing you was to trick you? Had I wanted to be cruel, I could have said or done a thousand other things to hurt you. And if I'd simply wanted you to leave me behind in that dungeon cell, I could have hefted you over my shoulder and set you on the other side of the door before you knew what was happening."

The thought of Teryn picking her up with such ease sent heat building low in her belly. But the image fled her mind as he leaned down, planted his forearm against the trunk over her head, and brought his face mere inches from hers. His voice left his lips in a whisper. "I kissed you because I wanted to. Because I wanted to feel your lips against mine before I died. Because it was my desire."

"Desire," she echoed. The word sent her knees quaking.

"Yes, desire."

Mother Goddess, she was losing hold of everything. Of her anger, her logic. That spark of hope was growing, searing through her carefully constructed walls.

She forced herself to straighten, to hold his gaze and pretend every inch of her wasn't burning from the inside. She waved her hand in a flippant gesture. "So now you want to go straight from desire to an engagement? Is there nothing missing between those two steps?"

"Oh, there's plenty missing. Could I disentangle our necessary betrothal from my feelings, I would, for that would allow me to court you the way you deserve to be courted. And I'll do it no matter what. Our engagement need only satisfy King Verdian, and we have a year before we're expected to wed. A year for you to change your mind. A year for me to win you over. Regardless of your answer, of whatever is expected of us, I'll woo you, Cora. I'll court you as befits strangers. Lovers. I'll deny myself the pleasure of kissing you until I've fully won your heart."

Cora's cold façade crumpled. His words cleaved through all remaining resistance, obliterated every argument she had in her arsenal. She could no longer deny the truth she'd tried so hard to suppress—that when Queen Bethaeny had offered the proposal, she'd *wanted* it to be with Teryn. And when he'd kissed her in the dungeon, she'd *wanted* that kiss.

Wanted him. She slackened against the tree trunk and surrendered to Teryn's relentless barrage. "All right," she whispered, and her chest pulsed its satisfaction.

"All right," she said again, louder this time. The spark of hope ignited, melting the remainder of her walls, heating her blood, and filling her head with the most tantalizing euphoria. "But under one condition. I want you to kiss me now."

25

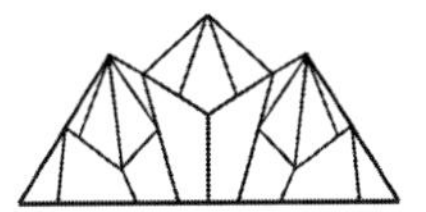

Cora's request sent heat radiating through Teryn's chest. His eyes dropped down to her full, slightly parted lips, wondering if he hadn't imagined the words that had left them. As if in silent confirmation, she tilted her chin, lashes fluttering closed.

That was all Teryn needed. All the agonizing seconds he could resist before he lowered his mouth to hers. She met him halfway, her lips impossibly soft as they crushed against his. Her arms wound around his neck, fingertips sliding into his hair and sending a shiver down his spine. He pressed her closer to the tree, one hand snaking behind her back while the other trailed down her hair, the side of her face. Then, cradling her jaw, he gently tilted her chin, allowing their kiss to deepen. Her lips parted, and their tongues met in a languorous sweep. His hand stiffened on her back, pulling her ever closer. She yielded to him, her soft, small body somehow fitting perfectly against him. Their breaths grew heavy, sharp, and with the next sweep of his tongue, she released the most delicious of moans.

It nearly unraveled him, nearly made him slide his

hands to places better left explored in private. He ached to palm her backside, to untie her apron and feel at least one less layer between them. Yet, despite his near-feverish desire, he remained vaguely aware of the two guards nearby. Guards that were surely getting an eyeful regardless of where Teryn kept his hands.

Cora arched into him, releasing another soft moan, her fingers clawing into the hair at the nape of his neck. Teryn was about to throw caution to the wind and heft her into his arms to close more of the sparse distance between them—when Cora suddenly pulled back with a gasp. And not one of pleasure. Of...something he couldn't comprehend.

Teryn froze. Had he done something wrong? Had he let his passion get out of control after all? The tightening in his trousers suggested as much, and she certainly would have noticed *that*, but—

She gasped again. Only this time he realized it wasn't a gasp at all but a snort.

Of laughter.

Which might have been worse than whatever he'd been imagining.

Still, her smile sent a fluttery feeling to his chest, and he found his lips lifting too. Her arms were still around his neck, her body still close to his. "What is it?"

She pursed her lips, gaze lowered. Then she lifted her dark eyes to his and her smile grew. "It's Valorre," she said, her voice quavering with restrained laughter. "That smug little bastard is smirking."

Teryn cast a glance over his shoulder but saw only the edge of the cliff and the wildflower meadow. The other direction revealed nothing but trees and the forest path. Well, that and the pair of guards who were absolutely looking at them. Perverts.

"I don't see him," he said.

"He's not here," she whispered, "but he is close by. I can *feel* him smirking."

Awe washed over him. "You really can communicate with him, can't you?"

Her expression turned timid, but she gave him a small smile. "Yes."

Seven gods, she was incredible. Their moment of passion may have been broken by Cora's sudden amusement, but it hadn't changed his feelings. With his hand still pressed against her back, he gently stroked his thumb over the wool fabric of her dress. "I wish you didn't have to hide who you really are. You are too godsdamned amazing for that."

Her expression took on a teasing quality. "I think I liked it best when you called me formidable."

"You're always formidable."

She leaned against the tree, placing space between them. Her hands slid from around his neck but lingered over his chest. "I never did thank you," she said, eyes flashing toward the guards. "For keeping my secret. About my magic, about...well, a lot of things."

He gave her a wry grin. "Yes, I seem to recall you being too busy yelling at me when last we spoke to properly thank me."

She playfully swatted his chest, but he caught her fingers and brought them to his lips. Holding her gaze, he planted a kiss over the back of her bare, gloveless hand, right over the rounded curves of her knuckles. She bit her lower lip as if that could hide the grin splitting her face. And if it wasn't the most beautiful godsdamned smile he'd ever seen. He didn't think she'd ever looked at him like that, and now that he'd seen the expression, he was determined to inspire it a thousand times more.

Her face fell slightly, eyes darting toward the guards again. “We should probably get back before we lose our senses and give them another show.”

Losing his senses was exactly what Teryn wanted to do with her. Just the thought of how good she’d felt against him, against that tree, nearly had him pulling her into his arms all over again. But she was probably right. So instead of kissing her swollen lips and eliciting another one of those glorious moans of hers, he took her hand and placed it at the crook of his elbow. Angling his head toward the path, he said, “Shall we?”

THEY FELL INTO SILENCE AS THEY MADE THEIR WAY BACK toward the castle. Berol soared overhead, sometimes swooping low enough that he could hear the beat of her wings. As much as Teryn wanted to fill the void with conversation, he was grateful for the quiet, for it allowed him to simply enjoy the feel of Cora’s company, of her slender hand warm against his forearm, of the pound of his heart dancing in rhythm with their steps. A pinch of fear crept up now and then, and he’d worry their silence was shifting into the awkward sort. But then he’d glance her way and she’d grin back.

Perhaps there was some awkwardness to their silence, but it was a good kind. One that marked new beginnings. Two people getting to know one another in an entirely new way.

In fact, all of this was new to Teryn. While he’d had his share of lovers, he’d never entertained anything serious. His marriage prospects had always been filtered through political advantage. Which, of course, had resulted in his engagement to Mareleau. Regardless, he'd always been resigned to his fate. After seeing what love had done to his parents and his kingdom, he'd been determined to accept his duty with a cold heart.

But meeting Cora...

She'd changed him in such a short time. He'd made mistakes with her, ones that taught him the dangers of blindly following what he thought was his duty and going against his heart.

Now his duty and his heart were aligned. Because Cora was both.

"What will you do now?" Cora asked, finally breaking their silence. Ridine's towers peeked over the trees in the distance.

"Well, I..." Teryn frowned. "I don't actually know. My mind has been so consumed with simply getting here and speaking with you about our engagement, I haven't thought about what comes next now that the alliance is secure."

She arched a teasing brow. "Oh, so the alliance is all you came here for?"

"You know I came for more than that," he said. It was true, although he'd never expected their conversation would end in a kiss. He'd intended to tell Cora the truth. That regardless of her feelings, or lack thereof, his own ran deeper than politics. He hadn't realized just how deep they ran until she'd refused to entertain such a notion at all. Until he was forced to spell it out—both to himself and her—that he *wanted* their union to be a romantic one. A passionate one.

Had she told him she wanted to keep things platonic between them, he'd have agreed. Grudgingly, yes, but respectfully. But gods, was he thrilled she'd accepted his affection. He wasn't ready to call it love. Not yet—

"Will you stay?"

Teryn glanced at Cora and found her worrying a corner of her lip.

"Now that you've secured the…the alliance, will you return to Dermaine Palace, or will you…stay? For a while at least? Maybe until the peace pact is signed?"

He paused and turned toward her. "I'll stay. For as long as I can."

He hoped it would be long indeed and that Verdian and his brothers wouldn't interfere. He hated that they had a stranglehold on Ridine Castle and the kingdom at large. On *Cora's* kingdom. He hated that they treated her and her brother like they were still prisoners. Perhaps now that the engagement was secure, they'd respect her title more.

"I'd like that," she said.

A tendril of dark hair unraveled from her messy updo and fell onto her cheek, but before she could sweep it away, he gently took hold of it. He ran the silken lock between his fingers before tucking it behind her ear.

"My hair is probably a mess right now," she said, cheeks flushing.

"I like when it's a mess." And for the love of all things, he liked it when she blushed. The fact that he could make this fierce, gorgeous little creature blush made his stomach tighten.

She averted her gaze with a poorly hidden smile, and they proceeded toward the castle once more.

~

By the time Teryn returned Cora to the stairwell leading up to the tower room, she'd told him about the task she'd taken on. It gave him no small amount of terror to imagine her in that room surrounded by a dead mage's possibly enchanted belongings. He knew better than to ask her to stop her work. All he could do was offer his help, which she'd predictably refused.

At least she said yes to dinner tonight.

Teryn let that warm his heart as he left the stairwell, left Cora to proceed with her work alone, but it did little to calm his nerves. He trusted Cora's powers, knew she was so much stronger than anyone gave her credit for. And yet, he couldn't shake how she'd looked when he'd first climbed the staircase and saw her standing frozen, staring at...

At...

Teryn's mind went blank.

Hadn't she been staring at something? Something she'd held in her hand? The more he tried to remember, the hazier his thoughts became. That in itself was worrisome, not to mention the fate of Cora's lady's maid, Lurel. His muscles tightened, begging him to turn around. Begging him to take up post next to her useless guards and ensure she was safe every moment she spent in there.

But he couldn't.

He wouldn't.

He'd trust her. Believe in her.

Because he knew there were few others who did right now.

He released his worries in a heavy sigh and made his way through the castle halls...only to realize he hadn't a clue where he was going. This was only his second time at Ridine, and the first had been so fraught with tension that he'd hardly paid heed to the castle's layout. This time, his arrival had been overshadowed by his single-minded focus to find Cora. Master Arther had greeted him, given him a room, and set an appointment for him to be received by King Dimetreus that evening, but he'd evaded every question Teryn had asked about Cora's whereabouts. Which had left Teryn to investigate on his own. Thankfully, other members of the castle staff had been far more amenable to his inquiries, especially when they realized who he was. It seemed *some* respected royal title over the influence of two self-righteous lords who'd been given more power than they deserved.

Was Teryn bitter at seeing Cora's castle swarming with Ulrich's and Kevan's guards and staff? Yes. Yes, he was. And was he perhaps growing just a little too protective over her? Also yes, but that simply couldn't be helped, not after they'd shared that heated, incredible, mind-blowing kiss—

He rounded the next corner and almost collided with a figure coming his way. A feminine yelp had him leaping back a step, but it was followed by a familiar aggrieved tone.

"Ugh. You." Mareleau's lip curled at the sight of him.

Teryn returned her sentiment with a flat look. "Ugh. Likewise." He offered a shallow bow and stepped aside for her to pass. She started to sweep by but faced him with a roll of her eyes.

"I suppose you found her then, with no trouble from my uncles?" Her tone suggested she couldn't care less, but if that were the case, she could have said nothing at all.

"I did." He'd meant to keep his expression stony, but admitting he'd found Cora filled his mind with the memory of her lips.

Mareleau's eyes went wide. "Seven devils, I know that look."

His cheeks flushed. "What look?"

Her expression softened the slightest bit. "Larylis gets the same one sometimes."

"And?"

She popped a hip to the side with a huff, as if their continued conversation were becoming more and more offensive to her by the second. Finally, she deigned to answer him, her face impassive while her voice held a note of genuine curiosity. "You like her, don't you? The princess."

He gave her a pointed look. "Did you think I was going through all this trouble to see her because I barely tolerated her?"

She shrugged. "I assumed you were tasked with formalizing a betrothal to her now that Larylis was no longer an option. But just because you were assigned as her groom didn't mean you had to like it."

He gave her a humorless grin. "We'd both know a thing or two about that situation, wouldn't we? Regardless of politics, I do like her. She's part of the reason I was so set against marrying you. That and your revolting personality, of course."

She scoffed, but she seemed to take his insult in stride. "I'd be offended were I not so completely and utterly grateful for your dislike of me. I suppose we're even then? You have your beloved and I have mine."

He gave an exaggerated wince. "Not quite. You see, you and Larylis are already married, while Cora and I must wait a year. So how about we call it even on my wedding night? In the meantime, you can work off your debt to me by directing me toward the keep."

She crossed her arms. "I'm your queen, not your servant. Besides, I'm going to the kitchen."

The kitchen. That was on his list of places to visit too. He'd asked Cora to dine with him, but he hoped he could arrange something a little better than a public meal in the dining hall. Something to make up for everything Cora had missed when she'd refused to meet him in the garden at Verlot. He may not have access to a harpist or an elegant candlelit alcove, but he could do something to show her the efforts she hadn't gotten to see.

"You know where the kitchen is?" he asked.

"No, of course I don't. But I'm determined to find it, if only to prove to my maids just how incompetent they are. They've assured me there's no chocolate in this castle. Can you imagine? There has to be chocolate. At least chocolate cake."

Teryn resisted the urge to bark a laugh. Of course the pampered Mareleau wouldn't realize just what a luxury chocolate was in some places. However, he recalled seeing a chocolatier's shop in one of the cities he'd traveled through on his way here. He'd stopped before the window and considered going inside to buy a peace offering for Cora. Before he could act on it, he'd talked himself out of the idea, reminding himself that Cora might send him packing before he even got the chance to offer gifts.

Oh, how wrong he'd been...

He shook his head before memories of a kiss beneath a tree—of Cora's body against that tree—could render him brainless.

"How about this," he said. "I'll place an order for chocolate if you do me a favor tonight."

She threw back her head with a groan. "For the love of the seven gods, not again."

"It's a small favor," Teryn rushed to say. "I need to talk to the royal chef. If all goes well, I'll simply need your help procuring a spare table and maybe some candles. Perhaps a nice cloth. And, if you're feeling generous, you can locate somewhere Cora and I might dine undisturbed tonight too."

"Oh, that's all," she muttered with sarcasm. "Why do you call her Cora, anyway? And why can't you do any of this yourself?"

He ignored the first question, but it served as a reminder to call Cora by her royal name in front of others. To address her second question, he said, "I still have an audience with King Dimetreus to attend once he returns from his hunt, and I'm not entirely convinced your uncles won't thwart my efforts to enjoy myself while I'm here. They are your father's brothers, after all."

She nodded as if to admit *fair enough*.

"If you do it," he said, "you can tell your uncles it's for the sake of teaching the princess proper dinner etiquette. They'll believe that."

She narrowed her eyes and tapped her foot rapidly against the flagstones. Finally, she blew out a long breath and said, "You're lucky I'm bored."

"And you're lucky I know of a place that sells cream-filled truffles. Now, sister, if you don't mind, let us make haste to the kitchen where our mutual schemes might be realized."

She burned him with a scowl but it lacked venom. "Very well...brother."

26

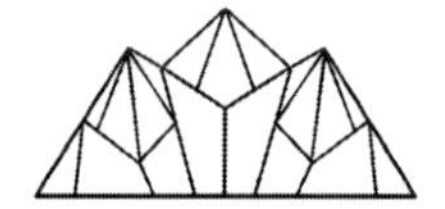

Cora's lips continued to tingle even hours later, forcing her to recall the feel of Teryn's mouth against hers again and again. It was a pleasant reminder, yet a dangerous distraction considering where she was and what she was doing. She bit her bottom lip, letting the pressure override the far gentler memories, and focused on what was before her—a hearth filled with flame, consuming pages of a very dangerous book.

She hated burning books on principle alone. The thought of permanently destroying knowledge, eradicating words that had been carefully recorded on paper for a distinct purpose, weighed her stomach down with guilt. She knew to cherish knowledge. Stories. Traditions. For six years, Cora had been raised by Salinda, the Forest People's Keeper of Histories. Passing knowledge of the Arts down from one generation to the next had been Salinda's job as one of the commune's Faeryn elders.

But Cora knew even Salinda would approve of her burning this knowledge now. Knew she'd insist upon it.

Cora shuddered with revulsion, recalling the unsettling images she'd found within the book's pages.

A wolf and a stag, facing off in the forest. One with bared teeth and raised hackles, the other with a lowered head of deadly antlers.

On the next page, the two creatures colliding in a battle of teeth and claws, hooves and tines.

On the following page, the animals collapsing in a heap of blood and torn flesh, eyes devoid of life.

Then, concluding the chapter, a single creature with paws and hooves, a sweeping tail, and a head crowned with antlers emerging from the two bodies...

She hadn't seen the word Roizan anywhere on the page, but she knew that was what it was. That was how Morkai had created his creature, his vessel for dark magic.

Part of her had been tempted to keep the book for informational purposes, if only to learn more about Morkai, his magic, how he'd constructed his spells—

And that idea had made her slam the book entitled *Mastering the Ethera* shut.

Her desire to keep the book hadn't been sinister in any way. There was logic to learning more about an enemy, even a dead one, especially when his dark magic lingered beyond his death. But the fact that she'd almost felt justified in keeping a book on the forbidden Arts had terrified her.

So now it burned. Just like the dozen she'd burned before it and the hundreds still left to toss into the flames. It was a slow process. She couldn't simply pick up a volume from one of the many shelves lining the circular room and chuck it in the fire. Instead, she had to extend her senses, *feel* for any threat radiating from the spine or cover. Then, handling it with care, she'd have to flip open the cover with the edge of her paring knife, investigate the pages, seek any sign that they were laced with poison or woven with enchantments that needed to be broken with salt or water before succumbing to fire and air.

She glanced around the room at the leagues upon leagues of books, bottles of poisons, and stacks of paper cluttered everywhere. Her shoulders sank with how heavy this task was. How lengthy. How vital. She'd only been working in the tower for a few hours today, and already she was exhausted. Her stamina nearly spent.

But she was the only one who could do this.

It would take time, but she *would* do this.

She watched the book turn to cinders and added more of the purifying herbs to the fire. Then, returning to where she'd found *Mastering the Ethera*, she assessed the shelf. One more book to burn and it would be empty. One more and she'd have cleared an entire shelf.

A glance out the window showed the sun was close to setting. Not only was she determined never to work in the tower after dark, but she had something very important to do tonight. Dinner with Teryn. The thought tugged her lips and reawakened her awareness of how they tingled. If she wanted time to bathe and dress and look something like a princess meeting her betrothed for a romantic meal, she needed to leave the tower soon.

But the near-empty shelf taunted her.

I suppose I can do one more.

She lifted her palms. They tingled at once, but she resisted stepping closer to the shelf until she reconnected with the elements: the stone beneath her feet for grounding and safety, the air in her lungs for intellect, the heat of the hearth for her strength of will, and the water on her tongue that connected her to her emotions, to the very root of her clairsentient magic.

Only then did she step closer to the book.

Her palms immediately pulsed with warning, tingling along every line of her *insigmora*. She breathed out deeply and brought her palm closer to the book, careful not to touch it with her flesh, only the extension of her Art. The spine felt neutral, as did the cover. Lowering her hand inch by inch, she carefully grasped the spine and angled the book to the side. The edges of the paper nearly shouted at her magic, and as she turned it farther around, she saw they were discolored. It wasn't from age, either. It was poison.

She cursed under her breath, knowing she couldn't burn poison. Without knowing exactly what herbs or botanicals Morkai had used, she couldn't guarantee they wouldn't carry on the smoke and kill everyone who dared inhale it. Instead, she gathered up a piece of cloth and carefully wrapped the book. She brought it to the table at the center of the room, setting it next to another book. The one that had killed Lurel.

The table had become her place for collecting items that would require extra care before being rendered harmless. That included most of the vials of poisons and bottled herbs Cora had found around the room. She didn't dare pour them in any soil or stream, for the same reasons she couldn't burn the poison-laced book; they could pose too great a harm. Those items she could only lock in a chest filled with salt and bury deep underground.

She glanced at the book that had killed Lurel and had the strangest sensation there was something missing from beside it. Hadn't there been another item...something she'd tried to clear this morning...

Her mind went blank.

Perhaps it was the book itself that made her uneasy, gave her the niggling thought that she was forgetting something.

She shifted her focus, narrowing her eyes on its leather cover. She'd already determined the book was too dangerous to destroy without knowing the extent of her stamina, but now she wondered if that hadn't been another justification. A temptation to keep it in the off chance that something within its pages could eventually serve Cora in some way.

The thought alone brought several *what ifs*...

What if it contains a spell to undo some other enchantment?

What if it holds information about the fae?

What if it mentions unicorns and where they came from?

What if...

Cora shook the notions from her head. While this book was clearly one of Morkai's most personal items, there was nothing that could justify keeping it for any extended period of time. Perhaps she should just throw it in the fire now.

Her stomach sank in warning.

No, she couldn't be reckless. Like everything else in this room, the book needed to be handled with care. Caution. Her Art.

With a deep breath, she assessed her connection to the elements and found it strong. Then, swallowing hard, she slid the book closer. From her apron pocket, she withdrew her knife and used it to carefully flip open the front cover.

It opened to the page she'd seen before, the one bearing the blood weaving that had sealed Lurel's fate. The rust-red color hadn't faded, nor had the design. Still, it was just paper and blood. It could be burned. As for the rest of the pages...

Her palms pulsed with heat, reminding her of why she'd chosen not to clear the book just yet. It wasn't like the other books she'd discarded already. While those contained instructions in the forbidden Arts, this one held more than that. It was laced with darkness. Personal intent. She should slam it shut. She knew she should.

But something inside it called to her. Not in a tempting way. Not like a siren's song. It was more like...a part of her. A missing piece of a puzzle she could recognize by size and shape alone. *This* was the feeling that called to her, coalescing somewhere in the middle of the book. It thrummed with an energy that matched the cadence of her pulse, vibrating alongside the darkness that compressed all around it.

Cora's throat tightened, fear strangling her chest.

But she had to know.

She had to.

Using the edge of her blade again, she tucked it between the pages, right at the center of the gathering energy. She lifted the pages and the worn spine complied, splaying open to reveal a spread of two inked pages. Unlike the page that had killed Lurel, the ink on these was not red like blood but black. Yet their design was of a similar nature, marking both pages in a complex pattern of crisscrossing lines. They may not have been actual blood weavings, but Cora felt with certainty that these were designs for ones. Blueprints. Curses invented to be forged with real blood later.

And at the top of each page was a name.

On the left, *Linette Rose Caelan*. Cora's dead sister-in-law and Dimetreus' dearly departed wife.

On the right, *Aveline Corasande Caelan*.

Cora's name.

Cora's fate.

Cora's death.

27

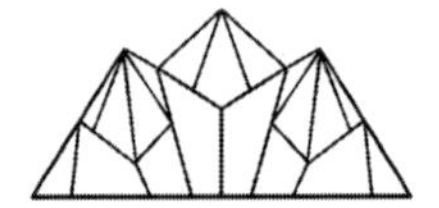

Cora hadn't forgotten about Morkai's blood weaving that had bound her fate with Linette's. But knowing about the curse was one thing. Seeing the origins of its inception was another. It made her stomach bottom out, made every hair on her arms stand on end.

When Morkai had confessed to her about the fate weaving—told her about it in this very room, no less—she'd felt violated. Shocked. Ashamed. He'd taken a twelve-year-old Cora's mistake and twisted it for his own sinister use. After Cora had publicly declared before the court that Queen Linette had been lying about being with child, he'd used that knowledge to forge a devious plan, killing the queen and gathering her blood. Then he took Cora's blood too, cutting her palm and weaving a horrible tapestry with it before her eyes. She'd fled the castle right after, unwitting as to why he'd cut her or what purpose that strange blood weaving had served.

But she knew now.

Morkai had bound her fate to Linette's so that she, like

her sister-in-law, would die childless.

All because of a prophecy he'd been determined to thwart.

Morkai's voice echoed through her mind, recalling the words he'd said the night he'd confessed the truth.

The unicorns. The mother. The child. Who do you think you are in that prophecy?

Then after that...

You are the mother and your child would have been my enemy.

Weaving your fate was the only thing I could do to let you keep your life.

She hadn't forgotten. No, she'd carried the burden of the curse, hating what he'd done if only because it robbed her of choice. And yet, she had grown complacent, hadn't she? Upon Morkai's death, she'd seen proof that his glamours had been severed. She'd assumed every bit of magic he'd cast had died along with him.

But that wasn't true. She knew that now. The evidence was all around her, mocking her from the shadows of Lurel's demise. Only the glamours, spells, and enchantments that had relied upon a continuous stream of magic from the Roizan had been broken when the creature died. When Morkai died. But everything else remained. Every curse he'd placed—using just a single instance of dark magic—stayed unbroken.

Which meant her fate was sealed. She'd die childless.

Her stomach plummeted further, taking her heart with it, but not for the reasons she expected. Having children might be a blessing she'd someday desire, but it had never been at the front of her mind. She was nowhere near ready for maternal responsibilities.

But that curse—that fate—was tangled up in something

else now. Something far more pressing. Present. Cherished.

More of Morkai's words rang through her mind.

You could never be Teryn's queen. Do you know what the prince's father did to his *queen? He tried to have her replaced with his mistress. Teryn would only do the same to you.*

She wanted to believe Morkai had been wrong. Her heart told her he had been. Teryn wouldn't cast her aside for being unable to bear him children.

No, he wouldn't, he'd…never…

He betrayed you before, came her own voice from deep inside her. It was stoic and steady, the part of her that remained within the walls she'd erected around her heart. *He said he desired you. He never said love.*

And even love could be broken. Even love could twist hearts. She'd seen it happen.

As much as Dimetreus had loved Linette, the queen had been so afraid of disappointing him that she'd lied. Pretended to be with child to keep his attentions from wandering. Back then, Cora had been perplexed over Linette's motive. Why would anyone—a powerful queen, no less—lie about being pregnant?

Cora understood, now that she was older. She knew full well the expectations placed on royal women, even more so after her recent experiences with Verdian and his brothers. Queens were expected to bear heirs. If they failed…

Teryn would only do the same to you.

She shook her head. Teryn was no longer beholden to the pressures of the crown; he didn't need an heir. He only needed to marry Cora to fulfill the alliance, and in turn, position Cora as Dimetreus' heir. His *temporary* heir. Once he remarried…

Cora stepped back from the table, as a complex layer of truth peeled back before her. In what world could she imagine Dimetreus—her hurt, traumatized brother who still agonized over his dead wife—getting remarried? If he didn't, Cora's place as heir would be permanent. She'd be expected to ascend to queen one day. A queen forced to carry all the same burdens and pressures Linette had caved under. That Teryn's mother nearly lost her crown over.

Cora had never wanted to reclaim her role as princess permanently. She'd only wanted to help her brother get his throne back and ensure Khero was taken care of. Agreeing to a loveless marriage alliance had been a necessary evil, and she'd still considered it something she could escape once her duties had been served.

Then came Teryn's confession. It had opened her heart, made her think that being stuck in her role wouldn't be so bad. Not with him by her side.

Half her heart told her she was in no danger of losing that now. This was Teryn, after all. He wouldn't reject her for being unable to bear children, even if he wanted them. But the other half of her heart shrank back, reminding her that all royal men—even those with lesser titles like dukes and lords—were forever fixated on heirs. On sons. On their legacies.

What if she couldn't provide that?

Regardless, if the worst came to pass and Cora ascended to the throne, the curse had potential to upend her life in the future. Wars sprung easily where bloodlines were broken. Where queens failed to produce sons.

Even if Teryn decided he didn't care about having children, could she truly subject him to the chaos that might one day ensue in her kingdom?

Mother Goddess, it was too much to think about.

Her lungs tightened. The room felt too small, the walls closing in around her, smothering her. She felt...trapped.

Trapped in a curse.

Trapped as her brother's heir.

Trapped in a game of royal politics.

Trapped under fragile, breakable hopes.

"Your Highness."

The voice sent her whirling away from the table and toward the door. Her guard stood on the other side of the rosemary bundles, his face cast in shadow from the stairwell. She glanced out the nearest window and saw the sun sinking over the horizon. How long had she been lost in her thoughts? Something small and wet landed on her collarbone. Belatedly she realized it was a tear, and more were pouring down her cheeks.

She cleared her voice and addressed the guard. "What is it?"

"His Highness Prince Teryn is here to see you."

Cora's heart leaped into her throat. He was early! No, she was late. They were supposed to meet for dinner, one she most certainly couldn't attend. Not in this state. Not with her mind so consumed with blood magic and curses.

"Tell him..." Her voice dissolved into a quaver. She found herself unable to continue.

"Cora." This time it was Teryn's voice coming from the other side of the threshold. She hadn't realized he was at the top of the stairwell too. Damn her guards. She'd have to tell the sentry at the bottom of the stairs to block all visitors from ascending from now on. Just because she was inside the room didn't mean it was safe. "Is everything all right?"

Before she could say a word, he brushed aside the hanging herbs. Their eyes met, and his grew wide. He surged forward, ready to cross the line of salt—

"Stop!" she shouted, charging toward the door. "Get out, Teryn!" Her voice came out harsher than she'd intended. A look of hurt crossed his face, but he halted in place—that was what mattered. It was too dangerous for him to step inside this room. He'd already done it once and she'd be damned if he made a habit out of it. Besides, she didn't want him to see her like this. It was too late, of course. Now that she was closer to the doorway, he could fully see her through the rosemary. His gaze slid to her cheeks, and his expression of hurt shifted into one of concern.

"Cora, what's wrong?"

She opened her mouth to try and shape her current state into words, but no sound would come. Instead, she breathed in the truth on an inhale, burying it in her heart, and donned a casual demeanor on an exhale. "It's nothing," she finally managed to say.

His voice deepened into a growl. "It's clearly not nothing. Who hurt you? *What* hurt you?"

"I'm fine." A lie. The deepest of lies. She had been hurt by someone and something, but how could she express that? The thought alone made her throat tighten all over again, summoning painful memories to the surface. She'd spent most of her life keeping secrets, and for good reason. Telling the truth had rarely served her well. Evidence flashed before her mind's eye.

Queen Linette condemning Cora's clairsentience, calling her a witch and begging Dimetreus to have her exorcized by a Godspriest.

Dimetreus ignoring Cora's strange powers and telling her that her insights were untrue.

The Forest People boasting of their distrust of royals.

Cora's meeting with the Forest People elders where some denounced her for her lies. Her secrets. Her identity.

Cora gaining the acceptance of Verdian's inquisitors only after pretending she knew nothing of magic.

Dimetreus' new council feigning that magic didn't exist. Fearing her relationship to the Arts. Mistrusting her motives in the tower.

She shook the memories away, reminding herself that this new situation wasn't like the rest. This was about her and Teryn. Even so, with these wounds still darkening her past—many of which were still fresh—she found herself shrinking deeper and deeper into herself. She wanted to talk to Teryn, but she was still learning how to open up to people, especially to him. This curse was no small matter, nor were the repercussions it could have on their relationship. On her responsibility as potential future queen. She needed time to prepare for that conversation.

"Please come out here and talk to me."

She shook her head. No. No, she wasn't ready.

Another look of hurt flashed across his face. "We can sit in silence then. Let me be there for you, whatever is wrong."

"No, Teryn." His name on her lips nearly shattered her heart in two. But it was nothing compared to the pain she'd feel if he rejected her upon learning about the curse. Teryn may desire her, but what if he desired furthering his bloodline more? She tried to tell herself such a fear was silly, but it didn't *feel* silly. It felt crippling. Smothering. Before she'd be ready to tell him the truth, she'd need to prepare herself for possible heartbreak. Fortify the walls she'd so recklessly abandoned, just in case she needed to retreat behind them once more.

She was nowhere near strong enough for that right now.

"I just need one night to be alone," she said, tone softening.

Teryn's throat bobbed, expression struck with agony. "I don't want to leave you."

"I need you to. Please. Just one night." She wasn't sure a

single night would be enough to sort through her feelings, but she hoped it would be. She forced a reassuring smile to her lips. "Please."

Teryn held her gaze for several silent moments. Finally, he gave her a nod and turned away. She watched his back until he was out of sight. Fresh tears trailed down her cheeks.

~

IT KILLED TERYN TO DO AS CORA HAD BID AND LEAVE HER behind. To think only hours ago she'd requested a kiss that he'd been all too eager to deliver. Now she was asking for space.

Every step that took him farther from the tower room made him question whether he was doing the right thing. He wanted to trust her. Believe in her strength. But seeing her like that, her cheeks glistening with tears, her shoulders hunched with grief...it nearly cleaved his heart in two. He knew she was capable of combating dark energies, of using her magic to accomplish incredible feats.

But what the bloody hell had made her cry?

Rage sparked in his blood, and his fists closed around air. He wished he held his hunting spear right now. If he did, he would chase down the source of Cora's distress and destroy it.

What if I'm the source?

The question sank his gut, but he had to consider if it was true. Had he pushed her too far? Had she changed her mind about him? About *them*? If so, he couldn't force his presence upon her. The best thing he could do was let her work through it. And if she had changed her mind...

He found himself outside the door to the guest bedroom

he'd been given. With a sigh, he pressed his forehead to it.

If she's changed her mind, I have to respect that.

Telling her about his feelings had already been a risk. He'd known she could have rejected him, and he'd been prepared for that. But to lose her now, lose the small, beautiful thing that had begun to bloom between them, tore him up inside.

Feeling as if his feet were made of lead, he opened his bedroom door and dragged himself inside, stopping only when he reached one of the windows. There was no balcony, no balustrade to lean upon, so the windowsill would have to do. He opened the glass pane, relishing the fresh air pouring in, and gathered lungfuls to counteract the tightening in his chest.

His eyes were unfocused, but not enough to miss the feathered shape darting from the trees outside the castle wall. Berol landed beside Teryn on the windowsill, giving his forearm an affectionate nibble. He reached into his pocket in search of the dried meat he always kept on hand for his falcon, only to realize he wasn't wearing his traveling vest but an elegant frock coat.

He'd changed his clothing before his audience with King Dimetreus, during which the king had granted him permission to dine privately with Cora instead of attending the meal in the dining hall. After that, he'd changed again, outfitting himself in the finest ensemble he'd brought. He didn't have the heart to join the main feast now, to sit amongst the king and his council, trying to pretend there wasn't somewhere else he'd rather be.

He was about to fetch his leather vest from where it was draped at the foot of his bed, when his hand brushed over a lump in his waistcoat. Had he tucked some treats in there after all and simply forgotten? He reached inside the pocket to extract what he expected to be a strip of meat...but came away with an amber crystal.

He blinked at it a few times, confusion blanketing his mind. Why did he have this? Was this...no. It couldn't be.

Yet the color, shape, and size were hauntingly familiar. There was no denying what this was. The last time he'd seen it, it had been attached to the dagger that had opened his father's throat.

Wait, that wasn't true.

The last time he'd seen it had been...

A memory snapped into place, of him changing his clothing and finding the crystal in his trouser pocket. The same confusion had struck him then. He hadn't understood why he had it or where he'd gotten it until—like now—his memories returned.

Now he remembered it all.

He recalled Cora standing frozen in the tower room, her fingers clutched around the crystal. She hadn't moved, hadn't responded to the sound of her name or the feel of his touch. Not until he'd wrenched the crystal from her hand and shook her by the shoulders once more. He must have tucked it in his pocket to free his hands then. And when he'd found the crystal while he'd been getting changed, he'd moved it to his waistcoat pocket with the intention of returning it to the tower.

But...he'd forgotten. Twice now.

The thought chilled his bones.

With a screech, Berol nipped at his fingers, then raked a talon over the back of his hand. He winced and dropped the crystal to the ground. It rolled toward the bed, and he watched it settle at the corner of the rug. Berol screeched from the windowsill again, wings splayed.

"Hush, Berol," he said to her, tone soothing. His eyes

remained locked on the crystal. He still couldn't fathom how he'd forgotten about it. Sure, he had his reasons for being distracted, but forgetting that he'd tucked a strange object into his pocket? It had to be enchanted. Possibly triggered by touch.

He frowned, stepping closer to it. Berol screeched once more, but he held out a hand to quiet her. "I know, Berol. It's dangerous. I won't touch it. I just need to tuck it somewhere safe until I can tell Cora about it."

Saying Cora's name wrenched his heart, but he was too preoccupied with the mysterious crystal to linger over his pain. Instead, he kept his attention on the stone, afraid to blink lest it somehow flee his memory like it did before. Inch by inch, he crept toward the crystal as if he were stalking prey on a hunt. He untied his white silk cravat from around his neck and stooped over the stone. Careful not to let his skin touch the object, he lifted it with the cloth.

He faced the window, ready to fold his cravat fully around the crystal, when shards of light exploded around him. The light from the setting sun had caught upon one of the facets. The glittering effect was...beautiful. He'd never seen that happen when the duke had carried it atop his cane.

His fear and trepidation fled his mind. What had he been so worried about a moment before? Entranced by the dance of amber light, he lifted the crystal higher, let the waning sunlight catch more of its facets...

Berol let out a sharp cry, startling him as she launched off the sill and into the room.

"Right," he said, closing his fist around the crystal and smothering it in the folds of his cravat. But when he looked back at his surroundings, all he saw was blinding white light.

28

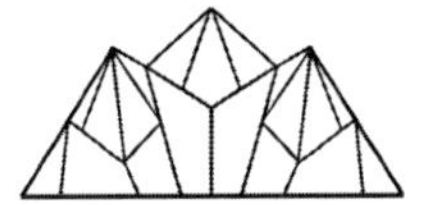

Mareleau had never arranged a bouquet with her own hands, and as she assessed the sparse collection of greenery and wild poppies she'd picked from the castle lawn, she realized there was a very good reason for that. If she'd seen such a sad spectacle gracing the vases at Verlot Palace, she'd have insisted upon whoever had made it be fired at once. But this wasn't Verlot. Nor was it the slightly more modest Dermaine. This was Ridine Castle, and the tiny bundle of drooping flowers was the brightest thing about it.

The bouquet sat in a cracked porcelain vase upon a small table. The table itself was nestled in a narrow courtyard surrounded by overgrown shrubs outside the kitchen. An array of half-melted candles lit the table's surface, illuminating two sets of empty dishes. Soon the dishes would be ladled with food, and Mareleau's mission on behalf of her brother-in-law would be complete. With the last vestiges of the sunset painting the sky from pink to indigo, the end result was rather charming, if she did say so herself.

Mareleau jumped at the loud clatter that carried

through the open kitchen windows. All right, so the noise was less than charming, but the location was the best she could find. Inside the kitchen, dozens of cooks and servants bustled about in preparation for the king's dinner. One she'd be expected to attend, same as she had every night she'd been here.

A pang of envy struck her as she glanced at the quaint dining area she'd arranged. While it wasn't the most elegant of spaces, she regretted that she wouldn't get to enjoy the fruits of her labor. Her gaze landed on the bottle of wine sitting beside two glasses. That was perhaps the most tempting part of the whole setup. Seven gods, she missed wine. She was so desperate for a sip, it made her sick to her stomach. Literally. Or...maybe the sudden nausea was more due to hunger. Regardless, she knew she couldn't imbibe, for her ladies were watching, and they'd report back to her mother and father. Until her ruse was up, she needed to act like the epitome of the careful, pregnant queen. That way, when she confessed to the surprising return of her moon cycle, she'd be blameless. Her father would have to carry that guilt, for she was fully prepared to lament over the castle's agonizingly chilly drafts and the musty air quality.

"It's lovely, Your Majesty," Breah said, coming up beside her.

Ann nodded in agreement. "You have a knack for creating elegance, Majesty."

The girls were pandering to her, but Mareleau didn't care. Despite her shoddy attempts at setting up a romantic meal, she couldn't ignore the pride flaring in her chest. She'd never done anything like this before. Perhaps she could do it for Larylis when she returned home to him.

The thought warmed her heart, and a soft smile curled her lips. Before her longing could dip into sorrow, she adopted a flippant tone and said, "It beats picking out hideous linens with Master Arther. Come. Let us prepare for dinner."

Sera released a groan. "I suppose I should fetch my lady from her horrible tower."

Mareleau cut a glare at the girl. She was so used to Sera's presence, she kept forgetting the girl was supposed to be serving the princess. "Sera, you should have readied her for dinner an hour ago."

Sera shifted from foot to foot. "I...I figured you were more in need of assistance than she, Majesty."

"Yes, well, *she* is supposed to attend a romantic meal with my brother. You can't have her looking like a pauper, for it will surely be the ruination of my efforts. Go get her cleaned up at once."

Sera's shoulders slumped, but she sank into an obedient curtsy before shuffling out of the courtyard and into the kitchen. Mareleau and her ladies followed just behind, turning toward the keep as they exited into the hall. She halted in place, glancing in the opposite direction to where Sera was heading for the North Tower Library stairwell. A strange feeling fluttered in her chest, and it wasn't entirely pleasant. She wasn't sure what to call it, but it might have been something akin to sympathy.

"The two of you go with her," she said to Ann and Breah before she could stop herself.

Her maids stared back at her as if she'd lost her mind. And maybe she had.

Breah's tone turned simpering. "Why, Majesty?"

"Sera will need your help to ready the princess with haste," Mareleau said.

"Don't *you* need our help?" Ann asked. "Surely you want to change into a new gown for dinner."

"Why? Is there something wrong with how I look now?" She knew it was only habit that drove her maids to expect a change of clothes, but she needed them to stop their whining. "I can manage looking appropriate for dinner just fine. The princess, on the other hand, needs all the help she can get. I won't have her making a mockery of all the hard work I did tonight. Now go. Follow after Sera and make certain the princess is presentable in the next half hour. Understand?"

The girls bobbed into curtsies before making their grudging departure. Meanwhile, Mareleau ascended the stairs to the keep. She had every intention of heading straight for her room, but when she passed the door she knew belonged to Teryn's guest quarters, she paused.

Again, that irritating feeling fluttered in her chest. It was less about sympathy this time and more about...was it care? Pride? All she knew was that she wanted to brag to Teryn that tonight's dinner was going to be fabulous, thanks to her. With her chin held high, she marched to his door and rapped on it with her gloved hand. The lamps illuminating the hall revealed several smudges of dirt on the white silk. She certainly wasn't used to seeing that.

The door opened in a rush, tearing her from her thoughts. Teryn's form stood on the other side of the doorway, but she could hardly separate him from the shadows. She frowned, wondering why he was in a dark room.

Some of her excitement waned, and she took a step back, folding her arms over her chest. "You better not tell me you've been napping while I've been doing all the hard work for you, brother."

"Brother," he echoed, a hint of taunting in his tone.

She frowned. That hadn't been the first time she'd used that word to his face, and he was the one who'd started it, calling her *sister*. Why did he sound so amused?

He stepped out of the doorway and into the light of the hall.

Mareleau's eyes went wide as she noted the gash on his cheek, then the way he cradled his hand. A white cloth—his missing cravat, perhaps—was wrapped around it like a bandage.

"Teryn, what the seven devils happened to you?"

He glanced down at his hand and huffed a chuckle. "Ah, that. I broke a glass."

It must have been quite the violent break for it to have sliced his cheek. And...was there a portion of his shirt missing? His ruffled collar appeared to have been torn. Maybe that was what he'd used to tie his hand. Whatever the case, he looked quite the mess.

She waved at him, motioning him back toward his room. "Clean yourself up at once. You can't meet Princess Aveline looking like this."

He narrowed his eyes, as if trying to decipher the meaning of her words. Then, with a shake of his head, he said, "For dinner tonight. The one I asked you to help me with."

There was something strange about the way he spoke, uttering each word slowly as if he wasn't quite sure what he was saying. "Are you still asleep? Go! Get changed. Princess Aveline will be coming by at any moment to do the same. I didn't offer my maids to her for nothing, and I'll be damned if the both of you embarrass me."

"Who are we embarrassing you before?"

Mareleau pulled her head back with a scoff. "Me, of course. For two people so madly in love, neither of you seem to know how to impress the other. Perhaps I'll have to play the mentor to you both."

He narrowed his eyes again. "Because you're at Ridine Castle to mentor Princess Aveline."

Once more with that careful way of talking. It almost seemed like he was asking a question rather than stating a fact. What was wrong with him?

"You know this," she said. "Now go before I lose my mind and promise never to help you again."

Teryn watched her with a probing look that was almost unsettling. Then he crossed his arms and leaned against the doorframe. "I regret that your aid will come to naught. The princess will not be joining me for dinner tonight."

"No, she's simply running behind. My ladies will return with her soon and have her dressed and ready in no time."

"You don't understand," Teryn said with a sigh. "I've already been to see her tonight and she refused to come to dinner with me."

"But...but my ladies—"

"She will refuse them. Trust me."

Disappointment sank her stomach. Then anger took its place. "Don't you dare tell me you're going to waste the wine I picked out for you. And the cake!" She clenched her jaw with a growl. It wasn't chocolate cake, but it was lemon chiffon. Mareleau had nearly burst into an inferno of rage when the baker told Teryn she'd make a small cake just for him and Aveline. Where was Mareleau's cake?

A corner of Teryn's mouth lifted into a smirk she'd never seen grace his face before. "Wine and cake, you say? Well, we certainly can't let that go to waste."

She huffed. "You seem awfully buoyant for a man whose dinner offer was rejected by his beloved. I would have expected you to be more upset." Or maybe she just didn't know Teryn well at all. She was finally beginning to warm up to him, but the way he was acting now...it didn't seem quite right.

"What is there to be upset about? She's simply busy. I respect her. There's no need to cling to someone you trust."

Mareleau felt abashed at that. She may not know her brother-in-law well, but she knew even less about separating love from obsession. She'd clung to her chance at love so hard, she'd lied for it. Betrayed the trust of the person she'd been fighting for. She waited for the guilt to come, but most of it had already faded when Larylis forgave her.

Larylis. Gods how she missed him.

She pushed the thought away. "You must really like her."

Teryn's expression shifted, his smile tightening with his jaw, eyes suddenly devoid of mirth. "An understatement."

"Then why don't you march over to that tower—"

"No." The word came out cold, edged with finality. It hung between them, chilling the air. Then his smile returned, and it was no longer angled into a smirk. "Why don't you join me for the meal you worked so hard to prepare, sister?"

"Me," Mareleau said with a grimace. "Dine with you?"

"You seemed quite passionate over the wine and cake. If anyone deserves to enjoy it, it's you, am I wrong?"

He had a point. She had worked hard, and if Aveline was going to force all that effort to go to waste, then the least she could do was enjoy it. "But...but my presence will be missed at dinner in the hall."

"Will it, though?"

Another good point. She doubted anyone would even note her absence. Besides, she was only going for cake. She could always join the feast after.

Her stomach churned, rippling with the same nausea she'd felt earlier when she'd lusted over the wine. Seven gods, she was ravenous. She supposed it made sense after all her hard work.

That left her only one answer she could give. "Fine."

By the time they reached the little courtyard, the plates had already been filled with food, and a small round cake rested upon a tray at the center of the table. Noise still carried from the kitchen, but with most of the staff busy in the dining hall, it was somewhat less chaotic. Still, Teryn didn't hesitate to close the shutters over the kitchen window and seal the door leading to the courtyard. It cut off even more of the noise, leaving them some semblance of peace.

Teryn lowered himself into one of the seats, his posture casual as he sank into the chair. He seemed...tired. Fatigued. As if he'd been the one slaving away over table decorations the last couple of hours.

Mareleau resisted the urge to sneer at his lax composure and dragged her chair far from his. When they were on opposite ends of the table, she took her seat. She leaned toward the glorious display of lemon chiffon, only to pause with her hand an inch away from the serving knife. Teryn had insisted that his dinner with the princess be unattended by servants, and while she'd found the notion crass then, it was even more so now. She'd never had to slice her own cake before...

Teryn released a soft chuckle and took the knife from under her hand. Then, with deft movements, he sliced the cake with two flicks of the blade and placed the piece on her plate.

"Thank you," she mumbled, taking up her fork. She was about to take a dainty bite as befitting a queen, when she decided—*to hell with it*—since no one of import was watching, she might as well shove the largest forkful she could fit. One with equal parts frosting and cake.

She closed her eyes as the sweet lemon flavor melted over her tongue. It made her want to dance in her seat. Were she a younger girl, she would have. She was far too reserved for that now.

The sound of pouring liquid made her open her eyes. Teryn filled his glass with wine, then did the same for hers. Her stomach rumbled at the sight of the ruby liquid before her. It took all her strength of will to force her eyes away so she could burn Teryn with a glare. "I can't have that."

He arched a brow. "Why not?"

"You damn well know why not."

He shrugged, taking a long pull from his glass. "Gods, it's been too long since I've tasted wine. Why can't you have any?"

She glanced around, but she already knew they weren't being watched. "The baby," she whispered.

"Ah. Right. You're pregnant with my brother's child."

"Why do you keep acting like that?"

"Like what?"

"Like...like you've forgotten things."

He leaned farther back in his chair and tipped his face toward the sky. "It's been a long day. A day that has felt more like months. So forgive me if I'm beyond caring whether you imbibe."

She studied him, studied his too-relaxed posture, his loose limbs. Maybe courting Aveline had done a number on his brain. Or was it more that...

Her pulse racketed as realization dawned.

"Did Larylis tell you? Is that why you're being so lax about this?"

"Tell me what?"

"About...my lie."

He swirled his glass and watched her over the rim of his cup. "He tells me many things. He's my brother."

She felt suddenly small. Abashed. While she couldn't blame Larylis for wanting to relieve some of the guilt he carried, she hated that he hadn't warned her in advance that he'd be telling Teryn the truth. "So you know I'm not truly with child."

An amused grin lifted his lips. "I do now. What an entertaining twist."

Heat seared her blood and crawled up her cheeks. "Did you just...trick me into confessing—"

"Seven devils, Majesty," he said with a roll of his eyes. "Drink. Enjoy yourself. Or don't. I care not about whatever lies you've had to tell to get what you want."

She was flustered beyond belief, unsure whether Teryn had been teasing her or if he still was. Either way, it didn't seem like he was at all concerned about reporting her actions to her parents.

"Fine," she said, snatching the glass from the table and bringing it to her lips. She swallowed half the glass in a single gulp, then drained the rest between bites of cake. While she knew she should savor the wine's taste—it was a lovely vintage, after all—she couldn't help but fear it would be taken away at any moment. If one servant exited the door, if one of her lady's maids came looking for her, she'd have to return to her ruse.

Just a few more days, she reminded herself. Her cycle was due soon. Or was it overdue? It didn't matter. As soon as she could release herself from her lie, she could have all the wine she wanted. Then maybe, just *maybe*, her remaining days at Ridine would be somewhat tolerable.

"Your Majesty," Teryn said, refilling both their empty glasses, "I think we should get to know each other better."

"I suppose," she muttered, mouth full of cake. She gathered another forkful, noting her movements were growing sloppy. Damn. She should have known better than to drink so fast. Especially with how long it had been since her last drink. Even so, she'd enjoy the wine while she could, no matter how drunk it got her. Rebelling against her own good sense, she drained the rest of her glass and poured more. She chased that with the rest of her cake. With her nerves so unwound, she leaned back in her chair and released a satisfied moan, luxuriating in the sugary fullness of her belly, the burn of the wine, the lightness in her head.

"Tell me, sister. What is your deepest secret? Aside from the one I already know about, of course." He said the last part with a wink.

"My deepest secret...is that I have no secrets." She snorted a rather unladylike laugh at her lie.

"Then what is your greatest desire?"

That she could confess. "That I was back home at Dermaine with my husband."

Teryn's expression fell with pity. "You've been treated unfairly, Majesty. You deserve better."

"You don't need to tell me that." She lifted her chin, and a wave of dizziness had her swaying in her seat. "I already know."

"It must be so hard for you to be here alone. Without friends. Without family. All the while watching Princess Aveline get everything she wants. Her home, her lover. And what do you get?"

His words rang true, yet they sounded wrong coming from his lips. Why was he saying these things about the woman he adored? A shudder ran down her spine, and the warmth from the wine, the tingling in her mind and stomach, no longer felt so pleasant.

She stood on unsteady feet but forced herself to seem composed. “I’ve had enough cake,” she said, voice slurred. “I’m going to bed now.”

“No, you should enjoy yourself more. Besides, do you really want people to see you swaying through the halls? Courtiers talk, you know.”

She glared at him, but a swirl of nausea had her dropping back into her seat.

Teryn brushed past her, pausing at the door that led to the kitchen. “If ever there is something you want, do tell me. You’ll find I make a formidable ally and a terrifying enemy.”

She forced herself to turn around in her chair. “Is that some kind of a threat?”

“An offer, Majesty. We’re on the same side.”

“What side is that?”

“The one where we get everything we want.” He winked at her and left, closing the door behind him. As soon as it was shut, she lurched to the side and heaved her precious cake onto the courtyard stones.

29

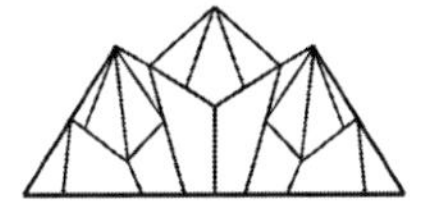

Teryn woke with a sudden start, though he didn't feel as if he'd been asleep. He felt more like he'd been...lost. Floating. Clinging to the fraying edges of his consciousness. Now wakefulness dawned on him in a violent rush. He sat up—at least he thought he did—but all he saw was blinding white light. Not even his body stood out against it. He glanced down at his hands, his legs, but there was nothing to see.

Panic raced through him, sending him teetering back toward the opposite edge of consciousness.

"Calm, Your Highness." A feminine voice reached his ears. It was a hollow sound, devoid of resonance, but the fact that there was someone near him, calming him, gave it a soothing quality.

"Where am I?" His voice held the same lack of resonance, but there was nothing soothing about it. The words left his lips, but instead of reverberating from his vocal cords, they simply took shape in the nothingness around him. That only renewed his sense of panic.

"It's all right, Prince Teryn."

"Who are you? Why can't I see anything?"

"My name is Emylia. I'm here to help you."

"Help me with what? Where the seven devils am I?"

As if in answer, the light grew muted, slowly fading into shadows. Those shadows spilled over the surface of white, like ink staining a blank page. But instead of pure darkness, the shadows took form, creating distinct edges, shapes, and textures, until it became a moonlit bedroom. *His* bedroom at Ridine Castle. He saw his four-poster bed, the flagstone floor, the tapestries decorating the walls.

He released a sigh of relief...but the breath leaving his lungs didn't feel normal. It tingled against his lips without warming them and it lacked the rushing sound he was used to. He glanced down at his body, and this time he could see hands. That was a small comfort.

"Just breathe, slow and steady," the woman named Emylia said. A woman he'd still yet to see.

He glanced up from his hands and nearly leaped out of his skin at the sight of the unfamiliar woman. If he had to guess, she was around his age, perhaps a year older. Her skin was a rich brown while her curly hair was the color of the midnight sky outside his room. A beautiful woman. And one who was only half dressed. The shift she wore was of a flowing, floor-length silk in a color he couldn't distinguish in the unlit room, but the way it bared her shoulders told him it had to be a nightgown at best.

Suspicion darkened in his mind. Averting his gaze, he set his jaw and said, "Miss...Emylia, who are you and what are you doing in my room?"

It was all he could do not to order her out at once. The last thing his relationship with Cora needed was a scandal. A nagging thought pulsed through him, telling him this was the least of his worries. But…why? Something had happened after his conversation with Cora…

Something that would explain the terror lurking in the back of his mind…

"I told you. I'm here to help you."

"With what?" He allowed his gaze to return to her and saw she now wore a capelet over her shoulders in the same flowing silk as her gown. It struck him as odd that her ensemble would change so suddenly, but he was more concerned with getting her out of his room. There was no way he was letting this stranger ruin what he had with Cora. "Never mind. You shouldn't be here. Please leave at once."

When she made no move to obey, he reached forward to assist her, determined to drag her out if he must.

"Don't touch me," she barked, leaping away from his touch.

Teryn froze.

The woman made a placating gesture, and her tone turned gentle again. "It's…it's probably fine, but we can't risk it."

"I don't want to touch you," Teryn said through his teeth, trying to ignore that his teeth felt…well, there was something wrong with them. Something wrong with *him*. Everything about his body felt…too light. Too fuzzy. Was he dreaming? It felt like a dream. But not even in his dreams did he fancy having a strange woman in his private quarters when he could have been dreaming about someone else. "I just want you out of my room before someone gets the wrong idea."

Her shoulders sank, eyes turning down at the corners. "Highness, we aren't in your room."

"What do you—"

"Do you remember anything about what you were doing before?"

"Before what?"

"What's the last thing you recall? Stay calm but try to remember. It's better if you remember on your own."

Teryn was torn between fear and irritation. A nagging notion—too hazy to decipher—continued to plague him, trying to remind him...

He closed his eyes, and a vision played through his mind. First he saw himself holding the crystal in his room, saw the light catch on its facets. Then there was nothing but white. He'd heard a woman's voice. Emylia's voice, he realized now. Then dark tendrils like black smoke took shape before him, forging legs, hands, a torso. Then a face. One he recognized. The shadowed figure was colorless, revealing neither Duke Morkai's dark hair nor his silver-blue eyes. But Teryn knew it was him. Emylia had shouted not to let Morkai touch him, but the voice had been too far away, too lost in the tumult of Teryn's fear and confusion. The figure reached out, grasped Teryn. Pain had surged through him, searing his skull as if it were being cleaved in two, and then...

Then nothing.

Teryn stumbled back, swiping a hand over his face. But when his palm made contact with his skin, it lacked the pressure he was used to. Instead, it simply...buzzed. Thickened the air. He drew his hand back and examined it. It was still his hand, but the closer he looked, the more he realized its edges were slightly blurred, its shape in a constant flux of swirling particles.

His breaths grew sharp and shallow. Breaths that didn't feel like true breaths.

"You need to stay calm," Emylia said, but her words only

reminded him of the wrongness of their voices. They still lacked resonance. Still struck hollow in the space around them.

"You expect me to stay calm? What the seven devils is happening? Where am I—*really*?"

Her expression sank with pity. "You're inside the object you know as Morkai's crystal."

Teryn glanced around the room, no longer trusting his surroundings. They seemed as tenuous as his form, something real but not real. This was wrong. All of this was wrong. He could only hope this was a nightmare and that he'd wake from it at any moment. But if this wasn't a dream and Emylia was telling the truth...

He was inside Morkai's crystal.

Not his body, though. He knew enough to comprehend that whatever he was now, it wasn't a being of flesh and blood.

A question formed on his lips, one he wasn't sure he was ready to hear the answer to. "Am I dead?"

"No, Teryn," she said with a gentle smile. "You're alive."

He swallowed hard. "Then what am I?"

She clasped her hands at her waist. "The part of you that exists inside this crystal is your ethera. You might call it your spirit. What you see now is the outer layer of your ethera, the part that most resembles your physical form."

"And you? What are you?"

She gestured at her body. "This too is the outer layer of my ethera. But unlike you, I died many years ago. I don't have a body to return to."

"Does that mean I can go back? I can get out of the crystal and...return to my body?" Referring to himself as something separate from his body ignited a fresh wave of panic.

"Yes, but you need to keep your breathing steady, Highness. It's your best defense against him."

Him.

The shadowed form of Duke Morkai.

"Was that...*thing* I saw...was that the sorcerer's ethera?"

She nodded. "He tethered it to the crystal as a way to fully evade death."

"But you said you're considered dead because your body is gone. So is his. He has nothing to return to."

Emylia wrung her hands before forcing them to still. "Returning to his *former* body isn't his goal."

The way she emphasized *former* sent a chill through him. She must have been implying that Morkai intended to forge some new body. What did that have to do with Teryn? Why was his spirit stuck inside a crystal—

Truth dawned like a dagger to his heart. "He wants to use my body."

Her nod of confirmation sent his head spinning. Or whatever part of this so-called ethera that felt like his head.

"He...already has," she said. "Somewhat."

"What the seven devils is that supposed to mean? Is his spirit in my body right now?" What were these words leaving his mouth? These kinds of things weren't possible. They weren't real. Months ago, he hadn't believed in magic. Magic had been a thing that existed only in faerytales. Then he'd met Cora, caught his first glimpse of a unicorn. Magic then shifted into a beautiful truth, one that gave Cora the ability to sense emotion and even go so far as to hide them from sight. But when Morkai came along, his view of magic changed yet again, and he'd learned of its dark side. One of wraiths and blood sorcery. Somehow, Teryn was now entangled in that malevolent kind of magic.

No, this can't be happening.

His chest tightened, lungs contracting. Or were they his lungs at all? Emylia had told him to breathe, but if he was separate from his body, then…then that was impossible. His legs-that-weren't-legs gave out beneath him and he slid to the floor. But the floor wasn't solid; it was nothing but a buzzing resistance against his thighs and hips.

Emylia crouched before him. "I can't answer any more questions until you strengthen your connection to your vitale."

"My what?"

"Your vitale, your life force energy. Your ethera is connected to it. Now close your eyes and focus on your breath. Breathe slow and deep."

It was hard to focus on anything except his growing panic, but she'd said breathing was his greatest weapon against the sorcerer, right? He didn't know how or why or even half of what was happening to him, but if Emylia was telling the truth, he had to try.

Closing his eyes, he took a breath. It was shaky and shallow, but he poured all his focus into making the next one deeper, stronger. Then the next.

"Can you feel the air moving through your lungs?" came Emylia's voice.

"Yes," he said, though he didn't understand how it was possible.

"Can you feel the beating of your heart?"

He shifted his attention to the rhythmic pounding. The thud of his pulse. The melody drained some of his fear, smoothing the edges of his panic. His next breaths were even deeper.

"Good. Sink your attention into what makes you feel alive. The pulsing of your blood. The workings of your heart, lungs, and other organs. That is your vitale. It is your life force, the part of your body you still maintain control over. Do not open your eyes until you feel like you can maintain this connection without conscious thought."

Teryn sat in stillness for countless minutes until his breaths were steady, his pulse uninterrupted by spikes of anxiety. Finally, he opened his eyes and saw Emylia sitting across from him. She no longer wore her dress and capelet but billowy silk pants and a matching tunic. It was yet another strange outfit, following neither current female fashions nor ones from the recent past. If Emylia's ethera resembled who she'd been when she was living, she hadn't been from the continent of Risa. The Southern Islands perhaps?

While his calmer state of consciousness allowed some curiosity to bloom, he had far more pressing questions.

"You said my vitale is the part of my body I still maintain control over. Does that mean..." His words snagged on a thorn of fear, but he quickly refocused on his breath, on the steady rise and fall of his lungs, on the steady beat of his heart. He tried again, and this time he managed to speak past the terror that threatened to overwhelm him. "Does that mean Morkai has control over the other parts of me?"

Emylia kept her tone steady. Gentle. "Morkai has control over your cereba. That is the spiritual aspect of your mind that allows your soul to animate your physical body. It controls movement. Speech."

Ethera. Vitale. Cereba. These were all strange words he'd never heard before. Were these scientific terms? Or did they have more to do with magic?

"If we're both souls, how are we talking?"

"Our etheras are beyond the restraints of the human body. We can communicate, even without forming words with our lips. However, the instinct to move our lips when we speak is deeply ingrained with the outer layer of our etheras."

"Are you saying we could communicate with just our minds if we wanted to?"

She pursed her lips. *Yes, we can. See?* This time, he heard the words despite her lips remaining pressed tight.

A shudder tore through him. If he had a body, his hair would stand on end.

"I figured you'd prefer it if we continued speaking like this," she said, moving her lips this time.

She was right. Speaking mind-to-mind was not something he was ready for.

Changing the subject, he asked, "How did this happen? You said Morkai tethered his ethera to the crystal. The last thing I remember from inside my body was looking at the light on the stone's facets."

"Eye contact with light from the crystal gave him temporary access to your cereba. He held you in place and drew your ethera into the crystal through that link."

Teryn shuddered, wondering if that was what had happened to Cora when he'd found her in the tower room. She'd had the crystal in her hand, but...she'd probably been looking at it too. He'd only taken the precaution of not letting the stone touch his skin, but he'd let himself look. Let himself become entranced by its dazzling light. How foolish could he be?

"Don't blame yourself," Emylia said. "Morkai wove countless enchantments around the crystal over the years, ones that were meant to be triggered upon his death, should it come to pass. As a result, the crystal is easy to forget, evading one's memory when it's out of sight. It's alluring, which makes one forget danger and want to look at it. And it's unbreakable. These enchantments were too strong for even the princess to break with her efforts."

"You know about Cora, then? I think she was stuck in here too, she—" His pulse racketed, surging out of his control. "Has he gained some hold over her ethera too?"

"No, you freed her before he could touch her ethera, and he...he didn't intend to touch hers at all."

That gave him some relief. Enough to steady his breaths again. "Does that mean when his shadowed form touched mine, he took control?"

"Yes. Touching your ethera with his own strengthened the link to your cereba. That allowed him to manipulate your body. A difficult task with such a temporary connection, but it was enough to force your hand to lift the crystal and hold it over your body's sternum. That closed the circuit, creating a sustained link from Morkai's ethera, to your cereba, to his heart-center."

Teryn furrowed his brow. "Heart-center?"

"The spiritual aspect of the heart. His is stored inside the crystal. So long as the crystal is near your body, within at least sixteen inches of where your heart-center should be, the circuit remains closed, giving him primary control over your cereba."

Primary control. Over *his* body.

Nothing good could come of that.

"Where is my body now? What is he doing with it?"

Emylia held his gaze, nibbling her bottom lip as if debating whether to answer. Then, with a sigh, she waved a hand. A ripple of shadow crossed his vision. As it settled, the bedroom grew somewhat sharper, the walls and furnishings more distinct. She stood and gestured toward the bed. Teryn rose too, feeling that strange buzzing resistance between his feet and the floor. Slowly, he turned toward the bed, dreading what he was about to see. He was right to feel dread. For there, upon the bed, lay himself. Asleep. His own body separate from the soul he was now.

"Is this real?" Teryn asked. "Is this truly my bedroom? Truly my body?"

She nodded. "I can utilize some of the magic in the crystal. With it, I can forge a likeness of any place I've seen. That is what I first showed you when you awoke. I muted the light of the crystal and showed you something familiar to set you at ease. But what you see now is real. In addition to casting illusions, I can create a window of sorts that allows me to project my ethera—and yours—outside the crystal."

"So we're free from the crystal now?" Even as he asked, he knew the hope was too good to be true.

"No, our etheras are tethered. Mine even more than yours, as I have no link to a living body. We can experience the crystal's immediate surroundings, but that doesn't make us free of our captivity."

Teryn wondered if Morkai had been able to project his ethera in the same way. If so, Morkai could have been watching Cora the entire time she'd possessed the crystal. Rage burned through him at the thought.

"Where is the crystal now?" he asked, stepping closer to the bed.

She angled her head at the sleeping Teryn's chest. "It's beneath your shirt."

"And Morkai is..."

"Resting his ethera. Controlling your cereba is taxing, especially since he has no link to your vitale. He'll need to sleep, and that is when you have the highest chance of regaining control. It will be hard, though. He maintains the primary connection even during sleep. To loosen his grip, we must move the crystal more than sixteen inches from your sternum and open the circuit between your cereba and his heart-center."

Teryn studied his body, saw the lump beneath his shirt that must be the crystal. If Morkai's spirit was sleeping, now was Teryn's chance. He surged toward his sleeping form and reached for the collar of his shirt—

His ethera's hands went straight through the cloth, resulting in nothing but that buzzing resistance. That thickening of the air.

"Breathe," Emylia said, and Teryn realized his lungs had begun to contract again.

Teryn took a few steps back, deepening his breaths and watching his body's chest rise and fall in tandem. "Seven devils, this is madness."

"I know, and you had the right idea. But before you have any chance of manipulating physical matter, you need to strengthen what little connection you have to your cereba. You maintain a slim link between it and your vitale."

"What can I do?" He had to do something. Anything. Morkai was in his body. He would wake. He would...

Teryn didn't want to think about what he might do. *Whom* he might do things to.

"For now," Emylia said, "align your ethera with your body and simply breathe. Feel your heart. Your pulse."

"You want me to just...lie down and breathe."

"Do not underestimate your connection to your vitale. So long as your awareness of it remains strong, you hold the upper hand. If you let fear disconnect you from it, you leave it open for Morkai to take. He isn't strong enough to take it yet, but he has plans to do so. I know he does."

What were his plans? And how did Emylia know so much about Morkai, about utilizing the crystal's magic?

Who was she aside from a trapped spirit? Could he even trust her?

Emylia opened her mouth, but before she could speak, he said, "If you tell me to breathe one more time, I'm going to lose my godsdamned mind."

She pursed her lips and gestured toward the bed with a pointed look.

With nothing else to do, he climbed upon the mattress, sank into his sleeping form, and tried to become one with a body that was no longer his own.

30

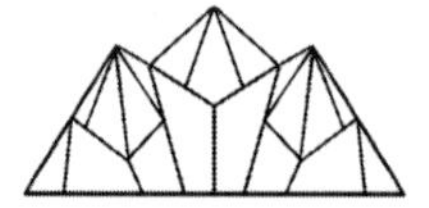

Morning dawned, but peace did not rise with the sun. Cora stayed in bed as sunlight streamed through her window, crawling up the walls and dancing over her ceiling. All the while she hoped she'd feel some of that light reflected in her heart. But she didn't. She remained burdened with the same dark revelations she'd stumbled upon last night. No matter how she wished otherwise, a curse placed by a dead man had invaded her life, throwing all her carefully laid plans into disarray.

And yet, when it came to said plans, she had to admit some of the folly lay with her. She'd been naive to think she could easily exit her role as princess. That all she had to do was ensure Dimetreus was secure on his throne. There was more to this political game than she'd anticipated. A game of heirs and royal bloodlines. Now, because of Morkai, she was unable to play the game at all. She'd lost the one piece that had made her a contender on the board.

The ability to further the Caelan bloodline.

She hated that something so small—something so intimate and personal—determined her worth as a royal woman. Hated it so much that it burned away the edges of her sorrow, replacing them with something sharper. Wilder. Fiercer.

Where last night she'd felt pain, only anger existed in her now.

It was enough to drive her out of bed, to make her throw back the bedsheets with awakening resolve. She stomped over to her vanity, splashed water on her face from the ewer, and set about getting herself dressed. Sera hadn't returned since Cora had sent her and Mareleau's other two ladies away when they'd tried to fetch her from the tower last night. Cora hadn't even deigned to deny them to their faces. Instead, she'd ordered the stairwell sentry to forbid anyone from coming upstairs. By the time she'd gathered her composure enough to leave the tower room, the three girls were long gone. Perhaps they'd been offended by her refusal to entertain their efforts, but Cora didn't have it in her to care.

She donned a linen summer dress that laced up the front, tightening each row with far more force than necessary. Each pull was infused with her rage. Her hatred.

How dare Morkai. How dare he make a lasting impact on her life in such an invasive, perverse way. How dare he have so much influence beyond the grave, great enough to shatter Cora's heart. To break what she and Teryn were beginning to forge.

Teryn.

Her hands went slack on her laces, and her shoulders dropped. The thought of him broke through her anger, blunting it with sorrow yet again.

Her eyes went unfocused as she tried to imagine what she should say to him today. How she should act. She couldn't avoid him after insisting she only needed one night alone. Yet she didn't know what to do. Didn't know how to tell him about Morkai's curse. Sure, she knew the words she needed to say, but it was one thing to *know* and another to actually confess something so deeply intimate, something that pertained to the inner workings of her body. Her heart. Her soul.

Her chest constricted, but she breathed the tightness away. Shifting her gaze to the morning light streaming through the window, she called upon the element of fire.

Light. Heat. Warmth.

Passion. Anger. Rage.

Life force. Strength. Transmutation.

The sunlight heated her insides, evoking her anger. It surged from her chest to her palms. With renewed vigor, she finished lacing her bodice and tied off the ends. Then, closing her eyes, she strengthened her connection to the other elements.

She rooted her feet to the stone floor.

Earth. Safety. Protection.

Took a fortifying breath, in then out.

Air. Thoughts. Intellect.

She acknowledged the element of water—*feeling, emotion*—but it was already too strong. She needed less water right now. Less emotion and more strength of will. Steady logic. Keen insight.

Calm settled over her. It wasn't the most peaceful calm, for she still didn't know how to express herself to Teryn. A night of agonizing over the situation hadn't given her any answers. Perhaps there weren't any. None that were easy, at least.

But she knew what she *could* do. What she *must* do.

She'd funnel her rage, her attention, and her energy into

the only suitable recourse: clearing Morkai's tower. And maybe—just maybe—if she was willing to take a risk and do something just a little reckless, she might be able to find the information she needed to break this damn curse.

TERYN HATED SITTING STILL. HE'D FORGOTTEN THIS FEELING. Forgotten the anxiety that had plagued him in the wake of his father's death. The time between Centerpointe Rock and Cora's official release from Verlot had been pure agony when he hadn't been moving. Doing. Fixing. He'd felt some relief after Cora had been given back her title, and every moment since had been filled with distraction—first helping his brother step into his role as king, then focusing all his efforts on reuniting with Cora.

Now sitting still was all he could do.

And it was torture.

He'd kept his ethera aligned with his body for hours on end. At least, he assumed hours had passed. His ethera didn't feel the passing of time the way his body had been able to. There were no hunger pangs, no bodily urges. His primary relationship to time now was his growing anxiety.

"Breathe, Teryn." Emylia's words made him want to clench his jaw, but the mild buzzing resistance his ethera generated lacked the satisfaction he was used to.

Which gave him no choice but to listen. To tune back in to the feel of his breath, the rush of his blood, the rhythmic pulse of his heart. Despite his irritation over Emylia's constant reminders, she was right. The strength of his connection to his vitale—the one bodily sensation he could consistently feel—always calmed his nerves. With his soul lying in perfect harmony with his body's shape, his spiritual heart-center aligned with his sternum, his ethera's eyes aligned with his body's eyes, his soul's feet nestled within his body's feet, he could almost pretend he was whole again.

"Good," Emylia said. "You're going to try some subtle muscular movements again."

A spike of panic flared inside him. He'd tried to control small muscular movements already and failed miserably. According to Emylia, if he had any chance at reclaiming his body, he needed to not only strengthen his connection to his vitale but also to the thin thread that linked him to his cereba. The only reason he even had that tiny link was due to his connection to his vitale. While Morkai reigned over Teryn's conscious movements, Teryn maintained a sliver that controlled his automatic functions like breathing, blinking, and swallowing. Emylia had surmised that if Teryn could intentionally create small movements related to these automatic functions, he could learn to control larger ones next.

He hadn't managed so much as a flinch the first time he'd tried, which had resulted in him flying into a panicked rage and losing his connection to his vitale entirely.

"You must start small and be patient," Emylia had said. "You will get there."

That same anxiety filled him now—of being inside his body, yet unable to move it. He tuned back in to his breath, his pulse, his blood, and felt the panic melt away.

Emylia kept her voice slow and gentle. "Now shift your attention to what's outside your body. Focus on the sensation of the blankets against your back. Feel the pillows cradling your head, brushing against your cheek."

He followed along, noting the various levels of resistance generated between each object and his ethera. It didn't feel quite the same as it should, but he tried not to dwell on that.

"Now focus on a single finger on your right hand," Emylia said. "Pour all your attention there. Feel the pressure of your fingertip against the blankets. The connection between the finger and your hand. Then your hand to your arm. Arm to shoulder. Shoulder to neck. Neck to spine. Spine to mind. Then follow it back down to your finger."

Teryn did as she said, following his awareness of each part of his body. Or was it just his ethera he was noting? He supposed it didn't matter. Emylia moved him through the exercise again and again until he felt a strange hum in his ethera, filling the space he was focusing on, rippling from his mind to his fingertip.

"Good," Emylia whispered. "Now send a single surge of awareness from your mind to your finger. Don't try to figure out how. Just trust. This is an automatic function. A flinch. You maintain that link. You can send energy through that circuit. That's all you're doing now. Are you ready?"

He breathed in deeply, felt his lungs expand. Felt the resistance between his back and the mattress shift with the movement. Felt the subtle sway in the energy from his mind to his hand, then back to his mind. He settled his attention at the top of his head. Then, with a rush of single-minded intent, he sent his awareness down his neck, his arm, his hand, and into his finger. The energy echoed back his intent with a flinch of movement.

"You did it," Emylia said, keeping her voice level despite the excitement it contained. "You moved your finger.

Teryn's pulse quickened in response to his shock. He... did it. He finally managed to move something—

A sudden wave of energy tore through his chest, and he felt as if he were torn in two. He shifted his attention to his surroundings, to the bed in the dark bedroom, the pale morning light creeping in through the closed curtains. His eyes fell on his own back, upright and no longer aligned with his ethera. His body moved of its own accord—no, Morkai's accord—glancing left and right, eyes blinking furiously.

This was the first time he'd witnessed his body being operated by Morkai, and it drained all the pride he'd felt in having made his finger flinch. What good was a damn flinch when Morkai could make his body sit? Stand. Walk. Talk.

Keeping his eyes on his now-awake form, he slowly shifted away from Morkai and slid from the bed. "You did great," Emylia said, standing at his side. "We will practice again next time he rests."

Teryn could only nod, eyes trained on Morkai.

The sorcerer ran a hand through his stolen body's hair, then threw back the covers.

Before Emylia could chastise him for his growing anxiety, Teryn focused on the sensations of his vitale, reminding himself that his heart was still his own. *His* breath kept his body alive. *His* blood pulsed through that body, even as Morkai made it walk across the room to the wardrobe.

"Does he know we're here?" Teryn asked. "Can he see us? Hear us?"

"No," Emylia said. "He's fully immersed in operating your body. He has no awareness of the spiritual plane we stand in now."

That gave him some relief.

"Now that he's awake," Emylia said, "you should rest your ethera. If you don't rest it on purpose, your ethera will eventually give you no choice. It's better you do so now so that you'll be at your best when Morkai sleeps. You aren't strong enough to wrest control of your body while he's awake yet."

Teryn debated the wisdom of her words, but he couldn't

stand the thought of resting while Morkai did devils-know-what in his body. "I want to see where he goes. What he does. I need to know what his plan is."

Morkai stripped off his nightshirt, giving Teryn the first glimpse of the crystal. It was wrapped in a thin strip of leather and secured around his neck on a long cord, the crystal itself resting at his sternum.

"We know what his plan is," Emylia said. "It's the same as it's always been. He intends to become the Morkaius of Lela."

Teryn whipped his gaze to her. "Morkaius? What is a Morkaius?"

She frowned. "Princess Aveline hasn't told you everything."

Mention of Cora struck him with a hollow ache. He recalled her tears last night, how she'd begged him to leave her alone. Now he'd give anything to take it all back, to storm up those stairs and refuse to leave her. He'd tolerate her rage, her ire, if it meant preventing what was happening now. If only he'd remembered the crystal. Perhaps she'd have had some idea how to destroy it...

Or would that only have gotten her trapped in his place?

Emylia's voice roused him from his thoughts. "*Morkaius* comes from the ancient fae language. It means High King of Magic. Morkai is not the sorcerer's real name but a title he's given himself. It means King of Magic. He intends to become Morkaius by ruling all three kingdoms of the land once known as Lela."

"Why?" Teryn shifted his gaze back to Morkai, saw him securing the buttons of one of Teryn's shirts, then donning a waistcoat.

"Ruling over Lela will allow Morkai to tap into an immense well of fae magic. That magic isn't meant to be wielded by a single person, and if he does harness it, he'll be able to do terrible things."

Teryn shuddered. He remembered how Morkai had boasted that he'd one day be King of Lela—that Dimetreus would conquer the three kingdoms, and Morkai would inherit rule after the king's passing. "If ruling over Lela has always been his goal, why did he even bother going through King Dimetreus and using him as a puppet?"

"To claim the magic," Emylia explained, "he must first inherit the land. Not through conquest either. Specifically, the crown must be *given not taken*, which suggests his best bet is to insert himself into the line of succession."

Morkai finished dressing and assessed his reflection in the mirror beside the wardrobe. Outfitted in Teryn's trousers, shirt, waistcoat, and jacket, no sign of the crystal or the leather strap could be seen. Seemingly satisfied with what Morkai saw in the mirror, he lifted Teryn's lips in a smug grin that looked nothing like his own.

"Are you starting to understand why Morkai chose you?" Emylia asked.

"What do you mean he *chose* me?"

"You were his target all along, which is why the crystal's magic was so strong with you. Why you forgot its existence so easily. Why you were so drawn to look at it. While the crystal is enchanted to have some semblance of self-preservation, its magic works strongest around Morkai's targets."

Dread filled every inch of his ethera. "And he specifically wanted me so he could..." He couldn't bring himself to finish, to even think it.

Emylia filled in the blanks for him. "He wanted your body so he could use your identity, your title, and your position to become Morkaius. To inherit the three kingdoms of Lela and control the magic of the ancient fae."

He still didn't understand the magic of the fae or even the full extent of what it meant to be Morkaius. The implications of Morkai's intent were enough to occupy his thoughts. If the sorcerer intended to use Teryn's body to accomplish his means, then his first step...

"It's because of Cora, isn't it?" His voice came out with a tremor, even though his words were no longer shaped with vocal cords. "It's because I am betrothed to her, and she is Dimetreus' heir. Through her, he could position himself as future King Consort of Khero."

Emylia's face fell with sympathy. "That is undoubtedly his first of many steps."

Teryn felt that agonizing urge to move, to act, to fix. Morkai was going to try to marry Cora in Teryn's stead. Surely she'd see through him! She had her magic, her ability to sense others' emotions. She'd notice Teryn wasn't who he appeared to be.

Wouldn't she?

Or would she continue to sense Teryn's soul as his own, oblivious to the fact that he was trapped in a crystal?

His only solace was that Cora and Teryn's marriage wasn't set for another year. If Morkai had the patience to play such a long game, Teryn could too. He'd strengthen his vitale, reclaim his cereba, and then—

A strange pulling sensation sent Teryn's ethera surging forward. Morkai had left the mirror and was now exiting the room.

"You and I are bound to the crystal," Emylia said, following after Morkai. "We are only able to project our etheras within the stone's immediate surroundings. So when the crystal moves, so do we. If not willingly, then by force."

Teryn caught up with the sensation pulling his ethera

and measured his steps behind Morkai's. Belatedly, he realized he probably didn't need to walk at all. Surely the act of setting one foot before the other was only for show. An instinct belonging to the outer layer of his ethera, like how Emylia had explained about their means of communication. Should he want, he could probably float in Morkai's wake.

The thought was as disturbing as speaking mind-to-mind had been. No matter what he was now—disembodied spirit or no—he would continue acting as alive as he could.

"Are you certain you wouldn't rather rest your ethera?" Emylia asked as they trailed Morkai through the halls of the keep. "Since I have no ties to a mortal body, I don't require rest the same way you and Morkai do now. I can keep watch and wake you if there's anything I think you should see."

He knew she was right, and he thought he could trust her. She was trapped, same as he. And yet, now that he knew what Morkai planned—that marrying Cora was his primary goal—he couldn't stand the thought of not witnessing his every move.

"Just a little longer," Teryn said. "I just want to see where he's—"

All thoughts fled his mind as Morkai rounded the next corner...and froze. It seemed Teryn and Morkai were of the same mind, equally as unprepared to see the person who halted before them.

Teryn's heart thundered in a chest that was no longer his own. He breathed her name in a voice she couldn't hear. "Cora."

31

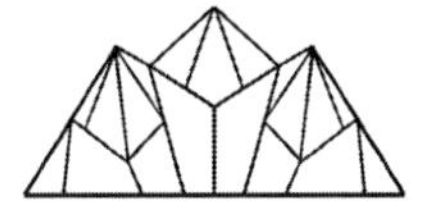

A thousand different things happened to Cora's heart in the split second that she realized Teryn stood before her. First was a joyful flip, an automatic response to seeing his green eyes, the tousle of his gold-touched dark hair, the broad expanse of his chest beneath the fine silk jacket he wore. Then came the sinking, the guilt over seeing his frozen posture, the tense set of his shoulders, his look of mild shock. Next, she felt a wave of anxiety along with the reminder that she still didn't know what to say to him. With the next beat of her rioting heart, Teryn's composure relaxed and a casual smile crossed his face. That sent a flutter of hope, a fragile, dangerous promise that everything would be all right.

"Princess Aveline," Teryn said with a bow.

She wasn't sure if his formality was more of a show for the passing servants or a response to her treatment of him last night. His smile remained present, but it only made her heart shift into a new emotion. This time it was shame. Shame because she knew—regardless of those precious hopes that all would work out as she wished—she wasn't ready to tell him about the curse.

Still, she couldn't pretend last night didn't happen. Nor could she avoid him. Certainly not while he was standing before her. Not when her heart was so tangled with his.

She took a step closer to him. Her muscles tensed, half with dread, half with longing, as she expected him to touch her. So badly she wanted to feel his reassuring embrace. Just as badly she feared she'd fall apart if he so much as held her hand.

But he didn't. He made no move to reach for her at all. He remained where he was, posture tall and stiff, hands behind his back. Was he merely being respectful after last night? She extended her senses, desperate to read what he was feeling, but she got back...nothing. Perhaps her own frazzled emotions were too loud.

"Teryn, I..." The overwhelming urge to fidget sent her fingers fluttering at her sides, so she folded her hands at her waist instead. She studied his face, as if she could read the words she needed to say, written somewhere on his visage. Her eyes caught on his cheek. The light from the hall window had cast part of him in shadow, but now that she was closer, she noticed a thin slice over his cheekbone. Concern replaced her anxiety. "What happened to your cheek?"

She lifted a hand to his face, but he took a step back. With a timid smile, he covered the wound with his hand. "Ah, that. It's embarrassing to say, but I accidentally cut myself with the straight razor while shaving. I suppose that will teach me not to travel without my valet."

"Oh." She frowned, noting how he hadn't let her touch him. Releasing a slow exhale, she searched his energy again, seeking whether he was truly shying away out of embarrassment...or if it was something else. Again, she sensed nothing. Not a hint of his emotions.

At least the unexpected topic had managed to banish some of her trepidation. Before her anxiety could return, she blurted out what she needed to say. "I'm so sorry about last night, Teryn. I shouldn't have pushed you away. I was just...dealing with something and I needed time alone."

He dropped his hand from his cheek. "There's nothing to be sorry about," he said, but there was something hollow in his words. Was he hiding his hurt after all? He continued to grin but she realized it didn't meet his eyes. "You were right to ask for space."

"I...was?"

His expression shifted into one of resignation. Or was it apology? His smile turned sad. "I was wrong to push you into something you weren't ready for. You accepted my proposal, but I pressured you for more."

Cora's brow knit into a furrow. Did he really think she'd asked to be alone last night because she hadn't been ready for their relationship to progress romantically?

Her heart raced as she spoke the next words. "That's not it, Teryn. I didn't ask for space out of some need to pull away emotionally. I...I just didn't know how to talk to you about what I was going through. But..." She swallowed hard. "I'm ready to talk now."

"You don't have to tell me anything."

Her stomach sank, though she wasn't sure if it was due to disappointment or relief.

"I trust you," he said. "You know that, right? You're free to keep your secrets. I'll never pry them from you or begrudge you your time alone. Besides, you have important work to do in the tower. It would be selfish for me to keep you from it."

Her lips flickered between a smile and a frown. While she'd hoped he wouldn't be too concerned over what had happened last night, she hadn't expected him to be so accepting. So dismissive. Was he posturing to hide any hurt he may feel? Or was he simply being supportive?

As if he could read the conflict in her expression, his tone turned warm. "My feelings haven't changed. We have all the time in the world to fall in love. There's no need to rush."

Before she could say anything else, he took a step back and gave her another formal bow. When he rose, his eyes danced with mirth, lips quirked in a sideways grin. Then, with nothing more than the word "Highness," he left.

Cora stood frozen for a few beats more, unsure how to feel about their exchange. Her emotions were still too tangled, too loud. Most of all, her skin felt cold, chilled beneath the broken expectations that she'd at least receive a kiss on the hand, if not a parting embrace. The absence of his touch was as painful as a slap, as was his failure to request her company for some later date. Instead, he'd just... walked away.

He'd given her what she needed though, hadn't he? The space to finish her work in the tower. Permission to keep her secrets to herself. She'd let that be enough.

In the meantime, she could do what needed to be done.

Clean the tower.

Learn how to break her curse.

She marched from the keep to the tower stairwell and up the stairs. Both guards acknowledged her with a bow of their heads. The room was as she'd left it, the windows having been closed for the night, the hearth filled with nothing but soot.

Summoning the fiery resolve she'd felt earlier, she set everything back in place—donning her apron, opening windows, adding fresh salt to the threshold and sill, tossing her blend of herbs upon the cedar logs in the hearth. Once she was ready to begin her work for the day, she strode to the bookshelf, selected a book, and analyzed its energy. Deeming it safe enough to touch, she brought it to the hearth. But instead of tossing it in the growing flames, she set it on her lap, retrieved her knife from her apron pocket, and flipped open the cover.

This time, without guilt or shame or worry that she was doing the wrong thing, she read.

And read.

And read.

TERYN FLOATED IN NOTHINGNESS, HIS SURROUNDINGS shapeless and awash in pale light. He vaguely noted that *this* must be how it felt to rest his ethera. It was the same sensation he'd had before he'd awoken inside the crystal for the first time. His mind lingered somewhere between rest and consciousness. Thoughts began to sharpen at the edges, forming his last waking memory.

Cora.

Beautiful, fearless, formidable Cora standing in the hall.

Cora, frozen in place as her eyes fell on his body.

Cora, trying to confess a hurt she'd endured.

Cora, crestfallen as Morkai's retreating footsteps dragged Teryn away from her, forcing him to follow the crystal's path.

He woke with a jolt and found himself in an unfamiliar place. Instead of the muted gray stone of Ridine's walls and regal tapestries, he found himself surrounded by pale marble carved in intricate patterns. Rugs covered the floor of the small room, and an array of bright pillows stood in lieu of tables and chairs. To the left was a low bed draped in gauzy curtains that hung from the ceiling, sheets the color of ruby and saffron haphazardly tucked in place.

"This was my bedroom when I was alive." Emylia's voice startled him, and he found her suddenly at his side. She was dressed in a sleeveless linen gown the same shade of saffron as the bedsheets. Her curly black hair was pulled into a bun at the top of her head. "I spend most of my time here. Is that all right? Or would you prefer I shape the crystal to mimic your bedroom at Ridine again?"

"It's fine," Teryn said, his mind still sharpening from the haze of rest. "But where are we really? Where is Morkai right now? How much time has passed since..." Fear clenched his chest as he realized he couldn't remember anything after he saw Cora. His ethera must have forced him to rest, just as Emylia had said it would.

"Connect with your vitale first."

He bit back a curse, but she was right.

With a deep breath, he focused on the feel of air moving through his lungs, the pulse of his blood, the beat of his heart. Calm settled over him.

Only then did Emylia answer his question. "A few hours have passed. King Dimetreus is holding court and Morkai is in attendance."

"Doing what?"

"Just watching."

Teryn arched a brow. "That's all?"

"For now."

Teryn had expected something more sinister, but as long as he wasn't anywhere near Cora, he could let himself relax.

Emylia gave him a sympathetic smile. "You're worried about the princess, aren't you?"

"How can I not be worried? He's using my body to marry her and become king. He—" His voice cut off as he recalled Morkai and Cora's interaction. He'd nearly exploded in a futile rage, expecting Morkai to put his hands on her, to touch her or kiss her the way Teryn would have. Instead, he'd kept his hands behind his back, maintained a steady distance between their bodies. Then there were the things he'd said, telling her she was right to ask for space. The fact that he knew about what had happened between them in the tower last night told him Morkai had indeed been spying on them, the same way Teryn had begun watching Morkai.

But why had he acted so cold?

Teryn faced Emylia. "If Morkai is determined to marry Cora, why did he try to keep her at bay today? Wouldn't it serve his purposes to keep her close?"

Emylia shook her head. "He will have to ensure your engagement remains secure while avoiding her as much as possible until the marriage contract is signed. Cora is dangerous to him because of her magic. The crystal likely keeps her from reading Morkai's true emotions, and it might be muting yours as well, but she may grow suspicious if she realizes she can no longer read you."

"You know about Cora's magic?"

"I've been in this crystal a very long time, and I've spent most of my time projecting myself outside of it, watching. I've witnessed every moment between her and Morkai, starting with when he first arrived at Ridine Castle. I watched her struggle with her magic as a child, long before she'd learned what she was. But I've always known she was a clairsentient witch. A strong one. She's what my people call an empath."

"An empath," Teryn echoed. He remembered Cora saying that word when she'd confessed about her magic. She'd told him about witches and their six sensory magics, said that an empath was a witch with the strongest form of clairsentience.

"I'm from Zaras," Emylia said, "in the Southern Islands. There we respect magic. Almost everyone feels a connection to at least one of the six sensory magics. The strongest in the Arts train as priests and priestesses at the Zaras Temple. This bedroom was where I lived while training as an acolyte at the temple. I was a promising seer before I died."

That explained why Emylia knew so much about magic, and perhaps why she could utilize the crystal the way she did. Yet it reminded him just how much he *didn't* know about her.

"How did you die? Why did he trap your ethera?"

"He trapped me for the same reason he trapped you. He has plans for me."

He didn't fail to note that she hadn't answered the first part of his question. Was she hiding something? He narrowed his eyes. "Why are you helping me?"

"Our goals are the same," she said with a shrug. "I want out. I want my soul to be at rest. And there's only one way to solve both our problems."

"What's that?"

"We must destroy the crystal."

Teryn's eyes went wide. "How?"

"I don't know yet," she said, wringing her hands at her

waist. "You need to strengthen your connection to your vitale and cereba first. You'll likely get only one chance to do what needs to be done. That flinch you created today? You'll need to do that with your whole body. If you can gain control over your movements, you'll have a chance at removing the crystal from your body. You must force it at least sixteen inches away, remember? That's the first step."

"What will that do?"

"Like I told you, removing the crystal from over your body's sternum will compromise the connection between Morkai's heart-center and your cereba. He will fight you for dominance, but without the crystal closing the circuit that gives him primary control, you'll have an equal chance at retaining motor function. You'll need to act at once to break the crystal."

He gave her a pointed look. "Didn't you tell me it's unbreakable?"

"Yes, but I'll work on figuring that part out. For now, you must get strong. You have time. I promise."

Teryn bristled despite her placating smile. He knew what empty promises sounded like, for he'd delivered his fair share, and hers rang as hollow as an unfilled vase. But that didn't mean he couldn't trust her. Right now, it was his only choice. And he did have time, didn't he? His marriage to Cora wouldn't commence for another year, and if Morkai was determined to avoid her until then, she'd be safe in the meantime. He'd be able to free himself before then.

Right?

Yes. He affirmed the word again and again.

Yes. Yes, I will do this.

No matter what it took, no matter how many sessions he had to spend laying in his empty body, trying to get his limbs to obey his mental commands, he'd get his body back.

And if he couldn't...

Well, he knew one thing that would prevent Morkai from attaining his goals. It would be a last resort. A dreadful one at that. But if it meant keeping Cora safe—keeping the three kingdoms he sought to control safe—then Teryn Alante was willing to die.

32

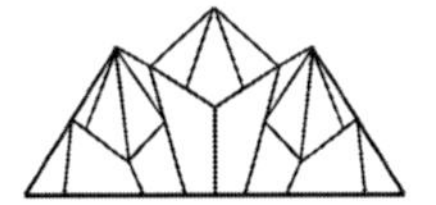

Witches didn't deal in curses. Cora knew this, knew every bit of information she pored through stood in contrast to her ethics. But if there was any hope in breaking Morkai's fate weaving, it had to be in one of these books. And yet by sunset, with over a dozen books read and burned, she'd found nothing to fuel that hope. Nothing of immediate value, at least.

Only three of the books had mentioned curses at all, and when it came to breaking them, all had said some measure of the same thing: *To break a curse, one must cast the same spell in reverse.*

That wasn't helpful. Cora may have had access to Morkai's blueprints for the fate weaving he'd cast, but she couldn't make heads or tails of the complex intersecting lines he'd drawn in his book. Would it be enough to draw the pattern in ink, or did she need blood? Would she have to suspend it in the air, make the pattern weave itself, like Morkai did? And if she was supposed to cast the spell in reverse, didn't that mean she needed to know which part of the pattern was the starting point and which was the end?

She'd found only one other option, a single sentence mentioned in the most recent book she'd read: *A curse may be rendered neutral if one casts a counter curse of equal or greater power to the opposite effect of the original curse.*

Yet another unhelpful piece of information. Because—as Cora had already surmised—witches didn't deal in curses. Even if she knew how to cast a counter curse, how could she make one strong enough to neutralize Morkai's dark magic? And what would the opposite effect be? A fertility spell?

She curled her fingers into fists as she watched the book burn, witnessed every page crumble to ash in the hearth. That single line of relevant, albeit unhelpful, text was all she let remain in her mind. Everything else, every unsettling spell, every instruction on using dark magic, she'd refused to take in. She may have decided to use Morkai's books as a means for education in a single subject, but she wasn't a fool. She wouldn't be seduced by the excerpts scrawled within these tomes, nor would she allow any excuse to save a single book from burning. Aside from those that couldn't be burned, of course, like the ones with pages laced with poison. But even those were fated to be discarded, not kept.

Even if she never found a way to unravel the weaving Morkai had placed upon her, she'd at least have the satisfaction of watching everything he'd owned be destroyed. That was where her true motive lay. This was less about gaining the ability to bear heirs and more about defeating a sorcerer who held too much power beyond the grave.

The sun began to set just as the last remnants of the book joined the ashes in the hearth. She debated returning to the bookshelf and selecting her next target, but she stopped herself, noting the heaviness of her bones, the fraying edges of her protective shields. As desperate as she was to do more, she knew better than to push herself. After expending so much energy sensing, reading, and clearing, she was at her limit. Her magic needed rest, as did her mind.

She set to the task of closing windows, putting out the hearth fire, and readying the room for the morrow. All the while, she couldn't shake her growing ire. She'd hoped she'd have gained something from reading Morkai's books today. Considering what little value she'd gained from the two excerpts she'd committed to memory, all she'd manage to accomplish was a slower pace than the day before.

Her frustration grew and grew as she left the tower and returned to the keep. Every step up the stairs carried the weight of her anger—an anger that hadn't diminished with her day's work.

All the better, she told herself. *It will carry me through tomorrow and keep me from thinking about...*

She cursed under her breath as Teryn entered her thoughts for the first time since she'd begun her day's work. Her mind had been too occupied to stray to him while she'd been reading and clearing, but now she remembered how his face had looked that morning. The smile that didn't reach his eyes when he'd told her she was right to ask for space. The distance he'd kept as they spoke. The rigidity of his spine as he'd stood with his hands behind his back, as if forcing himself not to touch her.

Or had he not wanted to touch her?

She shook her head, preferring her previous irritation to what she felt now, teetering on the edge of grief. She reached the main floor of the keep and saw the lamps had been lit in the hall.

Fire, she thought as she passed by the first, willing the element to grow within her, to spark the rage that served as a comforting barrier around her heart.

Fire, she thought again, striding past the next several sconces. She imagined the light dancing up her skin, settling over her core, and fueling her strength of will—

A startled squeak interrupted her focus, and she found Sera at the end of the hall, face pale as her eyes locked on Cora's. She lowered her eyes to the floor and dipped into a curtsy. Her voice came out with a mild tremor. "Highness."

A sense of guilt washed over Cora, but it wasn't her own. She'd left her mental shields as they'd been in the tower, strengthened only for protection, not sensing. Breathing deeply, she fully sealed them, but not before gaining a full understanding of Sera's state of remorse.

"I'm sorry I haven't attended to you today, Your Highness," Sera muttered, eyes still locked on the floor. She began to fiddle with the ends of her brown hair.

"It's fine," Cora said curtly as she reached the girl. "I had no need of your aid."

A rush of air left Sera's lips as she finally lifted her face. "That's a relief, Your Highness, for I couldn't have been spared to aid you even if I'd wanted to come. Queen Mareleau has been dreadfully ill all day, you see. She can hardly keep anything down."

Cora began to brush past the girl. "Do what you must. I'm sure the royal physician will take care of her." She paused. Did they even have a royal physician on staff yet? Surely such an appointment would have been a priority...

Sera lowered her voice to a whisper. "She refuses to allow any of us to fetch him or tell anyone about her condition. I'm only telling you because you're my current mistress, and I didn't want you to think—"

Cora rounded on the girl. "Her Majesty is ill and she refuses to be seen by the physician?"

Sera gave a frantic nod. "She insists she can cry and throw up well enough on her own."

Finally, Cora found an appropriate target for her anger. What was Mareleau thinking refusing help while ill? Wasn't she with child?

A dreadful thought occurred to her. What if she was having complications with her...her pregnancy? And didn't want to tell anyone? Cora's heart softened the slightest bit.

"Take me to her."

Sera blinked at her a few times. "To...Her Majesty?"

"Yes." Cora wasn't even sure why she insisted. Whatever Mareleau was going through was none of her business. But with the dreadful pressures of queens and royal women so fresh in her mind, she couldn't stand idly by if the woman was suffering.

Sera led her down the halls toward a familiar wing of the keep. Cora shuddered as they neared the late Queen Linette's former chambers.

Master Arther put her here?

It made sense considering both Cora and Dimetreus had refused to claim the room, and it was one of the largest in the keep. Of course the steward would appoint it to the visiting queen.

Sera opened the door and ushered Cora inside before quickly closing them in. Cora nearly gagged as the scent of vomit reached her nostrils. The windows were open, allowing a gentle evening breeze inside the room, but nothing could hide the smell of sick.

Cora took in the state of the room, saw ewers of water, soiled rags, and clothing haphazardly strewn about. There was no sign of blood, but that didn't mean the worst hadn't happened. Mareleau lay upon her bed, the back of her forearm covering her eyes. Her hair was slightly damp around her forehead and her cheeks were pale. Her two other ladies, Breah and Ann, fluttered about next to her, trying to coax her into taking a bite of bread.

"I don't want any more bread," Mareleau said with a grumbling moan. "Just leave me alone and stop fussing."

Sera led Cora to Mareleau's side. Cora addressed the queen's ladies. "What are her symptoms?"

With an affronted gasp, Mareleau threw back her arm, revealing her blue irises, the whites of her eyes bloodshot. "You can ask me myself. I'm not dead, you know."

"Fine," Cora said through her teeth. "What's wrong with you?"

Mareleau's eyes widened as she took in Cora's presence. "What the seven devils are you doing here?"

"I'm here to check on you, Majesty." Cora's barbed tone relayed just how much she was already regretting doing so. "Tell me your symptoms."

Mareleau scoffed. "Do you fancy yourself a physician?"

"Do you fancy yourself a fool? Surely you know better than to neglect your health in your condition."

"My condition?"

"Your pregnancy, Majesty." Cora was done dancing around the subject. If Mareleau wanted to be difficult, then Cora would be blunt. "The child you bear. Whether you're suffering from the condition itself, the loss of it, or some other ailment, it's folly to refuse proper care."

The queen's mouth fell open and color rose to her cheeks. "It's...it's not—who told you? Never mind. Get out!"

Cora lifted her chin. "No."

"I am the queen—"

"Not mine, though you keep forgetting. Now tell me your symptoms or I'll plant myself in this room until you do."

Mareleau bared her teeth with a growl of frustration. Her gaze shifted to her ladies. "Out! The three of you."

The maids exchanged wary glances, but as Mareleau added a sharp, "Now," the three scurried from the room and closed the door behind them.

Mareleau groaned as she pulled herself to sitting, struggling to arrange the pillows behind her. The shoulders of her silk gown hung loose as if the back had been left undone. Cora almost felt bad for the queen as she winced with every move, but her pride was too strong to offer help. Mareleau likely wouldn't want it anyway.

Once she was able to comfortably recline while sitting, she spoke. "It's not about the baby, trust me." Her eyes flashed to Cora's, then quickly away. A flicker of emotion—something like guilt or shame—crept past Cora's shields.

"Then what's wrong?"

Mareleau released a huff. "I'm nauseous, all right? That's all. It started yesterday. My stomach was rumbling most of the day. I worked too hard and got too hungry. Today, I can't keep anything down. My head is pulsing like it's about to split in two. I smell terrible. *Everything* smells terrible...and I...well, I simply ate too much cake last night, that's all."

Cora's muscles relaxed. What Mareleau described didn't sound too dire. But what reason did she have for refusing the attention of a physician?

"It's all your fault, you know," Mareleau said.

"My fault?"

"Yes, your fault. I spent hours—*hours*—slaving away in the courtyard behind the kitchen setting up the perfect romantic dinner for you and your beloved prince. I should have said no, but he begged me. Can you imagine? A prince begging a queen! But I said yes, and—"

"Wait." Cora frowned. "Teryn had you set up a private dinner for me?"

"Obviously. You refused to attend, did you not?"

Cora's mouth fell open but she couldn't find her words. When Teryn had asked her to dine with him last night, she'd imagined them sitting side by side at the feast in the dining hall, not a private meal made especially for her. Her shoulders sank, as did her heart. Though she supposed it made no difference. Even if she'd known about Teryn's efforts on her behalf, she still wouldn't have been able to face him last night. She'd needed that time alone. But now she felt the weight of her rejection, regretted that she never saw what he'd planned for her.

"You shouldn't spurn him, Princess," Mareleau said, oblivious to Cora's inner turmoil. Cora was only half listening as the queen continued. "I was just getting used to having a brother, but I daresay I liked him far less last night than usual. Still, I couldn't let all my hard work go to waste. If you weren't going to enjoy the bounty, I might as well, though I regret it now." She lurched as if about to be sick, but quickly settled.

Cora's mind sharpened, and her gaze snapped back to Mareleau. "Are you saying you dined with him in my stead?"

"Don't act jealous with me," she said with a scoff. "If you'd wanted to sit in my place, you very well could have. And I didn't *dine* with him; I only stayed for cake. One that was clearly underbaked."

Cora tried to ignore the pinching sensation in her heart and gave Mareleau a pointed look. "I highly doubt your nausea is due to an underbaked cake."

Mareleau pursed her lips and reached for a lock of silver hair. She began winding three strands into a braid but halted. With a grimace, she glanced down at her tresses where they tangled in something slick. With a whine, she dropped her hair and clasped her hands at her waist. Returning her attention to Cora, she rolled her eyes. "Fine, I admit it. I might have had wine too. Just one glass! All right, two."

Cora crossed her arms. "That's not what I meant either. I'm referring to the baby. Morning sickness. Though it isn't uncommon to be more sensitive to liquor while pregnant."

"Oh, and how would you know anything about it?"

"Pregnancy and childbirth were common occurrences amongst the people I lived with for the last six years. It wasn't a taboo subject like it is amongst royal society. We were open about it. Most of us trained in general aid, and I attended my share of births. While I've never experienced the condition myself—"

And never will, thanks to Morkai. The thought invaded her mind so suddenly, her breath caught in her throat. Breathing deeply, she forced the unwanted thought away and focused on what she'd been trying to say. "I have knowledge that can help, should you want it."

Mareleau quirked a brow, unimpressed with Cora's credentials. "And what knowledge is that?"

"First, that you really should see a physician when you're feeling ill. It isn't safe to neglect such care. Why did you, anyway?"

The queen shifted awkwardly in the bed, a hint of embarrassment on her face. "I didn't want him to know I'd had wine. If word got back to my mother...ugh. Must I spell it out for you? She wouldn't approve because of this..." She waved a hand at her belly. "*Condition*. Don't you dare say a word to anyone."

"I won't, but I doubt the royal physician would have been able to read your perceived sins through your vomit."

She lifted a shoulder in a shrug. "How should I know what a physician can and can't do? Is it not their job to read the inner workings of one's body?"

Cora would be amused if she weren't so tired. Now that she knew Mareleau wasn't in any immediate danger, she was desperate for sleep. Brushing her hands on her skirts, she took a step back from the bed. "I'll request a cup of ginger tea be brought to you at once, which you should have daily from now on."

"Why is that?"

"Morning sickness can last weeks, and you're certainly far enough along for it to begin."

"Surely I'm not. My wedding night wasn't yet three weeks ago."

"Oh, right," Cora said, tone flat. She recalled what Sera had said about Queen Helena preemptively spreading word that her daughter had conceived on her wedding night. All to cover the fact that her daughter was already with child. "Even if that *were* the case, it still isn't too soon for these symptoms to begin."

Mareleau released a disbelieving snort. "What do you know? I already told you it was underbaked cake and wine..." Her words dissolved, taking with it the color in her face. "Wait, what do you mean it's not too soon to experience...symptoms? That...that even if I'd conceived on my wedding night, I could..."

"It's exactly what it sounds like."

"No," she said with a light chuckle. "That's not possible." She held Cora's gaze with a hopeful grin as if waiting for Cora to agree with her. When Cora remained mute, Mareleau's expression went blank, eyes wide as they locked on Cora's. "No!"

A spike of the queen's emotions slammed into Cora.

Terror. Shock. Panic. They made Cora stagger back before she could strengthen her shields. Breathing deep, she closed her eyes and connected with the elements, weaving them tighter around her.

When she opened her eyes, Mareleau's face had crumpled.

"Seven devils, no," the queen said, chin quivering, before a sob tore from her throat. She hung her head and covered her face with her hands, shoulders heaving as she dissolved into a pool of tears.

Cora stared at the other woman, too startled to know whether she should comfort her or leave her in peace. She chose the latter and backed out of the room. The last thing she heard as she softly closed the door was Mareleau's distressed, high-pitched wail that ended in, "I'm gods-damned pregnant."

33

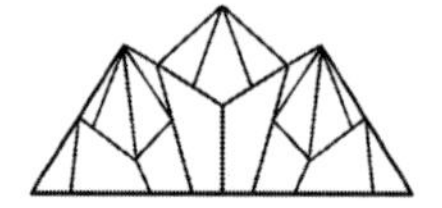

Larylis Alante never would have believed there was anything lonelier than being a bastard. Now that he was king, he knew it to be a far lonelier endeavor. He had guards. A bevy of attendants. His late father's councilmen. But being surrounded by all these people, most of whom were no better than strangers to him, made him feel even more alone than if he were in an empty room. Empty rooms, in fact, held a certain comfort no space filled with strangers could have.

He felt this now as he sat in King Arlous' place at *his* council table in *his* council room with *his* councilmen. As the king's bastard son, he'd never been allowed to attend such meetings before. Now, with his father gone and Teryn having abdicated, he had no choice but to attend them. He sat in his father's mahogany chair, wore his royal coat and crown of gold, yet he struggled to reconcile his change of station. The same doubt shone in the eyes of at least half of the councilmen who sat around the long oak table. They may address him as *Your Majesty* and pay him the outward respects required, but how many of them wished to see Teryn sitting in Larylis' place?

Larylis certainly did.

Or that Teryn was there, at least. Not that he had any intention of admitting as much to his brother. It wasn't pride that drove his silence but sympathy. He knew Teryn would come home at once if Larylis confessed just how much he could use Teryn's lifetime of knowledge as future-king-in-training. But Larylis was willing to suffer—willing to pretend he felt an ounce of confidence when he passed laws, made judgments on petitions, or sent correspondences marked with Menah's royal seal—if it meant Teryn had all the time he needed with Cora.

His own relationship may be temporarily stunted by distance, but that didn't mean Teryn's should be too.

Besides, Larylis had the means to adapt to his current struggles. He didn't have Teryn's lifetime of royal tutelage, but he had one reliable resource that had never let him down—books. Every night, he read about the kings of history. Great kings to emulate. Terrible kings to learn from their mistakes. During the day in his father's study, he learned from another form of the written word—his father's. He read over Arlous' correspondences, studied his diary, memorized the names of his allies, spies, and other important contacts.

He hadn't learned much to instill confidence in his capabilities, but facts, stories, and histories had always made him feel at least somewhat secure. They helped him pretend. If he could step into a role from fiction or history, he could separate himself from all his worries.

Right now, he was pretending to be Marsov, Fifth King of Rezkos, crowned Year 87 of the Sheep. Like Larylis, Marsov had been born a bastard. He, however, had claimed the throne without being legitimized and kept his crown despite many other contenders. It would have been an inspiring tale, were it not for the sixty years of war King Marsov put the Kingdom of Rezkos through, but that wasn't the part Larylis was emulating. Instead, he was mimicking the confidence he'd read about, the way King Marsov always sat with his chin held high, refusing to acknowledge any slight against his lesser birth.

Larylis wasn't sure if it helped or just made him look like an ass, but either way, his council continued to defer to him in every decision as the meeting continued. He wondered if King Dimetreus was receiving the same respect from his council. What was it like being served by a council made up of men from another kingdom? Larylis had that to be grateful for. Had it not been for Verdian's wariness of Dimetreus, the king may have tried to position his brothers at Dermaine instead.

Larylis' Head of Council, Lord Tolbrook, brought up the next subject for their discussion. "Are you certain you want to grant the Kingdom of Tomas inclusion into our trade with Brushwold?"

Larylis met the man's shrewd eyes and saw disapproval in them. His councilmen may have deferred to Larylis, but that didn't mean they ceased questioning some of his stances. Still, this was something he wouldn't budge on.

Sitting tall, he addressed the table in his best King Marsov voice. Or what he imagined his voice might have sounded like. Confident. Steady. "Prince Lexington came to our aid when my brother was captured by Duke Morkai. He fought at our side at Centerpointe Rock. His kingdom deserves to be rewarded for their prince's valiant efforts."

He didn't add that Teryn had promised the prince as much when they'd made a secret alliance during the Heart's Hunt, though he would if it came down to it. He'd learned that declaring something as *supported by Teryn* had its merits, for it proved that a change of heir would have made no difference.

Silence echoed over the table, and he felt his confidence waver. Then his eyes met those of Lord Hardingham, the councilman who had supported Larylis the most since he'd taken the throne. Hardingham had been his father's most trusted advisor, and unlike most of the others, he respected Arlous' dying wish to see his bastard son legitimized. Hardingham gave a subtle nod of encouragement.

With his confidence bolstered, he met Tolbrook's gaze without falter. "I will not yield on this."

"Very well," Lord Tolbrook said, tone grudging. "For the first time in forty years, we relinquish our exclusive rights to Aromir wool."

EVENING HAD FULLY FALLEN BY THE TIME THE MEETING CAME to its much-welcome close. His feet felt as heavy as bricks as he climbed the stairs to his sleeping quarters—chambers that once belonged to his father. Four guards followed in his wake, but he dismissed them once he reached his bedroom, along with his valet and other attendants who were ready to prepare him for bath and bed. Despite his fatigue, he wasn't ready for bed. His mind was simply set on being alone for the first time all damn day.

Alone yet far less lonely.

Part of his motivation was tucked in his waistcoat pocket,

inaccessible beneath the royal coat he'd worn to the council meeting. As soon as his guards and attendants exited the room and closed the doors behind them, he stripped off his jacket and extracted the piece of parchment that had been nestled against his heart all day. It was a letter from his wife. He'd gotten one almost daily since she'd left for Ridine, and they were the highlights of his days. This one, even before reading a single letter of her elegant, achingly familiar script, was no exception.

With a heavy sigh, he broke the seal and sank onto the bed. It was twice as large as the bed he'd had in his old chambers, which only made it feel emptier without Mareleau. But as he unfolded the letter and took in her words, a smile curled his lips. He could almost hear her voice, could almost pretend she was relaying her day's woes from beside him.

Ridine is a dark cruel place, my love. Is this a prison or a castle? I insist it's the former because they are highly lacking in sweet treats.

Larylis snorted a laugh at that. He'd have to send his reply first thing in the morning along with a jar of the finest cocoa. He knew how much she liked chocolate. With the speed a messenger horse could travel, she'd have her sweet treat in less than three days. His heart ached with envy. What he wouldn't give to travel by messenger horse himself. At least he didn't have to wait much longer to depart for Ridine; in two days, he'd start his journey north for the peace pact signing. But with the size of his retinue and the ridiculously slow agenda his council had planned for him, he wouldn't arrive until at least a week later.

He finished reading Mareleau's letter, then started over at the beginning, once again imagining every word in her sometimes playful, sometimes haughty voice.

My dearest Larylis—

A shuffling sound drew his attention from the letter. Sitting upright, he glanced around the room, seeking its source. The room still felt alien to him with its ample space, luxurious rugs, and elegant tapestries. Sound didn't travel the same way it had in his former bedroom. There could be a servants' passage behind one of the walls, for all he knew.

He heard the sound again, but this time he knew it was coming from his balcony. Frowning, he set down Mareleau's letter and approached the doors. The curtains were drawn shut, so he couldn't see the balcony beyond. He set his fingers on the handle, pausing to consider if he should call one of his guards inside instead...

Another sound, and this time it carried a note of familiarity. It was the telltale flap of...wings.

Larylis pushed the door open and found Berol staring up at him with what was undoubtedly an impatient look. Her wings were splayed, beak open, and before he could step out onto the balcony with her, she darted inside. She launched from the floor to one of his towering bedposts, then to his desk.

Larylis approached her, noting something tucked inside one of her talons. "Did Teryn send you?" From the agitated splay of her wings, he guessed she'd struggled to find him. It made sense considering she was used to the location of his former chambers. But why did Teryn send her? She could travel far faster than a messenger horse, and he was known to utilize her to send messages now and then. Regardless, her flustered state unsettled him.

He extended his hand and took the missive from Berol's talon.

Only it wasn't a missive at all.

Larylis stared at the piece of torn fabric, at the rust-colored splatter that looked an awful lot like blood.

His throat went dry as he was forced into a memory from not long ago.

It reminded him of...

Gods, he didn't want to think it.

But it was impossible not to see that scrap of fabric, the frantic splay of her wings, and *not* recall what had happened the last time she'd brought Larylis something while Teryn was at Ridine.

Why did she bring a scrap of cloth? Was this a piece of Teryn's shirt? Someone else's? Was he in trouble?

He sat at his desk and took out a quill and sheet of paper. He hadn't intended to write any letters until the morrow, but this one couldn't wait. Not with the dread sinking his heart.

It's nothing, it's nothing, he told himself again and again as he penned his inquiry to Teryn, asking if he was all right. If it truly was nothing, then he'd receive confirmation in less than three days' time. Sooner, actually, for he'd send a copy with Berol. There was a chance he'd get a reply as early as tomorrow evening.

It's nothing. Teryn's fine.

He rolled up the first letter and handed it to Berol. "To Teryn," he said aloud. She clutched it in her talons and set off at once. That was a good sign, right? She wouldn't have flown off if she didn't know where he was.

He tried to let that comfort him as he finished the second letter and handed it to one of his guards, insisting a messenger leave with it tonight. Then he returned to his desk and examined the torn strip of cloth Berol had brought him. He tried not to panic at the spatter of blood.

Yet try as he might, his mind kept wandering to the

worst-case scenario. Teryn injured. Teryn hurt. Teryn...*no.* That was as dark as he'd let his thoughts get. Whatever was happening, he'd sort it out soon enough.

In the meantime, he could only wonder...what the seven devils was happening at Ridine?

34

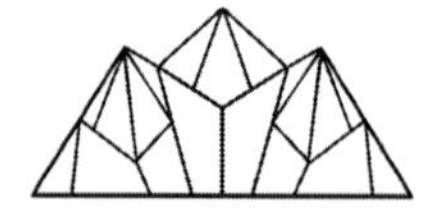

Teryn spent another night lying within the intangible bounds of his body, trying to influence muscle movement. After two hours, he managed another flinch of his finger. After three, a flutter of his eyelids. At least he thought he did. Unless it was merely coincidence that Emylia had witnessed Teryn's lashes lift just as he'd been directing all his intent to those minuscule muscles, he'd succeeded.

Yet it still wasn't enough. It was nothing compared to what he needed to do. Trying to force these subtle movements took all the strength of will he had. He couldn't imagine how long it might take to control enough of his body to remove the crystal from around his neck. He might go mad before then.

No, he told himself. *I will not give in to my own futility. I will build the strength required to do this or I will die trying.*

He shifted on the bed, feeling the edges of his ethera buzz from the contact it made with his body and the mattress beneath it. After connecting to his breath, blood, and pulse, he tried to refocus on his current task: parting his lips. No matter how he tried, his mind kept shifting to Cora. To worry. To fear.

He hated that Cora had no clue what was going on. Hated that she perceived Morkai's coldness to her as his own. At the same time, he was grateful for Morkai's outward indifference. If it kept Cora from getting too close to Morkai, Teryn would let her think anything at all. He'd sever ties with her for good if it prevented the sorcerer from using their relationship the way he intended. Furthermore, Morkai's avoidance of Cora gave Teryn the time he needed to reclaim his body. There wasn't much Morkai could do to further his goals until he was married to Cora. Right? Surely he could defeat this challenge by the end of a year.

Just the thought that it could take even a fraction of that time sent a flicker of anxiety through him...

"Breathe, Teryn," Emylia reminded him.

He clenched his jaw, creating a buzz of resistance tingling over the bottom half of his face, but he did as she suggested. He refocused on the air filling his lungs, on the steady thrum of his pulse, until his mind cleared of panic. Then he shifted his attention to his mouth, feeling the energy hum where his body and ethera were perfectly aligned. On an inhale, he experienced the air moving through his nostrils, unsure whether this sensation belonged to his body or ethera. Perhaps some place between where the two were connected. Slowly, he exhaled and felt the air tingle his upper lip. He repeated this meditation several times until he could imagine he was simply resting like normal—whole and alive. Then, on his next exhale, he shifted the course of the air escaping his lungs, sending it out his mouth instead.

His lips parted. The air left his mouth in a soft, easy breath.

Surprise sparked the edges of Teryn's consciousness, but he reined it in, determined to stay focused. He controlled several more mouth breaths, then shifted his attention to the back of his throat. To his tongue. The roof of his mouth. His vocal cords.

Excitement rippled through him as the idea took shape. If he could simply control his voice—form words for just the right person—he wouldn't need to wait until he could move his entire body. He could shout a warning. Get help.

His throat was warm with the heat of his breath, with the harmonious vibration humming between his body and ethera. On his next exhale, he sent a surge of energy, will, and intention, through his throat and vocal cords, lifting his tongue to the roof of his mouth—

Energy tore through him, ripping, separating, and his body bolted upright, leaving his ethera reclined on the bed. Morkai heaved a cough and pushed back the covers, motions agitated.

"Seven devils," Teryn cursed, leaving the bed to stand beside Emylia.

"Don't be discouraged." Her smile was warm, dark eyes glittering. Today she was dressed in billowing ivory pants and a knitted cream tunic. It occurred to him that he never had any awareness of his own appearance, much less what he was wearing. A quick glance down revealed the same articles of clothing he wore the night he was trapped in the crystal. It didn't matter to him, for it wasn't like he had any sense of comfort or discomfort when it came to his ethera's state of dress. He assumed it was merely a construct of his mind, anyway. Or perhaps a mirage shaped by Emylia's magic.

Emylia's smile grew wider. "You did really well this time.

You accomplished three muscular manipulations, and I could sense what you were trying to do at the end."

Teryn shook his head. "I failed. It woke him up."

"You didn't fail. You've already gotten stronger."

Teryn narrowed his eyes at the sorcerer who paraded about the room in Teryn's body, donning clothing with haste.

"You should rest your ethera," Emylia said. "It must be exhausted after what you accomplished."

"No, not yet," Teryn said. "Not until I see what he plans to do today."

TERYN AND EMYLIA FOLLOWED MORKAI THROUGH THE CASTLE as he strolled, dined, and greeted courtiers and councilmen. He seemed to lack an agenda until he began making inquiries of servants and staff, asking whether the king was holding court today and if Teryn had received any new correspondences. Teryn saw no sign of Cora, and he wasn't sure whether to feel sorrow or relief.

Finally, Morkai left the great hall to enter a separate building Teryn had never seen before. Its outer walls were crumbling and marked with ivy-shaped shadows that suggested the trailing vines had recently been removed. The building rose into a tall arch, its apex carved with a circle bearing seven interlocking spheres, marking it as a Godskeep. Teryn's eyes trailed back down the building, landing on two guards who stood outside the door. As Morkai approached, the guards made no move to open it.

One guard stepped forward. "His Majesty is at prayer."

"I too came for prayer," Morkai said, far more brazenly than Teryn would have dared. "I am soon to be the king's brother-in-law. He will not mind my attendance, for we pray for the good of the same kingdom."

Teryn cringed at the sound of his voice. It was *his* voice, *his* tone, but the way Morkai spoke...it sounded nothing like him. Yet of course these guards wouldn't know that. They'd been planted at Ridine from Selay. The only person here who could possibly see through Morkai's ruse was the very woman the sorcerer was determined to avoid.

When neither guard showed any sign of allowing Morkai inside, he lowered his voice. "To be honest, Lord Kevan asked me to come here for reasons I'm sure you understand."

The guards exchanged a look that set Teryn's teeth on edge. Despite now serving the king, they clearly maintained allegiance to Kevan. Had Morkai already gleaned the tense power dynamic here at Ridine? Did he know Dimetreus was still under scrutiny by Verdian and his brothers—the men who were supposed to be the king's new allies? If Morkai had been able to project his ethera outside the crystal the way Teryn and Emylia could, then he must have been able to collect at least some intel before having taken over Teryn's body. Not to mention the fact that he'd been off on his own much of yesterday while Teryn had been resting his ethera.

"I'll inform the king of your request," one of the guards said and entered the Godskeep.

Teryn frowned. What did Morkai want with the king? Whatever it was, it filled Teryn with a sinking sensation.

"Are you certain you wouldn't rather rest?" Emylia asked, tone wary. He met her eyes and found trepidation in them. She wrung her hands but stilled them when the movement caught Teryn's gaze.

"Is there something you know that you aren't telling me?" he asked.

She released her arms to her sides, donning a casual posture. Too casual.

Teryn *could* trust her...right?

"I'm telling you what's for the best," she said. "If you overexert yourself, you'll be forced to rest anyway. Remember what happened yesterday?"

Teryn knew she was referring to the way he'd lost consciousness after witnessing Morkai's conversation with Cora. He shrugged. "So be it. I want to know what business Morkai has with Cora's brother. I will watch their interaction for as long as I can."

"Just...just know that there's nothing you can do right now." She spoke slowly. Carefully. "Whatever happens, whatever you overhear, we can only continue with our plan."

Teryn's sense of unease increased, but the guard returned, pulling Teryn's focus back to the Godskeep door.

"The king will see you," the guard said, opening the door for Morkai to pass.

Teryn and Emylia shadowed Morkai through the antechamber, then to the nave. It was much smaller and darker than Dermaine's, with no bright tapestries, no painted ceiling, and no stained-glass windows. Its only adornments were a red carpet that ran from the doorway to the dais, a long wooden table that served as an altar, and seven statues of the seven gods that rested upon it. At the foot of the dais, Dimetreus kneeled. He was dressed in ceremonial robes in Khero's violet, embroidered with threads of gold and the kingdom's black mountain sigil on the back. A simple gold circlet rested upon his brow, while a bejeweled dagger hung at his waist. Teryn's gaze slid to Morkai's hip, relieved to see he was unarmed. Even if the sorcerer had thought to bring a weapon, the guards would have disarmed him upon his entrance to the Godskeep. Only the king and his guards could enter a Godskeep armed.

Morkai strolled past the rows of benches until he reached the king. "Your Majesty," he said with a deep bow.

Dimetreus nodded in reply. "Prince Teryn, how good of you to join me for prayer."

"I appreciate you allowing this intrusion."

"It's no intrusion," the king said, "for I am merely posturing. I've never been a man of prayer. A man of faith, yes, but not as faithful as I should be."

"Is that so, my king?" Morkai strolled up the dais and lit seven sticks of incense on the small brazier burning at the center of the table. Then he placed one stick before each of the deities before returning to the king's side. Teryn watched his every move with keen awareness, a tense wave of energy tightening his ethera. He expected Morkai to do something sinister, but he simply kneeled beside Dimetreus, positioned slightly behind as was deferential to the king.

Dimetreus spoke again. "Lords Kevan and Ulrich insist I make a show of being a penitent king to improve my image. Though I can't see how it would help when there's hardly a soul to witness me in here."

"I wouldn't say you're without witnesses, Majesty." Morkai gave a subtle nod toward the dais. Teryn's gaze followed to where the king's personal guard stood, two men on each side, nearly hidden amongst the shadows of the dark nave.

The king snorted a laugh. Lowering his voice to a whisper, he said, "I suppose you know more than anyone what position I'm in, as you had a strong hand in negotiating for my and Aveline's pardon."

"Yes, though I would have prevented Verdian's stranglehold on your castle if I'd held more sway. Kevan and Ulrich are too ambitious for their own good." Teryn hated hearing Morkai utter words that held true for Teryn. Perhaps the sorcerer was adept at playing this role after all.

"I appreciate you saying that, Prince, but...but I am in a situation of my own making. Though I wasn't of the right mind when I attempted to declare war on Selay and Menah, I can't change that it happened. I am willing to do whatever it takes to demonstrate my peaceful intent to my allies." His tone was dry, rehearsed.

"Majesty, I hope you won't fault me for being blunt, but you need not speak with caution around me. I'm on your side."

Dimetreus gave him a warm smile. "Of course you are. You were quick to forgive me, for you saw how I was being controlled firsthand when the sorcerer brought you here. Still, I bear the burden of having neglected to see Morkai's vile intent long before I named him duke. Even after, I'd had a choice. I could have listened to Aveline..."

His voice trailed off, eyes vacant. Haunted. Then he shook his head and rose to his feet. One of his guards rushed forward to offer him a hand, but he waved him off. The guard hesitated, then returned to his post at the end of the dais.

Morkai stood as well and faced the king with a bow.

"I'm glad my sister has you, Prince Teryn," Dimetreus said. "I can tell your affection for her goes beyond a betrothal contract."

Teryn was torn between feeling elated and enraged at the king's words. Though he said them to Morkai, the sentiment was true. Teryn's affection for Cora went beyond what he'd confessed to Dimetreus during the audience he'd had with him the night Teryn arrived. He was glad the king understood that.

But Morkai didn't deserve to hear those words, to receive them with that smug grin of his, one that made Teryn's face look nearly unrecognizable.

"You honor me, Majesty," Morkai said. "I am most *eager* to wed the princess."

Teryn tensed at how Morkai had emphasized *eager*.

"Next year, Khero will have regained enough stability to allow us to host a grand wedding," Dimetreus said.

"I await that day with the most ardent anticipation. However, I'm surprised your council has allowed for such a lengthy engagement."

Dimetreus gave a lighthearted chuckle. "I thought you were the one who'd suggested a yearlong betrothal, Prince. The marriage alliance had been your idea."

Morkai's face flashed with the slightest hint of alarm before he donned an easy smile. "Yes, I did propose the alliance, but I didn't set the timeline."

False, Teryn wanted to shout. He had set the timeline. He'd proposed a yearlong betrothal out of respect for Cora, out of consideration for the time he knew she'd need to adjust. The time they'd both need to fully enjoy their courtship.

"Ah," the king said, wagging a finger. "Your heart has made you impatient. I remember that feeling well."

"Yes, you are very right about that," Morkai said, but his voice lacked the warmth necessary to suggest the words were true. He furrowed his brow as if deep in thought. "I am concerned with one thing. Aren't you essentially without an heir until Aveline and I marry? Doesn't the peace pact state that your council will only accept your sister as heir after she and I are wed?"

"That's technically true," Dimetreus said. "It seems you are the key, Prince Teryn, for your neutrality secures

Verdian's trust as well as that of my council." The king's tone turned grudging as he spoke the last part.

Morkai narrowed his eyes. "You don't seem too happy about that."

Dimetreus forced a smile that crinkled the skin around his eyes, but there was no mirth in it. As he glanced over at his guards, it waned completely. He lowered his voice, eyes still on his guards. "It isn't a matter of being happy or unhappy. Aveline deserves to be heir in her own right. Yet the marriage alliance is a necessity. I'm only grateful it's a happy one."

Morkai's lips lifted at the corners in another smirk that had no right twisting Teryn's face. The expression disappeared as the king returned his gaze to Morkai.

"So, in a way," Morkai said, "I'm just as important of an heir as the princess is. When it comes to the council's point of view, that is. Wouldn't you agree?"

Teryn's pulse kicked up. He didn't like where this conversation was going.

Dimetreus frowned. "In a manner of speaking, I suppose you could say that."

"And you don't think you'll remarry?"

"No, my heart cannot part from my darling Linette. Due to my loss of memories, I feel like it's been far less than six years since her death. I have no intention of choosing a new queen. Aveline will further the Caelan bloodline, not me."

Morkai's face fell with false sympathy. "You must miss her dearly."

Dimetreus inhaled a sharp breath, and when he spoke, his voice held a quaver. "More than I can say."

"I bet you'd do anything to bring her back."

The king nodded.

"You'd sacrifice your own life, if need be, wouldn't you?"

"Without question."

Morkai stepped slightly closer. His voice dipped so low, Teryn had to move closer to hear.

"Teryn," Emylia said, a warning in her tone, but he couldn't be bothered to pay her heed. He *had* to know what Morkai was saying.

"What else would you trade, Majesty?" the sorcerer whispered. "Your kingdom? Your mind? Would you make a blood mage your heir in exchange for a promise that he could bring your wife back from the dead once he gained power over your kingdom? Or...or have you already done that?"

Teryn's heart slammed in his chest, his lungs constricting.

"Breathe, Teryn," Emylia said. "Keep your breaths slow and steady. Don't lose contact now."

Dimetreus took a trembling step back. "What...what are you saying?"

Morkai's voice shifted into a softer tone, one far more sinister than anything that left Teryn's lips before. It was so quiet, Teryn could barely make out the words. "Were you a willing participant after all, my king? Did you...*let* the duke take over your mind?"

"No, I..." Dimetreus' chest heaved, his eyes going unfocused. "No. No, it can't be. I wouldn't have..."

"I'm still here, my king. We can make the deal again. Give me your mind and I'll give you your wife. I'll bring her back—"

"No!" The roar leaped from the king's throat. His lips curled up in a snarl, eyes wild. "Monster! Demon! What are you? *What are you*?" In the blink of an eye, Dimetreus surged toward Morkai, the dagger at his belt suddenly unsheathed in his hand.

The guards darted from the dais, and Morkai threw up his hands and stumbled back. He fell to the ground, eyes wide with feigned terror.

Teryn watched, frozen in place, as Dimetreus tackled Morkai and held the dagger to his throat—to *Teryn's* throat. A line of crimson erupted from his flesh, but Teryn couldn't feel the cut. No, just the frantic beat of his heart. The race of his pulse. The tightness in his chest.

Spittle flew from the king's lips as he shouted, "Demon! Demon!"

"What are you doing, Majesty?" Morkai's voice had returned to normal, brimming with horrified innocence. "Seven gods, Majesty, look at me. Look at me! It's me, Prince Teryn!"

Dimetreus shuttered his eyes and pulled the blade back just as the king's guards reached them. They hauled Dimetreus up at once, eyes darting between their king and Morkai. "What happened?" one of the guards shouted.

Dimetreus continued to blink rapidly, then stared down at the knife in his restrained hand. With a cry of alarm, he dropped the blade. "Seven gods..."

Morkai slowly rose to his feet, shoulders almost as high as his ears, expression wary. "The king attacked me. We were talking and then...and then..."

Teryn's blood burned with rage as the guards showed no sign of seeing through Morkai's farce. Even Dimetreus seemed to take his performance as truth, a wail escaping his lips. With his crown askew and spittle speckling his chin, he looked every part the crazed king. "I'm...I'm so sorry. I don't know what came over me. It...it was a moment of hallucination. I've never had one so strong, so..."

"Keep him restrained," one guard said to the others. "This is a matter we must take to Lord Kevan."

The king went willingly as the guards led him through the nave. Morkai followed just behind. With the guards' backs turned, the sorcerer's lips curled into a satisfied smile.

Cold certainty washed over Teryn. This must have been his plan all along. He wasn't sure of the repercussions, but they couldn't be good. No, they could be terrible indeed.

Emylia tried to remind him to breathe, but his breaths were already too sharp, too shallow, his vision going hazy at the edges. The next thing he knew, the Godskeep faded from view and sent his mind drifting into nothingness.

35

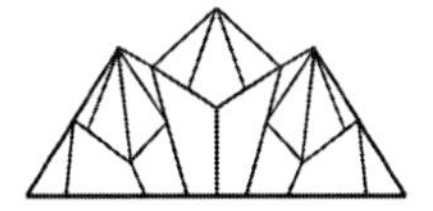

Cora had gotten used to the smell of burning paper, but she hadn't grown accustomed to the grim contents of Morkai's books. Nor the disappointment at finding nothing useful amongst all the references to blood magic, curses, and manipulations of mind and will. It was almost a relief to reach a portion of the bookcase filled with nothing but benign volumes—herbal encyclopedias, folk medicine, a regional guide to plants and animals. These made her feel far guiltier for burning them. Yet she followed her own rule: anything in this room that could be burned would be.

Her heart ached as she watched botanical illustrations blacken at the edges as fire lapped over a guide to flowers, but she reminded herself of the risk involved should she try to salvage anything. Should there be an unremarkable-seeming notation scrawled in the book, hidden amongst legitimate illustrations and documentations but bearing hidden treachery and dark magic, she'd be responsible should anyone find it in the future. She couldn't risk that.

Everything in the tower room belonged to Morkai, bore his essence, carried his energy. It all had to go.

As the book dissolved into ash, she tossed more herbs onto the fire and returned to the bookcase. It was three-quarters empty now. She felt accomplished so long as her gaze didn't stray to the multitude of other bookcases awaiting their turn at being cleared.

One at a time, she reminded herself. *No matter how long it takes, I will do this one at a time.*

In preparation to sense the energies of the next book on the shelf, she reconnected to the elements. Shifting her feet, she grounded her energy, rooting her stance upon the stone floor. Then she breathed in the afternoon air carrying scents of herbs and smoke. To connect to the element of water, she glanced at the basin on the floor, filled with clear liquid. Fire was easy. Not only did it fill the hearth, but the open windows drew in sunlight, filling the room with a golden glow, warming her skin, her hands. She cast her gaze out the window and looked upon the vibrant greens of the forest beyond the castle wall, the emerald mountains dappled in chartreuse.

A note of longing cut through her meditation. It was such a gorgeous summer day. What she wouldn't give to be outside, enjoying the scents of warm soil, a breeze that didn't carry dark energies and the ghosts of murdered books. She imagined the freedom of the forest, could almost feel the soft earth beneath her feet, could almost hear the birdsong increase.

Mother Goddess, if I could just be anywhere right now...

Her thoughts drifted to the Forest People's camp, and her longing deepened. She missed Salinda and Maiya so much more than she'd realized. The past several weeks had given her plenty to occupy her mind and time, and the same was true now, but such distractions had only prolonged her grief over losing her adoptive family. Would she ever see them again? She'd promised herself she would find them as soon as her kingdom was secure...

Her heart sank to her feet at the realization that the Forest People were no longer at the camp she'd left. It was well after Litha now, which meant the commune had already relocated, as they did with every season. To find them again would take tracking skills she didn't have.

Would she ever find them again?

We will, came Valorre's voice, and her heart trilled at the comfort it brought. *If you can feel them, we can find them.*

She wasn't sure if she *could* feel them, but she knew it was folly to worry about that now. Not when she had so much work ahead of her. Her kingdom wouldn't be secure until after the peace pact was signed. As for the tower room...that could take weeks longer. Months.

Darker thoughts lingered at the edges of her consciousness, questions she still had no answers to. Would she ever get the chance to take leave of the castle? Could she ever return to being the witch she longed to be? Was her role as princess shifting into a commitment as future queen?

You've been sad, Valorre said.

I have, she admitted.

But furious too.

Yes. She moved to the window, giving herself a better view of the castle's sprawling property and the towering walls that surrounded it. She felt how near Valorre was, could sense him on the other side of the wall, just out of sight.

You could sneak out again.

Her lips curled into a small smile. The offer was tempting, but she knew she couldn't risk it during the day. Night was the safest option, but lately she'd been so tired after her work in the tower, she hadn't even considered it.

Soon, she said and was about to apologize for neglecting him. Then she recalled his speech about treating him like a pet, and she decided to hold her mental tongue. Not that he wasn't likely reading her thoughts right now. She could sense the strength of their mind link, could feel his care and concern. And perhaps a note of confusion. He'd checked in on her enough the last couple of days to understand what she was upset about, but as a unicorn, he couldn't grasp the complexities of royal politics.

Valorre's energy turned distracted. *Oh, I know her!*

Cora frowned, leaning closer to the windowsill. She caught no sight of the unicorn or whoever had caught his attention. *What? Know who?*

The answer dove straight toward her, making her bite back a gasp. With her attention on the ground, she hadn't seen the falcon until it landed on the sill before her.

Cora hopped a step back, barking a yelp of surprise before she could stop herself.

"Highness," her guard called from the other side of the threshold.

"I'm fine," she assured him. She wasn't sure if he could see the window from his post, but at least he knew better than to enter the room. "It's just a bird."

Lowering her voice, she shuffled closer to the falcon. "What are you doing, Berol?"

The falcon's wings were splayed, head bowed. Her posture, along with the long string of chirps she uttered made her seem anxious. Upset. Then Cora noted the scroll of parchment in one talon. The falcon hopped closer, disturbing the line of salt on the sill.

Cora frowned, eying the paper. "Is that...for me?" A

spark of hope flitted in her chest. Perhaps Teryn had sent her a sweet letter and, instead of disturbing her with his presence, he'd sent Berol. She extended her hand toward the falcon. Berol uncurled her talon and dropped the scroll onto her inked palm.

Cora quickly unrolled the paper and found it was a short letter. Her eyes dipped to the bottom to find the sender's name. It was from Teryn's brother, King Larylis.

Teryn,

I hope this note finds you well. Berol delivered me something that looked like a scrap of your shirt, and it worried me. Please send her back with a reply letting me know if you're all right.

—Larylis

Cora cocked her head to the side. "Why didn't you deliver this to Teryn?"

Berol, of course, gave her no answer. Even when she tried to connect with the falcon's mind, it gave her nothing like the connection she could form with Valorre. Instead, all she felt was unease, agitation.

"Highness," came her guard's voice again, edged with a note of urgency. Berol took off from the sill, sending a gust of salt and rosemary in her wake.

Cora tucked the note in her apron pocket and turned toward the door. "Yes?"

A pause. Then, "Something has happened, Princess. Master Arther is here to escort you to speak with the king's council at once."

CORA'S HEART WAS IN HER THROAT BY THE TIME SHE MADE IT to the bottom of the tower stairwell where Master Arther awaited. After Berol's strange behavior and the letter she'd delivered, Cora couldn't help but think the worst. Something must have happened to Teryn. She hadn't seen him since yesterday morning. Had he returned home without saying goodbye? Had he been hurt or injured on his way? Even so, how had Berol had enough time to make it to Dermaine Palace and back? She supposed falcons were fast, but still...

"What happened?" she asked Master Arther, her voice both sharp and trembling.

The old steward wrung his gloved hands. "It's best you hear it from the council—"

"No, I will not take a single step farther until you tell me what happened."

Arther glanced around, but the hall was empty. Thankfully, the wing beneath the North Tower Library was rarely frequented by anyone but the guards. He released a sigh, and Cora braced herself for the worst.

Please don't say Teryn is...that he's...

"It's about His Majesty the King."

Her mind went blank. "What? Not Prince Teryn?"

Master Arther grimaced. "Well, it's about him too, Highness."

Her pulse hammered, setting her mind back to racing. "Please just tell me at once."

"You really should speak with the king's councilmen—"

"They are not your monarchs," she said, voice rising to a shout. "Tell me or I'll find someone else who will. And another steward while I'm at it."

She was too anxious to feel guilty for her sharp words. While she'd never made such an imperious threat, she was going out of her mind. Her mental shields were already beginning to fray, inviting in Arther's apprehension, and the curiosity of the stairwell guard behind them.

"Very well," he mumbled, folding his hands behind his back. "Highness, His Majesty attacked Prince Teryn. He drew a dagger on the prince inside the Godskeep during one of his..." The steward cleared his throat. "Moments."

Cora pulled her head back, unable to believe his words. "What? How could that...how would he..."

"Lord Kevan will tell you the details. The council has assembled and awaits your presence."

"Where is my brother?"

"He's in his room under guard—"

That was all she needed to hear before she darted from the steward and hurried through the halls toward the keep. The rush of her blood pounded through her ears. She paid no heed to Master Arther's pleading calls behind her, nor the sound of his feet as he shadowed her up the keep steps. She didn't slow, didn't stop, until she reached her brother's closed doors. Two guards stood outside them, men she recognized as members of Dimetreus' personal guard.

"Open the doors," she said, tone filled with cold authority.

"The king is at rest, Highness," one of the guards said, tone dry.

"Open the doors now."

They held their positions. Master Arther caught up with her, cheeks flushed pink, gray hair in disarray. "Highness, please—"

The doors began to open, drawing Cora's attention back to them. But she didn't have the guards to thank; they were opening from the other side. She nearly crumpled with relief at seeing her brother's face. His expression was wan, skin pale, reminding her too much of how he'd looked when he'd been under Morkai's control.

"Aveline," he said, eyes turning down at the corners. "You must have heard."

Cora glanced from her brother to the guards. The latter made no move to usher the king back inside his room or close the doors, which suggested he wasn't being held prisoner. Then again, he didn't invite her inside or cross the threshold into the hall.

She lowered her voice. "Can we speak in private?"

He gave her a solemn smile. "It's better if we speak here."

Her shoulders tensed. "What happened, Dimi?"

"What have you been told?"

She pursed her lips, eyes roving to the guards again, then to the steward.

Dimetreus held up a placating hand. "It's all right, Aveline. My guards saw what happened, and I'm sure Master Arther knows about the incident too. You may speak with candor."

Clenching her jaw, she inched slightly closer to her brother. "Is it true you attacked Prince Teryn in the Godskeep?"

He gave her a rueful nod.

"How, Dimi? Why?"

"It's as everyone feared. My mind...I'm unwell, Aveline."

She shook her head. "I don't understand. What happened?"

His expression turned haunted, eyes distant. "I saw *him*, Aveline. The sorcerer. I heard him, but he wasn't truly there. It seemed so real. Sounded so real..." He shook his head. "I pulled my dagger on the prince and nearly slit his throat.

Thank the seven gods my guards were fast enough to stop me. That the prince managed to get through to me, snapping me out of my hallucination."

Cora's stomach turned. She couldn't imagine her brother doing such a thing—

No, that wasn't true. While she couldn't imagine this version of Dimetreus acting so irrationally, she could imagine such a reaction from the man she met two months ago when he was being controlled by the sorcerer. The night Morkai had brought her to meet her brother in the dining hall, the king had been sweet and jovial one moment, then violent and suspicious the next. He'd called her sister, begged to see her dance, then ousted her as an impostor.

Had she been wrong to trust he could overcome the sorcerer's abuse?

"You know what this means, right?" he asked, rousing her from her thoughts.

She met his eyes with a questioning glance.

"My council has officially deemed me unfit to rule. According to the terms of the alliance we agreed to, I must abdicate at once and pass my rule to you and your husband. The peace pact will require it."

The blood drained from her face, making her knees go weak. "No. No, they can't do this. They're wrong—"

"They're not." His voice was so firm, Cora was forced to swallow her words. Stepping closer, he gathered Cora's hands in his. "I can't do this, Aveline. My mind is fraying. I'm in no state to rule this kingdom any longer. Not only that, but..." He shifted his jaw, then dropped his head, bringing his lips close to her ear. "My hallucination...it made me remember something. Something I'm not proud of."

She couldn't bring herself to utter a word, to do so much as breathe loudly.

"I let Morkai take my mind after Linette died. I gave him permission to use me, to warp my thoughts, in exchange for a promise that he could bring her back from the dead."

She pulled back slightly to meet his eyes. A chill ran down her spine. "That's not possible. He was already controlling you when she died. He made you believe that I..."

Her body went rigid. In learning to trust her brother again, she'd forgiven him for condemning her for his wife's death. She'd told herself Morkai had made him believe she could have done such a thing.

What if she was wrong? What if that enraged reaction at having found her in the room with the dead queen...had been genuine?

She forced the question from her mind. No, she remembered the strange sheen over his eyes when he'd ordered her to the dungeon. He hadn't been in his right mind back then, even before his wife's demise.

"It's just the guilt," she said, her voice uneven. "You're letting guilt get to you, brother."

Still holding her hands, he gave them a squeeze. "I'm grateful for your faith in me, but even if you're right, it doesn't matter. I've proven myself unstable."

Cora opened her mouth to argue but her brother spoke first.

"I'm tired, Aveline. So tired."

Her brother's sorrow slammed into her, destroying the last of her shields. She felt his exhaustion. His fear of his own mind. It was so potent, it made her breath catch.

"I thought I was a poor king because of a sorcerer, but the truth is, I am a shell of a man without Linette. Sometimes I wish I'd died on that battlefield. At least then I'd be with her now."

A spike of betrayal pierced her heart. How could he say such a thing? Was their kingdom not important to him? And what about *her*? Wasn't Cora enough to make him cherish being alive? "Don't talk like that."

"You will be the king I cannot be. Marry the prince and take my crown. You will serve this kingdom better than I ever could."

Panic laced her throat as she realized what he was saying; she was expected to marry Teryn *now*. To become queen *now*.

She shook her head. "I was never meant to rule, Dimi. I am here to help *you*. To reclaim your birthright and establish your legacy. I never intended..."

She couldn't finish. How could she admit that she'd seen her role as a temporary one?

Dimetreus' brows knitted into a furrow. "Are you not happy here, Aveline?" When she gave no answer—for what could she even say in such a frazzled state?—he spoke again, his voice barely above a whisper. "I know you could have abandoned me at Centerpointe Rock, but you didn't. That was selfless of you. Should you reject the burden I'm placing upon your head, I won't blame you. Never could I begrudge you a life of freedom if that is what you want."

Cora's chest expanded with a light feeling. He was giving her permission...to say no. To reject her birthright and leave Khero to...

To what? To ruin? To be conquered by King Verdian? With his brothers' positions, it would be easy to accomplish. Was that something Cora could live with? To end the Caelan line just to shrug off the burden of the throne and run free in the woods?

It was selfish to even consider such a thing. She was stronger than fear. Stronger than the weight of a crown.

Dimetreus spoke again. "Whatever you choose, I will support you. But I must make one request—consider love, Aveline. Don't shy away from it if that is what makes you hesitate. You and I have lost much in our lives. Our parents. Linette. But I promise you, love is worth it, even if you lose it in the end."

Cora's mind went to Teryn, to the curse that still stood between them—between the future of her kingdom—should she fail to break it. Everything was happening too fast, too soon, and her heart was struggling to keep up with it.

Regardless of the racing in her heart, the nausea shredding her stomach, she knew what had to be done.

It was time to tell Teryn the truth.

36

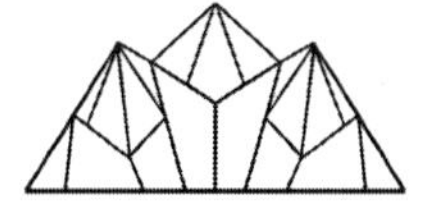

When Teryn returned to consciousness, it was to the sound of Cora's voice. It was distant, soft, barely brushing against the edges of his awareness. Yet the sound of it called him from nothingness, and when his surroundings took shape, they weren't the bright light of the crystal or even Emylia's temple bedroom illusion. Instead, he found himself before a door. The door inside his bedroom at Ridine Castle.

Cora's voice echoed from the other side, along with a rumbling knock.

"Teryn, are you there? It's Cora."

Teryn's consciousness sharpened. He connected to his breath, his pulse, the hammering of his heart. The events he last recalled—Morkai tricking Dimetreus into attacking him—surfaced in his mind, but he anchored his focus with the sound of Cora's voice. He was pulled to the melody of her tone, the sensation so strong, he felt it could draw his ethera straight through the door. But as he tried to take a step through the physical matter, he felt a much stronger pull against his back. Glancing behind him, he saw his body resting in his bed. This was as far as his tether to the crystal would let him go.

"Teryn, please. We need to talk."

He whirled back toward the door. Everything inside him begged to answer, but he knew his voice wouldn't travel to reach her. Not from whatever plane of existence his ethera was on. So he pressed his palm to the door, felt the resistance hum. She knocked again, and the vibration rang through him like ripples on smooth water.

"Are you there?"

"I'm here," he said, his voice hollow against the resonance of hers. It didn't matter that she couldn't hear him. He was there. He was there and he'd fix this.

She knocked once more, and he welcomed the reverberation like a caress.

Gods, this was as close as he could get to touching her. To being beside her.

He stayed like that for several long moments, even after he realized she'd left.

"You projected yourself outside the crystal on your own this time," Emylia said, suddenly beside him.

"It was Cora's voice that brought me here."

She released a heavy sigh. "You shouldn't have overexerted your ethera, Highness. It's dangerous to wait until your ethera forces you to rest."

He turned away from the door to face her with narrowed eyes. "Why?"

"Your ethera requires rest and recovery, just like a human body does."

"I know that, but why is it so dangerous for me to be forced to rest after overexertion? What haven't you been telling me?"

She nibbled her bottom lip before answering. "Being forced to rest abruptly severs your connection to your vitale, the same way fear or panic does."

Teryn folded his arms. "And that's a bad thing because..."

"Because it causes your body's functions to begin to shut down."

Teryn blinked at her. So that was why she was always reminding him to focus on his breath, to strengthen his vitale. It had been less about maintaining his strongest connection and more about preserving his body's functions. Did that mean...

"Could that...kill me?"

She nodded.

Anger sparked inside him. "Then why the seven devils didn't you tell me?"

"I didn't want to worry you," she said. "I knew it would only make you panic more." Her voice was brimming with apology, and yet...

He remembered how nervous she'd seemed when they'd followed Morkai into the Godskeep. How she'd tried to get him to rest before Morkai spoke with the king. Had she only been anxious over the prospect of him overhearing something that would cause his fear to spike, tearing him away from his vitale and forcing his ethera to rest? Had her concern been due to precaution...or premeditation?

Teryn's fingers curled into fists. He hated that he was starting to get used to the way the gesture buzzed, the way he was beginning to forget what being made of flesh and blood felt like. "Did you know? When we entered the Godskeep, did you know what Morkai had been planning to do?"

She shrank down, shoulders tense. "I had an inkling, but

I didn't want you to panic. You can't focus on what he's doing. You can only focus on regaining control of your cereba."

"So I can remove the crystal from my body and destroy it. Which we still don't have a solution to."

"I have an idea."

Teryn tightened his jaw. "Why the seven devils haven't you told me?"

"Because it's just that—an idea. Actually, it's less of an idea. It's simply...knowledge. I know how Morkai made the crystal unbreakable. A year ago, he wove its fate to a unicorn horn, focusing on the horn's indestructibility. The crystal now has the same properties that a unicorn horn has. It cannot break, burn, or crack."

Teryn was torn between feeling daunted by such facts or elated that he finally had something to work with. There had to be a solution now. He pondered what he knew about unicorn horns, most of which he'd learned from the now-dead Prince Helios. "You said the crystal can't be cracked or broken, but there must be a way. If it has the same properties a unicorn horn has, then it can be cut. Horns can be carved."

She shook her head. "Only severed horns can be carved. The horn Morkai used was still attached to the unicorn when he cast the fate weaving."

"Then what is your idea? How do we use this knowledge to destroy the crystal?"

"To break a curse, spell, or enchantment, one must go through the motions that were placed upon it but in reverse. Morkai used a bastardized version of an ancient Elvyn magic called *weaving*. Elvyn weavers used sky, but Morkai was never able to utilize this magic. Instead, he used blood. He'd draw out blueprints for complex patterns to execute his spells and cast them using blood. Since the crystal and horn were both inanimate objects, he had to use his own blood for that weaving, along with most of the magic he'd currently stored in his Roizan."

Teryn's mind spun with the information. Weaving. Ancient Elvyn magic. The Roizan. Teryn had witnessed the sorcerer utilize blood in such dark ways. He'd even attempted to kill Teryn with that very magic at Centerpointe Rock. The Roizan, however, he only partially understood. During Cora's interrogation, she'd told the inquisitors that the creature he'd known as the Beast had a name. *Roizan*. He'd learned the intel during his own interview. One of many he'd endured to prove Cora's identity. "What exactly is a Roizan?"

"A Roizan is a creature born from death, a sorcery of the forbidden Arts of the sanguina and ethera—blood and spirit. Neither alive nor dead, it becomes a vessel for magic that can be drawn from at will. It amplified Morkai's own magic, allowing him to do things he never could have done on his own. Large feats of magic either empty or destroy the Roizan, but the beasts are essential for doing magic beyond one's means."

"You said to nullify the enchantment that makes the crystal unbreakable, we would need to reverse the spell he'd placed on it. How the seven devils can we do that?"

She gave him an exasperated look. "I don't have all the answers yet, but I'm working on finding a way. One thing we'll need is Morkai's blood—the blood from his original body. He'll have some stored somewhere, and we can count on him to retrieve it himself. There are certain spells he won't be able to cast with the blood from your body alone. He'll need his own. The second thing we'll need..."

She paused, expression falling.

"…is the blueprint for the pattern he used to bind the qualities of the crystal to the unicorn horn."

"Do you have a way of finding this blueprint?"

"Not exactly," she said with a grimace. "He never showed it to me. He has the power to block me from projecting my ethera outside the crystal. It takes constant focus, so he couldn't do it all the time, but he must have been doing so when he drew the blueprint. I watched him weave the spell, but I couldn't see the pattern he used clearly. It was complex. Miniscule from where I stood."

Teryn rubbed his brow. "How are we to reverse a spell with a pattern we don't know? How do we reverse a spell at all? Is that something you have the power to do?"

"No, that is not something I can do. You'll have to be the one to reverse the spell."

Teryn's eyes went wide. "I don't know the first thing about casting magic."

"You don't need to. Blood magic follows rules. Patterns. That's why Morkai relied on it so much. Once we have everything we need, and you've strengthened your connection to your cereba as much as you can, you'll need to take over your body and draw the pattern in reverse using Morkai's blood. On paper, on a stone, it won't matter. You simply must reverse the lines he drew. As for the pattern itself…do you remember how I told you I was a seer when I was alive? I still maintain some of my abilities. I can watch my own memories. I've been trying to study my memory of Morkai casting the spell, watching it from different angles to see if I can untangle his movements. I've also sought the greater Art of seeing, seeking answers from the spiritual plane beyond. I haven't glimpsed the pattern yet, but…" Her eyes unfocused. "I have seen that we must stay the course. Keep doing what we're doing."

"That's all? Stay the course?"

"It's an imperfect Art, especially for someone no longer alive. I don't *see* as strongly as I used to. Even if I do manage to catch glimpses with the sight, when it comes to Morkai, everything is shrouded in these tangled...threads. I don't know what else to call them. All I know is that they're working against him. So when they pull me forward and tell me to stay the course, I listen."

Teryn leaned against the doorframe, felt the energy thrum against his back. Gods, no wonder she hadn't told him this. It didn't help at all. Perhaps Emylia was used to blind trust when it came to magic, but Teryn still felt lost in this world of fate and blood sorcery. There was so much he didn't know. So much he didn't understand. His mind wandered back to the Godskeep, saw Dimetreus draw blood from Teryn's own throat.

His gaze locked on Emylia's. "You said you had an inkling about Morkai's plan in the Godskeep. What were his reasons behind it?"

Emylia held up her hands in a soothing gesture. "If I tell you, you must remember that there's nothing you can do—"

"Just tell me," he ground out.

She folded her hands at her waist. "Morkai's plan was to destabilize the king and prove to the council that he's incapable of ruling. The council has made their decision. You know what happens next."

Teryn's pulse quickened. "Cora will be forced to ascend to the throne."

Emylia nodded. "But first she must marry you. Morkai has spoken to the council in your place and has agreed. I don't know about Cora, but as of now, your marriage contract is set to be signed first thing tomorrow morning."

It took all of Teryn's focus not to lose touch with his

breathing, with the rapid thud of his heart. "He's going to marry her...as me. Tomorrow."

"Yes."

His voice came out cold. Sharp. "What happened to *you have time, I promise*?"

"You still do have time. Maybe not as much as you thought, but enough to do what must be done."

"I have until tomorrow morning to regain control over my body before he..." He couldn't say it out loud. No, that would make it too real. Gods, he thought he had a year, not a matter of days. In what world did Emylia consider that enough time?

"He won't attempt to consummate the marriage, if that's what you're worried about. He'll continue to try and maintain his distance for the time being."

"Why is he forcing her to ascend to the throne so soon, to finalize the marriage alliance so suddenly?"

"He wanted to act before Cora could catch on," Emylia explained. "This way, even if she does grow suspicious, he secures his role as king consort while he puts all the other pieces of his plan into place."

"What is his plan? I know he intends to rule Menah, Khero, and Selay as one, and that he wants to use my marriage to Cora to make that happen, but...how?"

"I don't know, but I have a feeling he'll execute it at the signing of the peace pact."

Teryn's heart raced. Seven devils, the signing was to take place at the end of the month—eleven days from now. Larylis and King Verdian might already be on their way. When they arrived, Morkai would have every monarch—every person who stood between him and total rule—under one roof.

He cursed under his breath.

"There's something else he'll be working toward," Emylia said, her voice barely above a whisper.

"What?"

"Once your marriage to Cora is secure, he'll pour all of his focus into making his takeover of your body complete."

Teryn straightened, a chill running through him. "What does he need to make the takeover complete?"

"He needs to forge a fate weaving. To do that, he'll need your blood, his original body's blood, and a Roizan. Your blood will be easy, for he merely needs to cut your flesh. As for his blood, well, I already told you about that; he has vials of it hidden somewhere. He always kept a stash of his own blood, as a precaution against using all the blood he'd stored in his crystal. Since Cora's attempts to energetically clear the crystal emptied it of blood, his hidden store is his only option."

Teryn's mind spun as he worked to keep his breathing steady. "What about the Roizan? How long does it take for him to create one?"

"A Roizan can be forged in a single night, but it normally takes years to strengthen it with magic, to fill it with enough power for a fate weaving."

"That's some relief. I'll be able to reclaim control by then. If not to remove the crystal and destroy it, then to figure out how to work my voice. Tell Cora the truth. She'll see through him—"

Emylia hung her head with so much defeat, he swallowed his words. Her voice came out small. "It may take years for a Roizan to be strong enough to work great magic, but Morkai doesn't have years. Not even a single year. Perhaps not even a month."

Teryn's breaths grew shallow, but he couldn't bring himself to speak.

She lifted her head and met his eyes with a mournful expression. "Being forced to rest your ethera isn't the only thing that deteriorates your body. The mere act of being split like this will slowly wreak havoc upon your inner functions, day by day. There are only two things that can happen. Either Morkai succeeds and makes the takeover complete, or you reclaim your body and force Morkai out. Otherwise...you'll die."

His eyes went wide as dread sank every inch of his incorporeal form. He sagged against the doorframe once more. "Why didn't you tell me this from the start?"

"If I'd told you early on," she said, "you'd have succumbed to your fear. Fear and panic are what detach you from your vitale. Detaching from your vitale harms your bodily functions and prevents you from connecting to your cereba. You must keep that connection strong. Regardless of what you think I should have told you, it doesn't change what must be done. You have one choice. One course of action."

"Reclaim my body. Break the crystal." The words came out flat. Even more hollow than they normally sounded on the spiritual plane.

"You focus on the former. I'll work on solving the latter."

He gave her a pointed look. "You mean the memory you can't clearly see? And the vision that keeps telling you to stay the course?"

"It's the best we have." She gestured toward his sleeping body, dozing upon the bed. "Now is your chance to practice your side of the plan, Highness."

Fueled with a stronger sense of determination—if not a

deeper sense of dread too—he made his way toward the bed. He reached the side and glanced down at his sleeping form. A sick feeling coursed through him as he noticed the hollows of his cheeks, the bags under his eyes. And...was that a wisp of silver at his temple? Teryn leaned forward to get a better look at the strand. It was mostly hidden beneath his dark waves, but it was there. It reminded him too much of King Dimetreus' hair, a silver-streaked brown that belied the king's true age of nine-and-twenty.

Whether he had himself to blame for overexerting his ethera or if these physical signs of bodily strain would have begun to show regardless, he knew not. Either way, Emylia was right; his body was deteriorating.

He shifted his gaze to her. "How do you know so much? About Morkai? His plans? About what's happening to my body?"

She gave him a sad smile. "I've been here for a long time. I've seen much of what Morkai does, and you aren't the first soul I've encountered inside this crystal. You ask me why I kept the secrets I kept? Because I've seen this all before. Again and again. I've witnessed the dangers of knowing you're running out of time. The madness that ensues. The futility that follows."

He shuddered. "Has Morkai ever succeeded at fully possessing another body?" If so, then the body he knew as Morkai might not even be his original one.

"No," she said.

Teryn was relieved at that. Yet, as he settled into his body's frame, he realized something; just because Morkai hadn't ever successfully transferred his soul to another body didn't mean the previous souls had survived. More concerning than that was the question of why the sorcerer had ever considered possessing another body when he'd had his own. Before his death, he wouldn't have had any need for a new body. Had he trapped other souls simply as a precaution?

Or was there more Emylia had left unsaid?

37

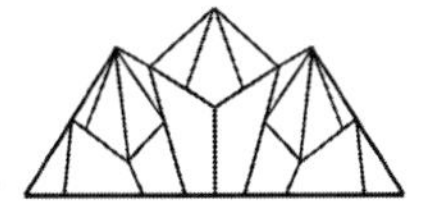

Cora left Teryn's door, her heart heavy with disappointment. Where was he? This was the second time she'd come to find him that day. A servant had insisted she'd seen him enter his room not long ago, but he hadn't answered when she'd called, just like the first time. He couldn't have been with the physician, for she'd gathered enough intel to learn that his wound had already been tended and hadn't been too deep in the first place. Even so, he may have been given something for the pain after his cut was treated. He could be sleeping. When she'd extended her senses, she'd felt *something* that suggested he was inside, but it was nowhere near as strong of an emotional impression as she normally received. But if he was sleeping, was he going to do so until morning? They didn't have time for that.

Cora was all too aware of the ticking clock.

She'd spent the previous hour talking with the council. Or being talked *at*, to be more accurate. No matter how she'd tried to argue in her brother's defense, the truth was that she and Dimetreus had already agreed to give Dimetreus' council the final say on the king's abdication. These terms had been necessary to forge the alliance with Verdian and would be written into the upcoming peace pact. Cora knew Verdian would refuse to sign it if she tried to go back on her word, and there was no talking the council out of their decision. Especially since the king had wholeheartedly agreed.

All that was left was for Cora to marry Teryn.

But she couldn't do that until they had a chance to talk. She couldn't enter their marriage with the secret of her curse.

She wandered through the halls of the keep, unsure where she intended to go. Returning to work in the tower would be too dangerous in her current state of mind; she knew she couldn't focus on clearing with her head so full of this newest burden. But as she passed the wing that led to her room, she found herself unwilling to turn. No, she couldn't sit idly in her bedroom either. She glanced out one of the windows in the hall and caught a glimpse of the early evening sun. There was still plenty of light left in the day. Perhaps she could sneak out after all...

She turned down a corridor that led to a portion of the keep that had yet to be refurbished, her mind set on entering the servants' passage—

She pulled up short as a figure, hunched at the base of the far wall, came into view. At first, she saw only a curtain of silver hair draped over dark blue silk, but as she took a step back, the woman's face lifted from her hands, revealing Queen Mareleau's tear-filled eyes. Startled, Mareleau bolted upright and pushed to her feet, swiping her cheeks with the backs of her hands.

Sorrow surged against Cora's shields, and she was too fatigued to block it. It swept over her, sinking her heart. Or perhaps it simply rested alongside a heart already sunk. Cora could tell Mareleau was embarrassed at being caught crying, so she dipped into a curtsy and turned to leave.

"I'm pregnant," Mareleau said to Cora's back.

Cora turned back around. "Oh?"

"My moon cycle is overdue. I'd lost track during my travels, but that and the emotions I've been having, not to mention the—" With a grimace, she put a palm to her stomach. "The nausea. I...I think you were right. I'm pregnant."

Cora frowned. Her voice sounded so empty. So resigned. "Did you not know, Majesty? I thought it was merely a well-kept secret, not something you were unaware of."

She crossed her arms and lifted her chin. "Who told you in the first place?"

"Lady Sera," Cora admitted, feeling no guilt about ousting her. "She mentioned instructions your mother had given your maids, insisting that you'd conceived on your wedding night, and that they were to forbid you from drinking wine."

"Mother." Mareleau bit out the word like a curse.

The queen's emotions surged against Cora's shields again, a medley of annoyance, guilt, and grief. At least this time Cora's nerves were more at ease, allowing her to connect with the elements and thicken her mental wards. Apparently focusing on someone else's problems were enough to distract her from her own. As much as Cora lacked any sort of friendly feeling toward Mareleau, maybe the distraction was what she needed. And from how the woman had stopped Cora from leaving with her statement that she was with child, perhaps Mareleau needed someone to talk to.

She supposed it wouldn't hurt to be that someone. For now. She took a few steps closer. "If this was something your mother already knew about, then why do you seem so surprised?"

Mareleau narrowed her pale blue eyes, lips pursed tight. Then, with a sigh, she spoke. "I lied."

Cora arched a brow. "About what?"

Mareleau averted her gaze and wandered to the nearest window. Lacing her fingers through her hair, she wove a messy braid as she stared with eyes that didn't seem to see anything beyond the window. "I lied about being with child so that my father would allow me to wed Larylis."

Silence stretched between them in the wake of her confession. Cora could hardly believe what she'd heard.

"No one else knows but Larylis—and Teryn too, now—so don't tell anyone." Her voice was nearly monotone, devoid of the barbed ire Cora expected from her.

Cora moved closer and lowered her voice. "Why are you telling me this?"

"I don't know. Maybe because my lie no longer matters. It's true now."

"And you aren't happy about that?"

Mareleau shook her head, lips curved down in a frown. "I'm not ready. I wanted more time with my husband. More time to...just be a woman in love. My parents kept me and Larylis apart for three years. Now that I have him, I just wanted it to be us for a while." She shifted her gaze to Cora. "You think I'm selfish, don't you?"

Cora could tell her that this new development neither added nor subtracted from her opinion of her. She expected the queen to be selfish. Cold. Haughty. That was all Mareleau had shown of herself so far.

Instead of saying that, she admitted something that hit far closer to home. "At least your position as queen is secure. You've managed to fulfill your singular duty."

"No," Mareleau said, whirling toward Cora with a clenched jaw. "I haven't fulfilled my duty, I've only taken the first step. The first of many exhausting steps, and one I wasn't even ready to take. Do you know what happens next? Next everyone will speculate whether it's a boy. When I birth my child, I'll be praised if it is. If not, I'll be consoled. Then I'll be expected to try again. Again. Again."

For the first time, Cora found herself able to relate to the queen. She too felt the burdens of such a role. But she wasn't ready to express their similarities. "It doesn't need to be a boy. You and I are both women and heirs."

Mareleau snorted a humorless laugh. "Are we though? Are we truly heirs? You know how they judge us. How they see us as less than a male heir."

Cora wasn't sure who Mareleau's use of *they* referred to. The people in general? Her parents? Her uncles? She supposed it didn't matter, for all were likely true.

Mareleau's tone turned sharper. "My father was so afraid of what my uncles would do to me as his heir. According to him, the only way I can keep my throne is if Larylis and I merge our kingdoms upon Father's death. Had I tried to rule as queen with only a consort of a lesser title at my side, my uncles would have fought to take my birthright. He went so far as to suggest they'd kill me for it."

Cora suppressed a shudder. The men she spoke of—Kevan and Ulrich—now had a stranglehold on Khero's council, on her very kingdom. She knew they were overly ambitious men, but were they truly as devious as Mareleau had said?

The queen seemed to be thinking along the same lines. "I wonder if he positioned them as your councilmen for this exact reason. To have them so preoccupied in your kingdom that I might have a fighting chance at keeping mine."

Cora bristled. Mother Goddess, was she right? She hadn't gotten the impression that Verdian thought too highly of his daughter, but what if he'd had more than one motive in appointing his brothers to Dimetreus' council?

Mareleau turned back toward the window. "Whatever the case, it isn't fair. Why must this be all we're worth as royal women? As nothing more than vehicles for our kingdoms' future kings. Why are we not kings ourselves?"

Cora nearly sagged with the weight of her words. With the truth of them. Yet Mareleau had something Cora didn't. "Being with child may not be something you're ready for, and it may be unfair that bearing heirs is expected of you, but what else can you do? At least with an heir, regardless of gender, you hold a weapon against your uncles' claims to your birthright."

Her lips lifted in a sneer. "Children shouldn't be weapons. Or pawns. Or...anything but what they are."

Cora's mouth snapped shut. Again, she found herself agreeing with her. Understanding her. But what was there to do about it? Mareleau was in a position where she could rebel against the norms. She was already queen. Her husband was king. An heir was on the way. How would she feel in Cora's position, if the choice and capability were taken away from her like it had been done to Cora?

Anger heated Cora's blood, and she let it rise. It felt better than feeling lost. Uncertain. Trapped. "You know what? You are selfish. No, children shouldn't be weapons or pawns, but here you are complaining when you could be grateful you can have children at all. Do you know what it's like for royal women with the opposite problem?"

Mareleau scoffed. "No, do you?"

Cora pursed her lips against her own rage, against the truth that scalded her tongue.

The queen suddenly straightened. She must have seen something in Cora's face, for her own paled. "Aveline...are you..."

"I was cursed." The words came out sharp yet trembling. "The sorcerer who once invaded my home—the man who forced my brother to wage war on Menah and Selay—cursed me to die childless."

The same silence that thickened the air after Mareleau's confession now settled in the aftermath of Cora's.

Mareleau's eyes went wide. "So you can't..."

Cora shook her head. "Not unless I can figure out how to break the curse. Which makes me an inadequate heir. And I don't know where you've been all day or what you've heard, but my brother is being forced to abdicate. I'm expected to marry Teryn first thing in the morning and take on the mantle of queen. A queen who may put an end to the bloodline she's expected to further. I haven't even told Teryn yet."

"Why not?"

"I'm afraid he'll value having children more than marrying me." Saying it out loud made her wince. Hearing her words somehow made her fear seem even more unfounded.

"Why would he care? It's not like his kingdom would suffer from lack of heir. Only yours."

Cora gave her a pointed look. "As king consort, Khero *will* be his kingdom."

"Well, fine, I suppose that's true. But all hope isn't lost. You have relatives, don't you?"

Cora shook her head. One of the first things she'd learned during her interrogations was that her nearest relatives—most of whom had served her brother at Ridine before Cora was forced to flee the castle—had died, leaving none alive to corroborate Cora's story. It hadn't been hard to glean why none remained living. "Morkai ensured all contenders to the throne were eliminated."

Mareleau furrowed her brow. "Oh. Well...that doesn't matter either. With your marriage to Teryn, you'll have new family ties. Teryn and Larylis have younger brothers."

Cora had never considered such an option, but appointing the role of heir to the nearest male relative wasn't unheard of.

Mareleau spoke again. "Where do you think my father got his crown? He wasn't born a Harvallis. He wasn't even a prince, which is why my uncles are only lords, despite having a king for a brother. My father was simply the eldest living male blood relative of the former King of Selay. I know a distant relative doesn't have the strongest claim, not nearly as strong as a child. And maybe you can't further the Caelan bloodline, but do you honestly care about bloodline politics?"

Cora's answer came easily. "No, I only care about the safety of my kingdom."

"Then it's settled. You'll tell Teryn about the curse, you'll marry, you'll appoint an heir, and once your reign is strong, you'll crush every last hope my uncles have at gaining more power than they deserve. Meanwhile, I'll do the same from my kingdom."

Cracks began to form in the heavy shroud of Cora's fears. For the first time in days, she felt hope. Hope that remained even if she couldn't break her curse. To think she had Mareleau to thank for such a shift in perspective.

She couldn't stop her mouth from lifting at the corners. "I didn't know you were such an optimist, Your Majesty."

Mareleau lifted her chin. "Apparently all it took to improve my mood was to hear about the dire hand you've been dealt."

Cora rolled her eyes. "I'm glad my plight has brought you such amusement."

The queen stepped closer, her haughty composure back in place. "You know, you aren't horrible. I don't hate you."

"And you are tolerable yourself," Cora said dryly. Then she softened her tone. "I'm glad you don't think children should be pawns. You'll make...an okay mother."

Mareleau smiled back at her. It was probably the first smile she'd ever received from the queen. But her face crumpled so suddenly, Cora hardly knew what was happening. Not until Mareleau did the absolute last thing Cora expected her to do...

She threw her arms around Cora...

And hugged her.

Mareleau was so much taller than Cora that she found her face nearly buried in the other woman's bosom. Still, she was too shocked to move.

The queen heaved with sobs. "I'm sorry," she said, voice strangled by hiccups. "I'm just really...emotional lately and I can't control it. I don't even like hugs."

"Neither do I," Cora muttered. And yet neither broke away. Instead, they stood a little closer, held each other a little tighter. Maybe they both needed an embrace with all they were going through, and they were simply tolerating the comfort of the last person they wanted it from. Or maybe it was more that they'd found an anchor in the other. A mirror. For in this world of cruel games and royal burdens, Cora and Mareleau were perhaps the two people who understood each other the most.

38

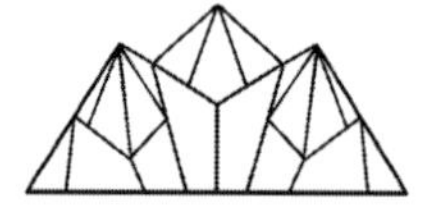

This time, Teryn didn't need all night to make progress. The first hour he lay in the space of his body, he managed to flinch every one of his fingers on both hands. The second hour, he moved his left leg. That had woken Morkai up enough that he'd rolled over and shifted Teryn's body on its side, but Teryn wasn't daunted. Instead, he adjusted his ethera to fit the proper bounds, aligning his hands, feet, torso, shoulders, and face, filling his form the way his soul was meant to.

Now it was time to work on the task he'd come to consider his highest priority: forming speech.

He breathed deeply, feeling his lungs expand, the air moving through his nostrils. His heart beat a steady rhythm while his pulse sang with his blood. He lost touch with the passing of time, focusing instead on the perfect harmony between his ethera and vitale. The singular connection that ensured he was—undoubtedly—still alive. That this body was still his.

Once he was fully settled into this awareness, he poured all his focus into repeating the feat he'd only barely accomplished last time. Shifting the course of his breath, he exhaled out of his mouth. His lips parted to release the warm air, and he breathed again. As the air left his lungs, he felt it tingle against the sides of his throat, the roof of his mouth. A hum of energy rose around him, surging through his blood, merging his body and ethera. The energy was as tangible as the vibrations from a string quartet, a beautiful melody that elucidated Teryn's control. His capabilities. Now all he needed to do was shape that energy into movement and sound.

Teryn.

His name wove through this melody and stitched itself into his consciousness. He didn't let it break his concentration, even as he searched his mind to identify the voice. Was Emylia talking to him? No, she'd returned to the bounds of the crystal and had left him to practice alone. Besides, this voice filled him with warmth. With purpose.

It was Cora.

At the door again.

"Teryn, I know it's the middle of the night but...but that also means you're in there. I know you are."

I am, he thought, but it wasn't enough to think it. He had to speak it.

A new sense of urgency—of need—filled him. Cora was right there, on the other side of his bedroom door. All he had to do was tell her.

"I'm not leaving until you open this door. I'll get Master Arther to unlock it if you won't do so yourself."

Teryn directed his attention to the inside of his mouth, the placement of his tongue. Slowly, his tongue lifted, the back of it connecting with flesh at the roof of his mouth, and his lips formed an *O* shape.

"I don't even know how badly you were hurt." Her voice

came out with a quaver, a sound that nearly cleaved Teryn's heart in two. But instead of breaking, he used it as fuel, gathering his pain, his desperation, and sending it out in a surge of energy through his vocal cords.

"Please. I *need* you right now."

"Cora!" The word left Teryn's mouth in a shout. A bit uneven, perhaps, but it was clear.

He'd done it.

But in that same moment, Teryn's body bolted out of bed, and Teryn was no longer in control of it. No matter how he tried not to feel disappointed after such a success—even one so short-lived—it was impossible not to. Especially when Morkai's eyes slid to the door.

"Teryn, I heard you," came Cora's voice. It was oddly more muted now that he was out of his meditation. Somehow, she had sounded so much closer before. Like she'd been speaking directly to his soul. "Please let me in."

Morkai glanced around the room, eyes wild, then stormed over to the door. He gripped the handle...but halted. Doubling back, he retrieved a discarded black jacket from the foot of the bed and hastily shoved his arms through it. He secured the jacket's buttons as well as the laces of his ruffled shirt collar, hiding not only the thin cut at the base of his throat but any sign of the crystal he wore. Only then did Morkai return to the door and fling it open.

Teryn finally moved from the bed. A sense of loss fell over him. In the wake of having regained temporary control of his body, being nothing more than his ethera felt wrong. Broken. How had he forgotten everything he'd been missing as a body?

Those worries fled his mind as soon as he saw Cora's face. She blinked up at Morkai from the doorway, dressed in only a white chemise draped in a floor-length velvet robe of violet and gold. Her expression alternated between relief and anger.

The latter gained dominance over her features. "Where have you been? I looked for you all day. Have you any clue how many times I've knocked on your door? You didn't attend dinner. You forbade servants from entering—"

"I was resting," Morkai said, voice hoarse from sleep but still so much like Teryn's own.

"From your injuries?" Cora's eyes widened as they searched his face. Teryn knew what she saw—the dark circles, his gaunt cheeks. Her expression turned to one of panic. "Teryn, are you all right?"

"I'm fine."

She shook her head. "No, you look...unwell." Stepping in close, she lifted a hand to his cheek—

Morkai caught her wrist so abruptly, Cora froze. Teryn, however, found himself suddenly at Cora's side. Whether he'd run, floated, or simply transported his ethera from one space to another, he knew not. All he knew was the rage that coursed through him at the sight of Morkai's fingers clenched around her wrist like that. He hated that he could do nothing. That he could only watch, only feel his heart race as fear raked claws through him.

Morkai's expression hardened with startled anger, but it lasted only a split second. In the next moment, the look was gone. Had Cora noticed it at all? Her eyes were locked on Morkai's fingers.

With a too-convincing smile, Morkai loosened his grip and brought the back of her hand to his lips. After a brief kiss, he dropped her wrist and took a subtle step back. "I told you I'm fine. Please don't worry about me. We have much bigger things to face in the morning."

Cora narrowed her eyes, her hand still lifted halfway

between them. Then she took a deep breath and brushed past him into the room. The breeze she carried vibrated against the edges of Teryn's ethera. She planted herself in the middle of the room, facing away from him. Crossing her arms, she said, "That's what I'm here for. We need to talk."

Morkai's jaw tensed as he glared at her back. Then, with an aggrieved sigh, he closed the door with more force than necessary.

Cora jumped at the sound and whirled toward him. As soon as her eyes landed on his face, Morkai's smile returned.

Teryn's incorporeal form rippled with tension.

"Breathe, Teryn." Emylia appeared at his side. It was the first time he'd seen her since she'd left him to practice. "He won't hurt her. He needs her alive, remember? You need to stay calm."

Teryn couldn't bring himself to reply. Instead, he focused on keeping his breaths steady, his awareness of his vitale strong. Now that he understood the repercussions of overtaxing his vitale, it was more important than ever to take her reminders to heart.

Morkai closed some of the distance between himself and Cora but left ample space, hands clasped behind his back. "I've already agreed to everything the council has asked of me. You don't need to worry. We'll marry in the morning. The peace pact is safe, as is your kingdom."

Cora's brows lowered. "That's not what I mean. There's something else I need to tell you."

"Whatever it is, it can wait," he said, his tone so gentle it made a dismissive mockery of Cora's clearly flustered state.

Her cheeks flushed with restrained anger. "No, it can't. This is important."

"What could be more important than the safety of your kingdom? Is this about *us*? Don't you remember the promise

I made? I won't go back on my word. I'll woo you as I said I would. Court you as you deserve. Our marriage contract need not matter when it comes to our hearts. We'll take things slow—"

"I can't have children." The words burst from Cora's lips in an angry shout.

The only movement Morkai made was a mild narrowing of his eyes.

Teryn, on the other hand, felt as if he were being ripped to shreds. Less from the words she'd said and more from the pain behind them.

"That's all right," Morkai said, voice soft. "Truly."

"It's not all right." Tears welled in Cora's eyes, and her voice carried a tremor. "Morkai placed a curse on me. He bound my fate to Queen Linette's using our blood, ensuring I'd die childless like she did."

Morkai's face fell with false sympathy. He took a step forward, and Cora's shoulders sagged. She lifted her hands from her sides as if she expected him to embrace her.

But he didn't. He simply...stopped. His hands remained clasped behind his back.

Teryn's eyes settled on Cora, giving her the attention his body couldn't. Was this what she'd been struggling with the night he'd found her crying in the tower? This...this curse? Grief and rage tore through him. His breaths grew sharp and shallow, threatening him with a wave of panic, but he refused to lose his connection to his vitale.

Morkai tilted his head slightly to the side. "That's what you found so pressing to say? Were you worried I'd reject you?"

"It involves you. It affects the future of my kingdom."

He stepped closer again, slower this time. Still, he made no move to touch her.

She *had* to know this wasn't him. That Teryn would never act so coldly. Would never withhold affection when she so clearly wanted it. *Needed* it.

"There's nothing to worry about, Aveline. I'm here for you. We'll work through this later. Naming an heir isn't something we need to concern ourselves with tonight. Let us get some sleep. Tomorrow is an important day for us." Morkai extended his hand toward the door.

Cora remained rooted in place. Her eyes locked on his face. "Why did you call me Aveline?"

Morkai's expression went blank, but he quickly donned an easy smile. "You're going to be queen. It's time I get used to calling you by your true name."

Fingers curled into fists, Cora strode up to him. Morkai's breath hitched as he took a step back, but Cora closed that space too. Despite their height difference, Cora kept her eyes on his. "What's really going on? This isn't you."

Teryn's heart raced. *No, Cora. It isn't me. Please see that. Please see the truth.*

A tic formed at the corners of Morkai's jaw, but he said nothing.

"You're acting strange," Cora said. "What are you hiding? What is happening to you?"

"Nothing," Morkai said, finally stepping in to fill the space between them. Then, after an agonizing beat of hesitation, he lifted his hands and settled them on Cora's shoulders. It would appear like a gesture of comfort if it wasn't for how stiff Morkai was, as if he were waiting, dreading, poised for the inevitable...

Teryn waited too, waited for Cora to know, to realize, to *feel* what was missing...

She shook her head, lips curving into a frown. "I can't read you."

Morkai's fingers curled ever so slightly on her shoulders. "Why are you trying to read me?"

"Because something isn't right. I can feel that much, but I...I can't feel *you*. Not even when we're close. Not even when you touch me. It's like...it's like you're not really here."

Teryn wanted to believe this was a good thing. Cora could tell something was wrong. But her confession meant Morkai knew that touching her gave her no additional insight. Revealed none of the secrets he was hiding.

Dread wound deep inside Teryn.

Morkai's smile widened with a note of triumph. His posture relaxed as he smoothed out his hands and began running them down her shoulders. "I'm sorry things aren't going the way you hoped. I know we were supposed to have a full year together—"

"That's not it."

"Then what is it? What's wrong?"

"This still doesn't...feel right. Something between us has changed, and I don't understand what it is."

"What can I do to prove everything is going to be all right?"

She stared at him, eyes drifting over his face as if desperate to read the truth written over it. Then her gaze stilled, deepened, locked on Morkai's eyes. Her expression hardened. Lifting her chin, she said, "Kiss me."

Teryn's heart rioted in his chest. *No.*

She stepped in closer, and this time Morkai didn't try to step away. "Kiss me like you did under the tree. Kiss me like you want to be my husband."

Teryn's eyes darted between Cora and Morkai, blood boiling as he saw the smirk twisting Morkai's face, the tilt of his head as he began to lower it toward her uptilted chin. Teryn felt a strange pull, as strong as Cora's voice had been both times he'd heard it on the other side of the bedroom door. This time it was her body, the warmth of her presence calling to his soul, drawing him forward on an invisible tether that seemed to grow straight from the center of his chest. Without another thought, he gave in to the pull and settled into the space of his body.

"Teryn, no!" Emylia's warning barely made it past his awareness, for in the next moment, he felt his flesh against the sleeves of Cora's velvet robe, breathed in the familiar scent of her hair, her skin, felt her with his body, his mind, and his ethera. There was no part of him that wasn't aware of her. So when her lips crushed into his, it was *he* who kissed back. *He* who folded into the embrace of the woman he loved.

39

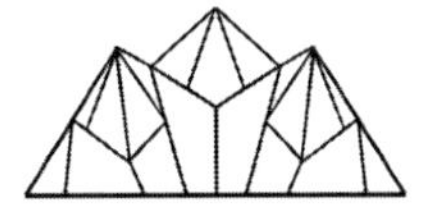

As soon as their lips met, Cora felt a rush of emotion. She nearly sobbed with relief as it flooded in. Opening her senses and dropping her shields, she welcomed more of the energy that was *his*. His affection. His attraction. His emotion. He'd been acting so strange since the night in the tower, his energy muted and nearly impossible to read. But now it wrapped around her, infusing their kiss with a silent promise. She pressed into him, desperate to erase every inch of space that he'd so stubbornly tried to maintain with her these last couple of days. The way he held her now, one hand cradling the back of her head, the other clutching her body tight against him, stood in contrast to the cold, formal man he'd become. She wound her arms around his neck, wishing he'd lift her off her feet already—

He stumbled back a step, breaking their kiss. She blinked up at him and found his eyes were closed, expression pained. Unlacing her hands from behind his neck, she palmed his cheek. Lightly, she ran her thumb just under the nearly healed cut on his cheekbone. "Teryn, what's wrong?"

"I don't have much time," he said, voice strained. "He's fighting me."

Her thumb stilled. "Who's fighting you?"

His body began to shake. A sheen of sweat coated his forehead. "Morkai," he said through chattering teeth.

Terror ripped through her, muting her sense of his emotions. Or were they growing muted of their own accord? "Teryn, what's happening? I don't understand."

His shoulders heaved with a shudder so violent, Cora was forced to release him. "No," he ground out, eyes still closed. "Touch me again. Keep your hands somewhere on me. I can hold on a little longer if I can feel you. Hear you. Just...say my name."

"Teryn," Cora said, the word laced with panic. She reached for his hand, gripping it as tightly as she dared.

His tremors subsided enough for him to open his eyes. "Morkai has taken over my body using the crystal."

"What do you mean, he's taken over your body? And what crystal?"

He plunged his free hand beneath the collar of his jacket and lifted a leather cord from around his neck. As he withdrew it fully, Cora saw a large amber crystal tied to the end. Memories tugged at the edges of her mind, so potent they nearly overwhelmed her.

The crystal.

The gem that once topped Morkai's cane.

The stone she took from the battlefield.

The object she'd tried—and failed—to clear. To break. To destroy.

Until she was trapped...in a realm of blinding white light...

Before she could remember anything more, he thrust the stone into her hand, closing her fingers around it.

"Take this, but don't look at it. Just...just go now. Keep

the crystal in mind and write this all down before it makes you forget. It's been enchanted to be as indestructible as a unicorn horn. You must find a way to break it, but don't let it come within sixteen inches of my body—" His voice cut off in an agonized shout. "Gods, he's fighting me. I can't hold him off much longer."

Cora's heart slammed against her ribs as she tried to take in everything he was saying. It was almost too much to comprehend. And what about Teryn? How the hell had Morkai taken over his body? It didn't make sense. Nothing made sense. And yet she felt the horrible truth of it. Felt the dreadful possibilities hidden in the palm of her hand where the crystal pulsed with that strange energy.

"You have to go," Teryn said, his voice barely above a whisper. He closed his eyes again and stumbled forward.

Her eyes went wide as they fell on a lock of silver hair beside his temple. No, both sides were now shot with a thick streak of white. "Teryn, your hair, it's..."

He lifted his face, teeth bared in a grimace.

Cora's stomach bottomed out as a crimson stream trickled from his nose. "Take this," he said, squeezing his hand around hers and reminding her of the crystal once more. "Run. Write everything down. Find a way to break the stone as soon as you can."

"I can't leave you like this."

His knees buckled, and he slid to the floor. "It's all right. You can. You must. Just go, and know that I—"

He winced again and tugged his hands from around hers, severing their physical connection. "Run."

That was the last thing she heard before his body went motionless, slumped to the side on the floor.

Everything inside her wanted to go to him, to help him, to ensure he was still alive.

But his words rang through her head, echoed by the pulsing warning that blared from her gut. She had to do what he'd said. She had to run.

Biting back an anguished cry, she ran for the door and tugged it open—

The door slammed shut just as fast. She froze, eyes locked on the hand pressed against the door, fingers splayed out, arm trembling either from weakness or rage. A lump rose in her throat, and the back of her neck prickled with fear. She felt the heat of the body caging her in from behind more than she felt any emotional presence. She couldn't turn around. Refused to. There was no way she could bring herself to look into the eyes of the man she loved and find Morkai's hatred—or even his false affection—looking back at her.

"Do you want him to die?" The voice was too close, brushing against the shell of her ear. Worse, it was Teryn's voice. His tone. Yet there was something wrong with it. Something she hadn't heard when the sorcerer had been acting under pretense. He must know now that there was no use pretending anymore.

When she made no reply, Morkai spoke again. "Teryn may think he's found a brilliant plan in getting you to take the crystal away from his body. Distance will certainly tear my soul from Teryn's body and make it impossible for me to control it. But what the prince doesn't understand is that the same goes for him. If I can't reenter Teryn's body due to physical distance, neither can he. Without a soul, the body will die. Teryn will have nothing to come back to even if you manage to break the crystal."

Cora's lungs constricted as she took in this new information. What was she supposed to do? Fight him off? Take the crystal and run, killing Teryn in the process? No answers came, only growing anxiety. She curled her hand so tightly around the crystal, it sent pain radiating up her arm.

Cora! Valorre's voice cut through her fear. *Danger. You're in danger.*

Yes, she sent back, unable to form anything more complex than that.

"Besides," Morkai said, voice deepening as he pressed in closer behind her, "the crystal is unbreakable. You haven't managed to sever a single one of the enchantments I've placed on the crystal, despite your best efforts. You will forget about the crystal as soon as your mind slips down a new train of thought. And when you next lay your eyes on it, it will take your soul instead."

Run away, Valorre said. *Please come here. Now.*

An image shot through her mind, of the castle wall, blanketed in shadows and a sliver of moonlight. Valorre was showing her where he was, just outside the hidden crevice on the other side of the wall.

So badly she wanted to simply *be* there. Without having to fight Morkai off. Without having to rely on running faster than him. Was there anything she could do to get through the wall before Morkai could catch her?

Her palms tingled in answer, not from the crystal she held, but from power surging from her chest, down her arms, and into her hands. It radiated down her legs, her feet. It was soft yet strong, yielding yet powerful.

Turn inward, her magic told her. It was the same feeling she'd gotten when she'd hidden herself and Teryn under the tree not long ago. Then again when she was locked in the dungeon, her magic smothered by her own resentment. And finally, she'd felt it on the battlefield when she'd been trapped under the horse.

Calm moved through her, stilling her thoughts. She

focused on the strength of the stone floor beneath her feet, the air that flooded her nostrils, the warmth of the blood rushing through her veins.

"What will it be, Aveline? If you don't play nice, I will make you. I've gone easy on you long enough. Do you recall when I offered you half my heart? I no longer have half to give, and I didn't come this far just to be stopped by you again."

She barely heard him. Barely let herself focus on anything but the elements moving through her, wrapping around her. On the Art that radiated through every inch of her body. Its presence was louder than Morkai's. Stronger.

But what was it asking her to do?

Hide, it had said the first time.

Forgive, it had urged the second.

Stop fighting, it had told her the third. Her mind settled there, on the battlefield at Centerpointe Rock. She recalled how her Art had somehow transported her through space, past physical matter and across a short distance in the blink of an eye. She needed that now. Needed to get to Valorre. To safety.

But how could she repeat that feat? She'd tried to replicate it a few times since that singular incident, but each attempt had been futile. She knew it had to be some form of astral travel, the rare gift witches only talked about but never performed. She knew no one who could do more than astral project—the invisible form of the Art that allowed one to project their souls during meditative states—and it wasn't something she'd ever trained in. So how had she traveled the once?

Feel, her magic told her.

She remembered then.

Emotion had driven her at Centerpointe Rock. She'd

moved because she'd had to. Because Teryn's life had been at stake. And then there'd been that time in the council room, where anger had made her feel certain she could take a single step and find herself on the other side of the table, confronting Lord Kevan in all her fiery rage. She'd stopped herself then, had written it off as simply a whim.

But she knew now it hadn't been. It had been her Art.

Morkai gripped her shoulders and whirled her around to face him. "The longer you keep that crystal from me, the more it hurts Teryn's body. The more it ages him. Kills him."

She shuddered but refused to look him in the eye, refused to lose focus. Valorre called out to her again and she latched onto his presence, to his view of the castle wall, to the smell of the earth, to the sound of his hooves beating an anxious rhythm on the forest floor.

"Give me the crystal or I'll take it from you." His hand covered hers. From how feebly he struggled to pry her fingers from around the crystal, she could tell his strength was waning.

If she wanted, she could wrest it from him. She could take the crystal far away, just like Teryn had asked.

And kill him in the process.

Or...

Calm settled over her heart, and she knew there was only one thing she was willing to do.

With a slow exhale, she closed her eyes, fully immersing herself into her connection with Valorre. She could almost feel the earth give way beneath her feet, as if she were standing beside him, could almost sense the mild summer breeze dancing through her hair.

Yes.

She felt it.

Felt everything about the location as if she were already there.

Tugging her hands from Morkai's, she opened her palm, dropped the crystal to the ground, and took a wide step back. Soft earth cradled her heels, rooting her upon moss and soil.

When she opened her eyes, she found herself outside the castle wall, a startled Valorre blinking back at her.

40

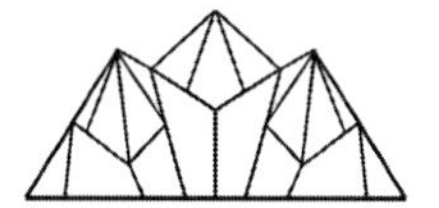

For hours they rode, stopping only when they were far enough away from the castle that Cora felt safe. She didn't think she'd been followed, but she wanted to place distance between herself and the castle nonetheless. The night was still dark when she finally slid down from Valorre's back. She groaned with relief, her legs aching from riding bareback after having spent so much of her recent time indoors. Valorre nudged her shoulder with his muzzle in a comforting gesture, and the sympathy she felt from him nearly brought a sob from her throat. But she refused to cry. She didn't have time to break down, no matter how deep her fatigue.

The sound of running water snagged her attention. A small stream trickled over a narrow rock bed, a soothing melody in contrast to Cora's frantic heartbeat. She crouched before it and gathered a handful of water in her palms. The cool liquid chilled her fingertips and tingled her skin, which served to sharpen her mind. After taking a few sips, she splashed some on her face. It was so cold it was almost painful, but at least it made her feel more awake. More capable of sorting through what had happened. What she'd learned.

Morkai was somehow alive.

In Teryn's body.

She didn't understand how Morkai had taken over Teryn's body, nor did she remember what she'd left behind that had made it possible. She knew there was...something. Some item that escaped her memory the more she tried to think about it. Whatever the case, she understood enough about the situation to guess Morkai had likely regained his strength after Cora left. He could be looking for her. Tracking her.

Which meant she needed a plan. Now.

A familiar presence entered her awareness, and thankfully it wasn't a threatening one. Glancing up, she found a falcon-shaped silhouette circling overhead.

She followed us from the castle, Valorre said, coming up beside her. He lowered his muzzle to drink from the stream while Berol flew down and landed on a nearby rock. Her wings were splayed with agitation, much like they'd been when she'd barged into the tower room with Larylis' letter—

The letter!

After everything that had happened since yesterday, she'd forgotten Larylis' missive. It remained where she'd left it last, in her apron pocket. She remembered the words, though, his inquiry over Teryn's well-being after Berol had brought him a scrap of his shirt.

Her eyes darted to Berol. "You knew it wasn't him, didn't you?"

She let out a sharp, keening cry.

Cora regretted that she couldn't send a letter back. Not that she could fully explain what had happened. What could she even say? *Your brother has been possessed by a sorcerer, but I cannot tell you how or why because some strange magic has made me forget. I promise I'm not crazy. Don't come to Ridine, or your own brother will probably kill you—*

Mother Goddess.

The signing of the peace pact.

Larylis *was* going to Ridine. In fact, he might already be on his way. Verdian too. In a matter of days, Morkai was going to have every monarch who stood in his way in one location. They were falling right into his trap.

She had to warn Larylis.

Cora rose to her feet and tore a scrap of fabric off the bottom of her chemise. Then she scoured the moonlit ground nearby, procuring a thin stick. Finally, she hastily dug beneath the underbrush, turning fresh soil. Gathering a handful of water from the stream, she made a thick paste. Overall, her writing materials were crude at best, but she had no other option. And while blood would serve as better ink than mud, she didn't dare use something of such value. Should Morkai get hold of this, he could use her blood against her.

With trembling hands, she dipped the tip of the stick in the dark paste and brought it to the fabric. She froze, still stuck with the same dilemma regarding what she could say. There was no way she could convey the dangers lurking at Ridine, especially with such limited accommodations. No matter what she said, she couldn't caution him from going to Ridine. His wife was there. She didn't know Larylis well, but if he was anything like Teryn, he'd make haste to reach Mareleau, regardless of the risk to himself.

Instead, she'd have to give him a warning that would allow him to make his own assessment.

Danger at Ridine. Teryn isn't Teryn. Trust no one.

—Cora

It probably wouldn't be enough, but it might at least put Larylis on guard. If anyone could see through Morkai's ruse, it would be Teryn's brother.

After letting the fabric dry for as long as she could stand being idle, she rolled it up and handed it to Berol. Only then did she ponder whether the falcon would heed her directions. Teryn had told her about the creature's intelligence in listening to his directions, but would she understand Cora?

It didn't matter. She had to try.

"To Larylis," she said, handing the fabric to the falcon. Berol gathered it in her talons and flew off at once. Cora watched her until she was swallowed by shadows, hoping beyond hope her letter would serve its purpose.

Warn Larylis.

Maybe save Teryn.

Her chest tightened at the thought, and her mind blared with the weight of her panicked realization.

I left Teryn behind.

Mother Goddess, I left *him.*

Guilt flooded her, even though she knew she'd had a reason. Yet whatever that reason had been was tangled up in the very thing she kept forgetting. What was that *thing*? Hadn't Teryn asked her to do something with it when he'd spoken to her as himself? And hadn't Morkai threatened Teryn's fate over that same nameless, shapeless, forgotten object?

She bit back a cry as she recalled the blood trailing from Teryn's nose, the streaks of white hair at his temples. It reminded her too much of what had happened to Dimetreus, how he'd aged under Morkai's control. Mother Goddess! She'd left her brother too. And Mareleau. None of them knew...

Cora cursed under her breath, truth dawning.

Her brother *did* know. He'd just suffered too much in his past to trust his own mind. He'd described his interaction with the man he'd thought was Teryn as a hallucination. He'd turned over his crown, his kingdom, all because of *him*. The sorcerer who'd already taken so much from Dimetreus. From Cora.

How much more would he take? How much time did she have?

No answers came, only a hollow dread.

She knew one thing for certain. Whatever Morkai ultimately wanted, it involved dark magic. Which meant there was only one place she could go for help.

"I have to find the Forest People," she said.

Valorre lifted his head from the stream. *Oh, I do like them. They revere me, as they should. As all people should.*

A small smile curled her lips, but it sank into a frown. "How can I face them like this? The last time I sought them out, I brought dark tidings and drew them into a war they wanted nothing to do with. Here I am, once again coming for help."

They are family, Valorre said. *They will understand.*

Family. The word echoed in Cora's mind, warming her chest.

He was right. While she knew there were many who resented her for having hidden her royal identity, there were some who loved her. Salinda. Maiya. Even High Elder Nalia had supported her. No matter how guilty she felt for having chosen her royal family over the Forest People, they'd understand, wouldn't they? They couldn't have expected her to come back with them after the battle at Centerpointe Rock. They'd made it clear Cora could never be a permanent resident amongst the commune again. Her royal identity went against one of their most essential rules—never get involved with royal matters.

But this matter with Morkai was one of magic. The fact that he'd defied death was no small concern. If he was alive in any form, the Arts—both fae magic and witch magic alike —were once again in danger.

Cold certainty stilled her worries. She had to go to them. Now her concern was how. The Forest People would have moved camps just before Litha. That was weeks ago. They could be anywhere now...

No, not anywhere. While the commune rarely ever made camp in the same area twice, they moved according to the fairest weather. In the summer, they chose areas with cooler temperatures, ample shade, and nearby sources of water that weren't at risk of drying out. They'd be near the mountains then. Close to a large river. But that still left too wide a net to cast.

She could try to track them from their previous camp, but that would take too long. She couldn't leave Teryn like that. Couldn't leave her kingdom at Morkai's mercy. She needed to find them *now*.

A ripple of energy ran through her forearms, warming her palms.

"I can astral travel," she whispered. The confession sent a shudder through her. She could no longer pretend the first time had been a fluke. Could no longer make up excuses for having misinterpreted what had happened at Centerpointe Rock.

The thing you did when you startled me out of nowhere,

Valorre said.

"Yes, but..."

How could she use that now, when she hadn't a clue where her destination was? Could she travel...to a person? Could she bring Valorre?

When she'd freed herself from under the horse on the battlefield, she'd traveled with everything that had been on her person, everything she'd carried. But not the dead horse. So proximity hadn't been a factor. Was it simply a matter of intent? The horse's body had been something she'd needed to be freed from, a location she'd wanted to leave.

Could she travel with Valorre by touch? Or perhaps through their mental connection?

Valorre left the stream and approached her. Lowering his head in an invitation for her to mount him, he said, *We can try*.

Steeling her resolve, she climbed back onto Valorre's back. A wave of exhaustion crested through her, but she breathed it away. She didn't have time to sleep. She hardly had time to think.

Closing her eyes, she shifted her attention to the elements around her, strengthening her connection to them. She breathed in the mild night air, filling her lungs with the scent of leaves and soil. Pressing her palms to Valorre's shoulders, she let her awareness radiate down his smooth hide, past his legs and hooves to the earth he stood upon. Through him, she rooted her energy to the earth. Next, she shifted her attention to the melodic trickle of the stream. Then tilted her face toward the sky to feel the light of the moon. The warmth of summer infusing the night.

Air. Earth. Water. Fire.

On a deep exhale, she filled her mind with thoughts of

Salinda, the woman who'd treated Cora as a daughter. She saw her brown skin, her long black hair, her dark eyes that crinkled at the corners when she smiled. She pictured the slight angle at the tip of her ears, marking her as a Faeryn descendent. Then she imagined the triple moon sigil that marked the tip of her chin, the ink that adorned her neck in complex geometric patterns, the *insigmora* that trailed over every inch of her arms down to her palms.

Cora's own *insigmora* seemed to hum in response, warming her blood, fueling her with the thrum that was her magic. She extended her senses and tried to *feel* for Salinda's presence. Her nearness. Her location.

She got nothing back.

Nothing.

Emotion, she reminded herself. *I need emotion to travel.*

She imagined Maiya next, the girl she loved as dearly as a sister. Her chest felt warm, but her heart felt so clouded with dread. Fear. Fatigue. Her emotions refused to rise past it.

No, I must feel. I must.

She thought of how the Forest People had cared for her. How they'd taken her in and taught her about the Arts. How they'd helped her recognize her clairsentience. Nurture it. Hone it.

Her heart began to lift.

They were my family, she said to herself. *My family. My home.*

Her emotions grew lighter. Richer. More potent.

She shifted her awareness to Valorre, welcoming his mind to connect with hers.

My family. My home. She said it again and again like a mantra, seeking some inkling that could guide her toward the location she sought.

My family. My home.

An invisible tug drew her forward, cleaving through her emotions. She followed it with her mind. Her heart—

My home. The words came not from her mind but Valorre's. Or was it simply a matter of their minds being connected?

I had another home before this.

This time, she couldn't decipher where the thought came from, but the sense of awe that accompanied it was so strong that it pulled her deeper into her emotions, strengthening that tug, that pull toward a place. A vision filled her mind now, a meadow of lush green grass in the most vibrant shade of emerald. Dewdrops glittered rainbow light upon every blade. Flowers in the most spectacular array of color shifted in a playful breeze, creating a susurration more melodic than any stream, any instrument.

It was...breathtaking. Unlike any place Cora had ever been. Was this where the Forest People were now?

Home. The word pulsed through her mind and filled her heart with longing. Another pull. Another tug forward. Everything inside her said to move. To step. To enter this new location.

Valorre shifted beneath her.

He took a step forward.

A flare of warm light kissed the other side of Cora's eyelids. Blinking them open, she greeted daylight. Her mind stumbled under the haze of her meditation, but as her senses sharpened, she realized she and Valorre were in the very meadow she'd seen in her mind. It was even more vibrant than she'd imagined, more stunning.

She dismounted from Valorre's back and fully took in their surroundings. The meadow was surrounded by towering willows, their waterfall leaves swaying in the warm breeze. Yet she saw no tent, not even in the distance. Found no sign that the Forest People were nearby.

Something pulsed inside her. A warning that this was very, very wrong.

Only now did the sudden daylight concern her. No matter where in Khero the Forest People had gone, there should have been no change in time. No hour difference. No way to account for having stepped from night to day. Unless...

Mother Goddess...did she move through time as well as space?

No, that wasn't part of astral travel. Not even astral projection could bypass the present.

I'm sorry.

She frowned, turning back toward Valorre. His muscles quivered, ears twitching in agitation. "What are you sorry for? I...I'm the one who messed this up—"

No. This was my fault. My fault.

Her blood chilled. "What do you mean?"

You thought of home, but I remembered. Remembered my first home.

She swallowed hard. "Are you saying we traveled to *your* home? The place you came from?"

Yes. This...this isn't good for you. I remember now.

Panic laced up Cora's throat. Wherever they were, it was far enough from Khero that it was daytime instead of night. Still, if she brought them here, she could bring them back.

She grabbed hold of his mane in preparation to mount again. "What kingdom are we in? What continent?"

A rush of sound erupted behind her. Cora startled and turned toward it in time to see an enormous sphere of swirling color perched at the edge of the meadow. Three figures strolled out of it as if it were a doorway. As soon as the three were fully outside the strange vortex, it disappeared, leaving Cora to stare at the strangers.

They appeared to be male, and beautiful at that. The one at the center had golden-blond hair the color of honey, fair skin, and piercing blue eyes. The second was shorter than the first, of wide build, and had curly hair in a fiery copper hue. The third was the tallest of the three with umber skin and long black hair laced with gold and silver thread that sparkled in the sunlight. All wore silk britches and an elegant knee-length robe belted with a wide sash. The style was unlike anything she'd seen of current fashions in *any* region. But that wasn't nearly as surprising as the angled tips of their ears. It wasn't a subtle angle either. Not an almost-imperceptible hint like some of the Forest People had. These ears came to a distinct and obvious point.

She couldn't pull her eyes from the three men. Their towering height, their unearthly beauty, their regal style...it was straight from a faerytale. And there was only one word she could think of to suit them.

Elvyn.

An ancient race of High Fae known to be extinct, even more so than the Faeryn.

Cora's heart slammed against her ribs as an impossible truth began to dawn.

We're not in your world at all anymore, Valorre said, finally answering the question he'd left hanging between them. *We're in my world. The fae realm. El'Ara.*

Cora sensed he was keeping himself from saying more. His silence didn't matter; the anger in the three Elvyn figures' eyes was universal enough for her to understand what he'd left unsaid.

She was not supposed to be here.

41

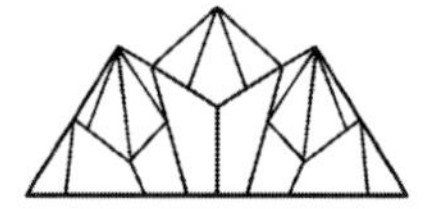

Teryn did not wake gently. There was no floating in nothingness, no subtle lack of consciousness. There was only an abrupt intake of breath, a startling sense of being alive.

Or...sort of alive.

As he took in his surroundings, he found himself reclined on the floor in the illusion that was Emylia's temple bedroom. She sat beside him on a stack of bright cushions, her expression heavy with concern. Before she could say what he knew she was about to, he tuned in to his vitale and connected with his breaths. They were short and shallow and came with a mild ache in his lungs. His heartbeat and pulse felt more distant than usual.

But that wasn't his primary concern. He settled his attention on Emylia. "What happened to Cora? Did she take the crystal like I told her to?"

The answer was already on her face. "She tried, but... Teryn, there was a reason our plan involved you removing the crystal from your chest and destroying it. I never told you to pass it off to someone else. You were never supposed to remove it in the first place until we were ready to execute our plan."

He pinned her with a hard look. "*Our plan* is nonexistent. I wasn't willing to wait for some hazy future hope."

"Don't you understand? If she'd taken the crystal far from your body and destroyed it, Morkai would have died, but so would you. You are tethered to the crystal, the same as Morkai. Your only link to the world of the living is through your body. And if your ethera is freed from the crystal while your connection to your cereba and vitale is severed...you'd have no hope of being whole again."

Her words sent a chill through him, but he couldn't bring himself to feel regret. Instead, he only felt more vindicated. "I would have been willing to risk my life if it meant destroying the sorcerer once and for all. If it meant keeping Cora safe from him."

Her eyes turned down at the corners. "We'll find a way, I promise."

Teryn bit back his argument. Hadn't she also promised he had more than enough time? "Where is she? Where is Cora now?"

"She got away."

"And where is *he*?"

"He's resting his ethera. He overtaxed himself and was forced to rest shortly after Cora disappeared. However, this is the one time I would caution against practicing with your cereba. Your body...it didn't respond well to what you did. To the two of you fighting for control."

Teryn remembered the blood that had seeped from his nose, the searing pain he'd felt when his body was being wrestled away from him. The only thing that had kept him in place for as long as it had was Cora's presence. That warm tether had remained, pulsing from his chest and anchoring him into his body. Had that been his heart-center? Had it overridden Morkai's?

It had...for a while at least.

Thank the seven gods she'd gotten away after he lost consciousness.

"You shouldn't have done what you did, Teryn."

"I *had* to try. I couldn't let her believe his lies a second longer. Couldn't let him kiss her, comfort her—" He recalled the reason she'd sought comfort in the first place. The reason she'd come to speak to him.

A searing ache pierced his heart.

He slid his gaze to Emylia. "Do you know about the curse Morkai placed on Cora? The one preventing her from bearing children?"

She shrank back slightly, shoulders stiff. Her dark eyes went wide, but she said nothing.

Teryn sat up straighter. "Do. You. Know. About. It."

She gave a sharp nod.

"Tell me."

"It's...it's not something you can change—"

His voice deepened, his fingers curling into fists. "Stop keeping things from me based on whether or not I can change them and just *tell* me, Emylia."

Closing her eyes, she lowered her head. Her voice came out muffled. "I suppose it's well past time for me to be judged for my sins."

Tension radiated through Teryn's ethera.

Slowly, she rose to her feet. Teryn followed, keeping his eyes locked on her hunched form. Her expression was wan, eyes distant.

"It's my fault," she said, voice barely above a whisper. "Everything he's doing. It's because of me."

It took all his restraint to keep his voice level. "Tell me what you know. Please."

"I can't. I'm too much of a coward to confess with words."

"Emylia—"

"But I can show you."

~

THE ILLUSION THAT WAS EMYLIA'S TEMPLE BEDROOM FELL beneath a sheer blanket of fog. When it dissipated, the tapestries and furnishings were left muted in color and clarity, while the light coming in from the windows seemed to shift between midday and early evening, then back again. When Teryn tried to focus on the details of the room—the pattern on the rugs, the designs on the tapestries—they'd change before his eyes. Whatever illusion he saw now, it had the same ephemeral quality as a dream.

"This is my memory," Emylia explained, taking up post against the far wall. Her expression remained hollow, shoulders slumped either with sorrow or resignation. "Or how I remember it playing out, at least. Memories are weaker than illusions, but this is as close to the truth as I can show you."

Teryn stood at her side, tense with trepidation. He had no idea what to expect or how her memories had anything to do with the curse Cora had mentioned.

The bedroom door opened and in walked another version of Emylia. She appeared to be a year or two younger than the Emylia he knew now, but perhaps it was the carefree smile, the sparkle in her eyes, and the buoyancy of her steps that made her seem so youthful. She wore a simple silk shift, belted at the waist with a red braided cord. A similar red cord framed her face, keeping her halo of black curls off her forehead, and ended in a bow at the nape of her neck. Her arms were full of leather-bound books.

Behind the Emylia of memory followed an older woman. She was tall with brown skin and short-cropped black hair. Her state of dress was slightly more elegant, her shift patterned with floral designs, and her braided belt was gold in color.

Neither figure paid any heed to Teryn and his companion. He and Emylia were merely spectators in this memory, not participants.

"He says he's from Syrus," the older woman said. Her voice was soft and slightly muffled, her tone inconstant, as if whatever magic Emylia was using to replicate this memory was unable to properly recall how the woman was supposed to sound. "He seems to be about the same age as you, and with the same fascination with books. For seven days, he's been in our library, asking questions that our archivists don't have answers to."

The younger Emylia set her books next to her bed and turned back toward the woman. "What does this have to do with me, Priestess Calla?"

"The young man is in need of a channel, either an oracle or seer. Moreover, I need him out of our library, and you need to hone your craft."

Emylia's eyes brightened. "You mean I can practice channeling for someone outside of the temple?"

"Yes. I believe you are ready. The man's search is of a nature that will provide you a challenge."

Emylia cocked her head to the side. "What is he asking about?"

"The fae."

Her mouth dropped open, expression falling. "The fae. He seeks answers to...faerytales."

Mother Calla gave her a knowing grin. "I told you it would be a challenge."

Emylia's face wrinkled with disgust. "It's a challenge because the fae aren't real. A channel is a seeker of truth. How can I act as his seer when the subject is one of myth?"

Mother Calla's mirth slipped from her face. "It is not a temple acolyte's job to judge what is and isn't real. If you are to become a Priestess of Zaras, you must open yourself to new possibilities. You cannot reject a patron based on your preconceived prejudice. You must be willing to seek before you judge, regardless of the subject."

Emylia stiffened, then bowed at the waist. "Forgive me," she said in a rush. "It was wrong for me to judge. Of course I'll channel for this patron."

"You will," Mother Calla said, then closed the distance between them. Placing her finger under Emylia's chin, she urged her to straighten from her bow. The older woman's eyes crinkled with clear fondness. "You're as bold as your mother, and just as stubborn. I believe in you, the same way I believed in her. You'll do her memory proud."

The image stilled. Teryn was about to ask what that memory had to do with Cora, when the fog returned and swept the room away completely. In its place, a new location formed, darkening the edges of Teryn's vision until it formed a cobblestone street bathed in shadow and moonlight. Both sides of the street were lined with narrow townhomes and clustered storefronts.

Teryn caught a glimpse of a hooded figure strolling up to one of the buildings before the image shifted again. The figure was now approaching the door of an inn. Teryn saw Emylia's telltale black curls peeking out from under her hood as the acolyte entered the building. The fog swept the image away once more and formed a small candlelit room.

Like the temple bedroom, the room shifted whenever Teryn tried to focus on details, but he was able to make out a narrow cot and a small desk.

Emylia entered the room, tossing back her hood as a young man closed the door behind them. Teryn assessed the man's fair skin, his pale eyes, his shoulder-length black hair. He looked young—perhaps a year younger than Teryn—but there was no denying his resemblance to Morkai. But unlike the duke, this man wasn't impeccably dressed. Instead, he wore plain brown trousers and a cream linen tunic.

The man faced Emylia, frowning as his eyes landed on her face. "*You're* a Priestess of Zaras? You look...young."

She scoffed. "Is that how you greet people in Syrus?"

His expression hardened. "I requested a priestess."

"Well, you got an acolyte. Shall I leave, or are you going to be a gentleman and introduce yourself?"

He ran a hand over his face, then crossed his arms. "Desmond."

Teryn frowned. He'd expected the man to introduce himself as Morkai, based on their striking similarities. Was this truly a younger version of the sorcerer as he'd first assumed, or a close relative? Was Desmond the sorcerer's true name? He glanced at the real Emylia to ask but found her lower lip trembling. A sheen of tears coated her eyes, and her expression sagged with longing.

"Is Desmond your surname?" The Emylia of memory stole his attention back to the scene playing out before him. She arched a brow at the man. "Or are we already on a first-name basis?"

"Desmond is the only name you need to know."

Her jaw shifted side to side. "Fine. Acolyte Emylia."

Desmond's only reply was to extend a hand toward the chair at the desk. "Take a seat and we can get started."

Emylia strode past him, burning him with a sneer on her way. With exaggerated moves, she pulled out the chair and planted herself onto it. Meanwhile, Desmond took a seat at the edge of the bed, elbows perched on his knees. One of his legs began to shake as he watched her. His steely expression cracked, revealing something softer. More anxious perhaps.

Emylia shrugged off her cloak and let it fall over the back of her chair. The candlelight glinted off a crystal she wore around her neck. It was wrapped in gold wire and strung from a chain. Even in the shadowed haze of the memory, Teryn knew this was the very same crystal his ethera was tethered to now.

Removing the chain from around her neck, Emylia set the crystal on the desk and cupped her palms around it.

Desmond's leg stopped shaking as his gaze landed on her hands. "What is that?"

"It helps me channel. It belonged to my mother when she was alive. She was a Priestess of Zaras."

His expression softened further. "Your mother died?"

"My birth killed her," she said stiffly. "Now, what is it you want to know?"

Desmond took a deep breath. "How do I get to the realm of the fae?"

Emylia rolled her eyes, a disbelieving smirk tugging a corner of her lips. Then, with a resigned sigh, she closed her eyes and settled into her seat, her body growing more and more relaxed as she breathed deeply. After several long moments, she spoke, her voice deep and even. "Show me the realm of the fae."

"That's not what I asked."

"I know," she said, tone calm. "Before I can ask how to get there, I must first see that it exists."

Desmond looked like he wanted to argue but remained silent.

Movement fluttered beneath Emylia's closed eyelids.

Desmond leaned closer, and Teryn found himself doing the same. Teryn didn't know much about fae lore, but he'd certainly never heard anyone refer to the fae as having belonged to another realm. Faerytales suggested fae creatures—unicorns, pixies, dragons, sprites—had lived long ago, along with two races of High Fae: the Elvyn and Faeryn. They were said to have inhabited the land once known as Lela—the land that was now divided into Menah, Selay, and Khero. All stories told that every kind of fae went extinct over five hundred years ago.

Teryn hadn't believed there was any truth to such tales. Not until he saw a unicorn with his own eyes. Learned magic was real. Confronted a blood mage who claimed to be an Elvyn prince.

The seer repeated her request. "Show me the realm of the fae."

A weighted silence fell over the room. Teryn folded his arms to keep from fidgeting.

Finally, she spoke again.

"The fae realms are many. They are here but not here. Layered upon this world. Parallel, but on separate planes."

Her eyes flew open, and she dropped her crystal to the surface of the table. "The fae are real," she muttered. Then, shifting in her seat to face Desmond, she said it again. "The fae are *real*."

His lips curled with the slightest hint of amusement, but he quickly steeled it behind an icy mask. "Yes, but how do I get to their realm?"

Emylia rose from her chair and began pacing the room. “I saw...many realms. There isn’t just one. Fae of different races and species exist on parallel planes. I can’t ask to see how to get to your particular realm unless I know more about it.” She halted before Desmond. “What is the name of the realm you seek?”

He pursed his lips. “I can't say.”

She propped her hands on her hips and stared down at him. “I can’t be of any help if you keep vital information from me. Honestly, I’m surprised I saw as much as I did, considering my skepticism. But what I’m seeing is taking me in too many different directions. I need to know the name of the realm if I am to see any more answers.”

Desmond threw his head back with a frustrated growl. “I can’t tell you because I don’t know.”

She arched a brow. “You don’t know?”

He stood and brushed past her toward the desk, planting his hands on its surface. His head hung low, sending his dark hair over his face. “My father sent me. He’s the one looking for the fae realm, not me. He’s its rightful heir, and I’m simply trying to return him to his throne.”

Teryn’s eyes widened. Desmond’s talk of fae heirs and blood rights reminded him too much of Morkai. Could Desmond’s father be...Morkai? While the sorcerer had looked only a handful of years older than Teryn, he was willing to entertain the possibility that he’d been old enough to sire this young man. If Morkai was truly Elvyn, he could have been ageless.

Emylia snorted a laugh. “Your father is the heir to a fae realm?”

His cheeks flushed. “I’m not joking, acolyte.”

“Right,” she said, trying to hide her amusement and failing miserably. “Open mind. I can do that.”

He glared at her for a few moments before speaking again. "He told me the fae realm has a name, but usurpers to the throne cursed him long ago, forcing him to forget. All I know is that it's the realm of the Elvyn and Faeryn."

Emylia nibbled a thumbnail, then gave a nod. She'd managed to rein in her mirth. "All right. I can work with that."

"You can?"

"It might take me days or weeks, but I can continue to channel. I'll seek the realm of the Elvyn and Faeryn and see if I can glean a name. Now that I know it's real…" She met his gaze with a wide smile. "This is actually exciting!"

He blinked at her a few times. Then, ever so slowly, a warm smile melted over his face. "So you'll come back? You'll come back and we'll try again?"

Her expression turned timid. "If you want me to."

"Yes," he said, voice soft, breathless. He reached a tentative hand and brushed his fingers against her wrist. "Thank you."

Emylia bit her lip, eyes locked on his. "Of course."

The image froze, and Teryn cast a glance at the real Emylia. Her expression was still brimming with mournful longing. "I don't see what this has to do with Cora," he said.

"You will," she whispered. "And you will hate me for it." She seemed so small, so defeated, as she turned to face him. "But don't worry. I hate myself for it too."

42

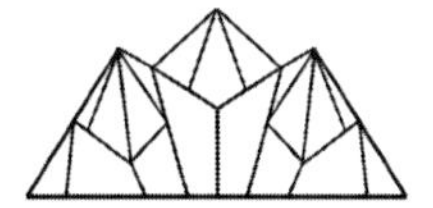

The fog flooded the room once again, forming image after image in rapid succession, as if representing the passing of many days. Teryn saw Emylia and Desmond reading in the library, followed by another scene of them sharing a smile from across a long table. Then they were elbowing each other playfully as they walked side by side down the cobblestone street near the inn. Finally, they exchanged a kiss over the desk in Desmond's bedroom.

Teryn didn't know why Emylia was showing him this. These seemed like private moments, not ones meant for great revelations. But as he glanced at the woman beside him, he saw the sad smile curling her lips, the hand she held over her heart. Perhaps she wasn't replaying these intimate memories for Teryn but for herself. Whoever Desmond was—whether he was Morkai himself, or the sorcerer's son—it was clear Emylia had fallen in love with him.

The memory shifted again. Emylia flung open Desmond's bedroom door and found him at his desk inspecting a book. He jumped and slammed the tome shut. Emylia frowned as Desmond shoved the book beneath a stack of papers.

"What are you reading?" she asked.

"Nothing but more boring texts," Desmond said with a wry grin. He ran his hand through his black tresses, revealing a hint of a slightly angled ear. Teryn's breath caught. Had Morkai had ears like that? Teryn couldn't recall. It hadn't been something he'd ever paid attention to. "You, on the other hand, are a far more interesting sight."

Emylia beamed and rushed to Desmond's side, taking his face in her hands. He wrapped his arms around her waist as they met in a passionate kiss. When their lips finally parted, Emylia kept her forehead pressed to his. "I found it," she whispered.

Desmond pulled back. "Found what?"

"I saw it, Des. It's called El'Ara."

His silver-blue eyes went wide. "The name of the fae realm? My father's true home?"

Emylia bounced on the balls of her feet, hardly able to contain her excitement. "Yes."

He bolted upright to stand. "So you can find it now? Find out how to get there?"

"That's why I'm here, aren't I?"

Desmond winked. "I assumed it was because you loved me."

She perched on her toes and planted a kiss on his cheek. "I do, but business first."

Desmond moved from behind the desk and let Emylia take her place in his chair. Like before, she removed her crystal from around her neck and brought it between her palms. This time, instead of perching at the edge of the bed, Desmond kneeled beside the desk.

Emylia settled into her meditative state. After a few deep breaths, she spoke. "Show me how to enter El'Ara."

Her eyelids fluttered, eyes darting side to side beneath them. For several long moments, she said nothing. Then, "I'm seeing something."

Desmond leaned closer to the desk. "What do you see?"

"A...wall. It's a wall of thread, and it's surrounding me, blocking everywhere I try to look."

"Cut the threads."

"They can't be cut, but...I think there's a window. A weakness."

Desmond's fingers curled at his sides.

"I'm getting something," Emylia whispered. "The way in. I see...truth. Someone is speaking from behind this wall of threads."

"What are they saying?"

She shook her head. "I'm a seer, not an oracle. It's harder for me to turn images to words, but...no, I see it."

Another stretch of silence.

"So long as the Veil remains," Emylia said, each word slow and careful, "the Blood of Darius cannot enter El'Ara."

Teryn frowned. Who—or what—was the Blood of Darius?

Desmond, however, wasn't concerned by the name Darius but something else. "The Veil? What is the Veil?"

"A ward woven to keep the Blood of Darius at bay."

"Can the Veil be destroyed?"

"When true Morkara is born, the Veil will be torn, setting into motion the end of the Blood of Darius."

Desmond's voice deepened. "Who is this *true Morkara*? How will they end the Blood of Darius?"

Emylia winced, her eyes darting rapidly now. "The true Morkara is the Blood of Ailan, born under the black mountain. He will unite three crowns and return El'Ara's heart."

"But who is this person? Where can I find the true Morkara?"

Emylia paused, head bobbing slightly side to side. "You will never know him."

Desmond's jaw tightened.

"But...but you may find his mother."

"Who is his mother?"

She winced again, and a sheen of sweat coated her brow. "She too is the Blood of Ailan, but with the beauty of Satsara. She has the blood of the witch, blood of the Elvyn, and blood of the crown. The unicorn will signify her awakening."

"What about this black mountain you mentioned?"

"A black mountain...over a field of violets."

"I've never seen such a place." Shaking his head, he stood and paced before the desk, hands clasped behind his back. "But if I can find it, then...then how do I put an end to the true Morkara?"

"If you end the true Morkara, the Veil will never be torn. The Blood of Darius will forever be barred from El'Ara."

"But if I don't end the true Morkara, he will end the Blood of Darius?"

"Yes," Emylia said.

Teryn's mind reeled to comprehend what he was hearing. *Morkara* sounded so much like Morkai, but he didn't know what it meant. Was it a name? A title? And while Desmond seemed to know who the *Blood of Darius* was, Teryn hadn't a clue. Then there were the other names: Satsara, Ailan.

"There has to be a way," Desmond said. "Tell me a way! Where do I find the black mountain over a field of violets?

What is the true Morkara's name? His mother's name? Who are Satsara and Ailan?"

Emylia began to tremble, and her voice came out weak and strained. "Desmond, that's too much. I can't...I can't see any more than that. I need to come out of the channel—"

"No!" His shout made her jump in her seat. He softened his tone. "No, Emy, you're doing great. We can keep going. I'll find a better question." He hung his head and planted his hands at the end of the desk. "It isn't El'Ara my father needs. Not for what he needs to do. It's the power of the Morkaius."

Morkaius. Another word that sounded so much like Morkai.

He returned to Emylia's side and kneeled on the floor again. "Can one claim the power of the Morkaius without entering El'Ara? Can one become Morkaius of *this* world?"

Emylia shifted in her seat, shaking her head. "I don't like this. I'm seeing too much darkness."

"You can do this, Emy. I believe in you. I *need* you to do this."

She shuddered but settled back into her trance. After a deep exhale, her voice regained its steady tone. "To gain the power of the Morkaius, one must first become King of Magic, a crown given, not taken, and reign over El'Ara's abandoned heart."

"What is El'Ara's abandoned heart? Where do I find it?"

"A land left in the wake of the Veil. A heart that once was one, now split by three crowns. One crown rests upon the birthplace of the mother you seek. To become Morkaius of El'Ara's heart, harness the magic that seeps from its center."

Desmond's face broke into a grin. He grabbed paper, ink, and quill from the desk and began to write. "A crown given, not taken. Reign over El'Ara's heart. Harness the magic—"

"He who harnesses the magic will be destroyed by it."

His pen stilled over his paper. "What?"

"El'Ara's magic is too strong to be contained by any man, neither mortal nor fae. It will eat through living flesh and burn living blood. No Morkaius shall survive the harnessing."

His eyes shot to Emylia, and he pursed his lips so tight, they lost color. Then, with a shout, he shot to his feet and swept his arms across the desk, sending books, ink, and paper flying. Emylia opened her eyes and let out a cry, backing away from him, chest heaving.

Silence enveloped the room while the two remained motionless, surrounded by the last of the fluttering papers.

"What's wrong with you?" Emylia finally shouted. "You could have hurt me, forcing me out of a channel like that!"

As his eyes met hers, his face twisted with anguish. He ran to her and gathered her in his arms. "Forgive me, Emylia. Forgive me."

She remained stiff in his arms for several long moments until she softened against him and wrapped her arms around his waist. "I'll try again, Des. We'll find the answers you need."

"I fear what you told me was answer enough," he said, voice muffled as he spoke into her hair. "My father's mission is impossible. And yet, we must find a way. Father must become Morkaius."

She pulled back and glanced up at him. "Why? What does that word even mean?"

"It means High King of Magic, and it's Father's birthright. Becoming Morkaius will give him access to magic beyond what we know."

Emylia frowned. "What kind of magic?"

His expression hardened. "The kind that can bring my mother back."

"Your...mother."

He nodded. "She died, like yours, but not during childbirth. She died of illness."

Emylia's face sank with pity. She brought a gentle hand to his cheek. "Des, no one can bring someone back from the dead."

"The Morkaius can."

"But how can your father become this...this Morkaius? You heard the words. He who harnesses the magic will be destroyed by it."

Desmond shook his head. "Father will find a way. Either that or he will find this mother the prophecy spoke of and end her."

Teryn shuddered at the ice in his tone.

"You can't be talking about...killing someone, Des. That's not what you mean, right? Your father isn't an evil man, is he?"

He smiled down at her but made no attempt to answer her question. "Thank you, Emy. You've helped me so much. I'll return home to Father next week and tell him what you've told me. It has to be enough for him. It will be. Whether in this world or in El'Ara, my father *will* become Morkaius."

Emylia's throat bobbed as something like fear settled in her dark eyes.

The image froze, and Teryn faced the real Emylia. His heart hammered, mind reeling to comprehend everything he'd witnessed. If this was supposed to have been about Cora...

About the reason Morkai cursed her to die childless...

His voice came out with a tremor. "Are you trying to tell

me that Cora was supposed to be the mother in this…this prophecy? Are you certain it's truly her?"

Emylia looked even more hollow than she had before, eyes distant. "*Blood of the witch, blood of the Elvyn, blood of the crown*. That means the prophesied mother is part witch, part Elvyn, and royal."

"Cora never said anything about being of Elvyn descent."

She shrugged. "She likely doesn't know. But this clue will convince you. *The unicorn will signify her awakening*."

Teryn's heart sank. "Valorre."

She nodded. "Her relationship with Valorre is the final piece that makes me certain she's the mother. Yet Morkai acted long before he saw the first sign of a unicorn, long before he even knew who Princess Aveline was. Instead, he followed my prophecy to find the Heart of El'Ara, as it and the mother were connected by the black mountain over the field of violets. It took him years to find the place he sought, but it shouldn't take you nearly as long to figure out."

He closed his eyes, but the closest image he could conjure was the cliff Cora had taken him to. Beneath it, the wildflower meadow stretched out before the Cambron Mountains. If only the flowers were fully purple, then—

"Seven devils," he said, opening his eyes. "It's not a place. It's a sigil."

The vision came to him now—the silhouette of a mountain over a purple background. The symbol of Khero.

"Yes," Emylia said. "Because of the words I spoke, Morkai sought to end Cora's life."

A spike of rage shot through him, but he was too fatigued to hold on to it. "Morkai didn't kill her, though. Why? Why did he curse her instead?"

Emylia rubbed her brow. "Mother Goddess, there's...so much more to tell you, but—" She froze, eyes widening.

"But what?"

She nibbled her lip before answering. "He's awake."

Dread filled every inch of Teryn's ethera. He needed to know the rest of Emylia's tale. Needed to understand the full truth of Desmond, Morkai, and the prophecy.

But just as badly, he wanted to see how Morkai would react now that Cora had escaped his clutches. What would the sorcerer do now that the marriage alliance—his one link to royal power—was compromised? If Teryn's body was beginning to shut down, then Morkai was running out of time.

They both were.

"We follow him," Teryn said, tone resolute, "but as soon as he's asleep once more, you're showing me the rest of your memories."

She gave him a sad smile that almost looked relieved. "And finally my sins will be laid bare."

43

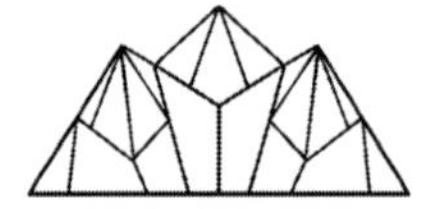

Cora had no time to feel awed over the sight of the three Elvyn males, for the anger on their faces was second only to the rage in their tones. If that wasn't enough, she could *feel* it. Their shock, their ire, their...fear. Or was that her own? Before she could so much as gather her bearings, they charged across the meadow. Her gaze fell on the swords they carried at their hips. Though each had a hand resting upon the hilt, none drew their weapons. Even so, Cora found her hands flinching toward her waist, her shoulder, seeking weapons that weren't there. Only then did she recall what she was wearing—a thin linen shift and velvet robe. She didn't even have her apron and paring knife.

They were nearly upon her now. With every step they took, they shouted at her in a language she couldn't understand. The golden-haired Elvyn at the fore of the group lifted a hand, pressing his thumb to the center of his ring finger and turning his wrist slightly.

Cora didn't know what the gesture meant, but it sparked

within her enough urgency to mount Valorre and make an escape.

Only...she found her body frozen.

And it wasn't fear that stilled her, nor any other internal source.

Instead, an invisible force pinned her arms to her sides. Her gaze narrowed on the golden-haired Elvyn's hand, still curled in that strange gesture.

Valorre reared back on his hind legs, kicking out with his front hooves, but the same fae male extended his other hand. With the same gesture, he forced Valorre back to all fours. The unicorn bucked and thrashed, but it was no use. It was as if he'd been harnessed by an invisible bridle.

The other two Elvyn flanked the first. The one with umber skin and dark hair stepped forward and spoke in more words Cora couldn't comprehend. Yet she noted the placating nature of his tone. Unlike the golden-haired fae, whose lips were peeled back in a sneer, blue eyes cast in a glower, or the copper-haired fae who simply looked amused, the dark-haired Elvyn had a much gentler energy. Cora's panic was almost strong enough to drown out the emotions of the three, but she could still bet which of the fae she'd have the best chance of appealing to.

He spoke again, slower this time.

"I don't understand what you're saying," she said, voice edged with hysteria. She tried to focus on deepening her breaths, on rooting herself to the earth beneath her feet, but that only reminded her that she was in another gods-damned *realm*. Whatever the hell that was supposed to mean. And she was still trapped under the unseen force the golden fae was using.

The dark-haired fae released a sigh and lifted a hand. He crossed two of his fingers and slid them through the air in a horizontal line. "What are you?" he said, and this time Cora could understand him.

"Are you human?" asked the golden fae. His words made sense now too, but she realized they didn't match the shape of his lips. Perhaps the dark-haired fae had cast a translation enchantment. Was that something the Elvyn could do? All she knew of Elvyn magic was that they utilized what the Forest People had called the Magic of the Sky. Unlike the Faeryn, who revered the earth and lived in harmony with nature, the Elvyn were said to value beauty, art, music, and luxury. She knew the Elvyn specialized in an Art called weaving—the very magic Morkai tried to emulate with his blood tapestries—but she didn't know what it entailed.

"I'm...I'm human," she finally managed to say.

The copper-haired Elvyn dipped his chin at her lower body. Now that he was near, she could see an array of bronze freckles dotting his tan skin. "What's on her arms?"

The golden fae flicked his wrist, and she found her arm thrust suddenly forward. She winced as the invisible force twisted the limb, yanking it at an uncomfortable angle until her inked forearm showed clearly.

"Fanon," the dark-haired fae said, casting a stern look at the golden fae, "show a little restraint. We don't know if she's guilty."

The word *Fanon* remained untranslated, so she assumed that must be the golden fae's name.

"If she's human, she's guilty," Fanon said. He folded his arms over his chest in a slightly more relaxed posture. The pressure eased from her forearm, returning it to a natural angle. She expected to be freed from his invisible magic altogether, but her arms simply snapped back to her sides. Even though he was no longer actively making that strange gesture, both she and Valorre were still trapped under his magic's influence.

"But those looked like Faeryn *insigmora*," said the stout fae. Belatedly Cora realized his lips had formed the last two words, matching up with what she'd heard.

"She's not Faeryn, Garot," said Fanon.

Despite the disgust and trepidation wafting off the three strangers, Cora saw an opportunity to forge some kind of understanding between them. "You're right, they are Faeryn *insigmora*. Where I'm from, I lived with a group of people who are Faeryn descendants. They took me in—"

"There are Faeryn descendants in your realm?" the copper-haired Garot asked, his green eyes alight with renewed curiosity.

Fanon and the dark-haired fae exchanged a brief look. When Fanon returned his gaze to hers, it was no longer quite so cold. His throat bobbed before he spoke. "Are there any Elvyn survivors in your world? Or...descendants?"

Cora sensed a subtle spark of hope in him. Her heart sank. Why did he have to ask that? She knew her answer would only disappoint him. "I've never met anyone of Elvyn descent."

Fanon's dark glower returned, and with it came a string of clipped words that remained untranslated. Based on his tone, she could only assume they were expletives.

"How did you come here?" the dark-haired fae said. He was now the only one whose name she didn't know. His eyes were a ruby-tinted brown, and the way they crinkled at the corners set her at ease. She got the distinct impression that he was the eldest of the three, despite their equally youthful appearances. Somehow, all appeared to be both young and ancient at the same time, but the dark-haired fae held a weight to his energy, one that bore centuries of life. Of wisdom.

She realized his question still hung between them. She was about to confess what had happened—or at least try to put it into words—when Valorre's voice entered her mind.

Tell them I brought you here. Anxiety rippled from him. *Do not tell them about your magic.*

She glanced at him, saw his muscles quivering against his invisible restraints. *Why?*

Because it was *my fault. I invaded your thoughts with my memory of home. I took a step and brought us here using your traveling magic. But...more than that, I've come to learn the value of a lie. If you do not lie, I fear...something. I don't remember what, but I fear it. They will not like your magic.*

He sounded so uncertain in her mind. So unlike the overly proud creature he normally was.

She returned her gaze to the dark-haired fae. "Valorre brought me."

"What is...Valorre?" Garot asked.

"My unicorn companion."

Fanon scoffed. "The unicorn is your companion?"

"More concerning," said the unnamed Elvyn, "is that she's suggesting he came from her world." Then to Cora, he said, "Please explain."

"Unicorns were considered extinct in my world for five hundred years. Only recently have they reappeared." She tried to keep her voice level. It was easier said than done with the tremors racking her body, coursing with waves of panic over being restrained by a force she couldn't see. Not to mention the fact that she was referring to where she'd come from as *her world.*

Mother Goddess, was this really happening? All her life, she'd thought of the fae as creatures who'd once existed and had simply gone extinct. Now she was supposed to reconcile that they'd come from another world. But how?

"And you befriended this one?" The unnamed male glanced at Valorre.

"Yes," she said, "and we came here by mistake. He accidentally brought me to his home."

Fanon's eyes went wide. He whipped his face toward the dark-haired fae. "What does this mean for the Veil, Etrix?"

Etrix. The final name.

He rubbed his jaw. "It might be torn."

Fanon took a forbidding step closer to Cora, leaving only a foot of space between them. She wanted to flinch back but she still couldn't move. Valorre released a guttural whinny, but he too remained trapped in place. All Cora could do was tilt her head and meet his gaze. She swallowed hard, realizing he was even taller than Teryn. And Teryn was one of the tallest men she'd met. Fanon's build, however, was leaner. That didn't make him any less intimidating.

"Did you cross through the Veil?" he asked with clenched teeth.

"I don't know what the Veil is."

"Then are you a worldwalker?"

Cora was struck with the most potent hatred, and her answer dried in her throat. Similar emotions came from the two fae behind Fanon, but theirs was tangled with far more fear. Fanon's contempt, on the other hand, was too strong to carry much else.

Whatever a worldwalker was, he despised it with a violent passion.

Tell them we came through the Veil, Valorre said.

She shuddered beneath Fanon's icy stare but finally managed to find her words. "I…I think we came through the Veil."

He watched her for a few silent moments, then reached toward his waist. Her heart slammed against her ribs as she expected him to unsheathe his sword—

To her relief, he simply extracted something from inside his robe. Her eyes widened as she took in the strange item. It looked like a large cuff made from two pieces of curved obsidian that ended in tapered points. Like talons. Or claws. A wide gap remained between the sharp tips, and as Fanon tugged on both sides, it widened further on a hinge.

He stepped even closer, bringing the cuff-like object toward her neck.

"What is that?" Cora asked, voice trembling. She struggled against her invisible bonds but they were just as strong as ever. Valorre gave another futile whinny.

"Fanon," Etrix said, his tone brimming with warning. "You don't have to—"

Fanon ignored his companion and proceeded to hook the cuff around her neck. She couldn't see when he closed it, could glimpse no part of it beneath her chin, but as she felt a sharp pain bite into her skin, she realized he hadn't hooked it *around* her neck; he'd hooked the tapered points into her flesh.

Vertigo seized her, first from fear, then from...

A hollow feeling crept upon her awareness. An empty void. An unsettling quiet.

It took her several long moments to realize what was happening.

Her magic...

Her awareness of outside emotion, her connection to the dance of the elements all around her...

It was...gone.

This wasn't the quiet that came from using her mental shields. This was an absence of clairsentience altogether. A rent in her very identity. Frenzied grief rattled her bones, sent her head spinning, lungs tightening, tears springing to her eyes...

"Is this entirely necessary?" Etrix said, striding up to Fanon. With hollow awareness, Cora realized the translation enchantment remained in place. It seemed the strange collar only affected her own use of magic. She cast a glance at Valorre, tried with all her might to convey some silent thought to him.

She didn't know if it worked. Didn't know if he understood the words she couldn't form.

Then she heard a subtle, *I'm here.*

It was simple. Stilted. It reminded her of how they'd begun to communicate when they'd first met. Perhaps their connection was weak when only one of them could use their magic. At least they could converse at all.

Etrix spoke again. "She said she isn't a worldwalker. Even if she was, no worldwalker can move through the Veil. She can't leave, with or without the collar."

"We don't know that," Fanon said, his cruel gaze still on Cora. "The Veil was woven to keep a worldwalker from entering our world; one could still worldwalk out. Besides, if the Veil is torn, who knows what a worldwalker can do? I won't risk letting her escape until we've sorted out the truth."

With that, he turned his back on her and began walking away. He was no more than a few steps ahead before Cora found herself pulled forward by that unseen force. She stumbled to keep her feet beneath her, and when she finally managed to match the pace she was being dragged at, it was too fast. Or was she simply too drained? Too broken in the wake of her stolen magic?

Valorre trotted beside her. Though he too moved against his will, his presence provided some semblance of comfort.

"I'm sorry," Etrix said, keeping pace at her side, "about the collar. I know it hurts, but it's a necessary precaution."

The physical pain she felt biting into the sides of her neck was nothing compared to the absence of her magic. "Where are you taking me?"

"To the Veil," Garot said, grinning over his shoulder like the situation was nothing more than run-of-the-mill amusement to him. He outpaced Fanon and paused at the edge of the meadow. He made a complex gesture with both hands, and the landscape turned to a swirling vortex of green and brown that opened into some sort of tunnel. It was just like what the three males had emerged from when they'd first appeared. Fanon strode straight into it, while Garot waited at its entrance for Cora and Etrix to bypass him.

"Don't worry," Etrix said as they approached the unsettling whirl of color. "So long as you aren't a worldwalker, you have nothing to fear from us."

Cora pursed her lips. She wasn't certain what a worldwalker was, but she could guess. It was a type of human they abhorred, someone who could enter their world at will.

She shuddered.

What if she *did* have something to fear?

What if a worldwalker was exactly what she was?

44

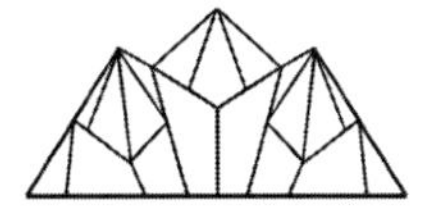

Dawn had risen while Teryn had been watching Emylia's memories. Now morning light streamed through the windows into the halls of Ridine, bathing the flagstones in pink and gold. It would have been a beautiful morning were it not for Teryn's dread. And the fact that he was a disembodied spirit, of course, but that was hardly novel anymore. His feeling of unease grew with every step Morkai took down the quiet halls, mostly empty save for the servants who were already busy at work. The servants bowed when they saw Morkai, recognizing him as Prince Teryn, and Morkai gave them all friendly smiles.

It was his smile—his overly calm demeanor—that chilled Teryn the most.

Having projected their etheras outside the crystal, Teryn and Emylia followed in the sorcerer's wake. Teryn had expected an air of frantic urgency to surround Morkai after having lost the most vital piece of his plan. Instead, Morkai walked with poise. Purpose. Fearlessness.

If that wasn't unsettling enough, the streaks of white running through Morkai's hair—*Teryn's* hair—sent a splinter of panic through him. He hardly dared look too long at the deepening hollows in his cheeks, the purple rimming his eyes. Emylia had warned him that his body hadn't responded well to his fight with Morkai for control. His only solace was that anyone who got close enough to the sorcerer would surely notice these things. The servants hadn't acted like anything was amiss, but they were trained to be polite. Anyone else, though...Master Arther, Mareleau...*someone* would notice there was something seriously wrong with the man pretending to be Teryn. Right?

Finally, Morkai came to the closed door of the king's study. Teryn had been there before. He'd met with Morkai there after the duke had captured Cora and hauled her to Ridine under the pretense of returning her to her place as princess. That was before Teryn had fully understood what was happening at Ridine. Even then, he'd regretted his betrayal. Hated the duke.

Morkai opened the door to reveal Lord Kevan behind the king's desk, brow furrowed as he read over what appeared to be a contract. At his side stood Lord Ulrich, expression somehow both bored and smug at the same time. Morkai closed the door behind him and approached the desk. Emylia went to the window behind Kevan and stared outside at the blushing sunrise, a note of longing in her face, as if she remained haunted by the memories she'd shown him. Teryn took up post beside the desk where he could see all three men clearly.

Kevan glanced up from the contract. His eyes went wide as they darted up to the top of Morkai's head. "What the seven devils happened to your hair?"

Teryn's pulse quickened. *There.* Someone did notice.

Ulrich huffed a laugh. "Have you slept, Highness? Or were you kept up with premarital jitters?"

Morkai simply smirked at the questions as he lowered himself into a chair at the other side of the desk. "What, you don't like my natural color? Not all of us are skilled at maintaining the façades of ink and dyes." He winked at Ulrich, whose dark bowl cut glittered with gray at the roots. "Perhaps I got tired of hiding. I think it's time we all show candor, don't you?"

Kevan returned his gaze to the contract, already disinterested in the man he thought was Teryn. "Where is Princess Aveline, Highness? The Godspriest will be here any moment. You and the princess—well, I suppose I should call her queen—must sign your marriage contract at once."

Morkai leaned back in his chair, one ankle crossed over his knee, hands interlaced at his waist. It was very much the duke's posture and not Teryn's. "I've already sent a message informing the Godspriest we'll have no need for him this morning."

Kevan's eyes bulged as he looked up from the contract once more. "Why the seven devils—"

"Aveline is gone."

Silence fell over the room. Emylia slowly turned from the window to watch what would happen next.

Ulrich cleared his throat, breaking the quiet. "What do you mean she's gone?"

"She ran away in the middle of the night."

Kevan stood in a rush. "Excuse me?"

"I don't know what drove her away. Perhaps the pressures of the crown were too much for her."

Kevan burned him with a scowl. "Do you jest, Highness?"

Morkai met his stare without falter. "No."

"Verdian will be here within days for the signing of the pact," Kevan said through his teeth. "He entrusted Khero to us. If he sees the kingdom has fallen apart under our watch, he'll—"

"He'll what?" Morkai let out a dark chuckle. "You're councilmen of Khero now. Verdian has no power here."

"On the contrary, Highness, Verdian can usurp Khero in the blink of an eye. That was implied from the start when he and Dimetreus negotiated his and Aveline's freedom."

"Then shouldn't he be grateful to you? Or am I to believe he was being generous in staking such a firm claim on this kingdom? If anything, it seems like he wanted Dimetreus' regime to fail, and the two of you along with it."

Kevan's face burned red, lips pursed tight.

Ulrich took a step forward, teeth bared. "Watch how you speak about King Verdian, Highness."

Morkai shrugged. "I speak only the truth, and I'm going to speak true now. Verdian was right to suspect Princess Aveline and King Dimetreus as incapable of ruling Khero. Dimetreus is a madman and Aveline is both too soft and too volatile for the pressures of the crown."

"That we can agree on," Kevan bit out.

"Which is why," Morkai said, "you should name me King of Khero."

Teryn and Emylia exchanged a startled glance.

Kevan and Ulrich seemed equally as perplexed. "Why the seven devils would we do that?" Ulrich said with a disbelieving laugh.

Morkai slowly rose from his chair and stood before the desk. "Before Dimetreus had his mental fit and tried to kill me, we'd had a candid conversation. He'd confessed that I was just as much his heir as Aveline. And we all know that Aveline's ascension to the throne was entirely dependent upon her marrying me."

Kevan planted his hands on the surface of the desk. He

clearly meant to appear intimidating, but with Morkai standing at Teryn's body's full height, the lord seemed more meek than threatening. Especially with how Morkai stared down his nose at the man. "You have no claim to Khero aside from being king consort," Kevan said. "A title which is invalid without the princess."

"And what right does Verdian have?" Morkai shook his head. "You may think I'm out of line for speaking against your dear brother, but we can at least agree that his motives were hardly genuine when he appointed the two of you here."

Kevan said nothing, but Ulrich asked. "How so?"

Morkai spoke with practiced ease. "You went from the heads of Verdian's council in Selay to the heads of council in Khero. I'm sure you were promised new lands and titles upon the signing of the peace treaty, and it seems a lateral move in terms of position. But we know the truth. Verdian's real aim was to get you out of Selay to strengthen his daughter's position as heir. A position she should no longer have now that she's married into a new kingdom. He isn't satisfied with her being Queen of Menah through marriage. No, he wants her to inherit Selay too. Wants to see two kingdoms join as one."

The red seeped from Kevan's face. He maintained his position with his palms on the desk, but Teryn could see the sudden interest that flashed in the man's blue eyes.

Morkai spoke again. "You should be princes, both of you. At the very least, you should be Verdian's heirs. Instead, he's brought you here. And, like you'd begun to suggest, he'll blame you for Khero's current state, for its crazed king and missing princess. If you lose your positions on this council, you know he won't welcome you back onto his. Your places have already been filled. And if he does decide to usurp

Khero, he won't keep the two of you in power. He'll only be adding yet another kingdom to his reign. A reign his daughter will inherit."

"You don't know what you're talking about," Kevan said, but his tone held little conviction. "Half of what you say is considered treason."

"Like I said, I speak only truth. Let us not pretend otherwise."

"So you think we should back you as king instead," Ulrich said. His tone was brimming with disbelief, but his eyes were keen. Hungry.

"Dimetreus admitted that I am his heir," Morkai said. "Despite Verdian's lack of respect for his brothers, he did give the two of you ultimate power over accepting the line of succession should Dimetreus fail his duties. Back me as king and I'll give you more than land and titles. Kevan, you should be Verdian's heir, plain and simple. Support my claim, and I'll support you as heir to Selay. We'll work it into the negotiations over the treaty. And you, Ulrich, will be named Duke Calloway. You shall inherit the Calloway lands left by the former Duke Morkai."

Ulrich's eyes flashed with greed and a half smile tugged his lips.

Kevan, on the other hand, dropped into his seat and rubbed his thick brown beard. "There's a reason neither of us were named Verdian's heir," he said, tone infused with a hint of indignation. "We have no royal blood. We are unrelated to the former king and are only related to Verdian through our shared mother. She remarried after the death of Verdian's father, and it was his blood that put Verdian on the throne."

Morkai barked a laugh. "They named a bastard a king. If

they can do that, then surely a king's brother can be named heir."

Teryn bristled, hands curling into fists.

Kevan scoffed. "You say *they* like you weren't a part of those negotiations. You abdicated your claim and supported your bastard brother."

Teryn watched closely to see if Morkai showed any surprise, any sign that he was caught off guard by what Kevan had said. Morkai may have gleaned much about Cora, Dimetreus, and the current state of political unrest, but he knew little about Teryn's personal matters.

Morkai, however, was unfazed. He turned a calculating grin on the man. "Just like I'm supporting you. If you must know why I refused my birthright, it was because I would have had to marry Verdian's daughter to keep it. I wasn't willing to do that. On the other hand, I was more than happy to wed Aveline, but she's proven to be as weak as her brother. Now I only want what is best for Khero, and I am certain that is me. And what's best for Selay is you, Kevan."

Ulrich stepped closer. "You think we can get Verdian to agree to these terms? He could refuse."

"He won't refuse," Morkai said. "Refusal can lead to war, and you're only asking for what's fair. Besides, you've taken away a portion of his military. The men who serve under your houses fight for *you*, which means they now fight for Khero. He won't want to go up against that."

Kevan narrowed his eyes. "We are not resorting to war with Verdian."

"These negotiations will be friendly, trust me. We'll hold them during a celebration. A hunt. Instead of signing the pact here, we'll solidify the treaty outdoors, where the environment feels neutral. The three of us will stake out a private place to hold our grand hunt, and when Verdian and Larylis arrive, they will meet us there."

Kevan and Ulrich exchanged a weighted look, one that spoke of greed, desperation, and trepidation.

"Is there a reason you're proposing an isolated location for the meeting?" Ulrich said, brow arched.

Morkai lifted his chin. "Should there be?"

Neither man answered. They exchanged another questioning glance, but this time there was no trepidation. Only hunger. Avarice.

Teryn glanced at Emylia. "Is he using magic right now? A...glamour? Like what he did to Dimetreus?"

She shook her head. "He isn't strong enough to create any lasting glamour. Not without a Roizan. All he's doing is playing into their desires."

Teryn shuddered. It was far more unsettling than if he'd been using magic, for this showed exactly what kind of men Kevan and Ulrich were.

"If you'd rather stand opposite me," Morkai said, "by all means say so at once. But I'd rather have your support, Prince Kevan. And yours, Duke Calloway."

Teryn was tempted to hold his breath for their answer, but he forced himself to keep his breathing steady, drawing air evenly into his lungs.

Kevan finally spoke. "Very well, Your Highness—"

"No. I'll need you to address me as Your Majesty now. I will take my place as king from this moment on. We'll keep it between us until after the pact has been signed. For now, it is enough that my heads of council name me king and show obeisance."

Kevan flushed, jaw tense as if he were about to argue.

Ulrich shared no such hesitation. He fell to one knee, head bowed. "My king."

Morkai nodded. "Duke Calloway."

Kevan's eyes were steely, but he bent into a stiff bow. "Your Majesty, King Teryn."

"Thank you for your support, Prince Kevan." With that, Morkai exited the study, a figurative crown upon his brow. One he'd managed to claim without magic. Without war.

The prophetic words Emylia had spoken in her memory echoed through his head.

To gain the power of the Morkaius, one must first become King of Magic, a crown given, not taken...

The prophecy had said nothing about official coronations or ceremonies. Had given no other stipulations. Which likely meant all Morkai needed was the outward acknowledgment of those qualified to give it. Based on the alliance terms Dimetreus had accepted, Kevan and Ulrich were qualified.

Morkai—with Teryn's name and body—was King of Khero.

The sorcerer had only two crowns left to earn, and he'd make his move during this hunt he'd concocted for the signing of the pact. Teryn couldn't imagine how the sorcerer would succeed without using force that would be considered *taking*, but after what he'd just witnessed, he harbored no hope that Morkai didn't already have a plan.

45

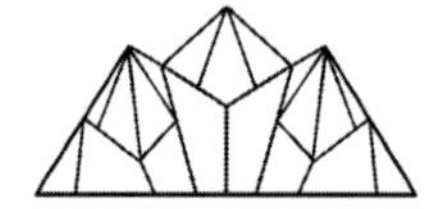

Cora thought she might retch if she was forced to endure the swirling colors of the tunnel much longer. Green, blue, gold, and brown, along with the occasional brighter hue, whirled before her in a horizontal vortex as far as she could see. It looked as if the landscape and sky had warped and spun to form this strange passage. The sensation it created was like riding through the forest at a breakneck pace but significantly more disorienting. While the ground felt smooth and steady beneath her feet, she almost lost her balance several times. With her arms pinned to her sides, she couldn't use them for stability. Instead, the only thing keeping her from falling was the invisible tug that forced her to follow in Fanon's wake.

Cora was about to send a volley of curses at the Elvyn male's back, demanding he slow down or free her from this nauseating place, when the tunnel ceased spinning. The greens and browns spread out like a wave from her feet while the blues and golds formed the sky overhead. They were in a dense forest, the mossy floor the brightest shade of emerald. The tree trunks were thicker than any Cora had seen, their branches towering high overhead. Some held clusters of glowing pink or white mushrooms that were nearly as large as she was, while unfamiliar birdsong filled the air. Tiny insects with jeweled wings flitted in clusters here and there, but none came close enough for Cora to get a good look. Were they pixies? She would have been enchanted by the stunning environment were it not for the current situation. The pain of the collar piercing her neck. The void she felt without her magic.

Fanon rushed on ahead, giving Cora and Valorre no time to adjust to the sudden change of terrain. His magical tether tugged them along, and now Cora had plenty of obstacles to avoid tripping over.

"Fanon," Etrix called, still beside her. "Release the human and unicorn. Let them proceed at their own pace."

"If the Veil is torn, we don't have time to dally," Fanon said.

Yet, despite his words, Cora felt that tug disappear. Though her arms were still pinned, she no longer felt as if she were being dragged. She paused to regain her equilibrium, but she managed only a single breath of relief before the tug returned. She was forced to step forward. This time the pressure disappeared as soon as she began walking on her own. Fanon's unspoken threat was clear: stop walking and he'd resort to dragging her again.

That made any chance of running away impossible. Besides, where would she go? She needed to get back home. Find the Forest People. Return to Ridine. Save Teryn from Morkai. To do any of that, she needed to astral travel. Needed her magic back. Needed to free her arms and get this damn collar off her neck.

She glanced at Etrix, careful not to angle her head too far to the side. Any drastic motion sent a renewed sting of pain where the collar dug into her flesh. At least she felt no trickle of warm blood, which told her the wounds weren't too deep. The Elvyn met her gaze with a tense smile. Whether he kept close to her out of care or caution, she wasn't sure. All she knew was that, so far, he was the only one of the three who'd shown her an ounce of concern. Perhaps he'd help her. First, she needed to better understand her situation.

"What is the Veil?" she asked.

He narrowed his eyes. "You confessed that you entered through the Veil. If that's the case, how do you not know what it is?"

Her mind raced, but she found her answer easily. Keeping secrets and telling lies to cover them was as familiar to her as her own skin. "I know I came through the Veil, but I don't understand what exactly it is."

"You're asking about the Veil?" Cora was startled to find Garot suddenly between her and Valorre. Before now, he'd been walking behind them.

"Garot," Etrix said with the same warning tone he'd used on Fanon.

Garot shrugged. "What? She's clearly not dangerous."

"We've yet to establish—"

"The Veil is like a curtain between your world and ours," Garot said, a smile stretching over his round face. His tone had taken on a whimsical quality, like a bard telling a tale.

That explanation did very little to clarify anything for Cora, but it sounded like a way back to her world. If she couldn't use her magic, then perhaps she and Valorre could escape through the Veil—

Wait. Would Valorre even want to return with her? Her eyes flicked to him, trotting on the other side of Garot. This was his true home. The place he'd come from.

I stay with you, Valorre conveyed in that same clipped style of communication as before. She wondered if it was his magic or the translation enchantment that allowed their connection to remain. It didn't seem like he could speak to the three Elvyn, and they hadn't bothered to address him when they'd inquired about him having come from her world. Once again, her connection with Valorre defied reason. Well, all but one.

The witches amongst the Forest People had kept pets now and then, and some had even claimed an animal as their familiar. She'd always scoffed at the claim. To her, it was another unimpressive quiet magic she hadn't put much value in. But she valued quiet magic now. Very much so.

Which made her wonder...was Valorre her familiar?

You are my home, he said, and she didn't need her magic to glean his conviction. *This is no more home. Sorry I brought us.*

Her heart warmed and broke all at once. *Are you in danger here? Is that why you left?*

Don't remember.

"I'm sorry I couldn't take us any farther by Path," Garot said, stealing her attention. "We can't use the *mora* once the Blight begins, which is why we're proceeding by foot."

Several words stuck out to her. *By Path. The Blight.* But one lingered in her awareness. No, it was...two. When he'd said *mora*, she'd heard two words at once: *mora* and *magic*. His mouth had formed an *O* to suggest the former had been in his language and the latter had been the translation. That was the first time she'd heard two words simultaneously. Did that mean...she *sort of* knew the word in its native tongue?

Insigmora.

Morkai.

Morkaius.

All those words contained *mor* or *mora* in some form, and they'd all come from the fae language, as far as she knew. She recalled that *Morkai* meant *King of Magic* and *Morkaius* meant *High King of Magic*. She'd never been told there was any translation for *insigmora*, but now she understood what part of it meant. Of course her tattoos were named for magic.

Now for her remaining questions. "What did you mean *by Path*? Was that the tunnel we walked through?"

Garot puffed out his chest with a proud nod. "I'm a pathweaver. I can navigate vast distances in a short time by weaving a portal."

Her next question was on the tip of her tongue. She hesitated before speaking, ensuring her tone came out as nonchalant as she could manage. Anxiety still crawled up her throat while grief at losing her magic weighed heavy on her shoulders, but the hope of returning home once she reached this Veil helped her keep her composure. Or at least pretend to. "If I'm unable to return home through the Veil, could you take me by Path—"

"No," Garot said, his grin disappearing. He glanced at Fanon, still leading their party from far up ahead, and lowered his voice. "Traversing worlds is something only a worldwalker can do. And worldwalking is a repulsive, invasive magic."

Damn it. She supposed there was no point appealing to his carefree nature in hopes that he might offer her aid. Still, she appreciated that he was at least answering her questions. "What is *the Blight*?"

"Did you not see it when you entered?" Etrix said from her other side. Though she'd first deemed him the kindest of the three, she was starting to realize he was the keenest too. "If you entered through the Veil, you would have seen it."

"I was asleep on Valorre's back," she rushed to say. "I didn't realize what had happened until I'd woken up and found us in the meadow. That was when Valorre told me he'd accidentally taken me home by crossing the Veil."

He studied her for several beats too long.

"You'll see the Blight for yourself soon enough," Garot said, pointing a finger straight ahead. "We're almost there."

Cora followed his line of sight to where the forest was beginning to thin. Thick tree trunks gave way to slim saplings, then disappeared into a gray fog. Where she stood now, a blue sky shone above the towering canopy of leaves, the sun comfortably warm, but at the edge of the woods, it almost looked like winter lay ahead. As they drew closer, Cora grew more unsettled. The saplings weren't simply small. They were frail. Decaying. And the forest didn't end in a fog; it lost color. Vibrancy. Life.

They emerged from the line of trees and stepped onto a gray path. From here on, there was no more mossy earth or glowing mushrooms. No more birdsong. No insects or pixies. The sky and golden sun were the only sources of color, and they did nothing to brighten the rotting landscape that stretched as far as Cora could see. The smell of rot filled her nostrils, making her wish her arms were free of their invisible restraints, if only to allow her to cover her nose and mouth.

She glanced at Garot. "This is the Blight?"

He gave her a somber nod. "It stretches all around the Veil and spreads farther into El'Ara daily."

A dark shadow passed overhead, blotting out the sun and casting them in momentary darkness. She froze, turning her eyes to the sky. An enormous beast with a long, sinuous body and a wide expanse of wings flew above them. It let out an ear-splitting screech that had Cora's shoulders shooting toward her ears. That, in turn, shifted her collar, causing its sharp tines to tear at her pierced flesh. She forced her shoulders to relax, eyes locked on the flying beast. In a matter of seconds it was far ahead, leaving Cora trembling with awed terror.

Mother Goddess, that was a...a dragon.

Don't like those, Valorre said. *I remember that.*

Did they create this? The Blight? Based on the faerytales Cora had grown up with, she knew dragons could wield flame. That could explain why the land was suddenly devoid of color. Perhaps it had been burned.

Don't think so, Valorre said. *But don't remember.*

Cora cast her gaze back to the path ahead and found Fanon striding on with his hurried pace as if the dragon were no concern. Garot trailed behind him, his steps somewhat less buoyant than before. Only Etrix remained at her side, watching the tiny speck that was the dragon until it was gone entirely.

"I thought perhaps she would come for the unicorn," he said.

"She?"

"Ferrah. The dragon. She's been seen chasing unicorns, especially any wandering through the Blight."

"Why?"

"We aren't certain. The dragons have been restless for months."

Do not like, Valorre said.

Etrix gestured for her and Valorre to proceed. Before she had to suffer one of Fanon's irritating tugs, she started walking again. She kept her eyes on the sky for several moments, worried the dragon might come back. She had no desire to find out what the creatures did to the unicorns they chased. When she saw no sign of its return, she dropped her gaze to the gray landscape. A wash of color and movement caught her eye.

Half hidden behind a patch of gnarled stumps was a cluster of humanoid figures. They crouched on the ground, palms pressed flat to the colorless earth. They were petite in stature with pointed ears, their skin in every shade of brown and tan, their hair and clothing in the richest earth tones. One was a male with long hair as black as midnight and a tunic of woven moss. Another had hair and eyes in shades of rich green, her leather dress adorned with sparkling beads of morning dew. The nearest figure, a male with hair made from autumn-colored leaves, lifted wide gray eyes to watch them pass. That was when Cora glimpsed the black patterns marking his arms and neck. In fact, all the figures bore such markings on every inch of skin not hidden by clothing. The symbols were more intricate than her own tattoos, but she recognized the *insigmora*.

"Faeryn," Cora said.

"They try to heal the Blight," Etrix said, "but their use of *mora* does little to help. They merely manage to slow the Blight's inevitable course."

"What is the Blight from?"

"The Veil," Etrix said and nothing more. She almost wished Garot was nearby again, for maybe he'd have given a more substantial answer.

She couldn't take her eyes off the Faeryn as they walked by. Unlike the Elvyn, whom she knew little about, she'd heard so much about the Faeryn from the Forest People. The commune's very way of life was dedicated to preserving the Faeryn's ancient ways, their traditions, their harmony with nature. In a way, these figures were like family to her. Not by blood, of course, but an unseen bond.

A sudden spark of hope ignited in her chest. Perhaps if she ran to them, showed them her *insigmora*, and implored them for help, they'd free her from her captors. But as each turned to watch her pass, she caught the ice in their collective gaze, the curl of their lips as they studied her human form. It was enough to tell her they thought no better of her than Fanon did, regardless of the markings on her arms.

She cursed under her breath. It was clear she'd find no allies here, in this realm where humans were feared. Hated. She couldn't fully rely on her own knowledge of the fae either, for the stories the Forest People had told were obviously wrong. The fae weren't extinct. The Elvyn and Faeryn hadn't killed each other in a war five hundred years ago. They were *here*. Alive. Just in another realm.

She could only rely on herself and Valorre, and their primary hope was to get to the Veil and pray to the Mother Goddess there really was a way to cross through.

Only then could she get back home and find some way to save Teryn—and her world—from Morkai.

46

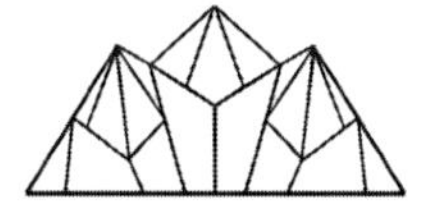

After Morkai left the king's study, Teryn rested his ethera. He had no desire to add more strain to his already failing body. But as soon as he awoke, drifting from his state of floating unconsciousness to bright awareness, he had but one thought. One need.

He opened his eyes and found himself in the illusion of Emylia's temple bedroom. She sat cross-legged at his side, expression resigned as if she knew exactly what he was going to say.

"Show me the rest of your memories."

With a trembling sigh, she nodded.

They rose to their feet. Emylia lifted her hand, and a fog rolled in, covering the floor, walls, and ceiling. When it dispersed, it left behind the muted tones of Desmond's dark room at the inn. Teryn and Emylia stood at the far end while two figures sat at opposite sides of the small desk.

"Are you ready?" the Emylia of memory asked, an edge of excitement in her voice. "We're getting so close, Des. I can feel it."

Desmond nodded, but his expression held a hint of

apprehension. “This is our last session before I return home to Syrus to report to my father. I hope what we’ve learned is enough for him.”

“How could it not be? We’ve done so much work on his behalf, more than he’s ever been able to do on his own, right?”

His lips quirked up at one corner. “When did you become such an optimist?”

“Only when it comes to you,” she said with a wide smile.

His face fell, voice deepening into a whisper. “I don’t know how long I’ll be gone, Em. I hate not knowing when I’ll be back.”

Her smile remained, but it no longer reached her eyes. “Then let’s hurry. I don’t want to spend our last night together working.”

He nodded and anxiously ran his palms over his thighs while Emylia closed her eyes. Desmond kept his voice low and steady. “Where is the mother of the true Morkara now?”

Teryn’s breath caught, knowing this man was asking about Cora. The woman he loved.

Emylia, crystal in hand, remained still while her eyelids fluttered. “Unborn.”

“When will she be born?”

“The year of the Great Bear.”

Teryn was startled to realize how long ago this memory must have been from.

Desmond rubbed his dark brows. “That could be three years from now, thirteen, twenty-three, or more. How many years from now will she be born?”

Emylia remained silent.

Desmond released a frustrated groan. “Fine. What will she look like?”

Again, silence.

He ran his hand through his black hair, sending wayward strands into his pale eyes. His expression brightened. "Wait. She is said to have the beauty of Satsara. What does Satsara look like?"

Emylia tilted her head to show her disbelief. "Just because the mother has the beauty of Satsara doesn't mean they'll look exactly the same. Besides, we don't even know who she is. Every time I've channeled for information on her or Ailan, I get nothing."

"Just try anyway. It could be a helpful clue."

Emylia wore a skeptical frown, but she settled back into her trance. Soon her eyes began to dart behind her closed lids. "I see her," she whispered. "At least...I think I do. She's...beautiful."

"And?" Desmond leaned closer to the desk. "What does she look like?"

"Eyes and hair as black as a raven's wing. Golden skin. She's tall. Slim but powerful. Pointed ears. Mother Goddess, Des! She's Elvyn. A true, beautiful Elvyn." Her voice was rich with awe. "I can't believe I'm seeing one."

Desmond's face melted as he watched her. "She can't be any more stunning than you."

She slowly fluttered her lashes open. "How am I supposed to get any work done when you compliment me like that?"

Desmond rounded the desk and pulled her from her seat. He brushed his hand along her cheek. "We've worked enough. Let's make the rest of tonight about us."

Emylia flung her arms around his neck and they dissolved into tangled limbs and heated kisses.

The true Emylia waved her hand, and the image was swept away in a blanket of fog. When it settled, Teryn found himself on the moonlit cobblestone street outside the inn.

The Emylia of memory sprinted past sleeping storefronts, her dark hair flying wild in a mass of bouncing curls. She looked the same age as the true Emylia did now—a year or two older than she'd been in the previous memory. As she reached the door to the inn, she pulled up short. A figure stood just outside the door, back facing her, a long cloak hiding their form. Then the figure turned and revealed Desmond's face beneath the hood. He ran to her and gathered her into his arms.

"I missed you so much," Emylia said, a wide smile stretching her lips. She lifted her eyes to his vacant expression, the sorrow tugging his lips. Her face fell. "What's wrong?"

Desmond took her by the hand and led her inside the inn. They bypassed the dining room and wove through a narrow hall until they arrived at the same small room as before. "Father lied to me," he said as he ushered her inside and closed the door behind them.

The Emylia of memory wrung her hands. Even Teryn could tell this wasn't the reunion she'd been expecting. "About what?"

Desmond unclasped his cloak and tossed it onto the cot. He was dressed in dark slacks and a long black coat buttoned high to his neck. His hair was longer now, reaching several inches past his shoulders, and his cheekbones were sharper. He began to pace the room, hardly sparing Emylia a glance. "He can't bring my mother back, even if he becomes Morkaius. He doesn't have her ethera."

Emylia tilted her head. "Her ethera? Why would he have her ethera in the first place?"

"I've been reading about the magic of the sanguina and ethera, trying to figure out what Father would need to bring my mother back. While there is no clear formula, I do know he would need her ethera. When I asked him about it, he tried to brush me off. But I asked and asked until he told me the truth." He halted his pacing and met her eyes. "He lied to me. He never planned on bringing my mother back when he became Morkaius. He's been using that story this entire time. Using me to find answers to *his* questions, to override the curse that makes him forget his past."

With slow steps, she approached him. "Des, I'm so sorry. I...I did warn you that it wasn't possible—"

His gaze deepened into a glare, but it quickly softened. He closed the remaining distance between them and embraced her. She rested her cheek against his chest, her head tucked beneath his chin. "Yes, you're right, my love. You warned me."

She pulled away just enough to meet his eyes. "What did he say about the information you've gathered for him?"

His jaw shifted side to side. "He said it isn't enough. He told me I have to keep looking until I find the Heart of El'Ara."

"Are you still going to help him, even though you know he lied?"

Desmond shrugged. "I don't know what else to do. He's my father, and this is a matter of his birthright. A birthright that will one day be passed on to me. He can't claim it without me. Not only has he been cursed to forget, but he is physically weak. He can't leave Syrus the way I can, not until he has a clear destination. And that destination is the Heart of El'Ara. Wherever the hell that is, with its black mountain and violet fields. Have you found this place for me yet?"

She shook her head. "I've read up on flower varieties specific to different regions, unique mountain ranges. I've asked foreign visitors. There are several possibilities, but nothing certain."

He closed his eyes, his frustration made clear in the tense line of his jaw.

"I'm sorry, Des. I'll keep trying. You know I'll do anything for you. And if you're determined to continue serving your father, I'll help. Always."

Teryn tried not to wince at the desperation in her tone. How was she so enamored with the man that she didn't see the darkness lurking in his eyes? The very real threat his quest posed? Teryn had seen love make a fool of his father, nearly tearing his country in two, and he'd given up a crown for the love of his brother and for Cora. But this...this was something else. Everything inside Teryn blared with warning.

The real Emylia stared at the floor, a hint of shame coloring her expression. She met his eyes for a moment, nodding as if to confirm his thoughts. That she too regretted this part of her past.

"Is that a promise?" Desmond said, drawing Teryn's attention back to the figures of the memory. He clutched Emylia's cheeks between his palms. "Will you do anything for me?"

Her throat bobbed, but she said, "Anything."

The image faded, then shifted. The two figures were now sitting at the desk on opposite sides. Emylia held her crystal like she always did when preparing to use her sight. Closing her eyes, she said, "What would you like to ask this time, Des?"

His voice came out cold. Firm. "Find my mother."

47

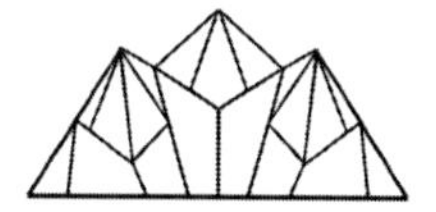

Her eyes flew open at once. "What?"

"I need you to channel my mother's ethera."

She shook her head. "I'm a seer, not a medium. I don't commune with the dead."

"If you can see her, you can draw her forth. I told you; I've been reading about the Art of the ethera and sanguina. I've studied your Art too. You can use the sight to channel my mother."

"Des..."

"You're powerful enough to do this. I know you are. If I'm not going to see her again like Father promised, then I must at least speak to her." He paused, then added, "You said you'd do anything for me."

Emylia pursed her lips, and for a moment Teryn thought she might refuse. Then her expression softened. Her voice came out small. "I'll try."

"Thank you," Desmond said. "Please find her. The spirit of Morgana Solaria."

Her eyes widened. "Morgana Solaria," she echoed. "The Queen of Syrus? You...You're..."

"Prince Desmond Solaria. Son of King Darius Solaria."

A look of hurt crossed her face. "Why didn't you tell me?"

"You loved me for me. I wanted *someone* to love me as I am. For once." Emylia stared back at him, brow furrowed. A tic formed at the corner of Desmond's jaw. "Besides, Father always told me being a royal of this world was nothing when we were the true monarchs of the fae. Now will you find her or not?"

She gave him a curt nod and settled into her meditation.

The room fell under a tense silence as seconds ticked past. Then minutes.

Desmond remained in place at the other side of the desk, hands perched upon his knees. The only sign of his anxiety was the slight jitter of his leg.

"I see her," Emylia whispered.

Desmond sat upright, posture rigid. "You...you do?"

"Yes," she said with a smile. "She looks just like you."

"Make eye contact. Draw her to you."

"I...I don't know—"

"Do it."

Emylia returned to silence. Then, "I made eye contact. She...she doesn't look happy."

"Draw her soul to yours. See yourself connecting with her mind. When she's close, touch her ethera."

Emylia trembled from head to toe. "She...she doesn't want me to touch her."

"Do it, Emylia," Desmond growled. "Do it now."

Emylia let out a strangled cry, then her eyes shot open. Rage darkened her expression. "Desmond," she said, but her voice sounded wrong. Too deep. Too lilting. "What have you done?"

Desmond clasped a hand over his mouth, his expression

twisted with emotion. His throat bobbed. Once. Twice. Finally, he lowered his hand and approached Emylia. "I wanted to hear your voice again, Mother. I miss you so much."

His mother's voice hesitated before it emerged from Emylia's mouth again. "I missed you too, my darling, but this isn't right. You should leave me at peace."

"I want you to come back."

"That isn't possible."

"What if it is?" With slow, deliberate movements, Desmond leaned forward. One palm covered Emylia's hands and the crystal within. The other reached for the collar of his jacket and began to loosen the buttons, one at a time.

"What are you doing, Desmond?" his mother's voice asked.

"I want you back, and I'm willing to sacrifice half my heart to get it." He now had the top of his coat unbuttoned. He pulled it back to reveal a strange marking on the white shirt he wore beneath it. It was a complex pattern drawn over his sternum, illustrated with a dark ink Teryn suspected was blood.

"No!" his mother's voice shouted, erupting from Emylia's lips. A cyclone of air spiraled around Emylia, blowing the seer's hair back and sending papers soaring off the desk. "I don't want to come back! Leave me at peace!"

"No, Mother," Desmond said calmly as he lifted Emylia's hands and brought them toward the marking on his shirt. "I need you."

The wind increased, and Desmond struggled to bring her hands the rest of the way to his chest. The lanterns lighting the room flared in a roar of fire, casting it in an orange glow. Emylia's face angled up at Desmond, her lips peeled back from her teeth. "Let. Me. Go."

Teryn wasn't sure whose voice spoke then, for it seemed both Emylia and Desmond's mother cried out in tandem.

Desmond's eyes went wide as he looked down at Emylia, at her twisted expression. He seemed to falter, and the cyclone of wind increased. Desmond stumbled back, breaking contact with Emylia's hands. She, in turn, dropped the crystal and tumbled from her chair.

In the next moment, the wind was gone, the lanterns extinguished save for one.

Teryn blinked to adjust to the shift in light.

"Why, Mother?" came Desmond's trembling voice. He stared at the ceiling, blinking back tears, shoulders slumped. "Why didn't you want to come back? Is your love for me so weak?"

Only silence answered.

With a heavy sigh, he lowered his gaze. Teryn saw the motionless heap on the floor before Desmond did.

"Emylia!" Desmond called out, rushing to her side. She was sprawled beside her chair, lips pale, face coated in a sheen of sweat. Her crystal lay a foot away from her empty palm. He fell onto the floor and pulled her into his lap. "Say something. Please!"

She mumbled incoherently as blood trickled from her nose.

"No, please no." He rocked her in his lap, tears streaming from his eyes. "I'm so sorry. Forgive me, Em. I did this. I didn't know this would happen."

"Des," she said, voice weak. She lifted a hand toward his cheek but dropped it before it could make contact. Her face went slack, body limp. Fresh blood trickled over her lips, her chin.

Desmond stared down at her, eyes wide with terror. "No, no, no. Emylia!"

She was silent. Still.

A sob broke from Desmond's throat. He pressed his hands to her cheeks, her neck, her wrist, hands trembling with every move. As he released her wrist, his eyes fell on what lay discarded beside her. The crystal. His trembling ceased. With a chilling calm, he grabbed the amber stone. Then, folding her limp fingers around it, he pressed it to his chest, directly over the blood marking his shirt. As soon as the crystal made contact, Desmond heaved forward with an agonized grunt. He stayed like that for several moments, eyes pinched tight. Then his face relaxed. Slowly, he let Emylia's hand slide from around the crystal, from his chest, to the ground.

He cradled the crystal to him. "I'll make this right, Em," he whispered. "I'll bring you back. I've given up half my heart to do so. It belongs to you now."

He crouched beside Emylia's lifeless body and caressed her brow. "Forget my father. Let him stay cursed." He brought his lips close to her ear. "I'll find the Heart of El'Ara myself. I'll find the mother and make sure she never bears this true Morkara. Then when I am Morkaius, I'll find you a new body and we will rule together."

Teryn felt colder than he ever had before. He no longer held any doubt about who Desmond was. He wasn't Morkai's son, but the sorcerer himself. And he'd trapped Emylia in the crystal out of a dark and treacherous love.

Teryn slowly turned to face her and noted her pursed lips, her empty eyes. "He didn't wait until he was Morkaius," she said, voice hollow.

She waved her hand, and their surroundings shifted. Teryn found himself in a candlelit bedroom he'd never seen before. From the gilded portraits lining the walls and the elegant furnishings, Teryn guessed it was inside a palace or manor. The only thing that belied the room's grandeur was the table that stood at the far end of the room, its surface littered with books, vials, and stacks of paper. It reminded Teryn of the contents in the tower library.

Beside a large four-poster bed stood Morkai—and this time Teryn could see all the signs that he was a slightly older version of Desmond. He had the same ageless grace that the former duke had when he'd been alive, but the tender sorrow he'd glimpsed in the younger man's eyes too. He stared down at the bed. Or, more accurately, the female body that laid upon it.

She was slim with hollow cheeks and black hair streaked with silver. Morkai trembled. "We'll try again, Em."

The image stilled, then shifted. The room stayed the same but there was a new body on the bed. Another young woman. This one thrashed and cried as blood streamed from her eyes and nose. With a sudden lurch, she went still. Morkai threw his head back. "We'll try again."

Another image.

Another body.

Another.

Another.

Teryn watched the images flash before him, each one more gruesome, more heartbreaking, than the last.

Emylia waved a hand and the final scene froze. "Morkai knew there was no hope until he had the power of the Morkaius. Too late, he'd learned that to bring an ethera back to life in another's body, one needed blood from the original body. By now, my body was long since gone. Still he tried."

Teryn swallowed hard before voicing the question he

needed an answer to. "You...you tried to do what Morkai is doing to me, didn't you? That's why you know so much. You've not only been in my position, but Morkai's too; the trapped spirit and the invading entity."

She gave a solemn nod. "For the first few attempts, I participated. I was a willing accomplice in trying to take over another's body. He chose women who were unwell. Women who would have died even without our magical interference. It was a mercy, he'd said. But it was clear that what we were doing wreaked havoc on a victim's body. I stopped participating before he moved on to healthy women. By then, he'd also begun sacrificing lives to extend his own. It wasn't his Elvyn blood that made him ageless, but the forbidden Arts. I realized then that the man I'd loved was gone. My refusal to participate in his efforts to bind me to a body made his attempts even more impossible. Years passed before he gave up altogether. Instead, he poured all his focus into finding the Heart of El'Ara and the mother of the true Morkara. He stopped looking for potential candidates for me. At least, for a while he did..."

She waved a hand, and their surroundings shifted yet again. They were now in the tower library at Ridine, the only light coming from the fire blazing in the hearth. Morkai stood beside one of the two chairs facing the hearth, his cane planted beneath him. Cora stood opposite him, in a puddle of spilled tea and broken porcelain. A tea table lay on its side.

Teryn's heart raced as he strode between them. He knew this was only a memory, but he couldn't help wanting to protect her from him.

Morkai stepped closer just the same. "I can give you half my heart."

"Half your heart?" Cora said with a sneer. "Is that what

you consider a proper proposal?"

"The other half doesn't belong to me. But you could. I think my heart would like you. It's a jealous heart, but it could come to understand."

Teryn recalled what Morkai had said when he'd first trapped Emylia inside the crystal. How he'd cried out when he'd brought her hand and the stone to the marking on his shirt.

I'll bring you back. I've given up half my heart to do so. It belongs to you now.

"Working with the ethera takes great sacrifice," Emylia said. "To trap me, he had to sacrifice half of his heart-center —the spiritual aspect of his heart. That's what made him colder. Deadlier."

She waved her hand again, but the scene had only slightly changed. Cora was now doubled over, and a shaft of an arrow was protruding from Morkai's ribs.

"I will give you time to choose me," the sorcerer said. "And you will. You will choose one half of my heart willingly, or you will take the other half unwillingly."

The image froze in place.

"Morkai no longer has even half a heart remaining," Emylia said, "for binding his soul to the crystal with his dying breath stole the second half. He is heartless now, both halves trapped in the very crystal that holds our etheras."

Teryn frowned at her, unsure why she was telling him this. Was she trying to make him understand the sorcerer? Pity him? But a far more pressing realization rose to his mind. "He said if she didn't take half his heart willingly, she'd take his other half unwillingly. Does that mean..."

His mind spun. He couldn't bear to say it out loud.

Emylia did so for him. "Yes. With his goals so close to being realized, he'd chosen his next target. He selected Cora to house my soul. Once he has the power of the Morkaius, he'll do to her what he's trying to do to you. With the power he seeks, Cora won't have a fighting chance."

Rage tore through him, boiling his blood, quickening his pulse. It took all his restraint to steady his breaths. "Tell me the truth, Emylia. What do you want? Whose side are you on?"

"Yours," she said, but her voice was empty. Tired. "I don't want to come back, Teryn. I just want to be at rest."

Teryn studied her for a few silent moments. She'd lied to him. Kept vital facts from him. After what she'd shown him, what she'd confessed to doing, he was even less sure he could trust her than he'd been before.

And yet, she was his only hope. He needed her to unravel the weaving in her memories, seek the pattern Morkai had used to strengthen the crystal's density. Only then did they have any chance of getting free.

Unless...

Had Emylia been telling the truth when she'd said her memory had been too hazy? That she'd been too distant to see the pattern clearly?

She narrowed her eyes, and her expression hardened. "Think what you want of me. Hate me if you must. Distrust me. Just please believe that all I want is to be free from my cage and take the monster who trapped me here with me."

Teryn was taken aback by the sudden ferocity in her tone. The rage that rippled through her, strong enough to match his own.

He gave her a curt nod. "Then we continue with our plan."

"We take him down," she said.

To himself Teryn added, *And protect the woman I love, no matter what it takes.*

48

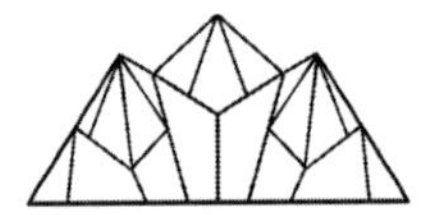

For the first time all day, Mareleau was no longer nauseous. She wanted to believe her calm stomach heralded a finite end to her morning sickness—a misleading term, by the way; she'd thank the seven gods if her roiling gut were relegated to morning—but her relief was likely due to the piece of candied ginger she'd just popped into her mouth. It was a welcome deviation from her constant refills of ginger tea and was all thanks to Ridine's cook. Mareleau had recently learned that if she came to the kitchen to request a refill of her tea in person, the cook would dote on her and hand her a plate of the latest sweet she'd whipped up. The most recent gift being the handkerchief full of candied ginger she now held in her hand.

Mareleau suspected the woman had gleaned the reason behind her constant need for tea, hence the doting. While she'd normally be averse to such babying—she was a queen, after all—she rather liked the woman's attention. And she certainly preferred the candied ginger over the tea.

She meandered away from the kitchen toward the keep

but found her feet moving past the correct staircase in favor of a different one. One she'd already visited twice today and was forbade entrance—

She pulled up short once she reached the stairwell in question. It was...empty.

She'd never seen the tower library stairwell unguarded. Not that she'd ever paid much attention to it before this morning. She'd come to call on Princess Aveline, and since the girl hadn't been in her room, she figured she must already be at work in the tower. But when Mareleau inquired with the guard, he'd insisted she wasn't there. Mareleau's anxiety increased after that, right alongside her incessant nausea. She'd been looking for the princess all day to no avail. She tried to tell herself she was simply bored, but after their strangely comforting conversation the day before, she had to admit she wanted to check in on her. Especially since today was the day she and Teryn were to be wed. Had Aveline managed to tell Teryn about the curse? Had she made peace with her sudden marriage? Had their hushed wedding already taken place?

Mareleau knew a thing or two about such matters. Her own wedding had been hurried, but at least she'd been given a feast afterward. Yet it was already nearing sundown and Mareleau hadn't heard a word whispered about the princess' nuptials or her impending rise to queen.

She cast a glance down both ends of the hall, which were empty, and approached the stairwell. A shudder coursed through her as she glanced up the narrow staircase. Her ladies had whispered time and again that this was where Lurel had taken her fall. A pang of grief struck her heart, but she swallowed it down—along with a fresh piece of candied ginger, for good measure. Then, with wary steps, she began to climb.

The door at the top of the stairs was unguarded as well, left open to reveal strands of herbs hanging in the doorway. The waning evening light cast the stairwell in shadow, as well as the room ahead. Perhaps it was only the rumors that sent apprehension crawling up her spine, but whatever it was, it made her want to keep her steps slow. Silent. She lifted her skirts higher, careful not to step on her hem.

She reached the landing and slowly approached the doorway. The scent of rosemary and old smoke wafted into her nostrils. She frowned at the hanging herbs blocking the top of her view and ducked down for a better glimpse of the room. It looked like total chaos, with crowded bookshelves, a cluttered table piled with objects wrapped in cloth, and two large basins beside an empty fireplace. Mareleau had no desire to step inside the room, for she'd surely find herself covered in dust, soot, and whatever the white substance was that lined the threshold. She was about to call out for Aveline when movement caught her eye.

At the far end of the room, near one of the bookcases, a male figure kneeled. She ducked lower, catching sight of brown hair streaked with white, dark trousers, a linen shirt, and a dark blue waistcoat. He was reaching into a hole in the stone floor. She watched as he extracted two small items that looked like glass vials. He pocketed them, then reached for a large object at his side—a square stone—and gingerly set it into the hole. The sound of stone scraping stone set her teeth on edge. When he was done, there was no sign of the hidden compartment.

The man rose to his feet. Mareleau startled and took a step back, reminding herself just in time that she was at the top of a stairwell. She cast a glance behind her and flung out a hand to catch herself against the wall. When she returned her attention to the room, the man was just on the other side of the doorway. But it wasn't just any man. It was Teryn.

Her eyes went wide. "Teryn, your...your hair! What happened?"

"Ah, yes. Everyone wants to know about my hair."

She arched a brow. That did nothing to explain the white streaks. Equally as concerning were the dark circles under his eyes, the pallor of his skin. "Are you unwell?"

"I'm perfectly well, thank you for asking," he said, voice smooth and disinterested. His smile held an edge she didn't understand. Perhaps she wasn't supposed to see him rifling around in here, digging in that hidden hole.

Well, lucky for him, it was Aveline she was concerned with, not him. She couldn't care less about her brother-in-law. Especially if he was going to continue to act so strange. What did Aveline see in him, anyway?

"Where's Aveline?"

He smirked. "You've come to know her on a first-name basis, yet you call her Aveline and not Cora?"

"She hasn't asked me to call her Cora, and I've only decided as of yesterday that I sort of like her." Though now that he mentioned it, she most certainly would start calling her Cora. Even Larylis referred to her as such. And Mareleau was nothing if not at least a little competitive. If anyone would prove to be Aveline's—no, Cora's—closest friend, it would be her. She'd see to it.

But first she had to find the girl.

"So," Mareleau said, giving him a pointed look, "where is she? I've been looking everywhere."

"Why?"

She lifted her hand, showing off the white gold and sapphire bracelet that dangled from her wrist. "I wanted to give her this and tell her she can't keep it."

Teryn gave her a questioning look.

"Something borrowed," she said. "Obviously. It's her wedding day. I thought she could use at least one small tradition." To be honest, the bracelet was merely meant to serve as an excuse to talk to Cora so that she wouldn't have to admit she was concerned for the girl. Mareleau may have decided making friends with someone might not be the worst thing in the world, but she still had her pride.

"Oh, of course," Teryn said.

Yet still he failed to answer her question.

"Are you trying to be evasive or are you just naturally annoying?" she asked, planting her hands on her hips.

Teryn gave her a simpering grin but said nothing.

She pulled her head back. Where was his clever quip? His insult? Mareleau respected people who had the gall to volley her with scalding banter, and if that made her a masochist, so be it. At least she could trust someone who did more than flatter, pander, and praise. Teryn's teasing wit was what had finally endeared him to her, and her unanswered question practically begged for a clever return, but he...said nothing.

Mareleau released an exasperated groan. "Where is she, Teryn? Where the seven devils is Cora?"

He stepped over the threshold to join her on the landing. She descended the next step down to put space between them. "My darling wife will be in seclusion until the signing of the peace pact. We're keeping our marriage a secret for now, and in the meantime, she is taking the time to properly come to terms with her change in status. It's a great responsibility, becoming queen, as you well know."

His words sparked her pride, and she almost answered with an automatic *Of course I know*, but she stopped herself. He still hadn't given her a clear answer.

"She isn't in her room," she said, "and Master Arther claims not to have seen her since last night."

Teryn's mouth tightened, but he quickly donned an easy grin that didn't meet his eyes. "As my wife, she no longer needs to stay in her own room."

She blushed at what he was suggesting, but that didn't change the fact that she'd had Master Arther unlock Teryn's room this morning too, when he hadn't answered his door. Thankfully the steward was amenable to Mareleau's commands, despite being only a visiting queen, but now she was more perplexed than ever. Did Ridine perhaps have a wedding chamber like the one she and Larylis spent their first night in? If so, why would Cora be there all day while Teryn was out here? Alone?

"Surely, she'll accept my visit—" Her words cut off as Teryn handed her an envelope.

"A letter arrived from your husband this morning."

Her heart stuttered as she tore the envelope from his grip and immediately flicked open the seal. Before she could read its contents, she glanced back at Teryn. "Why do you have my letter? Why wasn't it delivered directly to me?"

"Larylis had a letter for me as well, so the messenger delivered them together. I offered to bring you yours."

That was an adequate excuse, she supposed...

"Don't expect too many more before his arrival," he said. "He'll be traveling by now and likely won't have time to write. And you have your own travels to prepare for."

Excitement flooded her. Larylis was on his way! He'd be here soon, and after the pact was signed, she could return home with him. Was that what travels Teryn was referring to? Surely she didn't need to prepare for departure just yet.

"You may not have heard," Teryn said, "but the signing will now take place on a celebratory hunt. In a few days, we'll make camp not too far from here and await the arrival of your husband and father."

Her eyes went wide. "We? As in...me? Going...hunting?" She wrinkled her nose. She'd never been on a hunt before, and she certainly didn't like the sound of camping. Sleeping at shoddy inns on her way to Ridine had been bad enough.

"I want you there. Cora wants you there. As Queen of Menah and heir to Selay, you're an important part of this pact. Besides, it will allow you more time with your beloved husband. He will be going straight there regardless of whether you attend."

Mareleau narrowed his eyes. There was something about the way he'd phrased that last part that almost made it feel like a threat.

Teryn's smile softened. "What will you call it?"

She paled. Was he referring to the baby? Last they'd spoken, she'd confessed to having lied about her condition. Had her newest change of fortune already spread through the castle?

"Your two kingdoms," Teryn clarified, dousing her anxiety. "Once you're queen of both Menah and Selay, what name will give your new land?"

She gave a flippant shrug. "I haven't considered it."

He took a step closer, his feet reaching the edge of the platform. Mareleau descended another step. "You should think about it. You're a powerful woman, Majesty. Power should fill your every thought. I know it fills mine."

She lowered her brows with a dark glower. "Shouldn't your new wife fill your thoughts instead?"

"Oh, she does. It is because of her that I am here. To give her peace of mind, I'll tidy up her work in the tower. It's merely a matter of redecorating. Surely even I can do that."

Then why the hell had he asked *her* to set up his private

dinner with Cora a few nights back? Furthermore, the odd clusters of hanging herbs and basins on the floor made it seem like there was something other than redecorating going on. She was about to say as much but thought better of it. Brother or no, she didn't like conversing with him when he was in this strange mood. A mood he'd been in since the dinner they shared, she didn't fail to note.

She left him with no other farewell than an irritated scoff and descended the stairs. Her muscles were coiled with agitation. She still hadn't figured out where Cora was. Nevertheless, she'd find her. Until it came time to leave for this grand hunt she was now expected to attend, she'd have little else to do.

At least she had one source of comfort. She opened her husband's letter and sank into the solace of his words.

49

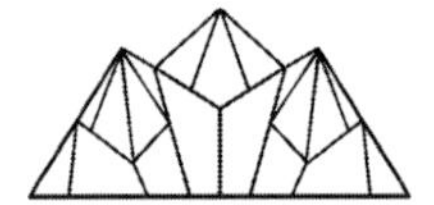

Teryn stared down the stairwell, even after Mareleau had gone. He and Emylia had witnessed her exchange with Morkai, and it left Teryn with a hollow pit of dread where his stomach should be. Teryn had realized something when they were talking; Cora wasn't Morkai's final option for getting everything he wanted. Mareleau could provide it in the same way—everything from her two kingdoms to a body he could use for Emylia.

All Morkai would have to do was get Verdian and Larylis out of the way. Force Mareleau to be his bride.

Teryn's lungs felt tight. While he'd managed to protect Cora somewhat, he now needed to find a way to save everyone else. Larylis. Mareleau. King Verdian.

"Teryn." Emylia's voice, pitched with urgency, stole his attention from the empty stairwell. Morkai had now returned to the tower room and was poring over a book on the cluttered table. Emylia stood beside the sorcerer, watching the pages that flipped by.

Teryn made his way inside, eyes locked on the sorcerer's

waistcoat pocket. He and Emylia had projected themselves outside the crystal in time to catch him lifting the hidden stone in the floor and extracting the two glass vials. Emylia had been right; Morkai had hidden stores of his original body's blood. A necessary ingredient for Teryn and Emylia's plan. Only one essential remained: the pattern that would allow Teryn to unravel the spell on the crystal.

"What is he doing?" Teryn asked, standing at the other side of the table. His eyes fell on the pages of the book Morkai thumbed through. Each was either scribbled over in an elegant script—one he had a feeling belonged to Morkai himself—or bore intricate patterns rendered in ink. He lifted his gaze to Emylia's.

She gave him an affirming nod. "This is his personal book of spells and blueprints."

"What's he looking for?"

"Probably the weaving he utilizes for his Roizan. Now that he has his blood, that's his next step."

Teryn tried to recall what Emylia had told him about the Roizan. He knew Morkai used it as a vessel for magic, and Emylia had said the creatures were born from death, neither alive nor dead. "How exactly does he create a Roizan? What is it made from?"

"In short, a Roizan is forged from two living creatures who suffer violent deaths during combat with each other, resulting in the two dying at the same moment. Morkai utilizes blood weavings to control the time of death for each animal and prolong the fight."

Teryn's lip curled into a sneer. "He makes them suffer?"

"Pain and violence fuel the forbidden Arts."

Teryn shouldn't have been surprised. This was the sorcerer who'd commanded his bands of hunters to capture and torture unicorns. He cast a dark glower at Morkai, though the mage couldn't see it.

Emylia returned her gaze to the pages Morkai continued to flip through. He paused on one that was filled with notes cramping every spare inch of the margins, scanned it briefly, then turned to the next.

Morkai suddenly went rigid and slammed the book shut with a force that made the table shake. Emylia jumped at the sound and leaped to the side. Morkai's head snapped up, eyes locking on Teryn's. Teryn took a stumbling step back, but Morkai's gaze didn't follow. Instead, it hovered straight ahead.

Teryn released a sigh. Of course he couldn't see them.

Morkai narrowed his eyes to slits. His voice came out cold. Slow. So unlike Teryn's own, it made him shudder. "You're watching, aren't you?"

Teryn's eyes found Emylia's; she looked just as startled as he.

"I know you are," Morkai said. "You're hoping you can fight me. Stop me. Well, I assure you, your hope is futile. Watching me will only make it hurt more when you fail. When you breathe your last breath and I take over your lungs. Your life. Your name. You will be nothing. You'll have nothing."

Teryn's fingers curled at his sides. He was half tempted to step into his body and wrestle control then and there, even if for a short time, out of spite alone. But the edges of his rage cooled as he took in his silver-shot hair, the dull green in his eyes, the hollows in his cheeks. Considering how much damage his single instant of repossession had done to his body, he likely only had one more shot. While he could continue to practice strengthening his connection to his cereba, it would be foolish to fully take control again until they had everything in place.

With a slow exhale, he focused on his breaths, his pulse, his pounding heart.

Morkai's lips curled into a cruel grin. "How about I grant you mercy? Trust me. You don't want to see what happens next." He reached into his waistcoat pocket and extracted one of the vials. With his other hand, he lifted the leather-wrapped crystal from under his shirt and let it rest on top of his waistcoat. Lifting the stopper, he dropped a single drop of ruby liquid onto the tip of his finger and brought it to the surface of the crystal.

Everything went white.

Panic crawled up Teryn's throat as the blinding light surrounded him. He tried to will his ethera outside the crystal, but...he couldn't. No matter how he tried, he remained in place.

"Teryn, it's all right." Emylia's calming tone reached him through the white light. Then, starting with the edges of his vision, the colors dulled. Soon brown, red, and saffron washed over the light, forming Emylia's temple bedroom. The seer stood before him, wringing her hands.

"What happened?" he asked.

"He's blocking us now. Remember how I said he used to block me from projecting my ethera outside the crystal when he wanted to? That's what he's doing to us."

"How long will it last?"

"It's just a simple spell. A temporary seal he created with his blood. He still isn't strong enough to do anything permanent. Not until he has his Roizan."

That wasn't entirely comforting. "What if the seal doesn't break until it's too late? I can't step into my body unless I can project my soul outside the crystal. I can't practice connecting to my cereba if—"

"Teryn."

He frowned, noting the way she continued to wring her hands. He thought it was from anxiety, but now he saw the light dancing in her eyes, the ghost of a smile tugging her lips. "What is it?"

"We have something else to do now."

His pulse quickened. Before he could ask her to elaborate, she waved her hand, sending the temple room scattering in a wash of light. It was replaced with a still image of the tower library, exactly how it had been moments before. Morkai stood at the table, eyes narrowed on a page in his book. If they were unable to project themselves outside the crystal, then this must be from Emylia's memory.

She approached Morkai's side. It was uncanny watching her move through an image while Morkai remained frozen. "Look," she said, beckoning Teryn to stand beside her. She pointed at the page.

Teryn leaned forward, taking in the complex diagram of intersecting lines and loops that marked both pages. The pattern was the same on each page, creating a mirror image. Teryn was about to inquire what significance they held when his eyes fell on the script marking the top of the pages. The left-hand side bore the word *Crystal*, while the right said *Unicorn horn*.

He met Emylia's gaze and she gave him a nod. Her eyes were wide, barely concealing her excitement. "We have it, Teryn. This is the pattern."

He glanced back at the complex markings, feeling both daunted and exhilarated at once. He could barely make heads or tails of the pattern. It would take forever to learn how to replicate it. But…this was it. The final piece of their plan.

"Are you ready to learn how to draw it yourself?"

Teryn swallowed his fear. In its place, he felt relief. A growing sense of determination. That gnawing inertia he'd felt after his father's death had compounded ever since he'd gotten stuck in the crystal. Practicing with his cereba had barely taken the edge off. But now, with such a formidable task at hand, and a clear road ahead to do it, Teryn felt strong. Sure. Tenacious.

"Yes," he said. "Let's unravel this damn spell."

King Larylis ached for silence, his wife, and a decent book. Only one was at his disposal, in the form of the empty balcony he stood upon, attached to his borrowed bedroom for the night. Today marked his first day of travel to Ridine Castle, and since he was still in the Kingdom of Menah, his overnight accommodations were provided by an eager lord. Lord Furrowsby's manor was vast, but his hospitality was even more so, which included a musical performance in his grand parlor and a five-course dinner. Larylis had wanted nothing but sleep and solitude when he and his entourage arrived at the manor, but instead he'd been forced to grin and socialize until half past midnight, all while donning the persona of king.

Now that he was finally alone on the spacious balcony, he could let his posture slip, his shoulders slump. He ran a hand through his hair—which was now expertly styled by his valet each morning—loosening it from the stiff gels and waxes that had held it in place all day. He found himself missing the days when no one paid his appearance much heed. Now everything mattered. His hair, his dress, his stride. At least he'd managed to avoid the powdered wigs his valet had suggested. They were popular in Selay, especially with King Verdian. His valet had insisted they'd make him appear more distinguished. Larylis had no desire to don a wig, no matter how fashionable they were, so he'd compromised by subjecting his hair to daily styling.

With a fatigued groan, he leaned over the balcony rail, resting his elbows on the balustrade.

Six more days, he said to himself. Three more days traveling through northeastern Menah, staying at a different lord's house each time, then another three days traveling through Khero. In Khero, he could finally be free from the hospitality of his lords and stay at fine inns instead. When that was all over, he'd reach his destination. Only then would he finally see her again.

Mareleau.

His wife.

His beloved.

What he wouldn't give to shake free from these painfully slow travels. Were he allowed to travel on his own, he'd take a messenger horse and arrive at Ridine in two or three days. Were he allowed to oversee his own schedule, he'd travel with haste and rest only after nightfall, and reach his destination in four days. Instead, his travels had been turned into a political move, a way to engage with his noble subjects.

He understood the reasoning behind it all. He was a king now, and he had responsibilities. Protocols. Impressions to make. Loyalties to secure.

But seven gods, was he tired.

It was safe to say he far preferred reading about kings over being one.

A familiar cadence reached his ears, a soft beat punctuating the quiet night. He stared into the distance, beyond the trees that surrounded Lord Furrowsby's manor, until he saw her. Berol. Moonlight illuminated her wings as she circled over the manor, then made her descent. She landed beside him on the balustrade, one talon curled around something.

Larylis' pulse kicked up. He hadn't received a reply from his brother yet, but the messenger had likely only arrived at Ridine that morning. But Berol would have reached him faster.

He extended his hand toward the falcon. She uncurled her talon and dropped a soft roll of what felt like cloth. Furrowing his brow, he unraveled it, and found a messy scribble of smeared, faded ink. Or was it ink at all? It was too dark to make out the words with moonlight alone, so he rushed inside his temporary bedroom and brought the cloth beside a lantern perched on the bedside table.

His heart leaped into his throat as he read the words. He read it over again. Again. Dread filled his stomach.

Danger at Ridine.

Teryn isn't Teryn.

Trust no one.

What did it mean? It was signed by Cora, but why had she written this message in whatever messy substance marred the cloth? And was the cloth itself...a piece of clothing? It reminded him too much of the blood-splattered scrap Berol had brought him.

None of it made sense. None of it explained anything that was happening. He'd received no other warning. No rushed messages that told of issues at Ridine. His recent letters from Mareleau had contained her usual musings, nothing more.

Larylis bristled with tension. He couldn't wait a week. Couldn't bear to dine and dance when something strange was happening. When his wife could be in danger.

He strode through the room and began to dress in his riding attire. His hands trembled as he laced up his pants, donned his gloves, threw on his coat.

Royal procedure could go to the seven devils. He didn't care if he offended nobles or enraged his guards. He didn't care if leaving now shaved only a few meager days off his travels. If he couldn't act on his instincts, then he was a puppet, not a king.

With hasty steps, he left his room and rapped his knuckles on the next door over. After a few long stretches of silence, a tired face answered the door. But it was the face he trusted most when it came to those who served him—Lord Hardingham. Aside from having been his father's most loyal councilman, he'd always treated Larylis with respect, bastard or no. He'd been at Centerpointe Rock. He'd seen the same terrors Larylis had. Though Hardingham had mourned Arlous' death, he'd stated his support of Larylis' impossible decision, even when the other councilmen continued to question their new king in whispers behind his back.

Only Hardingham would follow Larylis' next demand without question.

"Keep this quiet," Larylis said. "Gather a small selection of guards and meet me in the stables. We make haste for Ridine at once."

Hardingham's only reply was a widening of his eyes, followed by a nod.

Soon Larylis and a modest retinue took off under the blanket of night. His heart raced with fear, the excitement of his rebellion, and a pinch of shame. He knew he could be overreacting. He could be compromising everything.

But with every inch of distance he closed between himself and Ridine, he felt lighter. Freer. He let his thoughts go, lulled by the beat of horse hooves and Berol's wings flapping high overhead.

50

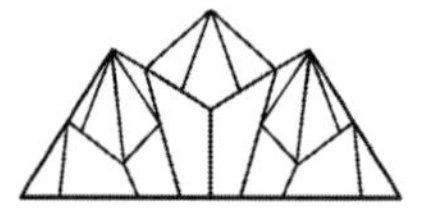

Night had fallen and still Cora and her unwanted companions continued to walk. Her legs ached with fatigue, her neck stiff from trying so hard not to jostle her collar. She'd lost all sense of time, but surely they'd been walking for at least half a day now. Under normal circumstances, a lengthy walk was no problem. She'd traveled on foot plenty during her time stalking Morkai's hunters with Valorre. But this was different. This was walking without rest. Without food. Without any sense of how near or far they were in relation to their destination.

At least the dying landscape of the Blight made for very few obstacles to navigate, but that was of little comfort with the exhaustion that tugged at her bones. She wasn't certain how much time had passed since she'd left Ridine, but she knew she'd been awake for far too long. Thankfully, Etrix had offered her a skin of water—which had been the sweetest, most refreshing water she'd ever tasted—but she wasn't sure how much longer she could go on that alone.

"Can we rest?" she ground out for what felt like the hundredth time.

"No," Fanon said from up ahead. Not once had he fallen back from his position several yards in front of her.

"Then can I ride? If I can just get on Valorre's back, we can travel much faster." She kept her tone pleading and pathetic to hide the truth; if she mounted Valorre, she could outpace all of them and give her and the unicorn a chance to escape through the Veil on their own. If there was a way through, that is.

Fanon glowered over his shoulder. It carried the depth of his ire even with the nighttime shadows muting her vision. "I think not, human."

"I have a name," she said. "It's *Cora,* not *human.*"

Fanon had nothing to say to that and simply increased his pace.

"You must forgive Fanon," Etrix said. Both he and Garot strolled at her side. As annoyed as she was with her captors, having the two close by was some comfort. The Blight was an eerie place. Too vast. Too empty. Too quiet. She constantly expected some faerytale creature to leap from the shadows with pointed fangs and threaten to claw out her eyes. Or perhaps a return of that enormous dragon. Now and then she was certain she could hear its screech in the distance, and she hadn't forgotten what Etrix had said about the dragons chasing unicorns. Thankfully, she'd seen no such creature. In fact, she hadn't seen a single soul aside from her companions since they'd passed the group of Faeryn.

Etrix spoke again. "Acting as Steward of El'Ara is a great burden to bear."

The way Etrix had said *steward* made her think the title was one of respect, and far higher in rank than a castle steward like Master Arther. She frowned at Fanon's back. *He* held a position of power?

"He's no Morkara." A note of sorrow crept into his voice. "We haven't had a true Morkara in a very long time."

The unknown word piqued her curiosity, and she debated asking what it meant. The *mor* portion meant magic, of course, but what about *kara*? It sounded too much like *Morkai* or *Morkaius* to ignore. While she'd kept quiet during most of their walk, focusing only on thoughts of getting home, it occurred to her that her companions might hold vital information about her enemy. Morkai had claimed to be an Elvyn prince, after all. Still, she didn't dare bring him up directly. For all she knew, these three could be the lost prince's most fervent supporters. But she could mine them for knowledge just the same.

"What is a Morkara?" she asked Etrix.

"Morkara is much like a steward, but the burden is given by blood, birth, and *mora*. They hold the highest position in El'Ara and are responsible for directing the flow of *mora* through our entire world. Satsara was the last Morkara we've had, but she died about seventy-five years ago. Fanon has been acting as steward in her place ever since."

"What happened to Satsara?"

A flicker of emotion passed over Etrix's face before he steeled it behind a stoic mask. "Your kind found its way to El'Ara. A human. A worldwalker."

"Oh, let me tell the rest," Garot said, stepping closer to Cora's other side. "You're terrible at telling stories."

"This isn't a *story*, Garot. It's a dark blot in our world's history. Why would you relish telling such a tale?"

Fanon glanced over his shoulder with another scowl. "Why are you bothering to talk with the human at all?"

"I thought she should know the deeds her kind are responsible for," Garot said, but when Fanon faced forward again, he gave Cora an exaggerated wink. She was starting to like the copper-haired Elvyn more and more. Where at first she'd been annoyed by his arrogant amusement over her plight, she'd come to realize his demeanor at least lacked cruelty.

"Fine," Fanon said with a grunt. "Make sure she understands her people's darkest deeds, not just the parts you like to talk about."

Garot puffed his chest and stood tall, and his tone took on the same whimsical quality it had when she'd asked about the Veil. "Morkara Satsara's reign was still new when she met Prince Tristaine, a human lost in El'Ara. He was more than a human, though. More than a prince. He had human magic. A witch, I think your kind call them. And this witch had one of the most dangerous powers we'd ever heard of. One that allowed him to travel anywhere in the blink of an eye."

Cora bristled at hearing him describe a type of magic she held. One the Elvyn considered dangerous. She briefly met Valorre's gaze. *Do you know of this tale? Is that why you told me to lie?*

No. Still don't remember.

Garot continued. "Rumors tell that Prince Tristaine had used scent-based magic to travel. That was how he'd found El'Ara. On Samhain—the day when the barriers between all worlds are at their thinnest—he caught a smell he'd never experienced before and followed it with his magic. That was how he'd crossed worlds for the first time and found himself suddenly in El'Ara. After that, he needed only to recall the scent to return. If you haven't already gleaned, he had the power of a worldwalker."

She gave a sharp nod. His words confirmed everything she'd suspected; a worldwalker was a witch who could astral travel. Not only that, but it sounded like this Prince Tristaine had used clairalience—clear smelling—to do so. Where Cora needed emotion to travel, this worldwalker needed scent.

"You're getting ahead of yourself, Garot," Etrix said, a note of fatigue in his voice.

"Ah, you're right. I was telling you how Satsara first met Tristaine. To explain their first meeting, I must mention the triggers we have woven throughout our land. They alert the Morkara—or the steward, in today's case—of non-fae intruders. On that Samhain eve, when Tristaine first entered El'Ara, a trigger went off and alerted Satsara. As a ward-weaver, she took it upon herself to banish the intruder personally. Instead, she met him and fell in love. She didn't weave a ward around the prince to banish him like she was supposed to. No, she wove a secret ward in a forest alcove where she and the prince could meet again. They began an affair, and it continued well after she was forced to marry her Elvyn consort. Satsara eventually found herself the bearer of the human's child. Upon the child's birth, Satsara could no longer keep her secret. She confessed about her human lover to her consort and her tribunal. All agreed that she must banish Tristaine once and for all. So, finally, she met him one last time and wove a ward around his body that would keep him from ever entering El'Ara again. The child, on the other hand, was permitted to remain."

"A mistake," Etrix said. Cora glanced at the dark-haired fae and was surprised to see the deep furrow in his brow, the distant look in his ruby-brown eyes.

"A very grave mistake," Garot agreed. "This half-witch, half-Elvyn child named Darius grew up alongside his Elvyn sister, Ailan."

Cora tried not to let her surprise show at the name Darius. When she'd brought news of Morkai to the Forest

People, they'd told her about the Morkaius, a man they'd called the Blood of Darius. She'd never learned who Darius had been, or if he perhaps was Morkai himself.

Garot continued. "Despite Darius' tainted blood, Satsara loved him deeply. It caused her great strife when it came time to name her heir."

"The eldest child of the Morkara is always named heir by blood right," Etrix said, "but as Darius was half human, the tribunal encouraged Satsara to choose the younger, pureblood child."

Garot nodded. "As Darius grew, the wisdom of the tribunal became harder to ignore. The boy was tainted with his father's dark magic. He could worldwalk, just like his father could, and left time and again to the human world. Satsara and her tribunal feared he'd use his power for ill, should he be made Morkara. Eventually, Ailan was named heir instead. In a violent scheme of revenge, Darius tricked Satsara's dragon, Berolla, into wounding his sister, which confirmed everyone's fears about him."

"Berolla?" Cora echoed. She'd heard that name in stories. Faerytales told of a legendary fae queen and her faithful dragon. Even Teryn knew the tale, for he'd named his falcon after her.

"Every Morkara is bonded to a dragon," Garot said, "and Berolla was Satsara's bonded companion. Berolla hadn't meant to hurt Ailan, and Darius' cruel trick nearly ended his sister's life. Because of that, Satsara had no choice but to banish Darius. She had to use the very same wardweaving she'd used on his father years before."

She furrowed her brow. "How many kinds of weavers are there? And what exactly does each power do?"

"There are many," Garot said. "More than I can name. But I'll give you a few examples. As I've said, Satsara was a wardweaver, which meant she specialized in creating barriers infused with a protective purpose. As a pathweaver, I manipulate distance for fast travel. Etrix here is a speech-weaver, and he specializes in translation. And Fanon is a skyweaver, which allows him to give shape, form, and pressure to air."

She supposed that accounted for her invisible restraints. A question burned the back of her throat. Her heart hammered as she prepared to voice it. "Is there such a thing as a fateweaver? Or a bloodweaver?"

Garot arched a copper brow. "We have skinweavers who specialize in healing, if that is what you mean by blood-weaver. And we have truthweavers who seek out hidden knowledge about the past, present, and future. Is that what you mean by fateweaver?"

"Not exactly," she said, keeping her tone nonchalant. "Is there any kind of weaver who can change or control another's fate?"

"The Elvyn do nothing of that sort," Etrix said, voice brimming with reproach. "Our magic is neither invasive nor harmful."

She couldn't help but give him a pointed look. If she could move her arms, she'd gesture toward the collar.

Etrix, however, seemed to understand. He gave her an apologetic nod. "Not unless it is out of protection. Like what we're doing to you now. Or like what Satsara did to Darius."

"What she did to Darius was essential indeed," Garot said. "If only her attempt had succeeded. But as she'd begun to weave the ward around her son, Darius realized what was happening. With the power of the worldwalker, he disappeared into the human world before the weaving could take hold."

"Only to return many years later to kill his mother and

destroy the balance of El'Ara." Etrix's words came out in a rush.

Garot frowned at him. "That's a terrible way to end the story."

Etrix's throat bobbed before he spoke. "We're here."

Cora looked straight ahead. With the night so dark and the landscape so gnarled and colorless, it took her a moment to see what he was referring to. Then she saw it, a wall of mist and shadow on the horizon. No, it was nearer than that, stretching out from side to side and swallowing the sky above. She shuddered at the sight. "That's the Veil?"

"Yes," Etrix said. "Though it looks like a sheet of dark mist, it is as impenetrable as a wall."

"What happens now?"

Fanon finally came to a halt and turned to face them. "Now we inspect the Veil and see if it's truly been torn. If it has, and we can surmise that you entered on accident with the unicorn, we'll let you go. If the Veil is torn, you'll be the least of our worries. We'll have war on our hands in a matter of weeks, if not days."

"That's a pessimistic take," Garot said with a sideways grin. "You've heard the whispers of the truthweavers. The Veil will only tear when our Morkara returns. If it has been torn, Ailan could be back."

Fanon clenched his jaw. "If Ailan was going to return, she would have done it ages ago."

Garot shrugged. "It's only been seventy-five years."

"Here, yes, but it's been closer to five hundred years for her. Time passes faster in the human realm. If she were able to return at all, she would have by now."

"We don't know what she's been dealing with in the human world all this time."

"She might not even be alive."

"Are you so afraid of hope, Fanon?"

"I'm not afraid..."

The two Elvyn continued to argue, but Cora's mind remained stuck on what Garot had said about the passage of time. Her heart leaped into her throat, sending a question surging from her lips, her tone frantic. "What do you mean time passes faster in the human realm?"

Fanon and Garot ceased their argument, but it was Etrix who answered. "Our two realms experience time differently, in both tangible and intangible ways. We have no exact calculation, but past events have suggested that one day here is equal to approximately one week in the human realm."

A wave of dizziness tore through her, almost strong enough to make her knees buckle. "You're telling me," she said, voice trembling, "that in the time I've been here, walking through the woods and the Blight, watching day turn to night, everyone I know and love has already lived through several days in my absence."

Etrix had the decency to don a sympathetic frown, but Garot only grinned as he said, "Precisely."

This time Cora's knees truly did give out. They crashed into the soft, decaying soil. She sat back on her heels to keep herself from falling forward. "I have to get home," she whispered. Then louder. "I have to get home *now*!"

Fanon sneered at her. "Is that not why we're at the Veil? Like I said, if there's a tear in the Veil, we'll send you home."

She shifted her jaw side to side, burning him with a glare. "And if there isn't?"

His lips curled into a cruel smile. "Then I suppose that would make you a liar."

Mother Goddess, she hoped there really was a tear. Hoped there was a way to cross through. And if not, then she had to find a way to free her hands from Fanon's bonds and remove the collar, all without using her magic.

She glanced at Valorre.

We go, he said.

She gave him a subtle nod, understanding what his clipped words were meant to convey. No matter what it took, no matter what they had to do, she and Valorre were getting out of there.

51

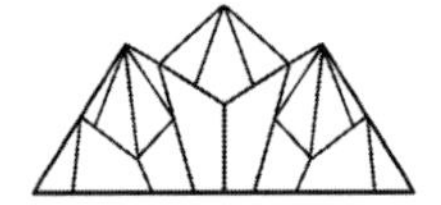

Mareleau hadn't been at the newly erected campsite for more than an hour when she decided she already hated camping. The location was charming, she supposed. She hadn't paid much attention to the scenery on the brief journey here, but now that she'd arrived at her destination, there was little else to do. The wide meadow dotted with bright wildflowers was so lovely, it almost seemed like it had come from a painting. Mountains loomed behind her while a short cliff surrounded by lush forest stood at the other side. The sun was high in the sky, the afternoon warm, but that was where the charm of this supposed hunting expedition ended.

Half of the beautiful meadow and the flowers within it were now crushed by an array of pavilions set up throughout it, leaving only a small area left to wander through. And it was too damn hot for that. Which meant all she could do was sit under the open-air tent that served as a makeshift parlor with her ladies and try not to lose her mind.

Just a few more days, then Larylis will be here, she

reminded herself. *Just a few more days after that, and I get to go home with him.*

Mareleau sank deeper into the cushions of the divan she reclined on, grateful she had no one to put on airs for. There were no courtiers in attendance, only servants, and the men were in their own tent at the other side of the meadow, preparing for their hunt. Breah, Ann, and Sera lounged in chairs around her, gossiping with the same ease they always did. How were her ladies so adaptable, regardless of circumstance? Did none of them miss Selay? Verlot Palace? Did none of them yearn for the stability of their new home at Dermaine Palace like she did?

Instead of voicing any of her questions aloud, she filled her mouth with sweets. Reaching across the tea table, she plucked up a lemon cookie and a piece of candied ginger from a porcelain plate. She chose one of each, less out of hunger and more out of boredom. Gods, she was miserable. There was even less to do here than there'd been at the castle. At least at Ridine she could wander alone and find some empty hall to cry in—something her emotions demanded on a whim these days—but here there was nowhere to go beyond this tent or the meadow. Unless she fancied a trip into the woods where she could get eaten by bears, mosquitoes, or both.

At least no one expected her to attend the hunt itself. Teryn, her uncles, and King Dimetreus would depart for the day's adventure any time now. Mareleau cast a glance toward the men's pavilion, and saw only silhouettes as they lounged, drank, and laughed. Around them, servants gathered supplies and readied horses. She was surprised King Dimetreus was here, considering what Cora had said. Dimetreus was technically no longer king. But of course, to abdicate his position, he'd need his sister to take his place.

A sister who was eerily absent.

Mareleau hadn't caught a single glimpse of Cora the last few days, much to her growing dread. Whenever she'd asked Teryn about her whereabouts, he'd insist she was under severe protection and wouldn't publicly show herself until after the peace pact was signed. It made sense, she supposed. If Cora was now queen, she'd need far more protection than when she'd been a princess. But this seemed excessive. Especially considering just how little anyone regarded Mareleau's safety, and she'd been queen for nearly three weeks longer than her new friend.

Breah shifted in her seat and turned toward Mareleau with a wide grin. "Are you comfortable, Majesty? Do you need more tea? More pillows?"

Well, at least *someone* paid attention to her well-being.

Before she could answer, Sera leaped from her seat and began pouring a fresh cup anyway. "You must stay hydrated in this heat. And eat as many sweets as you like." She shoved the plate of cookies a little closer.

Breah scowled at Sera, but the other girl paid her no heed.

Sera batted her lashes. "What else do you need, Majesty?"

Ever since Cora had taken up confinement, Sera had returned to Mareleau's side. It seemed the girl was now desperate to prove she was indispensable. Her efforts, though, bordered on annoying more often than not.

Ann, not wanting to be left out of whatever competition was brewing amongst the queen's ladies, stood from her chair. "How about a bath, Majesty? I saw a tub in one of the wagons. I can boil water for you and scent it with oils. Oh, and wildflowers from the meadow!"

Mareleau didn't want to encourage their petty rivalries,

but seven gods, a bath sounded divine. She already felt filthy after this morning's journey, not to mention the sweat caused by the afternoon sun blazing through the open sides of the tent. Additionally, a bath meant privacy. Time alone. Some semblance of peace and purpose in her boredom.

"Very well," she said to Ann, which earned the girl dark glowers from both Breah and Sera, "you may draw me a bath."

LARYLIS WAS NOTHING MORE THAN RAW NERVES DRESSED IN human flesh as he rode through the forest toward his destination. A page in Lord Kevan's livery led the way, guiding him from Ridine Castle to some undisclosed location in the woods nearby. Apparently, the signing of the peace pact would take place on a royal hunt. Thankfully Larylis wasn't alone, otherwise his imagination might have carried him away to the worst possible scenario. However, it wasn't Lord Hardingham at his side, calming him down with cool logic; it was King Verdian.

Verdian had been the last person Larylis had wanted to meet on the road, but two days ago, Larylis' small entourage had caught up with Verdian's much larger one. Larylis had no choice but to tell his father-in-law of Cora's strange letter to explain why he'd left his retinue. He'd expected a barrage of insults at having acted so recklessly, and Verdian certainly had a few choice words to say, but after reading Cora's fading letter a time or two more, the king had calmed down. He'd still insisted the letter was simply the result of a lovers' quarrel, but his subsequent actions had belied his confident words. Like Larylis had done, Verdian had selected a small group to ride with haste to Ridine.

Thus, Larylis earned his unwanted companion.

He had to admit the king steadied his nerves somewhat. He hoped with all his heart that Verdian was right—that Cora's letter was the culmination of a simple quarrel and nothing more.

"We're here," the young page said, guiding their party into a wide clearing. A sunlit meadow stretched ahead, filled with several pavilions. At the edge of the meadow, a group of men on horseback entered the woods. Larylis thought he could make out the figures of King Dimetreus and Lord Kevan. Closer, another group mounted their horses. Lord Ulrich was amongst them, and…was that Teryn?

Larylis hadn't recognized his brother first, for his back had been facing them. But now that Teryn turned, Larylis saw his face beneath a tricorn hat. Larylis frowned. Since when did Teryn wear tricorns on a hunt? He didn't think he'd ever seen his brother don a hat.

Teryn tugged his horse's reins and faced the approaching party. "Brother. King Verdian. I'm glad to see you've arrived early. We were just about to depart for the day's hunt. Will you be joining us?"

Larylis frowned. That was Teryn's voice, but his tone was too formal. The hat cast Teryn's face in shadow, but Larylis was almost certain his cheeks appeared thinner. Paler.

Verdian said nothing to Teryn and rode straight for Ulrich. Larylis watched as the brothers spoke in hushed tones, their horses side by side. There was something smug about Ulrich's countenance, and he gave only short answers to Verdian's questions, most of which were too quiet for Larylis to hear.

He forced his attention back to Teryn, who remained

seated on his horse. Keeping his voice casual, he said, "Are you well, brother?"

"Quite. And you? How were your travels?"

He was too polite. Too stiff. He was acting different, but that didn't suggest anything outright sinister. "We met no trouble on the road. Where is Princess Aveline?"

"She'll be with us shortly." He shifted in his saddle and pointed to the other end of the meadow. "Your wife is in the last tent."

Had that been...a diversion? If so, it worked. Larylis' eyes locked on the elegant pavilion. He recognized Mareleau's lady's maids chatting outside the closed front flap. From the ease of their postures, the animated manners in which they spoke to each other, he sensed nothing amiss. Nothing to suggest Mareleau was in danger.

He returned his gaze to Teryn and saw his brother smiling back at him. It was a familiar grin, as comforting as a warm embrace. Larylis was starting to believe he really had overreacted.

"She's missed you terribly," Teryn said, lowering his voice. His previous air of formality was gone. "I'm sure you already knew that."

Verdian broke away from Ulrich. "I'll see my daughter at once."

"I believe she's bathing, Majesty," Teryn said, prompting a flush of color to rise to the king's cheeks. "At least, that's what I've guessed based on the many buckets of boiled water I saw one of her maids dragging into the tent for the better part of an hour."

Teryn was back to that formal tone again. Was it simply an act he was putting on in front of Verdian?

Larylis glanced back at his wife's pavilion, heart pulsing with longing. While he had many questions to ask Teryn, he needed to see Mareleau. Needed to confirm she truly was safe.

"Why don't you stay here, brother?" Teryn said. "Verdian, you should join us on our hunt. We have much to discuss regarding the peace pact, and what better time to start than now? If we are to take advantage of the daylight, we must leave at once. Dimetreus and Kevan already have a head start." He nodded toward the edge of the woods where the first party was now hidden beyond the trees.

"Very well," Verdian said, giving Larylis a subtle nod. Larylis knew what he was wordlessly trying to convey: Larylis would check on Mareleau while Verdian assessed the situation with Teryn and the others. Verdian ordered two of his guards to remain behind with Larylis while the other two would accompany him on the hunt. Larylis had left Lord Hardingham and his own guards back at Ridine to keep an eye on things there.

"Let's be off then," Teryn said, then cast his smile at Larylis again. "You'll join us on tomorrow's hunt, though, won't you? It will be like old times."

Larylis mirrored his brother's grin. Was he pulling at straws trying to find something malevolent in his brother's eyes? Of course this was Teryn. This was his brother. His best friend. "Like old times."

Only...where was Berol? She'd accompanied Larylis on his journey until he'd met up with Verdian. After that, she'd made an appearance now and then, reminding him she was still following, but her absence struck him now. Why wasn't she perched on Teryn's shoulder, elated to see him? Or at the very least circling overhead?

"Give her this." Verdian's voice roused Larylis from his thoughts. The king pulled his horse up beside Larylis' mount and thrust out a small package.

Larylis took it, brow furrowed.

Verdian's cheeks pinked again. "It's for the baby. My... grandchild," he muttered between his teeth, then pulled his horse away.

Larylis watched after him, a lump caught in his throat. While Larylis knew Mareleau's condition was fabricated, Verdian's gesture moved him. Perhaps he really had come to regret the awful things he'd said to her when they'd last spoken.

Larylis watched the party depart, a sight that made his gut feel heavy, then rode for the other end of the meadow. With Verdian's gift clutched in his hand, he dismounted and made a beeline for Mareleau's tent. Her three ladies caught sight of him and dipped into hasty curtsies.

"Majesty," Breah said, eyes wide, "the queen is inside, but—"

He didn't let her finish. Ignoring their flustered warnings, he charged into the tent, his heart racing with every step.

The air was heavy inside, even warmer than the outdoor summer temperature, infused with jasmine-scented steam. It wafted from a copper basin at the center of the tent. And in it was his wife.

She bolted upright when she saw him, rising from the tub in a rush. "Larylis!"

He pulled up short, eyes falling on her bare torso, taking in the rivulets of water trailing down her neck, her breasts, the planes of her stomach. He'd known she was bathing. Known she'd likely be naked. But seeing her like this, the surprise on her face, followed by the way she immediately sank back into the tub, filled him with an aching sense of self-awareness.

He turned abruptly around. "I'm sorry," he called over

his shoulder, not daring to look at her. "I thought you'd be behind a screen."

He heard nothing in reply, only the pounding of his heart.

Seven devils, had he embarrassed her? Offended her?

He'd been too caught in his worry, his passion, his desperation to see her, that he hadn't stopped to consider one important thing: that even though they'd loved each other for years and were now married, their relationship was still new in many ways. They'd been estranged for longer than they'd been lovers and had spent most of their marriage apart. While Larylis was confident when writing love letters, able to bare his soul and express the depths of his heart behind the safety of a quill and paper, he suddenly found himself feeling very much tongue-tied and vulnerable. How was he supposed to act with her in person? Could he voice aloud the things he'd said in his letters?

As for seeing her naked...well, they'd only been wholly intimate once. That hardly granted him permission to barge in on her while she was bathing. What had he been thinking? Still, the memory of their single night of passion surged through him now, mingling with the sight of seeing her in the tub. It sent heat coursing through him that he wasn't sure was entirely appropriate in this moment. Never before had he felt less like a king and more like a fool.

He swallowed hard and took a step forward, prepared to bolt from the tent—

"Larylis." This time Mareleau's voice held no surprise, only softness. "Turn around, you idiot."

The taunting in her tone set his nerves at ease, encouraged his lips to curl up at the corners. Slowly, he shifted back to face her.

She was standing again, but this time her chin was lifted,

her shoulders thrown back. Again, he couldn't keep his eyes from wandering down her figure. Now that he had her permission, he let himself savor every inch of her slick skin, her ample curves, the pale hair that framed her shoulders. He lifted his gaze to her eyes, saw hunger in them, as well as a dash of timidity that matched his own. She grinned, biting a corner of her bottom lip.

"Come here." Her words were whispered, but there was command in her tone. "Get in the tub with me."

His stomach tightened, his mind going blissfully empty.

He dropped the gift and shrugged off his jacket and sword belt in quick succession, letting them fall to the floor before he strode straight for his wife. With every step, he loosened a button, discarded one piece of clothing, then the next, until he stood bare before the tub, his lips pressed against hers. She pulled him tight to her, angling her head to deepen the kiss. Her tongue swept against his, and he released a throaty moan.

He no longer felt an ounce of apprehension between them. His fear melted away, as did his self-consciousness. In this moment, he was the confident king he'd been in his letters. Every promise he'd made, every embarrassing poem he'd drafted during their time apart now filled his lips, his tongue, his fingertips, reaffirming his affection for her.

Stepping blindly into the tub, he erased every inch of space that separated them. One hand circled her bottom while the other explored the generous curve of her breast. She arched against him as if she yearned to be even closer than their flush bodies would allow. He breathed in every kiss she gave him like it was air, touched every part of her like he was committing the feel of her to memory. Desire seared his core, coalescing in a hungry roar that pulsed between them, infused their shared kisses and groping hands. He sank into the basin, his fingers tangled in her sodden hair. She followed him into the water, straddling his hips as she lowered herself on top of him.

She pulled her face back slightly, eyes locked on his. "Gods, I missed you, Lare."

He opened his mouth, but she didn't give him a chance to say anything back. Instead, she kissed him again. With a rock of her hips, she lowered herself further onto him, sparking new sensations of pleasure. Larylis forgot his fears, forgot everything but her as they lost themselves in each other's bodies, in their love, and made up for lost time.

52

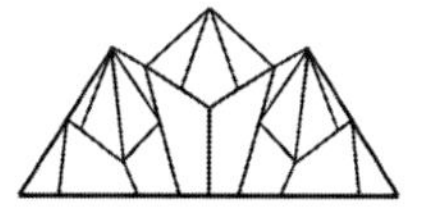

Mareleau had never heard a sound more beautiful than Larylis' heartbeat. It thudded against her ear, echoing the pound of her own. They reclined on the pallet that was nestled at the far end of Mareleau's tent, their bodies tangled in blankets and furs. Based on the lack of light streaming through the canvas walls, and the darkening shadows that grew around the single lantern lit inside, it must be night now. Mareleau had lost all sense of time during her impassioned reunion with her husband. The memory of their time in the tub—then on the floor, then again on the pallet where they now lay—flooded her with warmth, and a tingling heat built between her thighs. It seemed her desire for him would never be satiated. Her body, on the other hand, was spent.

She shifted her face to prop her chin on his chest and assessed her husband's countenance. Gods, he was beautiful. His eyes were closed, but she'd drunk in their emerald hue when she'd been astride him earlier, studying his every expression, his every sound, as he'd wrung pleasure from her, and she from him. Their love was both long-standing and new. She was determined to know every angle of him, all the quirks and facets she'd never learned, and any she may have forgotten in their three years apart.

His dark lashes fluttered, and he glanced down at her with a sleepy grin. She lifted a hand and lightly brushed the curve of his bottom lip, then trailed it across the hard edge of his lightly stubbled jaw. His throat bobbed as she brushed the column of his neck, then his collarbone. Her fingers drifted behind his head to where his hair curled slightly, damp with sweat and bathwater. She liked seeing him like this. Undone. Rugged. She liked the way his body tensed as she shifted against him. Lifting herself slightly, she planted a kiss on his lips. His mouth met hers in a tender softness that had been absent between them earlier. With their desires quenched, there was a slowness to their kiss now. A promise.

His hands came to her hips, rounding her curves in a way that had her stomach tightening, her center tingling. Perhaps their desires weren't so quenched after all.

She was about to deepen the kiss, but Larylis pulled away. "I wish we could do this all day."

"Look around, Lare," she said with a chuckle. "We already did."

A furrow formed between his brows. He pulled himself to sitting and glanced around the tent. When his eyes fell on the solitary light glowing from the lantern, a sideways grin took over his lips. He returned his gaze to her. "I suppose you're right. But still..."

She sat upright before him and pushed out her bottom lip in a mock pout. It had the effect she'd been after. His eyes dipped to her mouth. Then to her bare torso.

A groan built in the back of his throat. "You make it very hard—"

"I know." She let her eyes dip to his waist.

"—to talk about anything serious," he said, his words dissolving in a laugh.

"Must we? There are so many better things we could do tonight."

His mirth slowly began to drain from his face. "There... there are some things we should talk about."

She didn't like where that was going. His words almost made her feel like she was in trouble. More than that, they reminded her that she had something very serious to tell him too. Something she hadn't dared confess by way of letter. Her hand went impulsively to her belly, soft and curving in the way it always was, yet too small to reveal the secret growing within. She snatched her hand away and batted her lashes. "Like the gift you brought me?"

Maybe she was a coward for changing the subject, but she wasn't ready to lose the sweetness of their reunion.

"The gift?"

"I saw you carrying a package when you entered. Was it for me?"

His smile returned, but it wasn't as bright as before. "It was, but it wasn't from me. It's from your father."

"My father?" Verdian was an even drearier topic than the one she was trying to avoid. But...had he really gotten her a gift? If so, why did Larylis have it?

Larylis threw back the blankets and left the pallet, making his way across the tent to gather his discarded clothing one piece at a time. Mareleau took the opportunity to admire his lean build, his bare broad shoulders, and the perfect view of his backside. Her shoulders slumped as he hid the latter beneath his trousers, then the former beneath his shirt.

Not wanting to be the only one naked, she retrieved the

chemise and robe Ann had left out before her bath. She pulled the chemise over her head and belted the silk robe at her waist. Larylis reached the package he'd left by his jacket and sword belt and brought it back to the pallet with him.

"I crossed paths with your father on my way here," he said, holding the package out to her.

Gingerly, she accepted the gift and lowered herself back onto the pallet. The package was a bundle of brown canvas tied with string. Whatever was inside, it was soft and shapeless.

Larylis planted himself beside her, but there was a tenseness in his posture. "We traveled here together, but when we arrived, he left for the hunt with Teryn, Dimetreus, and your uncles. He asked me to give this to you. But...but I don't know if you want to open it."

She lifted her eyes from the gift to find a grimace on Larylis' face. "Why not?"

"He said it was for the baby. For his grandchild."

Mareleau's heart stuttered. Heat rushed to her cheeks, renewing her panic over what she needed to tell Larylis. But beside her anxiety was something tender. Something laced with guilt and love.

She dropped her gaze back to the package and slowly worked the knots in the string. One by one, they fell away, followed by the canvas wrapping. As it unfolded, it revealed a bundle of cloth. She lifted the item, finding a small blanket made from the softest red velvet on one side and elegant white and gold brocade on the other. The pattern was of vines and roses—white ones to represent Selay's sigil—with woodland creatures weaving through the brambles.

Tears stung her eyes.

Her father had gifted this to her. To the baby. His grandchild.

While she couldn't banish the resentment that constantly burned in her heart, she felt the edges smooth out.

"I think he's sorry," Larylis said, shifting closer to her. "Though I know you'll eventually have to tell him..."

He didn't finish, but Mareleau knew what he was trying to say. Soon she'd have to tell her father that her condition had come to an end. That had been the plan, at least.

With the gift in her lap and the emotions building in her chest, the cruelty of her original scheme struck her like a knife to the chest. Yes, she'd been willing to do whatever it took to be with Larylis, but couldn't she have gone about it another way? She'd been desperate then, fueled by anger and indignation. But she'd lied about a subject that no longer felt like an easy pawn to play with. It felt fragile. Tenuous. Precious. Something that shouldn't be treated like a game. She remembered how Cora had praised her for not wanting to treat children like pawns. The princess had given her far too much credit.

Again her hand went to her belly. She hadn't made peace with her pregnancy and had no clue how Larylis would react. She remembered his bitterness over her lie, but that didn't mean he wanted children any time soon. Yet... something brighter than fear ignited inside her. A fierce and protective fire she'd never felt before. She let it grow. Let it warm her heart and soul.

Her vision blurred beneath a sheen of tears. She felt the pallet shift, then Larylis' arms gathering her to his chest. "It's all right, Mare," he whispered into her hair. "We'll tell him together. I'll support your lie in every way, then we'll never need to speak of it again."

Her pulse sped like hummingbird wings, drawing words to her lips. Once she said them, she couldn't take them back.

With a deep breath, she pulled away. He kept his arms around her shoulders, as if he feared she'd fall apart. Maybe she would. Her voice trembled, her tone a whisper. "It isn't a lie. Not anymore."

Larylis blinked at her several times. "What do you mean?"

"It isn't a lie. I...I'm with child."

His eyes went wide.

"At least I think I am," she said in a rush. "I haven't been seen by a physician, but the signs are rather hard to ignore—"

Larylis pulled her back to him again. His embrace was tighter this time, as if he too felt that protective fire. They stayed like that for endless moments, saying nothing, letting their shared tears relay the promises in their hearts.

THE EDGES OF TERYN'S CONSCIOUSNESS THREATENED TO FRAY, but he forced his focus to remain steady, narrowing onto the thin strand of light he drew with the tip of his finger. He didn't know how long he'd been drawing, but the pattern was nearly complete. A rectangle composed of interlocking loops and lines hovered midair beneath his hand. Just a few more lines remained...

Teryn turned his hand, executing a precise loop with the glowing light that trailed his finger like ink. Finally, he made the final mark, a straight line at the very top. With a gasp, he broke away from the pattern. Emylia stood beside him, remaining silent as he connected with his vitale. One breath. Two. He counted his heartbeat, sank into the rhythm of his pulse. Once his nerves had settled, he lifted his gaze to the pattern that hovered before him.

He and Emylia were in her temple bedroom, and the weaving glowed like an apparition in the air. Emylia had taught him how to manipulate the crystal's light, how to use it to cut through her illusions to create markings in the air. It took all of Teryn's concentration to focus on drawing with light, but without a body, much less paper and ink, this was the only way he could practice the pattern.

"It's perfect," she said, stepping closer and studying it from every angle.

Teryn nodded. He already knew it was. This was the seventh time he'd perfectly replicated the markings they'd found in the book from memory alone. Before this, he'd practiced tracing it, then copying the image beside the original. He'd lost count of how many unsuccessful attempts he'd made before his seven perfect ones, but he knew how many days had passed. Five since they'd discovered the pattern. Six since he'd had last seen Cora.

Despite Emylia's insistence that the blood seal would eventually fade, they were still unable to project themselves outside the crystal unless Morkai was sleeping. That wouldn't have been a problem, for Teryn would have an easier time taking over his body while Morkai slept, but the sorcerer was already a step ahead. Each night, he'd begun tying a wrist to the bedpost, and the vials of blood Teryn needed to draw the pattern with were always at the far end of the room. This meant Teryn had to first throw all his efforts into untying the binds around his wrists before he could attempt anything else. Even so, Morkai almost always awoke before Teryn could free his wrist. The one time he'd managed to free himself, he was so fatigued that he hadn't managed more than a single step away from the bed before he lost consciousness.

He hated his own futility. While he'd grown more adept

at seizing control over his cereba at night, it still wasn't easy. His moves were uncoordinated, erratic, his limbs too heavy as if they weren't his own. The only time he'd felt somewhat whole was when he'd stepped into his body to kiss Cora.

His heart ached at the thought of her. Where was she? Was she somewhere safe? He had no idea what was happening during the day. What dark deeds had Morkai accomplished in Teryn's absence?

He had no answers. All he could do was practice.

Practice.

Practice.

So that when the time came, he'd be ready to act.

He waved his hand through the weaving and the light dissolved. "Again," he said, and started the drawing all over again, working from the bottom up.

Emylia had shown him the memory of the original weaving. She'd been telling the truth about it being too far away for her to clearly see. The crystal had been resting on a stone in the forest while a pair of hunters held down a gray unicorn with iron chains. Morkai had stood in the shadows far from the crystal—beyond the radius Emylia could project from—while he'd woven his pattern of blood. Unlike Teryn, Morkai didn't use his hands to manipulate blood. Instead, the blood moved on its own above the sorcerer's palm. Still, Teryn had been able to make out one important detail: where the pattern started. It began with a straight line across before weaving downward toward Morkai's hand.

After studying the pattern, Teryn knew it had been forged of a single unbroken line from top to bottom. All Teryn had to do was draw it in reverse. To fully break the spell, he'd need to draw it with the sorcerer's blood, and to do that he'd need to memorize the pattern.

He had one step down. One step that he was determined to repeat over and over—

Teryn's hand froze, his newest drawing only a quarter complete. A sense of pressure eased from around him. It was a sensation he'd only begun to feel since Morkai had blocked him and Emylia from projecting, and he rarely noticed it until it was gone. The only time it dissipated was when Morkai was asleep.

His eyes met Emylia's, and she gave him a nod.

It was time to practice in a more tangible way. Perhaps this time he'd make it across the room to the vials of blood.

But as he and Emylia projected their etheras outside the crystal, it wasn't into the dark bedroom at Ridine Castle. It was a clearing in a dense forest blanketed by night, illuminated under shafts of moonlight that stretched pale claws through the treetops. Teryn's body was hunched on the ground. The sorcerer inhabiting the body curled his fingers, one hand digging into the earth, the other clutching his chest. His head was bent over several pieces of parchment that littered the mossy forest floor. On each page was a pattern inked in red.

Blood weavings.

Morkai's chest heaved, but it was Teryn who felt those breaths, felt the shallow pulses of air that moved inside him. Morkai sat back on his heels and threw his head back, letting the moonlight wash over his face. His lips twisted in a triumphant smile.

Teryn looked from the sorcerer to the bloodstained papers, then to Emylia. "What has he done?"

Her gaze was locked on something farther away.

Teryn followed her line of sight. His breath caught as he saw a hulking form half hidden in shadow. He stepped closer, noting the silhouette of a pair of antlers, an enormous set of paws. The creature shifted on those paws and took a lumbering step toward Morkai. Moonlight shone on brown fur and claws that dug into the earth. Another step revealed a boar-like snout with curving tusks, nostrils flaring over a mouth of serrated teeth. Teryn saw the antlers clearly now, each tine ending in a deadly point. But that wasn't nearly as unsettling as what rested below those antlers; where eyes should be, the creature had four fleshy faces.

Four faces with mouths locked open in a silent scream.

Four faces with hollow gazes.

Four faces Teryn knew.

Four faces that had now become a Roizan.

53

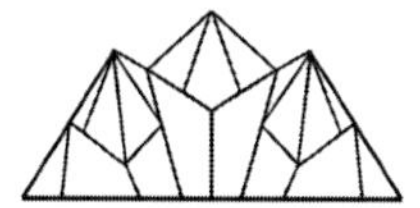

The Veil was even more immense up close. Cora stared up at the strange wall, watching it writhe with swirling particles of shadows and mist. When they'd first approached, Fanon had ordered her to walk through the Veil. His smug grin should have been enough to tell her it wouldn't work, but her hope had been too strong. Just when she was certain the Veil would be as yielding as a fog, she'd found herself against something solid. She'd first suspected Fanon's magic, but then she noted her hands were suddenly free, her palms pressed against the invisible wall. As realization had dawned, she'd immediately reached for her collar. But before her fingers could make contact, Fanon used his magic to pin her arms to her sides and fling her several feet back from the wall.

"Well, at least we know the wardweaving remains strong," Fanon had said. After that, he'd approached the Veil, pressed both palms to its swirling surface, and closed his eyes.

Then he'd stood there.

Unmoving.

For hours.

Or had it only been minutes? Now that she knew time moved differently here, she was unable to trust her own estimation. It certainly didn't help that she had nothing to do but stand painfully idle next to Valorre, Etrix, and Garot while Fanon faced the Veil doing...whatever the hell he was doing. Every second that crawled by was like a knife twisting in her heart. Because each of those seconds were minutes for her world. For Teryn. If day broke, they'd be approaching a week.

Mother Goddess, would Teryn last that long? What could Morkai be doing to her kingdom right now?

"I know you must be anxious to return home," Etrix said, stepping closer to her, "but we must give Fanon time. He's extending his skyweaving all along the Veil, seeking the source of a possible tear."

So that was what he was doing. If only Fanon's task took the whole of his attention. She'd tested her abilities to fight her restraints while he was so distracted, tried to approach the wall a few times, but each attempt had resulted in invisible pressure holding her back. She wasn't sure how his skyweaving worked, but his magic was obviously strong.

Garot shifted to face her. "Would you like to hear a story? I find stories relax me, and I never did finish telling you the history of your kind's dark deeds."

She bristled. So far his story had only revealed that a witch had used magic that brought him to El'Ara, and it didn't sound like a *dark deed* so much as an accident that resulted in a love affair. Their child, on the other hand, seemed a bit unhinged, but he wasn't *her kind*. He may have been half witch and a worldwalker, but he was half Elvyn too. After meeting Fanon, it wasn't hard to imagine Darius may have gotten his cruel streak from his Elvyn side.

Of course, there was likely much she still didn't know. Besides, a distraction might make the wait less agonizing. Especially if it provided more answers that could aid her escape.

"Will you tell me more about the Veil?" she asked, trying to sound more bored than desperate. "Has the border between our worlds always been here, or was it created to keep Darius out after he escaped Satsara's first ward?"

"The latter," Garot said, "though the fact that you can see it is proof that the ward is flawed. Had it been properly completed, it would be invisible to us all, and we'd never have to fear anyone crossing into our world again."

"Why wasn't it properly completed?"

Garot's tone took on that whimsical storytelling quality again. "Before I can explain that, I must first tell you of Darius' return. Feeling betrayed by what his mother had tried to do, he now came with invasion in mind. He insisted he was the rightful heir and would claim his place as Morkaius. Not Morkara, mind you, but as the self-proclaimed High King. Where the Morkara is responsible for distributing the *mora* fairly and evenly throughout the land, Darius sought to control it and harness it as he saw fit. War came. He used his worldwalking abilities to bring in human armies wielding weapons of iron. Many, many died."

Cora tried not to let the terrified awe show on her face. Darius was no doubt the first Morkaius Salinda had told her about. She remembered the story, about the illegitimate son of the Elvyn queen, how he'd sought to overthrow his sister as heir. Salinda had said the war ended in a final battle at a palace, and that an explosion had turned the structure into a ruin. She'd surmised that Centerpointe Rock had been that ruin. That was where Morkai had intended to harness fae magic from, after all. It had made sense when she'd believed the fae war had happened in her world, but how was there an Elvyn ruin in the human realm if the war happened in El'Ara?

Garot continued. "Our only hope was Satsara. As Morkara, she had the ability to make a ward stronger than anything any other wardweaver could conjure. So she and her tribunal agreed that she'd weave a ward all around El'Ara. From her seat at the palace, Satsara began weaving her ward, starting at the opposite end of our world, toward her. It took days upon days to weave, but it was almost finished. Only the land surrounding the palace remained when Darius arrived and killed her. In her dying breath, she relinquished the power of the Morkara, officially passing the role onto her heir, Ailan. But not before she secured the edges of the Veil and completed it where it had stopped—around a wide circumference of land surrounding the capital city of Le'Lana. What remained outside the Veil was pushed into your human world."

Cora blinked at him. The capital city of Le'Lana. That... must be the land once known as Lela. The land that was now divided into three portions, one of which was her own kingdom. "So you're saying the place I come from was once fae land?"

Garot nodded, eyes on the Veil. "The Veil surrounds the land that was left behind when Satsara finished her ward-weaving too soon. If you came from the land that lies on the other side of this wall, the place we call the Void, then you came from what was once El'Ara's heart."

Cora's mind whirled to reconcile old facts with this new information. The Veil wasn't simply a barrier between two worlds; it was an incomplete ward that surrounded a piece of land that had once existed in another realm. All the tales of the mysterious land that had appeared out of nowhere, suddenly attached to the continent of Risa where once there had only been a beach, made sense now. Those tales hadn't been exaggerated. They'd been true.

And no one...*no one* in her world knew. Not even the Forest People.

Garot continued his story, oblivious to Cora's stunned musings. "The Veil succeeded at locking Darius outside of El'Ara. However, when Satsara had tied off the edges of her wardweaving, she hadn't known Ailan had been at the palace too. Now her heir, our true Morkara, was stuck in the human realm too."

Etrix gave a somber nod. "Which is why Fanon, Ailan's consort, has been acting as steward ever since."

Cora's gaze flew to the golden-haired fae, still standing before the Veil. He was Ailan's consort? While she couldn't forgive him for his rough treatment of her, she could sort of understand his cruel demeanor. His consort was trapped in the human realm because of a war a world-walker had started. A war with human soldiers wielding iron weapons.

Garot lowered his voice to a whisper. "Not everyone thinks Fanon should have been named steward. Many would have rather followed Etrix."

"Garot," Etrix growled in warning.

"I'm just saying," Garot whispered. "You were Satsara's consort. Had she not relinquished the power of the Morkara before she died, you'd have been steward."

Cora's eyes widened. Etrix had been...*Satsara's* consort? The one Satsara had been forced to marry while carrying on her affair with Prince Tristaine? Cora was surprised Etrix had been able to bear Garot's tale with nothing more than the occasional furrowed brow. Then again, if what they'd said was true, over seventy-five years had passed since

Satsara's death. Perhaps Etrix had been able to move on where Fanon could not.

Complicated, Valorre conveyed.

She agreed. It seemed humans weren't the only ones who had complex marriage politics.

Etrix let out a dark chuckle. "You think I want that responsibility? I have enough work on my plate as Head of Tribunal."

"I suppose you're right," Garot said. Then he turned to Cora, including her in the conversation again. "I'm certainly happy to be without Fanon's burdens. Everyone knows he's only a steward and can't direct the *mora*, yet he gets struck by the people's ire over the Blight."

Cora shifted her gaze to the decayed landscape. It struck her as more significant now that she fully understood what the Veil was. "Why is the Blight happening?"

"Another unforeseen circumstance of Satsara's incomplete wardweaving," Etrix said.

"In other words," Garot said, "the Veil is to blame for the Blight, and that is due to how the *mora* moves through El'Ara. It is born at the center of our world, in the heart of our planet's core. From there, it travels to the surface in the fire dunes, the land at the complete opposite end of our world, then travels through veins deep underground. These veins crisscross the land until they join again at the polarity opposite the fire dunes. That polarity was located in the capital city of Le'Lana. The palace of the Morkara was built directly over that polarity, its very structure designed to funnel the *mora* straight from the conjunction of those veins of power. The Morkara has always been in charge of directing the flow of *mora* back into our world, distributing it evenly, fueling light, heat, and technology."

Cora frowned. "You mean it generated flame? Like

lanterns and hearths? Can you not produce flame without it?"

"Your technology is different from ours," Etrix explained. "Our light and heat come not from flame but the *mora*."

Garot's mouth quirked in a sly grin. "I once met a truthweaver who insisted the human realm would one day discover something similar. Do you have that yet? Instantaneous light? Means of travel fueled by combustion?"

Cora shook her head, having not a single clue what he was talking about.

"Disappointing," Garot said with a sigh. "I was hoping you could tell me some stories next."

Etrix frowned. "Is it not taboo to show interest in the human realm?"

Garot rolled his eyes, not bothering to answer the question. "Anyhow, because the Veil trapped the Heart of El'Ara —our very source of *mora*—in the human world, balance has been disrupted. The *mora* seeps through the Veil, traveling along those underground veins as if Le'Lana wasn't a world away. Without a Morkara, we have no one to call the *mora* back. No way to return the flow to our land. So the *mora* leaves our world and does not return. That is why the land is dying."

"That isn't the only balance that has been unsettled," Etrix said. "Without any way of directing the flow of *mora*, we have nothing to trade. We are unable to uphold our alliances with the Faeryn, which has made our relationship with them tense. They resent us for the Veil. Blame us for what is happening to the land. We fear war with them. But that's not all. While the Mermyn stick to the seas and the Djyn reside in the fire dunes, they too could pose a threat. The Blight hasn't reached them yet, but if it ever does, they could wreak havoc on our realm. The Mermyn could flood the world, or the Djyn could burn our land to cinders."

Cora was once again startled speechless. The Mermyn and Djyn...were these other types of High Fae? She'd only ever heard of the Faeryn and Elvyn. The fact that there were even more kinds of fae made her head spin. Yet the plight of the land sank her heart. "Is there nothing you can do about the Blight?"

"All we can do is wait for our Morkara," Garot said. "We don't know what happened to Ailan and Darius after the Veil went up. We only have our truthweavers to rely on. As far as we know, the Veil will tear when we have a true Morkara again. We hope Ailan is alive and will return, but most of our truthweavers have said our true Morkara will be born from her bloodline."

"Don't say that so loudly," Etrix said, eyes flashing toward Fanon.

Garot pursed his lips, expression abashed. "Right. Fanon doesn't like hearing about this prophesied heir, for it would suggest Ailan's heart has moved on in the human world."

"One's heart and body aren't always aligned," Etrix said. "One can love someone while physically being with another."

Garot gave him a sad smile, and Cora realized Etrix was probably referring to his relationship with Satsara. Had they loved one another, even with their forced pairing and infidelity? Or had he been the one she'd been with physically while loving someone else?

Garot spoke again. "Whether it's Ailan or this child of prophecy, we await the tear in the Veil."

Cora's pulse kicked up as his words triggered dawning realization.

The unicorns. The mother. The child. Who do you think you are in that prophecy?

Cora cursed under her breath.

This child they were waiting for, this heir of Ailan…

Was that…her future child?

The one she'd never have?

The one Morkai had ensured would never be born?

Her stomach bottomed out, adding to the hollow feeling that remained where her magic once filled.

Morkai's curse...

The fate weaving…

If left unbroken, the Elvyn might never have their Morkara again. The Blight could grow. El'Ara could be destroyed.

Panic crawled through her. She had to tell them. They *had* to help her—

"There is no tear." Fanon's voice rang out from near the Veil. Her eyes darted to him. The first blush of sunlight crept up from the horizon, illuminating his dark glower, his blue eyes pinned on her. "The Veil is fully intact, which means you lied. You couldn't have passed through the wardweaving. Worse, it means you're a worldwalker."

54

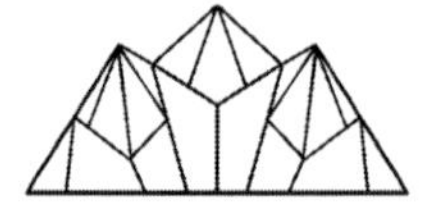

Fanon strode over to Cora, hand on the hilt of his sword. "Tell me how you got here, human."

Lie. Lie. Lie. Valorre's panicked words threaded through her mind.

Her shoulders sank with the weight of her own futility. She was tired of lying. Tired of pretending she was someone she wasn't. Lying about how she'd gotten here hadn't given her a way home. Hadn't gotten her through the Veil.

Beneath that lie was a mountain of others she'd told.

She'd lied to the inquisitors and claimed to know nothing of magic. It had earned her her place as princess, solidified Dimetreus' throne, but where were the fruits of such efforts now? Dimetreus' council still didn't trust her. Or him, for that matter. He'd lost his right to rule, was forced to abdicate according to the terms of an alliance that was supposed to be built on trust.

More recently, she'd lied to Teryn and told him nothing was wrong the night she remembered the curse, and he'd gotten possessed by a dead sorcerer.

She'd lied to Lurel. Told her the tower library wasn't dangerous. The girl was now dead.

She'd lied to the Forest People, kept her royal identity a secret. In later confessing the truth, she'd earned their distrust.

Lies upon lies upon lies.

She used to think they protected her. Saw them as a necessary precaution. But now she found they were circular. Perpetual. Simply a way to delay the inevitable.

Mother Goddess, she was tired of it.

She held Fanon's gaze, matching his glare with one of her own. *I am the very thing you fear*. The confession was perched on the tip of her tongue, moments away from leaving her lips, when Etrix stood between them.

Hands grasping the other Elvyn's shoulders, Etrix forced Fanon back a few steps. "You said the Veil is intact, Fanon. No worldwalker can move through the Veil. You know this. Even if it had been torn, there was no guarantee a world-walker could have gotten through."

He pointed a condemning finger at Cora. "Then how is she here?"

Valorre reared back and managed to lift off the ground, hooves flailing, before Fanon's magic brought him crashing back down to all fours. He let out an enraged whinny, but it was drowned out by a piercing screech that shattered the air in the distance.

Cora's blood went cold. She glanced at the sky and saw a familiar shape—the dragon—soaring toward them. Fanon shook loose from Etrix's grip, but instead of rounding on Cora, he faced the oncoming dragon. "Damn it, Ferrah, you unruly beast," he muttered.

"She wants the unicorn," Etrix said.

Valorre thrashed and neighed, but Fanon's restraints refused to give.

The dragon circled overhead, then began her descent.

Cora took a few steps back, angling closer to her unicorn companion. "What does she want with Valorre?"

Etrix's expression turned wary. "Like I told you, she's been seen chasing his kind through the Blight."

He didn't elaborate, but she feared the worst. She doubted the dragons only gave chase.

As the dragon drew nearer to the ground, Cora got a better look at the creature. She was massive, her sinuous body and tail the length of at least ten horses. Her scales were an opalescent white that glinted pink, blue, and purple in the rising sunlight. Her enormous wings were comprised of white feathers. Additional feathers framed her scaly face, and from her snout protruded long, trailing whiskers. Her eyes were a deep shade of violet with black slits for pupils. She landed with an earth-shaking thud several yards away.

Valorre quivered, ears twitching back and forth. *I remember her. Do not like. Not friends.*

The dragon took a darting step forth, but Fanon leaped forward too, hand outstretched. "Ferrah," he said, voice a deep growl. "Stay back."

To Cora's surprise, the dragon obeyed. Or was it Fanon's magic that held Ferrah at bay? The creature swiveled her neck to the side to get a look at Valorre. Her forked tongue flicked out of her mouth, carrying a hiss of steam.

Fanon spoke again, tone firm. "Stay. Back."

"Fanon," Garot said, wide eyes locked on the dragon. "The human said she arrived on the unicorn—"

"Let us not debate the human's lies until we've sent Ferrah back to the caves."

"Yes, but what if this has everything to do with Ferrah? What if the human is telling the truth?"

Fanon kept his gaze on the dragon a few beats more, then slowly shifted his eyes to Garot. He spoke through his teeth. "In what way?"

"What if unicorns can cross the Veil when no other creature can?"

"How is that possible?" Etrix asked.

"We know their horns have the strongest *mora*," Garot said. "Their powers haven't been compromised by the Blight unlike the rest of us. And we know they've been disappearing for the last two months."

"I thought Ferrah was to blame for that," said Fanon, turning his gaze back to the dragon.

"Yes, but what if she hasn't been chasing the unicorns to harm them? What if she's been chasing them through the Veil?"

I remember, Valorre said. *Yes. Ran from dragon.*

Cora's eyes went wide. If unicorns had been disappearing from El'Ara for two months but had been in her world for about a year now...it lined up, considering the time discrepancy between the two worlds.

Etrix frowned. "To what end?"

"The dragons have been restless for months," Garot said. "Particularly Ferrah. They've never been like this before, which means something has changed. What if Berolla's hatchlings sense the impending return of our Morkara? What if they sense Ailan or her heir and have sent the unicorns through the Veil to find them?"

Fanon scoffed. "That's a bit of a reach, isn't it?"

"Perhaps, but..." Garot glanced at Valorre. "We could test the theory. We do have a unicorn."

Etrix furrowed his brow, studying Valorre. "What do you propose?"

"We let the unicorn try to move through the Veil," Garot said. "If the unicorn slips through the wardweaving, we'll know it was the creature's horn that allowed him to pass."

Was my horn, Valorre conveyed to her. *Used your travel magic. But was my horn. It will work.*

Cora's chest sparked with hope. "You'll let us try to leave?"

Garot gave her a warm smile, but before he could utter a word of affirmation, Fanon spoke. "The unicorn can attempt to leave through the Veil, but not with the human. We must test the theory first. If the unicorn returns, we'll know for certain that the girl was telling the truth. Then we'll remove the collar and restraints and let her leave with him."

Her gaze darted to Valorre. Dread sank her stomach. She didn't like the idea of him leaving without her. What if Garot's theory was correct about how the unicorns had left, but not about their ability to come back the same way? Valorre had admitted that his horn had allowed them entrance into El'Ara, but that he'd used her ability to astral travel to get here. What if he couldn't return without her using her magic again?

Valorre voiced an additional worry. *What if Veil makes me forget? What if I don't remember you on the other side? I want to remember. Don't want to forget.*

Her anxiety only grew. Valorre could be right. When she'd met him, he hadn't remembered where he'd come from. Hadn't even been able to recall that he'd lived in another realm.

But this might be her last chance at getting home without engaging in further conflict with the Elvyn. She'd been prepared to tell the truth about her powers when it had seemed she was out of options, but this could really work. There was logic involved.

I'll do it, Valorre said. *Worried. But I'll do it.*

"All right," Cora said, her voice rough. "We'll send Valorre through the Veil, and when he returns, you'll free me and let me go back with him."

Fanon glared at her for a few moments but finally relented. "Very well. Unicorn, approach the Veil."

Valorre started to walk toward the Veil, head lowered. Cora took a step to follow but felt an invisible tug pull her back. She cut a scowl at Fanon, but he simply stared down his nose at her. Behind him, Ferrah shifted her head, tongue flicking as she watched Valorre with hungry interest.

Mother Goddess, Cora hoped Garot was right about his theory. With how the dragon kept her slitted violet eyes on Valorre, she seemed like a predatory beast, not a creature capable of masterminding a scheme to send unicorns through the Veil to find a lost heir.

Cora swallowed hard and returned her attention to Valorre. He was just a few feet from the swirling mass of mist and shadow now. Another step. Another. Now his horn was just inches from the Veil. He paused and swiveled his head toward Cora.

Will remember, he said.

Her throat went dry and burning tears pricked her eyes. She wished she had access to her magic so she could convey the full weight of her feelings—that she loved him. That he was her best friend. Her familiar. That meeting him was a miracle she'd never ever regret, no matter how much hardship had followed. But she couldn't touch her magic. She could only hope his was strong enough to read what was in her heart. With a somber smile, she gave him a nod. *I know you will.*

He held her gaze for several beats more. Then he returned to face the Veil. His next step brought his horn to the misty surface. Then his head. His neck. His shoulders. Then he was...gone.

He'd made it through.

She glanced at her companions, saw the bright awe in Garot's green eyes, the surprise in Etrix's raised brows. Only Fanon looked unimpressed. If anything, he looked annoyed. Ferrah, however, seemed calmer now. She'd settled onto her belly, legs curled up beneath her like an oversized feline. Her tail swished lazily over the colorless earth.

Cora turned back to the Veil and watched where Valorre had disappeared. Any moment now, he'd return. Any second, she'd see his horn pierce the misty wall. But with every breath she took, her sense of foreboding grew. These seconds that passed for her were minutes for him. Her minutes were his hours.

So why wasn't he coming back?

Pain lanced her heart as she considered the possibility that Valorre's fears had come to pass.

He'd...forgotten her.

No. No, even if he had, she...she'd find him again. She must.

Trembling, she faced the three fae. "Your theory was correct. Now you know how I entered your realm. Let me go home now."

"Unless you are a worldwalker, you cannot pass without a unicorn," Fanon said. "We will not send another of ours through the Veil."

Garot gave Fanon a scathing look. "You said she could leave if we proved she'd arrived like she'd said."

"I said the unicorn must return to prove our theory."

Rage simmered in Cora's gut.

"Fanon," Etrix said through his teeth, "we've proven enough. Let us find another unicorn and send her on her way."

"We cannot let her leave. She now holds vital information that will allow anyone to cross. The last thing we need is an army led by Darius charging in on the backs of our missing unicorns."

"You may be steward," Etrix said, "but you cannot decide this on your own. Take her to the tribunal if you must. Let us debate whether to send a unicorn with her so she can leave."

Fanon huffed a humorless laugh. "You know what the tribunal will choose. You may be soft, but the others aren't. They'll demand her head before she can utter a word in her defense. Better I grant her mercy now." With that, he unsheathed his sword and marched toward Cora.

Garot and Etrix tried to pull him back, but Fanon's invisible bonds pulled Cora straight to him. With a flick of his wrist, she was forced to her knees. The edge of his blade glinted in the early morning sun.

Cora's heart leaped into her throat, but she refused to let her fear show. Instead, she held his gaze, dared him to look her in the eye as he condemned her to her fate.

"Believe me, human," Fanon said, and there was a hint of pity in his eyes, "this is mercy."

Garot and Etrix fought to stop him, but he flung them back with his magic.

He lifted his sword.

"Kill me and you kill the blood of Ailan."

Fanon froze. "What?"

"You heard me. I am of Ailan's bloodline. Kill me and you kill any chance at getting your Morkara back."

His lips curled away from his teeth. "Explain."

Cora spoke quickly, every word laced with her rage. "I don't know who Darius is, but there's a man in my world who claims to be an Elvyn prince. He's been working against me most of my life because he knows I am the mother in a prophecy that claims my child would be his enemy. He calls himself Morkai and is trying to become Morkaius of my world. He plans to harness the magic that seeps from a place we call Centerpointe Rock—a ruin that once was the Morkara's palace. He will drain magic from this realm. He could come for you next and tear this entire Veil down."

Etrix and Garot both took stumbling steps forward, suddenly released from Fanon's magic. Etrix stared at her with wide eyes. "You...are of Ailan's blood?"

"Yes." It felt so wrong to say it. So false. Perhaps there was a part of her that still didn't believe it. Or maybe she just didn't want to. Admitting to such a role meant bearing the fate of two worlds. "I wasn't certain until I heard your stories, but now I know. And you can help me stop Morkai. You're stronger than he is, stronger than anyone in my world. If we don't—"

"You're not the blood of Ailan." Fanon's eyes narrowed to slits. "You haven't got a single drop of Elvyn blood in your body."

"You don't know that," Etrix said. "Only Elvyn blood relatives can sense their kin at close proximity."

"Then tell me, Etrix, is she your kin? If she's of Ailan's bloodline, then she's of yours too."

Etrix studied Cora for a few long moments, wrinkles deepening his brow.

Cora's heart racketed. What if she'd been wrong? What if Morkai had been? She held her breath, waiting for Etrix's pronouncement, words that would either condemn her as a liar...or confirm her claims once and for all.

He shook his head. "I don't sense anything—"

"Then she's lying."

"—but we have no precedent for meeting kin from a part-human, diluted bloodline. We don't know how many generations out she is from Ailan."

Fanon scoffed.

Etrix stepped in close to Fanon, brought them face to face. "Don't let your pride get in the way. If this girl truly is Ailan's kin, if she's destined to bear our true Morkara, then we must act rationally."

Fanon didn't balk at Etrix's proximity. "Very well. Let's act rationally. Come, Ferrah. There's one way to know if the human speaks truth."

"What are you doing?" Etrix bit out.

"A test," Fanon said with a smirk, "by dragon."

55

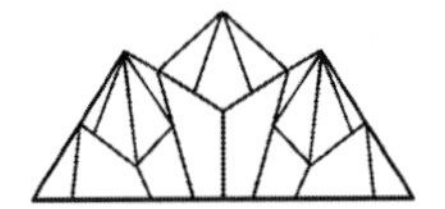

Cora was hauled to her feet by Fanon's unseen tethers. The sudden movement piqued the dragon's interest. Her pupils narrowed, and she slowly began to rise from her belly, planting her four slender legs beneath her. She splayed her white feathered wings before folding them onto her back. Her tongue flicked out several times, sending wisps of smoke curling into the air. The sun was climbing higher from the horizon, casting the gray landscape under a glow that did nothing to warm the stark appearance of the Blight. Nor did it thaw the ice in Cora's heart.

"What are you going to do to me?" she asked, voice trembling.

Fanon gestured over his shoulder for the dragon to approach. With slow, slithering moves, Ferrah crept toward them. "Only the Morkara's bloodline can bond with a dragon. Since I am Ailan's consort, I can command them and hope they listen, but I cannot bond with them. If you're truly of Ailan's lineage, you'll have no problem bonding with Ferrah."

"That could work," Garot said, expression brightening.

Etrix didn't share his enthusiasm. "This is reckless."

Fanon shrugged. "It's the only way we'll know for sure."

Cora's eyes darted from the approaching dragon to the three fae. She tossed Etrix a pleading look, but he gave Fanon no further argument.

Ferrah was just behind Fanon now, her slitted eyes locked on Cora. The creature was stunningly beautiful with her opalescent scales, her feathered wings, her long whiskers. She was a faerytale creature come to life. A fae she'd always fantasized about when she and Maiya had visited the hot spring caves. The Forest People's stories insisted dragons had once lived in the caves, and that—over time—the creatures had turned into the bioluminescent worms that now inhabited them. She'd never been sure if she believed those tales, but they had been enchanting. Charming.

The dragon who stood before her now was anything but charming. Beautiful, yes. Terrifying, more so.

Fanon stepped to the side, leaving only empty space between Cora and the dragon. Her muscles seized up as the creature stared down at her.

"Go ahead," Fanon said, a false smile tugging his lips. "Bond."

"What the hell does that mean?" she ground through her teeth.

"She doesn't know how." Etrix shifted his jaw side to side. "All you're doing is frightening her."

"Oh, that's all right," Garot said, tone gentle. He took a step forward but halted in place when Ferrah swiveled her head toward him with a sharp hiss. "Sorry, Ferrah. Allow me to show your new mommy how all of this works."

Cora paled. She didn't want to be this creature's *new mommy*. She already had a familiar.

Ferrah flicked her tongue at Garot a few more times, then took a step back. Cora noted the horrifying length of her claws, along with the deep gouges left in the soil where her talons had just been.

With slow moves, Garot shifted to the side, his gaze on Cora. "First, you're going to bow. Dragons are proud creatures and will refuse to bond with anyone—even someone of the Morkara's bloodline—who doesn't bow first. After that, you're going to hold your body as still as you can. One arm must stay loose at your side, fingers spread to show you hold no weapon. Your other must lift, palm forward, toward Ferrah." He demonstrated but did so away from the dragon.

When Cora failed to mimic him, he gave her an encouraging nod. "Go ahead. It's your turn. Face Ferrah and greet her."

She gave him a pointed look. "I can't move my arms at all."

Something loosened around her, and she found her arms suddenly free. Her muscles ached from disuse. The only time she'd been free since Fanon had trapped her was when he'd forced her to walk into the misty wall. But now... she was truly free. Her fingers flinched, tingling with anticipation. If she wanted, she could reach for the collar, remove it, and access her magic. She could avoid this ridiculous ritual and be back home before she knew it—

"Make any move but those Garot has shown you," Fanon said, "and I'll have your arms pinned in place again. Then you can be Ferrah's snack instead."

It took all her effort to keep herself from reaching for the collar regardless. But she knew removing the collar was only the first obstacle. She'd used her traveling abilities twice, and both times she'd needed time to tune in to her emotions.

"What are you waiting for, human?" Fanon let out a cruel chuckle. "Are you frightened because you lied? If you are the blood of Ailan, then you have nothing to fear."

Her stomach tied itself in knots. She *was* of Ailan's blood. Wasn't she? Morkai had been so certain of who she'd been that he'd cursed her. It was still so much to wrap her mind around. So much to doubt. To fear.

But...

But she had to try.

If this worked, she could earn the Elvyn's respect. Get them on her side. Encourage them to help her fight Morkai. Beseech them to find a way to reverse the blood weaving he'd placed upon her.

And if it doesn't work, this thing is going to eat me. That she was certain of.

"The dragon or my blade," Fanon said. "Choose which you'd rather greet. Now."

Gritting her teeth, she fully faced Ferrah. Every muscle in her body quivered as she lowered her head into a bow. She held the position for several long seconds before slowly straightening to her full height. She bit back a scream as she found Ferrah's face just a few feet from hers. The dragon studied her, shifting her head from side to side.

"Now lift your hand," Garot called in a too-loud whisper.

She didn't want to move at all, but she feared what would happen if she didn't.

Breathe, she chanted in her mind. *Breathe.*

Air flooded her nostrils, steadying her nerves the slightest bit. The sensation would have brought more comfort if she could feel the familiar magical connection to the air element. Without it, it was just air moving through her lungs. Nothing else. At least it was something. Routine.

Finally, she forced herself to move. With one arm loose at her side, fingers splayed to show her hand was empty, she lifted the other, palm forward.

"Level with her snout," Etrix said, but she couldn't bear to look at him. Of the three, his emotions had proved to be the most rational in any given moment. If his eyes held fear, her terror would grow.

She raised her palm until it was just a foot away from Ferrah's snout. Everything inside her told her to snatch her hand back. She yearned for her magic, yearned to feel the tingle of it surging through her palms. Then perhaps she'd know for sure whether she was doing the right thing.

Or if this was all a terrible mistake.

Ferrah flicked her tongue. Once. Twice. It tickled Cora's palm, while steam wafted over her face.

Cora's heart hammered so hard, she feared it would crack a rib. Her lungs constricted with panic.

Ferrah's throat rumbled with something like a growl. Her scaly lips lifted in a snarl, revealing the pointed tips of her teeth. The breath that brushed Cora's face became unbearably hot.

"It isn't working," Garot said, tone panicked. "Maybe her blood is too diluted. Maybe Ferrah doesn't recognize her as Ailan's kin."

Fanon let out a dark chuckle. "What happened to your theory that the dragons had sensed some great awakening of Ailan's heir? Here's proof that you were wrong."

Ferrah opened her mouth wider, revealing a bright glow at the back of her throat.

Cora stumbled a step back.

"No, Fanon," Etrix said, tone laced with panic. "Maybe

it's the collar. It's dulling the *mora* in her blood." Then louder, he shouted at Cora. "Take off the collar!"

"Do not—" Fanon's words ended with hiss as Cora reached for the collar with both hands. Pulling the two sides, she opened the cuff on its hinge and pried the tines from her neck.

Emotion surged through her in a rush. Warmth blazed from her chest, down her arms, filling her palms with a tingling heat. Fear echoed through her—her own mixed with Etrix's and Garot's. From Fanon, she felt anger and vindictive pride. And from the dragon...

Cora met her slitted purple gaze and was struck with the heat of Ferrah's ire. Her annoyance. Her enraged confusion. Ferrah's sinuous neck quivered with another growl, her breath so hot it scalded Cora's face. The glow at the back of her throat grew brighter. Brighter.

It's going to kill me. Cora was certain, whether from common sense or the return of her clairsentience.

To make matters clearer, a warning rang through her, filling her body with urgency. *Run.*

The dragon swung her head back and bellowed a screech.

"Get back!" Etrix yelled. He and Garot dove out of the way. Even Fanon looked panicked as he retreated several steps back. Ferrah lowered her head, but Cora didn't wait to see what happened. Turning around, she kicked up her feet and ran as fast as she could.

The ground trembled behind her, and heat licked her ankles. A bright blaze flashed in her periphery—purple flames—but she forced herself faster. Faster.

She knew what she had to do. And now that she'd removed the collar, she could do it.

With a deep breath, she called the elements to her. Air

in her lungs. Earth beneath her feet. Water in her blood. Fire chasing her steps. It wrapped around her, fueling her emotions. Fear. Terror. Worry. She sank into these feelings, affirmed their presence, their legitimacy.

The ground shook faster now, and another screech rang out behind her.

She closed her eyes and sought something lighter than fear. Something warmer than dread. Her thoughts immediately went to Teryn. A spike of worry surged through her, but she kept her thoughts on a softer path. A vision flashed in her mind's eye, of her and Teryn's kiss against the tree. Calm flooded her mind. Her heart. Her soul.

Yes.

That was where she could go.

She continued to run blindly, pumping her legs over the barren earth, trusting herself not to fall, and turned her thoughts over to Teryn. His lips on hers. His hands in her hair.

Her chest warmed. Her heart flitted.

She enveloped those emotions around her and visualized the tree under which they'd kissed. She saw its wide trunk, its bark, its bright green leaves. She saw the grass covering the cliff. Saw the wildflower meadow beneath it.

Every part of her felt like she was there.

Safe.

Home.

Heat scalded her back, but she ignored it, imagining it was sunlight blazing over the cliffside instead.

She sent a surge of magic into her feet...

And took a purpose-fueled step.

As her feet landed, the ground softened, the air shifted. She opened her eyes and flung out her hands, stumbling as she nearly collided with the tree she'd held in her mind's eye. Night surrounded her, as did the scents of the familiar woods. She'd done it. She was here. A cry of relief escaped her throat, and she sank to the base of the trunk, arms curled around her knees as she caught her breath.

She sat like that for minutes on end. Sobs tore from her chest, erupting with the weight of her emotions, the return of her magic, the terror of what had just happened.

Once she could breathe easily again, she unhooked her arms from around her knees and rose to her feet. She brushed out the skirt of her robe, frowning at its singed hem. A tendril of dark hair caught her eye, and she saw it too had been singed. Only then did she note the faint smell of burning in the air. How much hair had she lost? Was the back of her robe intact?

She reached for the lock of hair but realized she still held the collar in one hand. With a glare, she shoved it into her robe pocket with far more force than necessary. Then, stepping toward the edge of the cliff and into the moonlight, she assessed the charred strand. She ran her fingers through her tangled ends, relieved to find most of her hair still there—

Movement caught her eye from beneath the cliff. The moon illuminated the vast meadow below.

Cora bit her lip to smother her shout of alarm.

It wasn't the tents that startled her. Not the makeshift camp that had invaded what she'd once considered her most favorite and sacred location.

It was the monster that emerged from the trees.

56

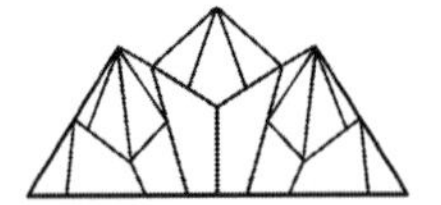

A thunderous roar reverberated through the night. It echoed through the tent, shattering the moment Mareleau and Larylis had been sharing. Sweetness had filled their embrace mere moments ago—mingling with the joy and terror that came with knowing they'd soon be parents—but now they both froze, tensing in each other's arms.

"What was that?" Mareleau whispered.

"A bear, probably," Larylis said, trying to appear composed. Though he'd gone on countless hunts with his brother growing up, he never fully understood its appeal. Hunting prey, delivering killing blows, hearing animalistic screams when a wound missed its mark and caused unnecessary pain...he'd hated all of it. The sound he'd just heard reminded him too much of those screams—an eerie, keening cry of pain.

"A bear?" Mareleau pulled back from him, face ashen. "Bears can't claw through tents, can they?"

He forced a reassuring smile to his lips. "There will be guards on patrol, ready to confront any hungry interlopers." Even as he said it, an unsettling chill fell over him. In the wake of the roar, he heard only silence. He was grateful not to hear a repeat of the sound, but he expected to at least catch strains of commotion coming from the camp. As far as he could tell, the roar had come from nearby in the woods, which meant everyone else would have heard it too.

But...now that he thought about it, he hadn't heard anything to suggest the hunting party had returned from their hunt. The darkness blanketing the tent walls told him it was well past nightfall, so they would have returned hours ago. Of course, it was possible he would have missed the party's return. He had been rather...*distracted.*

Ever since he'd first entered the tent and laid eyes on Mareleau, she'd consumed his every thought. In the hours that followed, he'd been immersed in pleasure, in the joy of their reunion. Then came her confession, which had brought an entirely new set of emotions to contend with.

But in the hollow wake of that roar, he was reminded of all the other reasons he had to feel uneasy.

He pulled farther back and met his wife's eyes. "Mare, I need to ask you some serious questions."

She shrank down a little, pulling the small blanket her father had gifted her to her chest. He knew she'd purposefully changed the subject when he'd first suggested they speak of serious matters, but they'd ended up on one of the most significant topics anyway. Still, he couldn't let her escape his line of questioning this time.

"There was a reason why I left my retinue to make haste to Ridine. That same reason drove your father to join me."

"What reason?"

Anxiety tickled his chest. "Has my brother been acting...odd?"

Some of the tenseness left her composure, replaced with haughty annoyance. "Odd is a word for it."

"How so?" Larylis held his breath, hoping her answer would be something mundane, dismissible.

"In the way he talks, I suppose. For a handful of days, I thought I could come to like him as a brother, but then he got...weird. There's something going on with him. Did you see his hair?"

Larylis frowned. "He was wearing a hat when I saw him."

She barked a laugh. "Of course he was. His hair has gone half white, like an aging old man, but he acts like it's nothing. He looks unwell lately, yet he refuses to acknowledge it."

His mind stumbled over her words. Teryn's hair had gone half white? He was unwell? Larylis didn't know what to think. The hat had hidden Teryn's hair and had cast his face in shadow, so he hadn't noticed anything too odd about his appearance. Then again, he could deem Teryn's sudden inclination for tricorns odd enough. Not to mention that too-formal tone he'd used.

"Did he and Cora quarrel?" he asked. "That you know of, at least? Have you seen her lately?"

Her brows lowered, revealing a hint of concern. "I haven't seen her since the day she found out she had to marry Teryn. She was worried about...about a certain conversation they needed to have before she'd feel comfortable marrying him, but I thought she'd made peace with it. I tried to see her on her wedding day, but Teryn said she'd taken to seclusion for her own protection. He said I wouldn't be able to see her until after the peace pact was signed."

His muscles tensed. He'd already been alarmed when she'd used the words *had to marry Teryn*, for that wasn't right. Teryn had come to propose to her and fulfill the terms of the pact, but he'd never force her into something she didn't want. That, however, wasn't the most troubling thing she'd said. "What do you mean their wedding day?"

"They were supposedly married five days ago."

"Why? The alliance terms should have given them a year."

She pulled her head back. "Has no one told you?"

"Told me what?"

"Dimetreus was deemed incapable of ruling by his council. Cora was forced to take his place and ascend to queen, but the alliance agreement states she must marry Teryn for the council to accept her rule."

A chill ran down his spine. He hadn't heard a word of this, and Verdian hadn't said anything either. He could understand some level of secrecy, but this...

This felt like something else.

He rose from the bed and began to pace. "You said you haven't seen Cora in how long?"

"Six days."

"And how long has Teryn been acting different?"

"A week at least."

He halted in place. He still didn't know what it meant. How could Teryn not be Teryn? And where was Cora? If she was in seclusion for her protection as Mareleau had said, then why had she sent that letter with Berol?

Another roar shattered the air, severing Larylis' train of thought. This time, the sound was closer. It had come from the other side of the meadow, if he had to guess.

Muffled shouts of alarm followed, but far fewer than he'd expect from a full camp. A rhythmic thud like galloping hooves sped by the tent.

Then came a scream.

Larylis charged across the tent, gathering up his sword belt and strapping it around his waist. Mareleau followed after him, panic lacing her voice. “What are you doing? Where are you going?”

“To see what the seven devils is going on out there.”

She clung to the front of his shirt. “Don’t you dare leave me.”

His resolve cracked, along with his heart. But he couldn’t hide when people were screaming. When something dark and twisted was happening around him. He pulled Mareleau to his chest, pressing a kiss to her forehead. As they broke apart, he reached for his belt and unsheathed a dagger. He pressed the hilt into her palm. “Stay safe. Hide. I love you.”

She was still blinking in confusion at the dagger when he fled the tent. As soon as he stepped outside, he was nearly bowled over by a charging horse—*his* horse. The palfrey paid him no heed as she darted past, disappearing into the trees behind another horse. The first must have been what he’d heard galloping by. He glanced down the other side of the meadow. He expected more chaos than a few fleeing horses. At the very least, he thought others would be out to investigate the sound. But the camp was too quiet. Too empty. He saw no other horses to suggest his brother’s party had returned. And where were the guards Verdian had left behind? Who had made the muffled shouts he’d heard? Who’d screamed?

He strained his ears for the slightest sound...

Shuffling movement had him whirling to the side. He reached for his sword, unsheathing it before pointing its tip at the cluster of shadows that hovered by the nearest tent.

A whine keened from the shadows. He blinked into the night, stepping closer, and finally made out the faces of

Mareleau's three maids. Relief uncoiled the knots in his stomach. "What are you doing?" he whispered.

The three were shaking, clinging to each other. "We heard that roar," Ann said, voice quavering. "We left our tent to go to our queen, and then...and then we saw a body."

Hair rose on the back of his neck. "A body?"

"A guard, I think," Ann said. "There was...blood."

His heart beat faster, and his sword arm began to tremble. "Do you know if the hunting party returned?"

Breah shook her head. "Not even the servants have come back. Only a few of us were left behind in the first place, but we haven't seen anyone in hours."

Seven devils, none of this was good. He pointed at Mareleau's pavilion and filled his voice with the command of a king. "Hide with the queen. Do not leave until I return."

With hasty nods, they shuffled away.

Larylis proceeded forward, eyes cast over the moonlit meadow. There was no sign of the creature who had made the noise. It would have been a comfort were it not for the missing hunting party and the body Ann claimed to have seen. He crept forth along the row of tents, seeking any sign—

A dark form was sprawled in the grass up ahead, and he suspected it was a body. He took a step forward, but the ground rocked beneath his feet.

One thud rumbled nearby. Then another. It was heavy and rhythmic like footfalls, but far too slow and deep to belong to a human or a horse. He turned in a half circle, trying to ascertain where it was coming from. It sounded like it was somewhere behind the tents. But as he faced the direction of the rumbling beat, a figure emerged from between the nearest pavilions, striding straight for him. The moon illuminated dark hair streaked with white, hollow cheeks, and a face as familiar to him as his own.

Teryn.

He stopped before Larylis. "Greetings, brother. Are you ready to join me on that hunt now?"

MARELEAU'S EYES DARTED BETWEEN THE TENT FLAP AND THE dagger in her hand. What was she supposed to do with a dagger? And why the hell had Larylis left her alone like this? Her legs trembled, torn between running after him and darting under the nearest piece of furniture. With the tent so sparse, the only thing she could hide under was a table.

Before she could do anything, the tent flap flew open. Her heart leaped into her throat, half with panic, half with hope, but neither danger nor salvation entered the pavilion. Instead, Ann, Breah, and Sera charged inside, uttering incoherent words as they closed in around Mareleau.

"Did you hear it?" Sera asked. "The roar?"

Now that her ladies were here, she felt some lessening of her terror. Stronger than her comfort, though, was the urge to contrast their fraying composures. She was queen. She couldn't act like them. Without intending to, she straightened her spine and threw her shoulders back. Tightening her fingers around the hilt of her blade, she lowered the dagger to her side. "Larylis said it's probably just a bear. There's nothing to get worked up about."

"Then what is *that*?" Breah's question hung in the air as a heavy thud shook the ground beneath them. With every trembling pulse, the sound drew nearer. Nearer.

"It could still be a bear," Mareleau said, but there was

less conviction in her tone. Why the seven devils should she be comforted about a bear in the first place?

The thudding was so close now, the walls of the tent rippled with every beat. It was coming from the back end of the pavilion.

The three girls crowded around Mareleau, clinging to her arms, her robe. Together they took a step back, then another. The thud stopped just behind the tent. What followed was a distinct snuffling, then something heavy rubbing against the canvas, scraping the other side of the cloth wall with an ear-splitting scratch.

Mareleau flung out the hand holding the dagger, then motioned for her ladies to retreat toward the tent flap.

They took one step back, then another, as the creature continued to rub against the back of the tent.

Something pierced the canvas, a sharp tine that protruded inside.

Sera smothered a scream behind her hand, and Mareleau had to bite the inside of her cheek to keep from crying out as well.

This creature wasn't a bear. A stag then? That wasn't encouraging either. Mareleau had no direct experience with any animals but her mother's lapdogs. When they misbehaved, her mother summoned their trainers. What the hell was she to do with an angry stag?

They stepped back again, careful to keep their steps soft. Only a few feet remained between them and the tent flap. But what then? Could they run? Hide? Based on the snuffling sounds that continued, the beast had a keen sense of smell.

The tine pierced deeper through the canvas. Then, with an echo of the roar she'd heard earlier, the tent wall split as the tine tore a diagonal line across it. An enormous, misshapen head protruded through the gap, followed by paws. Hooves. The light of the lantern illuminated fur, flesh, claws, and horns, too many different characteristics to belong to a single animal.

"Run," Mareleau whispered to the other girls. The demand was meant for her as much as them, but her legs were too wobbly to move. Her hand remained thrust before her, but the dagger looked more like a toy in the presence of her terrifying foe.

Anxiety crawled up her throat, tightening her chest, but it ignited something else inside her too—the same fierce protectiveness she'd felt when she'd confessed the truth to Larylis. It didn't shrink her fear, but it settled beside it, bolstering her legs, her arms. Her fingers closed tighter around the hilt of the dagger.

"Run!" she said again, her voice a shout, and this time her body and her ladies listened. They stumbled through the tent flap and darted toward the other side of the meadow. Breah was fastest, sprinting several feet ahead, but Ann and Sera trailed behind, sobbing with every uneven step. Mareleau glanced over her shoulder in time to see Sera fall. Ann reached for her, hauling her to her feet, but an immense shadow closed in behind, backlit by a sudden leap of flames. The tent lay in tatters and was now being consumed by what must be the remnants of a smashed lantern.

The beast bounded for Ann and Sera, who were still struggling to gain purchase and run. Mareleau glanced at Breah, who was almost to the other end of the meadow now, then back at the two girls. Without a second thought, she bared her teeth and rushed to her ladies, pulling them to their feet with her free hand. With her other, she flourished the dagger at the oncoming beast. Her heart hammered so loud, it drowned out its thundering steps, its roar. She was only aware of the heat of its breath as it closed in on them.

Ann and Sera finally managed to start running again, and she shoved them before her, away from the beast. She kicked up her feet, lifted the hem of her robe, and darted after them.

A flash of fur and flesh skidded before her, blocking her retreat. She thrust out the dagger again, leaping back.

The monster faced her, mouth gaping to reveal unnaturally sharp teeth. She lifted her face, taking in the sight of the creature clearly for the first time. It was larger than a carriage with clawed front paws contrasting rear hooves. Its boarlike snout was framed with tusks. A pair of overlarge antlers sprouted from its head. Its rear ended in a bushy wolflike tail.

But its eyes.

Above its massive snout, it had four sets of eyes from four human faces, skin pulled taut over what should have been the creature's upper skull. Each face was linked to the next, skin fused with what looked like scar tissue, then melting into the more animalistic features—the boar snout, the stag head, the bear neck.

The monster shifted to the side, pinning one distinct pair of eyes on her.

Her breath caught in her throat. The dagger slid from her grip and fell into the grass at her feet.

She knew this gaze, with irises as blue as her own. Eyes lined with creases she'd watched deepen over the years. A brow constantly furrowed in either anger or frustration whenever she was in its presence.

Bile simmered in her gut.

She forced her attention away from the face, but there was nowhere else to look but at these four terrifying visages.

Uncle Ulrich.

Uncle Kevan.

King Dimetreus.

And the one that continued to look at her with its eerie, lifeless stare.

A word left her lips in a cry. “Father.”

57

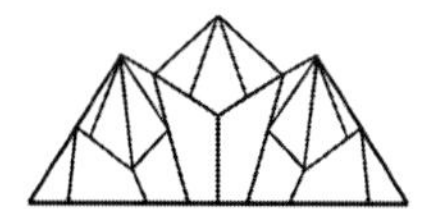

Cora's lungs heaved with trembling breaths, a muffled scream building in the back of her throat. She watched the meadow, vaguely noted the flames, the figures, but her brother's face was all she could see. The sight of it replayed before her eyes like a grotesque tableau, along with one undeniable truth.

Her brother was dead.

There was no way around it. She knew what the creature was. She knew what it meant to see Dimetreus' face protruding from the monster's skull.

Morkai had made her brother into a Roizan.

Along with Kevan, Ulrich, and Verdian.

He hadn't simply murdered those who stood in the way of his goals. He'd violated them. Twisted their bodies with blood magic.

She'd seen the process in the book she'd burned.

Two animals locked in battle.

Two animals dead.

Two animals reborn as one.

What did it mean that this Roizan had four faces?

Animal parts from at least four different creatures? Had they all died at the same time, in the same battle, to create this abomination? Or had he created Roizan after Roizan, and pitted them against one another?

It didn't matter.

Nothing mattered.

Dimetreus...was dead.

She'd known the creature that had emerged from the trees was a Roizan, even before she'd caught a clear glimpse. It had plodded toward her cliff, and she'd watched it with bated breath, inching closer and closer to the edge for a closer look. As soon as it had passed beneath where she stood, it paused, turning its monstrous face toward her. That was when she'd seen it. The faces. Her brother.

It had let out a bellowing roar then, one that had sent her stumbling back, clutching the nearest tree for stability. When next she dared look at the meadow, it was gone.

Gone.

Dimetreus was gone.

She heard another roar, this one from the other side of the meadow. The sound sent a shudder up her spine, a sensation so violent it sharpened her senses. Cut through her sorrow. Reminded her why she was here.

For Teryn.

If the Roizan was here, so was Morkai. So was Teryn.

She forced herself away from the tree and crawled back to the edge of the cliff. Fire leaped from a mangled tent, and the Roizan now circled a figure. Moonlight glinted off pale hair. Mareleau. The queen had fallen to her knees, eyes empty as the monster with her father's face paced around her.

Cora's heart stuttered at the sound of Teryn's voice. It

carried over the sound of crackling flames, but it was spoken with the sorcerer's lilt. "Ah, you've found her. Very good."

She squinted into the dark until she caught sight of Teryn's body stalking toward Mareleau and the Roizan. Another figure trailed behind, steps uneven, hand clutched to his chest.

King Larylis.

Morkai held his hand open to the side, palm facing up. Cora leaned closer to the edge. She couldn't see what he held, but she could guess. Now that Morkai had his Roizan, he could perform far more impressive feats of magic than he'd been able to without it. A ball of blood likely hovered over his hand, and based on how Larylis clutched his chest, it belonged to him.

Larylis doubled over and fell to his knees.

Mareleau let out a cry.

"Now," Morkai said, "it's time for us to come to an agreement."

MARELEAU DIDN'T KNOW WHAT WAS WORSE: HER FATHER'S lifeless face used as a monster's eyes or her husband's peril. The beast rounded behind her, giving her a clear view of Larylis. His shoulder dripped red, a gash splitting his sleeve. His face was twisted in agony. The way his fingers clawed at his sternum suggested he was fighting some invisible internal affliction.

Rage built alongside her terror, and she shifted her attention to the man who stood before her. He stared down his nose at her, a strange red bead hovering an inch above his open palm. He showed no fear for the beast that circled her, no concern for the flames that steadily burned away more and more of her tent. Pain pierced her heart as she remembered the gift she'd unwrapped not long ago, the beautiful blanket her father had given her, a symbol of his forgiveness and affection, now lost forever to the flames.

"What are you doing, Teryn?" She spoke with a quaver, fueled by equal parts fear and rage.

"He isn't Teryn," Larylis said, voice weak, strangled between his teeth.

Teryn shifted to the side to assess him. An amused grin curled his lips. "No?"

"I don't know how it's possible," Larylis said, "but you're Morkai."

The name echoed in Mareleau's head. It belonged to the duke who'd orchestrated the battle at Centerpointe Rock. The one who'd cursed Cora to never bear children.

She stared at the man who wore Teryn's face. It was impossible. Or it should have been. Aside from the graying hair, the pallor of his skin, and the overall signs of ill health, this *was* Teryn.

But his actions, his words, the subtle changes in his personality over the past week...

Not to mention the monster with four faces. A creation that shouldn't exist.

Larylis was right. He had to be. Somehow, this man was the former Duke Morkai brought back to life.

Larylis pinned Morkai with a scowl. "Where is my brother?"

Morkai patted his chest. "In here. This remains his body somewhat, though it won't be for long."

Larylis shifted, wincing as he tried to get a leg underneath him to stand, but Morkai curled his fingers inward toward the ball of blood. Larylis clutched his chest again and slumped back on his heels.

"Lare!" Mareleau tried to crawl forward but was intercepted by the creature. It pinned her beneath her father's empty gaze and sent her scrambling back. It rounded behind her again, returning her view of Larylis and Morkai. The sorcerer's eyes remained on her husband, that crimson ball still hovering over his hand. Was Morkai using the ball of blood to hurt Larylis somehow? To render him immobile?

Meanwhile, she was unscathed, guarded only by the monster. While the beast was terrifying, she realized something: Morkai didn't see her as a threat. Not the way he saw Larylis.

Of course Morkai wouldn't consider her a threat. He didn't know her. To him, she was just a simpleminded, pampered queen. He couldn't possibly know the full depths of her history. Her viciousness. The people she'd hurt. Lied to. Manipulated.

She could use that. The protective fire rekindled in her chest, her belly, encouraging her. Panic clawed her bones, but she could use that too. She could use all of it.

"What do you want from us?" she asked, letting her voice quaver even more, letting tears trail down her cheeks. Through her terror, she sought her trusty *magic trick*. Where normally she used it to don a confident outer shell, she used it for the opposite effect now.

Weak, she thought. *Frightened. Soft. Desperate*. The façade tugged her shoulders to her ears, raised the pitch of her voice, turned down the corners of her eyes. She hunched over the earth where she kneeled, hands digging into the soil as if she could barely hold herself up.

Morkai took a few steps closer to her. "Do not weep, Your Majesty. With your father's death, you've added yet another kingdom to your reign. Is power not worth celebrating? You are now Queen of Menah and Queen of Selay. I asked you before what you'd call your new kingdom once the two merged as one. Have you decided yet?"

"Why would I even think about such a thing at a time like this?" Her voice edged on hysteria. It was an honest illustration of her current state, but with her mind focused on crafting a weak outer persona, it helped her pretend it wasn't. Helped her detach. Feel like she was in control. "My father is dead. I don't care about what that means for me as queen."

Morkai gestured toward Larylis. "With your marriage, your husband has inherited a new kingdom as well. Your father was ambitious in setting you up as queen of one kingdom while keeping you as heir to another. It isn't unheard of for kingdoms to merge under such arrangements, but I daresay a bastard has never risen so far in such a short time."

Larylis narrowed his eyes, but his face twisted into another wince.

A sob tore from Mareleau's throat. "Stop hurting him!"

"Should Larylis die," Morkai said, "there would be quite a battle over who had the greatest right to the throne."

Terror sparked inside her. She wanted to flee from her fear, but she reminded herself that she needed it. Needed all these dark emotions to craft what she wanted Morkai to see.

She shrank down, cowering. *Weak. Small. No threat at all.*

Morkai spoke again. "As queen of the single entity that is your newly merged kingdom, you could continue to rule as reigning monarch. But without an heir, your claim will be weak. Especially when Prince Teryn still lives, and his blood right to Menah is stronger, regardless of the marital ties that have joined the kingdom to Selay."

She had to force herself not to react to the part about not having an heir. Force herself not to press a palm to her belly.

Morkai didn't know. Of course he didn't. She'd told the man she'd thought was Teryn that she'd lied. She made herself sniffle, crafted a miniscule tone of voice. "What are you trying to say? You...you're going to kill my husband?"

"In the unfortunate case that Larylis dies, leaving Menah and Selay in a contest of crowns, the most peaceful solution would be the one that creates the least amount of conflict. One that keeps bloodlines and land rights as they stand, with Menah and Selay as one. Better yet, why not reform Lela? Why not join three kingdoms? Do you understand what I'm suggesting?"

She shook her head.

"Then I'll spell it out for you. For the sake of peace, the best solution would be for you to marry Teryn, the new King of Khero."

Fire boiled her blood, and she didn't have to fake her rage as she shouted at the sorcerer. "I would *never* marry Teryn."

His gaze hardened, and he curled his fingers toward the ball of blood again. Larylis cried out, head falling forward as he clawed at his torso. "I don't have to give you a choice."

"Stop!" She extended a pleading hand. "Please stop hurting him! I take it back. I'll do anything you say. Is it my kingdom you want? Menah? Selay? They're yours. Take them. Take all of it. Just let me and Larylis go."

Morkai scoffed. "You're going to hand over your kingdoms, just like that? I thought you were stronger."

The amusement in his voice said the opposite. This was exactly what he'd expected of her. She was so lost in her fear over Larylis' fate, she wasn't sure if her words had been truth or bluff. Lies had always left her lips easily, but now... now she'd do anything to save her husband. Promise anything and mean it with her whole heart.

"Let us go," she said. "Let Larylis go and our kingdoms are yours."

He barked a laugh. "You don't expect me to—" He laughed again, so abruptly, it had him stumbling forward. He caught himself, hands on his knees. As he heaved again, she realized it wasn't laughter at all but a coughing fit.

Larylis slumped, face easing with relief as he was finally freed from whatever Morkai had been doing to him. Mareleau's eyes bored into her husband, willing him to realize this was his chance. Larylis' eyes locked on the sorcerer, his hand flying to his hip—

His scabbard was empty.

He scrambled to his feet anyway, took a charging step forward.

Morkai righted himself and thrust a palm toward Larylis. Mareleau's heart sank as her husband stumbled back, clutching his chest once more. Streams of red flitted through the air from the gash in his arm, dancing toward the sorcerer's open palm. It became a ball of crimson, like the one he'd held before.

Morkai's chest heaved. He swiped his free hand over his mouth, but when he pulled his palm away, his eyes widened. Mareleau wasn't sure what he saw in his hand, but the blood smeared over his lips made it easy to guess.

He'd coughed up blood.

Whatever was wrong with Morkai—or Teryn's body—it was catching up to him. Something like fear danced in his eyes as his lips curled up in a snarl. "You want to live?"

"Let my wife go," Larylis bit out. "Do what you will with me."

"No!" Mareleau called. "Let *him* go. Please! I'll make any promise."

Morkai's jaw was tense, all prior amusement gone from his face. "Fine. I'll give you a chance to survive, brother."

"Don't call me that. You're not Teryn."

Morkai reached for the sword at his hip and freed it from its scabbard. He tossed it to the side, letting it land in the grass several feet away. "If you can survive a fight with my Roizan, I'll let you and your wife live."

The monster leaped away from Mareleau toward her husband. Morkai turned his palm to the ground, and the bead of blood disappeared. Larylis straightened, freed from the sorcery, but the monster was just a few feet away. Mareleau's heart climbed into her throat as Larylis dove to the side, reaching for the sorcerer's discarded blade.

Morkai shifted before her, blocking her view. "Stay here and watch," he muttered, reaching into his jacket pocket. He extracted a vial with one hand and unsheathed a short knife with the other. She caught sight of him rolling back his sleeve and making a shallow cut in his flesh before he turned around, back facing her.

Of course he turned his back on her.

She'd succeeded in presenting herself as weak. To him, she was just a woman he could manipulate. A queen he could steal from.

She inched backward, lips peeled back in a snarl. Her hand closed over something hard. Glancing down, she saw the hilt of a dagger. It was the one Larylis had given her before he'd left the tent. She'd dropped it when she'd glimpsed her father's face on the monster, but now her fingers curled around it. Chest heaving, she rose to her feet, blade in hand.

58

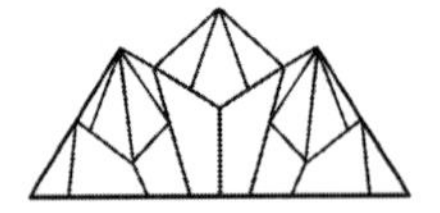

Teryn tried to step into his body, but it was no use. Morkai's grip on Teryn's cereba was too strong. It was nowhere near as malleable as it was when the sorcerer was asleep. The only time he'd managed to control his body while awake was when he'd intercepted Cora's kiss. He couldn't fathom what was different now, aside from Cora's obvious absence. Perhaps the Roizan was to blame. Already Teryn could tell the sorcerer's magic was stronger. No longer forced to rely on spells cast on paper, he could weave blood through the air like he had before he'd died.

Morkai was doing so now. A pattern formed over his open palm, one intricate line at a time. It was constructed from two strands—one emerging from the vial in his hand, the other from the blood that seeped from the cut in his forearm.

Teryn cast a glance at his brother and found him engaged with the Roizan. They clashed, a flurry of claws and teeth versus the sword Larylis had managed to snatch from the ground. Teryn's eyes flashed back to the weaving Morkai was creating, the strands of blood that danced through the air in complex loops and lines. He knew better than to trust what Morkai had said; there was no way he'd let Larylis live. He knew what his plans for Mareleau were—to provide Emylia a body—but even she would have to die to bring it to fruition. And since Morkai had Teryn's body to blame for all that he did, all that he forced Larylis and Mareleau to sacrifice, he had a workaround over the rule that the crown must be *given not taken*.

Teryn looked back at the fight. It had barely begun, but already Larylis had suffered a slice over his torso. Though Teryn had a feeling the battle was more than one of survival. If Morkai was forging a blood weaving...

"He'll make Larylis part of his Roizan," he said under his breath. With a renewed sense of urgency, he stepped into his body once more, felt the buzzing resistance all around him. His ethera fought against the movements of a physical form not under his control. He aligned his ethera's hands with his body's hands, tried to wrest control, turn his wrist, drop the blood—

"He's not making another Roizan." Emylia appeared before him, gaze locked on Morkai's palm. Her eyes lifted to his, wide with terror. "Creating a Roizan with multiple human lives made it strong enough to do what he needs to do next. Your brother's battle with the Roizan is a distraction. You saw how Morkai coughed up blood. He's running out of time. You both are."

Teryn glanced back at the pattern that continued to weave, studied the two distinct threads of blood that tangled together. Something tugged at the edges of his ethera, an unyielding pressure that grew with every beat of his heart.

"I recognize this pattern," Emylia said. "He's finalizing his possession of your body."

Cora didn't know where to look, what to do. Chaos filled the meadow as the fire continued to eat away at the tent, its flames now lapping up the sides of the next one over. Larylis was doing his best against the Roizan, focusing on dodging swipes and landing blows on its limbs to slow it down, but it was an unwinnable fight. His only advantage was the creature's bulk and lack of agility. Even so, the Roizan was a monster of magic. She had no doubt it could outlast a human's stamina. All it needed was one fatal swipe of claws. One violent kick of its rear hooves.

Then there was Teryn. She hoped his soul was safe for now, but Morkai was using his body to cast a blood weaving. She had to stop him. She had to do *something*.

Her hands went reflexively to her waist, her back, desperate for her bow or a dagger. The motions were futile; she already knew she'd find no weapon—

Except...there was *something* there.

The hand that clutched her empty hip brushed over a lump in her pocket. She patted it again, making out the curved shape of the collar that had pierced her neck not long ago, rendering her magic null. Calm certainty flooded her as she extracted the device. Her eyes narrowed on Teryn's body. She could cross the distance between them, collar him, and sever Morkai's magic. It wouldn't stop the Roizan from fighting Larylis, as the creature was its own vessel for magic, but she could at least stop Morkai from completing his weaving. It might even return Teryn's soul to its rightful place.

She hoped.

Breathing deeply, she forced her nerves to steady, her

mind to clear. She rooted her feet to the earth, gathered lungfuls of smoky air, let the flames dancing in the meadow fuel her fury, let her warm affection for Teryn guide her emotions, calling her to cross the space between them...

Light glinted off steel, and her eyes locked on the blade in Mareleau's hand. Her stomach clenched, threatening to shatter her concentration. She exhaled her panic, focused on Teryn's back, the familiar curve of his neck, the width of his shoulders, the sturdy feel of them beneath her palms.

Mareleau charged forward, thrust the blade toward the bottom of his ribs...

Cora closed her eyes.

Opened the two ends of the collar.

Took a step.

And felt the knife meant for Teryn sink into her shoulder.

Cora ignored the pain that radiated through her back, her arms, and instead focused on snapping the collar shut. Closing on its hinge, the pointed edges dug into Teryn's neck. He went rigid, a cry escaping his lips. From behind him, she pressed her palms to the sides of his face, stood on tiptoe, and whispered his name.

"Teryn."

THE SOUND OF CORA'S VOICE SENT TERYN'S ETHERA SURGING into his body. Pain erupted at the sides of his neck, and he fell to his knees. Then she was there, rounding to the front of him, her hands framing his face, her voice caressing his ears. Ears that were his. A touch he could feel. Her face filled his vision, her brow knitted with concern.

He was home.

Home.

His body was his own.

"Cora!" Mareleau's voice trembled as she crouched beside them. A dagger shook in her hand before falling to the ground. "Cora, I'm sorry."

Cora's throat bobbed. "Bind my shoulder," she barked at Mareleau. "Hurry."

Teryn blinked a few times, willing his mind to reconcile what was happening, the sensation of being whole again. Something still felt wrong. There remained a pull at the edges of his awareness. He shook the thought from his mind, more concerned with Cora. "Your shoulder," he said, voice far weaker than he wanted. "What happened?"

"Mareleau stabbed me," Cora said, though there was no ire in her tone, only cold logic. Her grimace, however, revealed her pain. Through her teeth, she said, "Luckily, she's lousy with a blade."

"It was meant for him," Mareleau bit out, then pursed her lips as she tore the silk belt from around her robe and began wrapping it around Cora's upper arm. "I...I thought he was Morkai. I thought Teryn was gone."

Teryn swallowed the dryness in his throat and tasted blood. "I wouldn't blame you," he said to Mareleau, "if the blade had met its mark. If it rids us of Morkai—"

"No." Cora's tone was sharp. She lowered the hand that belonged to the same side as her injured shoulder but kept the other on his cheek. Her touch was warm against his flesh. He was grateful for the pressure. It seemed to anchor him into his body. Did she know that? Was that why she wouldn't sever the touch? "You aren't sacrificing yourself, so don't you dare suggest it."

"Cora..." He lifted a hand, his moves slow and heavy, and managed to brush his thumb along her cheek. Even that much movement fatigued him. How long could he keep this up? As he dropped his hand, he felt a renewed surge of pain at the sides of his throat. "What is this?"

"It's a collar that suppresses magic."

He had no idea where she'd come across such an item, but if it was responsible for keeping Morkai at bay, he was grateful for it.

Something tugged on his awareness again. Pressure clawed at his ethera, trying to drag him out of his body. He winced. "He's still fighting me."

"And that thing is still fighting Larylis," Mareleau said, tone frantic. "We have to help him."

Cora whirled to the side, though she kept a hand on his cheek. Teryn frowned as something caught his attention. Hovering in the air above Cora's head, nearly invisible amongst the chaos and commotion, was a tapestry of blood. Two interlocking threads wove tighter and tighter, moving of their own accord.

His pulse quickened. Morkai's blood weaving...was finishing itself, even with the sorcerer no longer in control of Teryn's body. He glanced at the gash in his arm, the hand that had held the vial of blood Morkai had used for the tapestry. Crimson had ceased streaming from his cut, and the glass bottle lay on the ground, its contents seeping into the earth. Yet that didn't stop the tapestry from weaving higher and higher.

He lifted a hand and attempted to swipe his fingers through the pattern. An invisible force blocked him. Cora turned her attention back to him, then at the pattern suspended over her head. She gasped and shrank away from it. He tried again to swipe at it, from a different angle this time, but his fingers stopped an inch away.

The Roizan. It had to be the key, the reason Morkai's magic endured despite the strange collar Cora had put around Teryn's neck. And if the tapestry reached completion before Teryn could break the crystal...

Panic seared his heart, but alongside it was a cold and heavy sense of resolution. "I have to end this now."

Cora's brow furrowed as Teryn shrugged off his jacket and his waistcoat, then undid the buttons of his shirt. "What are you doing, Teryn?"

"I need a reed," he said, voice weak but surprisingly calm.

"A reed?"

"To write with." He reached the middle button of his shirt, revealing something underneath, strung by a leather strap. The nearby flames glinted off the facets of a crystal—

He paused and covered it with his hand. "Don't look at the light."

She averted her gaze, but memories surged through her. The unbreakable stone. The night Teryn had fought through Morkai's possession and told her the truth. The many enchantments that had forced her to forget about the object. She kept her eyes on his as he finished unbuttoning his shirt.

He spread the article on the grass before him and extracted a fresh vial from within his discarded waistcoat. "A reed," he repeated. "Please, Cora."

She jumped into action, plucking a tall slender stalk of

grass that hadn't been trampled by the Roizan. "What are you doing?" she repeated, handing it to him.

"Reversing the spell on the crystal so it's no longer unbreakable. Once I finish drawing the pattern, you'll need to take the crystal from around my neck, ensuring it's no longer touching my body—at least sixteen inches away from my chest—and shatter it." He unstoppered the vial and dipped the reed inside. Its tip dripped crimson as he brought it to the bottom hem of the back of the shirt. There he paused, eyes unfocused. Then he lifted his gaze to Cora's, his free hand brushing his collarbone. "You said this device blocks magic?"

She nodded.

He cursed. "This won't work unless we remove it. What I'm about to do is considered blood magic. I may not need to be a witch to draw the pattern, but...we can't risk it not working. This could be our only chance."

Anxiety raced through her. "The collar might be the only thing keeping Morkai at bay. You said he's still fighting you. What if he regains control without it?"

"I'll fight back," he said, but as the words left his lips, a trail of blood began to trickle from his nose.

She crouched beside him again, tone frenzied. "He's already hurting you. Teryn, you're bleeding!"

His face fell, but there was no surprise in his eyes. "I'll do whatever it takes. If he regains control, touch me again and call my name."

Tremors seized her. His battle with Morkai was killing him, that much was clear. The more he fought, the more his body suffered. But what other choice did they have?

"Remove the collar, Cora," he said, tone soft. Mournful. Resolute. "We don't have much time."

She tried not to read too far into his words. Tried not to

think what he meant by *we don't have much time*. Tried not to hear the resignation in his tone that told her he was ready to die.

With trembling hands, she reached behind his neck, separated the two sides of the collar, and pulled it away.

He offered her a sad smile.

And began to paint with blood.

59

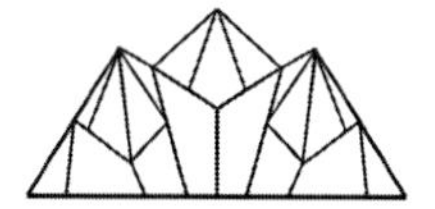

Larylis wasn't a warrior. He was hardly a king. He'd been trained in the art of the sword alongside his brother, but his strength had always resided in books. Knowledge. He'd read about warriors, survivors, wars, and battles. He understood combat both physically and intellectually, but he didn't consider himself a fighter. There were times when he marveled that he'd survived the battle at Centerpointe Rock at all.

That experience had certainly tested him, though he was convinced the only thing that had kept him on his feet was the incessant numbness he'd felt in the wake of his father's death. He'd felt fear then, yes, but it hadn't been as strong as his guilt. That guilt had allowed him to defy death, to risk everything, uncaring what happened to him.

He didn't have that luxury now.

Gone was his self-loathing, self-hatred. Gone was his desire to be punished for every good thing he'd been given.

I'm sorry, Father. I can no longer bear the burden of your death. I can no longer wish I'd have taken your place.

Because now, more than anything, Larylis wanted to live.

That *need* to survive generated waves of fear. It grew with every swipe of the Roizan's claws. Sent his heart thudding with every kick of the creature's hooves that brought him to the brink of death. He wasn't blanketed in numbness this time, no matter how he wished he could be. Instead, he was plagued by the selfish yearning to breathe another breath. To experience all the joys and pleasures life had in store for him.

Mareleau.

Their unborn child.

Every experience they'd yet to have.

He could tell himself he was fighting for the citizens he was responsible for too, but it wasn't the selfless desires of a king that kept his arms swinging. Kept his legs dodging. Kept his body rolling. Standing. Running. Swiping. Stabbing.

It was *her*. Their future. To hell with everything else.

The Roizan swung a massive paw. Larylis dove to the ground, but pain seared his thigh. He didn't have time to look at the wound, didn't have time to wipe the sweat from his brow. He rolled to the side, climbed to his feet, fighting the pain that screamed in every muscle, every bruise, every torn inch of flesh.

He rounded the creature, darting behind it on aching legs. The beast swung its head, trying to pin him beneath one of its four sets of eyes. With its rear hooves, it kicked out, grazing Larylis' ribs. His vision blackened, but he swung his sword again and again, grunting with the pain that radiated up his arms each time his blade met the thick hide of the Roizan. His next swing sank into the beast's slender leg.

The creature bellowed. It planted the wounded limb on

the earth, but the grass had been turned to mud. The Roizan slipped. Fell. Skidded to the ground.

Larylis charged for the injured leg. Gritting his teeth, he swung. Cleaved.

Whatever it took, he'd live.

He *had* to live.

MARELEAU HAULED CORA TO HER FEET BY HER GOOD ARM, though Cora was certain the girl wasn't being mindful of the wound she'd inflicted. "What are you doing?" Mareleau asked, eyes darting from Cora to Teryn. She gestured toward the field, teeth bared in frustration. "We have to help Larylis."

Cora spotted Larylis scrambling to his feet, moves lethargic. The Roizan hobbled after him, one of its hind legs missing. Larylis must have severed it to slow it down. The beast opened its maw, raking its tusks from side to side as it charged in close. Larylis rolled to the other side and dove to his feet, managing to sink his sword into the monster's neck. The Roizan let out a bellowing roar, then hobbled in for another charge.

Though Larylis fought relentlessly, Cora could see the exhaustion in his limbs, the ashen pallor of his skin. She cast her gaze throughout the meadow, seeking anything she could use to help him. The camp had been made as a base for a hunting excursion, but there were no weapons in sight. The hunting party must have taken them all with them.

Teryn cried out, drawing her attention back to him. His face contorted, and his hand shook as he fought to form the next line of his intricate pattern on the back of the shirt. In the next moment, his face went slack, eyes hard.

A chill shuddered through her.

She knew that look.

Knew it didn't belong to Teryn.

She rushed before him and framed his face with his hands. "Teryn."

His eyes rolled back. The sorcerer's steely gaze disappeared, and Teryn regained control of his body. She moved her hands to his shoulder, ready to intervene again if needed. He erupted with a cough, one that sent specks of blood flying from his lips, but he immediately returned to his task, dipping the reed back in the blood, painting a delicate slash of red, then a loop. Higher and higher the pattern climbed. He lifted his eyes, frowned at something in the air, and returned to paint another loop.

Cora squinted into the space above them where Morkai's weaving continued of its own accord. The pattern was more complex than the one Teryn was painting. It was taller too, and she feared that meant it was more complete. From the hasty speed of Teryn's brushstrokes, she got the sense that he was racing against this one. If only she could disrupt the pattern—

Something slammed against her, and she fell to her side. She looked up in time to see Teryn—no, Morkai—standing over her. Mareleau reached for her, dragging her to the side. She bit back a cry as her shoulder screamed in pain. Morkai released a growl of frustration and snapped his fingers. Suddenly, the Roizan turned away from Larylis and hobbled toward Cora and Mareleau, the four grotesque faces inching closer and closer.

Cora threw an arm around Mareleau and tried to focus on...on *somewhere* to use her magic to travel to, but her mind was racing too fast, her emotions too tangled, too panicked.

The Roizan opened its maw...

It froze, a bellowing screech piercing the air. Cora and Mareleau scrambled back. It shook its head as smoke wafted from one of the four faces—Ulrich. In the next moment, the fleshy visage blackened and charred until it sloughed off the creature in a puff of ash.

Morkai muttered a curse. He stood before his tapestry, studying it with intense concentration. The red threads continued to climb, but they were slower now.

The Roizan thrashed, bellowing in rage as the next face began to blacken.

Cora's pulse quickened, but not with fear. Hope bloomed inside her. Morkai's blood weaving must be using too much of the Roizan's magic.

With a deep inhale, she pushed her panic down and focused on the grass near Morkai's feet. On her exhale, she extricated herself from Mareleau, rose to her feet, and took a step through space.

Morkai leaped back at her sudden appearance. Before he could react, she touched his cheek and called Teryn's name.

RETURNING TO HIS BODY FELT LIKE TORTURE, HIS EVERY muscle aching, his stomach turning with bile. Yet Cora's voice cut through these sensations, bolstering him, giving him the strength to fill the space of his body. His hands became his own again, his legs under his command.

Wincing, he kneeled over his unfinished painting. His hands shook as he gathered up the discarded reed, dipped it in the sorcerer's blood, and picked up where he'd left off. His vision blurred, his lips chapped and bleeding. Every move he made grew increasingly heavy. Despite his efforts to deepen his breaths, his lungs felt shallow, uneven. His heartbeat failed to keep a steady rhythm, his pulse slowing with every second.

"You're almost there." Emylia's gentle tone entered his awareness. It sounded wrong to hear her voice with his true ears now that he was back in his body. Or was it still his ethera that heard her? She crouched beside him, the edges of her form wavering as she watched his progress. "You're so close, Teryn. You can do this."

"Why can I hear you?" He spoke the words, but they didn't leave his lips. "Why can I see you?"

Her mouth tugged into a frown. "Morkai's spell is almost complete. With every strand, it fights to sever you from your body, fights to trap you as an ethera for good. Even though you're in your body, you straddle the line between life and death. Your feelings for Cora are all that keep your connection to your cereba intact, linking it to your heart-center."

He felt Cora's hands then, palms against his cheeks, but it wasn't his flesh that felt her touch; it was the buzzing resistance of his ethera. His name left her lips over and over like a mantra.

The Roizan roared again, and Teryn felt a stronger tug, fighting to wrench him from his body.

"Teryn. Teryn. Teryn." Cora's voice kept him in place, while Emylia's urged him to keep painting. Don't lose focus. He was so close.

So close.

Cora said his name again, and this time it ended on a sob. He was vaguely aware of the blood dripping down his chin, tingling the surface of his ethera.

"One last line," Emylia whispered, the sorrow in her tone mingling with Cora's cries.

"Teryn, Teryn, Teryn..." Cora continued to chant, and he

felt her lips press against his cheek, felt her cradle his face, her tears mingling with his blood.

With a final surge of intent, he painted the last line and closed the pattern in a slash of red. Then, with all the waning strength he had left, he lifted the leather strap from around his neck and shoved the crystal into Cora's trembling hands.

"I love you," he said, but the words left the lips of his ethera, not his body. "I love you," he repeated, and this time he managed a garbled whisper before his hands slipped from the crystal.

CORA STARED DOWN AT TERYN, LIMP IN THE GRASS BEFORE her. Blood stained his lower face, trailed down his neck and over the puncture wounds that had been left in the collar's absence. His hair was now entirely silver, skin so pale she could see blue veins beneath it. She didn't dare look at his chest, couldn't bring herself to note if it still rose and fell.

The man she loved was dying, but there was still more work to be done.

She swallowed down her sorrow and turned herself over to logic. Safety. The anchoring element of earth cradling her knees, her legs. Breathing in, she called on the element of air to guide her intellect. The growing flames fueled her resolve. Her strength of will.

The watery realm of grief would have to wait.

"Where is your dagger?" she said to Mareleau, but the other woman's eyes were locked on the Roizan. It had ceased its attack, and now a third face sloughed off into a puddle of ash.

King Verdian.

Mareleau was too distracted to pay Cora's question any heed, but she needed something to break the crystal with. If only she could find the dagger and slam the stone with its hilt. Her eyes flicked to the pattern that was suspended in midair. It continued to slowly weave, which meant they still weren't safe. So long as the crystal was intact, no one was safe from Morkai.

Ignoring the heavy ache in her heart, she slowly inched away from Teryn's side in search of the dagger, a rock—

A curved black tip caught her eye. The collar. She'd dropped it when she'd removed it from Teryn's neck, but now the pointed tines called to her. She scrambled for the cuff and gathered it in her hand. Then, dropping the crystal to the ground, she pressed one sharp tip to the widest facet.

Splinters fissured in a radius around the point...

But it didn't break.

The Roizan bellowed again, tossing its head side to side. It pushed off from the ground, angled its face until its remaining pair of eyes—Dimetreus'—locked on hers. It charged forward, teeth bared. Larylis leaped into its path. Swinging his sword in an arc, he cleaved through the Roizan's front leg, severing its paw. It skidded to the ground, thrashing to rise on its two remaining limbs.

Cora returned her focus to the collar and the crystal, pressing harder. Harder.

Another crack.

White light streamed from the fissures, nearly blinding her.

She closed her eyes against the glaring light and pressed again. Again.

The brightness struck her eyelids, and for a moment she wasn't sure if they remained open or shut.

Gritting her teeth, she forced the tine deeper into the

crack. A splintering sound struck her ears, tinkling like a thousand shattering mirrors.

The pressure gave way beneath her, and she felt the sharp tine strike the soil under the crystal. The light disappeared, leaving darkness on the other side of her eyelids.

Fluttering her lashes open, she stared down at the ground.

The crystal lay in two broken halves.

The claw pierced the earth.

When she glanced up at where the blood weaving had been, there was only sky.

60

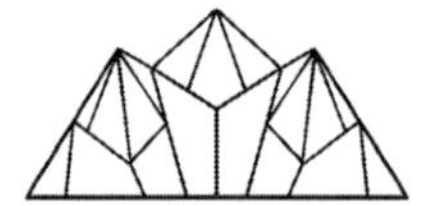

First Teryn was swallowed by darkness, his consciousness faint and floating in nothingness. No thoughts. No memories. Just a much-needed sleep. A final rest.

Then light bled into the void, splitting it into shards. It burned brighter and brighter until it was all that there was. All Teryn could see. It dimmed at the edges of his vision, shrinking inch by inch until it narrowed into two points of light.

Teryn's mind felt slow, heavy, as he took in his surroundings. They were familiar like a dream, and just as hazy.

A dark meadow bathed in fire and moonlight.

A beautiful woman crouched upon the earth.

Before her were two halves of a broken crystal from which the points of light glowed. The woman moved slowly, as if the passing of time had been reduced to a leisurely crawl. He watched as she gathered up the two halves of the crystal and brought them toward the blazing fire that lapped over the walls of a tent. It was strange seeing flames move so slowly, but even stranger to watch the woman. The longer he looked at her, the more certain he was that he knew her. The feeling only grew as she moved farther away from him. The wider the distance grew between them, the more desperate he was to draw her back.

Something warm and heavy condensed in his chest.

A name formed in his mind.

Cora.

And he remembered.

His memories brought a hollow ache, one that deepened when his eyes fell on a body sprawled in the grass nearby. He hadn't noticed it at first, not with his attention so absorbed by Cora, but now he saw his own slack face, eyes closed. Was he...dead? The world didn't look how it had when he and Emylia projected themselves outside the crystal. There was a haze between him and the plane of existence he watched. A discrepancy between time and space that sent waves of panic through him.

Stark illumination drew his attention away from his body. Even though Cora had taken the broken halves of the crystal to the fire, the two points of light remained on the earth. Beside it, another familiar figure kneeled. This one, however, didn't belong to the living world.

"Emylia," he said. His voice rang hollow, lacking all resonance.

She met his eyes briefly, lips pursed tight. While her form appeared as solid as it had inside the crystal, the edges rippled like smoke. She collected the pieces of light in her palms, as gingerly as one would handle their most fragile treasure. "I must act quickly," she said, voice as hollow as his. "We don't know what he'll become without his heart."

A bolt of alarm shot through him. "What *who* will become?"

It was fruitless to ask; he already knew the answer. A

dark shadow drew his gaze to the center of the meadow. It towered twice his height, a shapeless mass of writhing tendrils that lapped out in every direction, fluttering at a violent pace as if on an invisible storm wind.

Emylia strode straight for the shadow, her moves not restricted by the sluggish momentum that had fallen over the plane of the living. Belatedly, Teryn followed her, felt the buzzing pressure between his feet and the earth beneath them. "What are you doing?"

"An ethera without a heart-center becomes a wraith," she said, "but Morkai...he could become something worse. I have to save him."

Teryn hadn't a clue how Emylia planned to save the sorcerer, nor did he think Morkai should be saved at all.

He could become something worse.

Teryn didn't like the sound of that.

His ethera constricted with fear as they approached. The shadow that was Morkai's ethera gave no reaction. It had no face. No eyes. Nothing to suggest it was sentient at all.

Emylia stepped far closer to it than Teryn dared, the two orbs of light cradled in her palms. She stared up at the shadow. A desperate emotion twisted her features, tugged the edges of her lips, turned her eyes down at the corners. Whether it was hope or terror, Teryn knew not.

"You sacrificed the first half of your heart-center to save my soul," she whispered, voice trembling.

The shadow shifted, drawing closer to her as if to hear her better. The undulating tendrils began to contract, shrinking more and more until the shadow was only as tall as Teryn. Little by little, the edges of the shadow became smooth, taking on the semblance of hands, legs, a torso. It resembled a wraith now, its body colorless and semi-transparent. Only its face remained hidden behind the rippling tendrils.

Emylia spoke again. "You sacrificed the second half of your heart-center when you tethered your soul to the crystal. In return, you became heartless."

The wraith lifted a hand and brushed it over his shadowed head. His fingers smoothed the undulating tendrils, leaving gray flesh behind to form Morkai's face. Teryn tensed, eager to evade Morkai's gaze, but the sorcerer only had eyes for Emylia. Morkai stared down at the seer, expression cold. "Don't you dare condemn me, Emylia. Everything I've done has been for you."

Her brows lowered into a glare. "You didn't do this for me. I never wanted you to do the things you've done. I never wanted you to become Morkaius."

"You were the one who helped me learn how to become Morkaius. You gave me the knowledge I sought. How could I not use it to bring you back?"

"I regret what I channeled for you. I regret it with all my heart."

He bared his teeth. "You told me you loved me. That you'd do anything for me."

"You used me. Manipulated me." Her chest heaved, shoulders tense.

Morkai's throat bobbed. "Is that really how you feel?"

She nodded.

Rage flashed over his face, but it didn't linger. His jaw shifted side to side. When he spoke, his voice quavered with emotion. "I can't apologize. I did what I thought was right. Nothing you say will change that. Hate me now if you must. I will continue to love you as I always have, and I will cling to the love you gave me when you meant it."

Her chin wobbled. Tears glazed her eyes. "I don't hate

you, Morkai. I could never hate you. Long ago, you were the man I loved." She stepped closer. Morkai flinched, his ethera going rigid. He recoiled as she lifted a hand but froze as she brought it to his cheek. Shadows rippled beneath her touch. Her lips curled into a sad smile, her eyes mournful. "I loved Desmond and always will."

Morkai's expression softened with a startling tenderness. "Emylia—"

"But you're not him."

With the hand that still cradled the light, she thrust her fist into Morkai's chest. He cried out, stumbling back. Emylia retreated as well, hand now empty.

The points of light glowed from within Morkai's chest, burning brighter and brighter until they merged as one. The light coursed through him, from his chest to his hands, feet, and head. Color spilled over his gray flesh, painting his pale eyes, his dark hair, a simple shirt, and a pair of trousers. Years filled out his cheeks somewhat, until he appeared a slightly younger version of himself. Teryn recognized this manifestation from Emylia's memories—it was Desmond. Though the edges of his form weren't fully solid, he was no longer transparent like a wraith.

He fell to his knees, hand clutched over the center of his torso. "Emylia."

She ran to him, framed his shoulders with her hands. "Des!"

He looked at her as if seeing her for the first time. Elation filled his gaze, tugged his lips into a smile. He trailed his fingertips over the curve of her cheek, her neck—

His hand fell.

Clutching his chest again, he sat back on his heels. "What did you do to me?"

Emylia's brows knitted together. "I gave you back your

heart, Des. You won't be a wraith. We can move to the other-life, side by side."

His face twisted, teeth bared. His voice came out strangled. "Why does it burn?"

Her eyes dropped to Desmond's chest, where white light began to glow through his ethera. "Des, what's happening?"

"It hurts. Gods, it hurts. What have you done?"

The light burned brighter. With a shout, he threw his head back. The white light spilled from his mouth, spiraling over his form. Desmond's limbs flailed, arms fluttering as if made of paper, while the light streamed from his hands and feet. Emylia gripped the edges of his burning ethera, but every part she touched crumbled into ash.

It continued to burn until nothing remained, neither light nor shadow. Not even ash lingered.

Emylia sat before nothing, clutching at air. She trembled, staring at the place Desmond had been a moment before.

Teryn watched, not knowing what to say. What to feel. He wasn't sorry to see all that remained of Morkai burn away. He wasn't sorry Desmond's soul couldn't be saved. Then again, he wasn't happy either.

He was…numb.

The edges of his consciousness began to fade.

Where was he? Where had he been?

Hadn't his heart ached for someone?

Hadn't there been flames?

A field?

"Teryn."

He opened his eyes. When had he closed them?

Emylia stood before him, sorrow etched into the lines of her face. "Don't fade away, Teryn. I couldn't save him, but it's not too late for you. You can still go back."

He blinked a few times, willing his mind to clear, but the haze was growing, eating at his awareness, his memories.

A tingling sensation buzzed over his shoulders, and he found Emylia was shaking him. "Don't fade away! You have to go back." She forced him to turn around, and his eyes landed on something not too far away.

A woman with dark hair bent over a body. Tears filled her eyes as she gently slapped the man's cheeks.

No, not just any man. That was *him*.

And that woman...

"Cora." Her name warmed his ethera as it left his lips.

His mind sharpened again, his memories melting back into place.

"Hurry, Teryn," Emylia said. "Connect to your vitale. Feel your heartbeat, the air filling your lungs—"

"There's nothing." The realization cleared his mind further, this time with fear. Where once he'd felt his blood and breath, there was only a hollow void. His vitale...it was lost to him.

There was no heartbeat.

No breath.

No pulse.

He was...

Teryn.

The sound was felt more than heard. It sent a shudder through him, sent awareness through every inch of his ethera. From somewhere deep inside his soul, a heavy thud echoed.

He glanced at his body, saw Cora's lips beside his ear. Tears trickled down her face. A single drop fell upon his cheek. Something buzzed against the same spot on his ethera.

Teryn.

Another echoing beat. A thud that hammered in his chest.

"There's still so much more for us to do," Cora whispered. "So much more I need to tell you. I'm not done with you yet. Do you hear me? You promised to court me. Remember? I won't let you break that promise."

A thud.

A pulse.

A breath.

"Come back to me, Teryn."

A rushing intake of air.

61

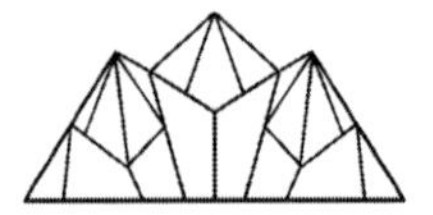

Dawn broke over the horizon, and with it came a summer storm. Cora didn't know if she had fate or magic to thank for the rain. She had prayed for it. Had sought the element of water with all her heart, begging every blade of grass to lend the meadow its dew, begging the clouds to converge if only for a day. Because rain was exactly what they needed.

Rain to stop the flames from devouring more of the tents, more of the meadow, more of the trees.

Rain to drench the earth where a mangled body had long since burned to ash, where two kings, two lords, and four animals had been laid to rest on a makeshift pyre of lantern oil and crushed wildflowers. It was the only dignity Cora and her companions could deliver those who'd died to become a Roizan. At least no one else would have to witness what had been done to them.

From under the shelter of a wide pine where the fire had yet to spread, Cora watched the downpour. Rain devoured the last remnants of the flames, leaving what had once been

Cora's favorite location scarred with scorch marks and the skeletons of half-eaten tents.

"This is the best I can do." Larylis' voice pulled her focus from the meadow. She glanced down at where he crouched beside Teryn. He'd constructed a pallet of canvas tied to two beams of wood—materials that had been salvaged from one of the unburned tents.

Her eyes lingered on Teryn's slack face, his hollow cheekbones. It broke her heart to see him this way.

But at least he was alive.

He'd taken a breath in her arms, muttered something she couldn't understand. Since then, his breathing had remained steady, his heartbeat strong. He needed medical attention and rest, but Cora had hope. She'd cling to it. Tether it to her heart and carry it herself if she must.

But she wasn't alone. Larylis carried the hope with her, and she suspected Mareleau did too.

"Are you ready?" Larylis asked, glancing from Cora to Mareleau. The latter sat at the other side of the tree trunk, hugging her knees to her chest. Ann, Sera, and Breah hovered around her. Larylis had found the three ladies not long ago, when Cora and her companions carried Teryn under the tree to keep him out of the rain. They'd been hiding at the base of Cora's favorite cliff, trembling, hardly able to say a word. Now they stared sightlessly ahead, arms linked as if desperate for the comfort of another's flesh.

Larylis rounded the tree and kneeled before his wife. Placing a hand under her chin, he gently lifted her eyes to his. "We must get Teryn back to the castle. We can't wait for your father's retinue to find us."

Mareleau flinched at the mention of her father, her eyes darting toward the charred field. "We're all that's left," she whispered.

Cora's chest tightened. While Cora had been able to smother her pain, tamping it down beneath a cool blanket of logic, Mareleau's composure seemed to be clinging to frayed edges. But Mareleau was right. They were all that was left. Not just of the camp, though that was certainly true. Larylis had scouted the area and found no other survivors. He'd located the bodies of two guards in the meadow, both mutilated by the Roizan. In a nearby clearing, he'd found more signs of slaughter—claw marks in the earth, on trees. Blood. Bones. Empty saddles drenched in gore. When Morkai had created his Roizan, he must have let it feed on the witnesses, the councilmen, servants, and horses he'd brought on the hunt.

But Cora was certain Mareleau meant something else—that Cora, Mareleau, Larylis, and Teryn were all that was left to rule their kingdoms. Verdian was gone. Dimetreus too. King Arlous had been the first to perish, at Centerpointe Rock.

It was daunting to think that Menah, Selay, and Khero now lay in their hands.

Mareleau's eyes were wide and haunted as she reached for Larylis, clinging to the bloodstained collar of his shirt. Cora had bound his wounds as best she could, but he'd need medical attention too. "What will we do?" Mareleau asked.

Larylis lifted a shoulder in a fatigued shrug. "Whatever it takes."

"But...what will we tell people?" Her eyes flicked back to the meadow. "No one will believe what happened here."

Cora took a step closer to them. "We'll tell the truth. Maybe not to the public, but to those we trust."

Larylis furrowed his brow. "Are you sure that's wise? Our council will think we're crazy."

"Then let them," Cora said. "I'm tired of lying about magic. I'm tired of hiding the truth and pretending I'm something I'm not. We defeated a sorcerer. A beast. Magic exists in this world, both dark and light. It's time we stop hiding that."

Mareleau and Larylis didn't seem convinced, but it didn't matter. They could do what they wished, and so would Cora. She was Queen of Khero now. Kevan and Ulrich were no longer around to control her. To tell her what she was and wasn't qualified to do. The peace pact was broken, as were its constraining terms. She didn't need anyone's permission to rule her kingdom.

She owed it to her brother to be queen.

She owed it to herself to be a witch.

She was both, and she wouldn't shy away from either. Not anymore.

Larylis extended a hand to his wife. "Come. We must hurry."

They managed to heft the four corners of the pallet between them. Even Mareleau's three ladies managed to assist, which Cora was grateful for. With her shoulder wounded, she had but one arm to use, and even that pulled on the hastily bound lesion. Their slow pace made Cora's nerves coil tight. Every second that ticked by was one Teryn endured without proper care. She kept her eyes on his face, his chest, thanking the Mother Goddess for every breath that left his lips. Her relentless focus on him prevented her mind from straying to topics she had even less control over.

Like Valorre.

Her heart ached whenever she thought of him. Whenever she recalled how he'd left the Veil, terrified that he'd forget her.

She understood what had been missing now, why he

hadn't come back. He'd only needed the magic of his horn to exit the fae realm, just like she'd only needed her magic to leave El'Ara. It was as Fanon had said: the Veil had been woven to keep worldwalkers from entering, not from leaving. But while she and Valorre had been able to leave with their own magic, they'd needed each other to enter. Without his horn paired with her worldwalking ability—a combination the Veil couldn't account for—he hadn't been able to get back in.

Either that or...

He'd forgotten her.

Stupid.

The voice flooded her heart, her mind, sending her pulse speeding. She was so shocked, she nearly dropped her side of the pallet. *Valorre?*

You are stupid to think I would forget you. My memory is mightier than that.

She nearly wept as she felt his presence. She couldn't see him, but she could feel his proximity. He was drawing closer by the second. *How did you get here?*

His smug façade faded away, replaced with genuine concern. *As soon as I crossed the Veil, it disappeared. There was no wall. Only forest in our world. I knew you'd find a way out, so I tried to return home, to where you'd go. I've been running for a day, trying to get here, but I was lost. I didn't know where the Veil had brought me.*

He'd been running for a day. To her, it had only been hours since she'd left El'Ara. *How did you find your way?*

She found me. Led me in the right direction.

She?

In answer, a rhythmic beat pulsed in the air. Cora glanced up in time to see Berol making her descent toward the pallet. Sera squealed, pulling her hands from the pallet as Berol landed on one of the wooden carrying posts.

"There you are," Larylis said. Though he tried to grin, the expression was strained. Empty. "Where have you been?"

Her wings were splayed as she shuffled down the length of the pallet until she reached Teryn's face. She tilted her head side to side, a barrage of frantic chirps erupting from her beak. She hopped from the post to the canvas, then gave Teryn's cheek a tentative peck, right over the fading scar that marred his flesh. There was something apologetic in the way she nipped at him. Had Berol given him that wound? Perhaps after Morkai had taken possession? Cora recalled how the falcon had brought Larylis' letter to her in the tower room instead of Teryn.

She nibbled his cheek again, this time a little harder. Cora was almost of a mind to shoo her away lest she injure him, but a soft smile flicked over Teryn's lips. "Berol." His voice was soft, a creaking whisper.

"He's awake!" Larylis pulled up short, forcing the rest of them to stop as well. Slowly, they lowered the pallet to the ground. The rain had ceased, and the morning sun was just beginning to peek through the clouds.

Cora ran to his side and brushed his silver hair off his forehead. "Teryn."

He caught her hand with his. His grip was loose, but he managed to squeeze her palm. "Cora...I..."

She hushed him. "Just rest. You're safe now. He's gone."

The memory of the broken crystal flashed in her mind. She'd watched it crackle and burn after she'd thrown it in the flames until there was no sign of it left. She had to trust that meant Morkai's soul was no longer able to possess anyone.

He spoke again, brow furrowed, but his words were too quiet to hear. She leaned closer and smoothed her hand over his hair. Berol chirped, nipping his ear. "It's going to be all right. It's over."

He blinked, and his green eyes gained steady focus as they locked on hers. "I...I don't think it's over."

Her hand went still in his hair. "What do you mean? Is Morkai—"

"He's gone, but...but I don't think he was the last threat to us. His father...Darius...Elvyn prince."

The name sent her stomach bottoming out. "Morkai's father was Darius?"

"Who's Darius?" Larylis said, leaning closer, but neither Cora nor Teryn took their gazes from each other.

"King Darius of Syrus," Teryn said. "He's the reason Morkai found Lela. Found you."

"King Darius of Syrus," Cora echoed. She'd heard that name. Her mother had been from the Southern Islands. She'd told Cora tales of Syrus, Zaras, and the other isles, though even if she'd had no personal knowledge of the location, the Southern Islands were hardly a secret. Selay had exclusive trade with them. Cora was certain Syrus' king—Darius Solaria—was still alive. But how did Teryn know about this?

"There's so much more I need to tell you," Teryn said. His face twisted with a wince.

She brushed her hand over his hair again. "Me too. But we have time."

He nodded, lashes fluttering shut, and sank back into slumber.

She exchanged a glance with Larylis, then Mareleau and her ladies. In wordless agreement, they hefted the pallet back up. Berol took off into the sky, soaring toward the castle.

I'm almost there, Valorre said.

She could feel him even closer now, a comfort that mingled with her growing dread.

If what Teryn had said was true, the danger they faced last night—and at Centerpointe Rock before that—might only be the beginning. Her mind whirled over possibilities.

A broken prophecy.

A fae realm, dying without its heart.

A true Morkara who would tear the Veil and make El'Ara whole.

And the mother who would bear this child, this savior…

She was no closer to breaking the spell that had been cast upon her.

Did that mean Morkai had won after all?

She shook her head, focusing instead on the rise and fall of Teryn's chest and the feel of Valorre's growing nearness. It was all she could do to face the crushing pressure as the fate of two worlds settled upon her shoulders.

EL'ARA

THE BLIGHT

THE VOID

LE'LANA
BEFORE THE VEIL
PALACE OF THE MORKARA
THE MISSING HEART OF ELIARA

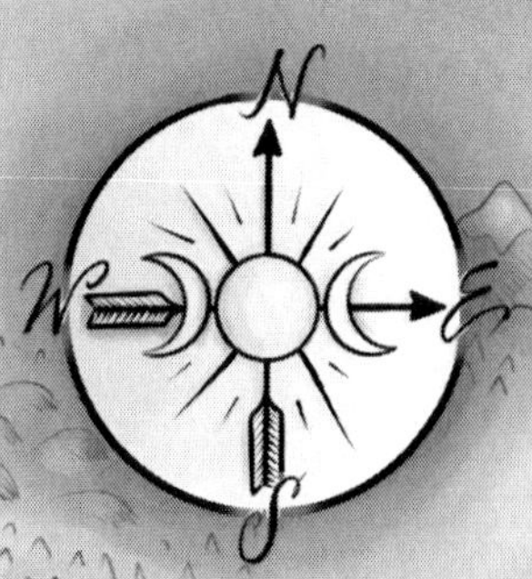
N
W
E
S

WANT MORE EPIC ROMANTIC FANTASY?

Keep the magic alive! The ***Prophecy of the Forgotten Fae*** trilogy concludes with ***A Fate of Flame***! Find out what happens to Cora, Teryn, Larylis, and Mareleau as they fight for the fate of two realms. There's more magic, more adventure, more romance, and more fae.

Still don't have enough epic fantasy in your life? ***The Fair Isle Trilogy*** is another series featuring epic magic and enemies-to-lovers romance! Set in a Victorian-inspired world, this series dives straight into all things fae romance. Start with ***To Carve a Fae Heart***.

ALSO BY TESSONJA ODETTE

Entangled with Fae - fae romance

Curse of the Wolf King: A Beauty and the Beast Retelling

Heart of the Raven Prince: A Cinderella Retelling

Kiss of the Selkie: A Little Mermaid Retelling

— And more —

The Fair Isle Trilogy - fae fantasy

To Carve a Fae Heart

To Wear a Fae Crown

To Spark a Fae War

standalone fae romance novella set in faerwyvae

Married by Scandal

Prophecy of the Forgotten Fae - epic fantasy

A Throne of Shadows

A Cage of Crystal

A Fate of Flame

ya dystopian psychological thriller

Twisting Minds

ABOUT THE AUTHOR

Tessonja Odette is a fantasy author living in Seattle with her family, her pets, and ample amounts of chocolate. When she isn't writing, she's watching cat videos, petting dogs, having dance parties in the kitchen with her daughter, or pursuing her many creative hobbies. Read more about Tessonja at www.tessonjaodette.com

instagram.com/tessonja
facebook.com/tessonjaodette
tiktok.com/@tessonja
twitter.com/tessonjaodette